SHASTA

An Adventure from the Dane Maddock Universe

DAVID WOOD
C.B. MATSON

Shasta- ©2020 by David Wood

The Dane Maddock Adventures™

All rights reserved

Published by Adrenaline Press
www.adrenaline.press

Adrenaline Press is an imprint of Gryphonwood Press
www.gryphonwoodpress.com

ISBN: 978-1-950920-09-9

What waits beneath the mountain?

When mercenaries abduct their friend, it's up to former Navy SEALs turned treasure hunters Dane Maddock and Bones Bonebrake to find him. With the clock ticking and powerful forces standing in their way, can Maddock and Bones unlock the secrets of ancient Lemuria and stop Pym Industries before it's too late! SHASTA is most action-packed Dane Maddock adventure yet!

BOOKS and SERIES by DAVID WOOD

The Dane Maddock Adventures
Blue Descent
Dourado
Cibola
Quest
Icefall
Buccaneer
Atlantis
Ark
Xibalba
Loch
Solomon Key
Contest

Dane and Bones Origins
Freedom
Hell Ship
Splashdown
Dead Ice
Liberty
Electra
Amber
Justice
Treasure of the Dead
Bloodstorm

From the Authors

SHASTA references characters and events from
MAUG- book two in the Dane Maddock Universe series.
It can be read as a stand-alone, but you will probably enjoy
it more if you read MAUG first.

PROLOGUE

Nahonka had watched Major Dickson's horse grow weaker over the past few months. Now it refused to eat, standing in the pasture, staring at the surrounding mountains, and shivering in the evening mist. The last surviving member of his tribe, Nahonka knew that his own fate was linked to that of the dying warhorse.

The Major, fresh from the Mexican War, had railed against his posting to the tiny mining camp of Chilcoot Creek and raged against all of its inhabitants. However, he saved his bitterest vitriol for young Nahonka. Every morning, he would summon the boy to his office and lift a coil of rope from beneath his desk.

"You take care of my horse, boy. That is your only job. The day my horse dies, you'll swing from the nearest tree."

Nahonka brushed the aging animal as the shadows lengthened and the smoke of a hundred cook fires rose in a gray haze across the valley below. He didn't want to die. Yet every day as the horse weakened, he felt a bit of his own spirit slip into the darkness. Every day the proud old creature refused to eat, Nahonka took no meals himself.

Now, as the sun slid toward the western horizon, he felt the rift between his world and the spirit world begin to open. Shadows of his ancestors flitted between the trees and tall spindly creatures lurked just beyond his field of vision. Stepping from the tales his grandmother told, the guardians of *Y'et*, the dwellers beneath the Mountain, walked openly upon the earth. Portents of change, young Nahonka read them as omens of his death.

The old warhorse whickered, flicked his ears, and raised his head. Nahonka spun about and found himself facing a young woman. Clad in buckskin and woven leaves, she could have been sixteen, she could have been sixty.

The woman cocked her head to one side and asked, "Why do you wish to die, Nahonka?"

Beautiful and terrifying, the woman rendered him speechless. She waited unmoving while he stammered for words.

"Who… how is it you know me?"

"I knew you in your mother's womb. I have known you since the winds first swept snow down from the sacred mountain. You are Nahonka, Watcher of the People, guardian of tradition."

"I am none of those. I am a slave of my father's murderer and tomorrow I will die by his hand as well."

"You have a horse. Ride him tonight and live tomorrow."

"I have nowhere to go."

"You have people of your own. Follow me and I will take you to them."

On a stolen saddle, with a stolen hackamore, Nahonka rode a stolen horse into the hills above Chilcoot Creek. As if in a dream, he followed the woman gliding between the trees. Sometimes she seemed to walk, a spirit of the woods, and sometimes it seemed to Nahonka that she rode a snow-white elk that climbed among the rocks and scree with all the delicacy of a yearling fawn.

As for his own mount, the dying horse had found some inner reserves and climbed the hillside with stoic determination. Among the pine shadows and out in the open moonlight Nahonka rode, oblivious to all but the flitting shape of the mysterious woman and her ghostly band of spirits. He'd lost sight of Chilcoot Creek by the time the moon rose high enough to shine above the surrounding hills.

Nahonka had no idea where he was being led. He didn't care. Death would come just as surely for stealing a horse as it would for allowing one to die. That night passed to the creaking of his saddle and the lonely cries of night birds in the forest.

As the sky lightened in the west, he and his phantom entourage crested a long ridge. Nahonka dismounted and walked the last few yards. Below him, the Sacramento River poured through its dark canyon. A scattering of gray and salmon-pink clouds floated in the turquoise sky, and as the mist cleared, Mount Shasta glittered pure and white in the new day's sun.

The mysterious woman appeared at his side, herself a thing of mist and clouds. "We must go, Nahonka. We traveled slowly in the dark, but now the men have found your trail and they follow behind us with murder in their hearts."

Nahonka led his aging mount down the east face of the ridge.

"You knew my name but tell me, by what name should I call you?"

"I am Killeli, keeper of the Fires."

Nahonka walked along in silent contemplation. He'd heard the name uttered in his grandfather's lodge. A woman from out of the dawn of days, she was the bringer of chaos, the mother of hard winters. Killeli walked with him as he descended into the shadows until the old warhorse began to fidget. "Ride now my child. Your enemies are close by and you still face a perilous river crossing before you reach the land of your ancestors."

Nahonka glanced back. Five riders crested the ridge less than a mile behind. He swung into the saddle and coaxed his horse into a gallop that risked disaster for both rider and mount. Grinning, the strange woman clung to her snowy elk and matched his pace stride for stride.

Crashing through the brush, the old stallion soldiered on. He cleared fallen logs and scrambled down the crumbling slope like a deer flees the wolf. Nahonka no longer tried to guide the animal, but simply clung to its back and prayed for a painless death.

They hadn't descended far when the first shot smacked into a tree a short distance away. Its report echoed back from the river canyon, a ghostly salvo from below. Nahonka allowed the horse to run, disregarding the other shots that spun sizzling of the rocks around him.

Closer, he could hear the river grumbling over its falls, and behind, the clatter of shod hooves on loose rock. Two more shots. The first burned through his left arm and the second caught his horse in the flank. The animal screamed and stumbled. Another shot through its neck dropped rider and mount, all tumbling bodies, flying limbs, and hard stones.

Somehow, Nahonka regained his feet and ran. The shots ceased as he headed for the canyon edge. His pursuers had fanned out. He knew they wanted him alive, to prolong the torment, to drag him back beaten and humiliated for their master, Major Dickson.

Gasping, stumbling, he reached the canyon rim. Looking down, Nahonka saw nothing but a black mass of churning water. Above him, five men descended with slow deliberation.

Killeli stepped to his side. "You must choose now. Jump and trust the river or stay and die at the end of a rope."

Clambering over stones and logs his pursuers closed around Nahonka. One raised his pistol, aimed and fired. The shot struck Killeli in the abdomen. She doubled over and tumbled into the water below. Nahonka glanced back, then leapt into the void after her.

The clench in his stomach as he watched the sky recede above him, the cold impact of the river on his back, they mattered nothing compared to seeing Killeli take that bullet. Nahonka burst to the surface, gasping for air. He was answered by a volley of shots that peppered the churning water. Diving deep, he let the current carry him downstream until his lungs burned for breath. Once more at the surface he became target of another volley. A numbness in his leg told Nahonka that he'd been hit again. Lifted to the crest of a steep wave, he felt rather than heard the deep thunder of water. A glimpse of white chaos, then he flew over the cataract.

Reeds and gravel beneath his chest, Nahonka retched and vomited a fountain of water and yellow bile. No shots echoed down the canyon. No bullets scattered stones about his feet. Shivering, he dragged himself to the riverbank where the first rays of sun crawled across the canyon wall.

Nearby, spinning slowly in an eddy, Killeli floated face down. Nahonka dragged her cold body to the shore, so real now that they had crossed the river. He touched her cheek. He felt her wet hair against his arm. Somehow, he knew he had reached his destination. Nahonka now stood in the land of Killeli, the land of his People at the foot of the great Mountain.

Dragging his injured leg, he laid her body on a pyre of splintered logs and river-washed branches. As Nahonka arrayed her arms and shut her sightless eyes, he noticed a jade green stone knife suspended from a chord about her neck. Holding it up in the morning sun, he heard the sound of a thousand voices. Chanting, lamenting, they called out in a language he barely remembered.

Down a narrow path, a line of People waited for him. Living People, his People, not ghosts, they approached bearing torches and beating drums. As the smoke of Killeli's flaming pyre reached up its arms to greet the morning sun, a tall spindly figure approached Nahonka. It took the stone knife from his hands and hung it about his neck.

"Welcome home, child. You are now our Watcher. Watch carefully, for someday, you will herald the new dawn when the Killeli returns to her Mountain."

1

At the foot of a broad ramp guarded by eight stone rams, Dane Maddock stopped and gazed up into the massive atrium. Sixteen tall columns supported a rectangular stone lintel. Primitive, almost cyclopean, the adjoining structure rose from the surrounding vegetation, an angular limestone block glowing in the afternoon sun.

Maddock, as he was known to his friends, wiped a bead of perspiration from his forehead and turned to the tall Cherokee standing at his side.

"Three thousand miles, and here we are at last."

Uriah "Bones" Bonebrake looked up from a scrap of paper he held. "Papyriform columns, definitely Old Kingdom, Egypt. But look at those vertical walls, and cornice work, Roman influence from two millennia later."

"You've been reading again. I told you not to do that."

"Screw you, Maddock. Don't make me smite you with a plague of frogs."

Just then, a smiling young woman in a colorful Egyptian dress walked up and said, "Welcome to the Rosicrucian Museum. Would you like a brochure?" Her name tag read Deana.

Bones grinned at her. "I certainly would. I'll take your number, too."

The young woman arched an eyebrow.

"A brochure would be great," Maddock said.

She handed Bones a folded glossy sheet before hurrying over to a group of Japanese tourists. His eyes followed her a moment, then he shook his head.

"Nice going, Maddock. You scared another one off."

"Yeah, we're on a mission. I don't want to get kicked

out before we can even make contact with Sally. She was supposed to meet us here."

Bones climbed to the top of the ramp and looked out over the museum grounds. "Yeah, Sally. She probably got distracted. I mean, craft beer, mac and cheese, along with a bit of you-know-who."

"Or she's waiting for us inside. So, what do we know about this place?"

Bones held a finger in the air and read aloud.

"The Ancient and Mystical Order Rosæ Crucis was established in the United States in 1909, being the true and proper heirs to the ancient Egyptian philosophy of The Primordial Tradition. Since the time of Sir Francis Bacon…"

Maddock grimaced. "Not that. I mean here, in the heart of Silicon Valley, their headquarters and museum. Does the brochure say anything about…" Maddock glanced back at the woman and lowered his voice, "…about the key?"

Bones held out the brochure and pointed to an ancient key decorating the second page. "You mean this one?"

"Nah," Maddock shook his head, "it can't be that simple."

Bones crossed the atrium and pushed through a gigantic pair of gilded metal doors. "Maybe it is. Sally said we needed to come here to find the key."

Sally, Maddock thought. *Five-foot, two inches of headache.* She'd been Bones' problem for a while, then the two of them managed to rope everyone else into the kerfuffle. By the time they'd escaped from Maug Island, she'd attached herself to Corey Dean. A year later, she'd dumped him for Willis. And now Willis had dropped off the radar. Maddock shook off his reverie as he stepped into the museum.

Bones had paused just beyond the doors and stood

gaping at an enormous golden sarcophagus. "That can't be real."

"It's a reproduction," a small voice answered from behind.

Maddock turned to see that the young woman had followed them inside. He noticed that in addition to the white robe, she wore a traditional wig of stranded beads and the iconic eye makeup of ancient Egypt.

She smiled up at Bones and shrugged. "I ran out of brochures."

Bones grinned back at her. "And you're here to give us a private tour."

"I don't know much, I'm what they call a Neophyte, a newbie—my name is Deana." She blushed and held out a hand.

Bones took it and made a slight nod. "I'm Bones, this is Maddock."

"Maddock, Maddock... oh, no. I was supposed to give you a message when you arrived." She began patting herself. "It's here somewhere."

Bones smirked. "Can I help you look?"

"What? No absolutely not. Oh, you're kidding, aren't you? Not funny." She reached behind her back and unclipped a small mobile phone case. "Here it is."

Deana's slender fingers tapped around on the screen before she handed the phone to Maddock.

"Who is this Letson guy anyway, and how does he know me?"

"A friend of ours. That explains a lot." Among other things, Jimmy was a hacker—one of the best in the business.

"What does it say?" Bones leaned closer.

"Looks like Sally isn't coming. She wants to meet us in San Francisco. Jimmy's arranged transportation."

"What? Right now?" Bones made a grab for the phone.

"Let me see that."

Maddock pulled back. "No, you'll break it." He held the screen up for Bones to read.

"No way. We're flying up in a private jet?"

Maddock nodded. "On my credit card, it seems."

Deana pushed between them. "Give me my phone back. You two are crazy. How'd this creep get my number anyway?"

"He likely checked your admin computer to learn who would be working the entrance." Maddock handed her the phone.

"I don't get it," Bones said, "why didn't he send you the text, or just call one of us?"

"That's been bothering me too." He turned to Deana. "Did anyone else talk to you today—I mean, anyone who seemed weird?"

"Only the two of you." She glanced over her shoulder. "Are you guys in trouble or something?"

"I didn't think so, but now I'm wondering."

"Augustus Pym has the resources to pull something like this," Bones said. Pym was a powerful businessman whom they'd run afoul of a while back. "We got back a year ago. I've been shaking out my shoes every morning, looking out for Russians in cheap suits, but 'til today, nothing."

Maddock watched the young woman. She hadn't reacted to Bones' admission. Still, something seemed off. A strand of beads fell across her face as she cocked her head.

"Back from where?" she asked.

"Maug Island," Bones said, as if that answered everything.

Maddock explained. "That's the northern end of the Mariana Island chain in the Pacific."

"Oh, the western boundary of Mu, the lost continent." Deana brightened. "You've actually been there?"

Bones did a doubletake. "You know of Maug?"

"Well, *yeah*. The Lemurians, they started all of this. They were the first Rosicrucians, after all. It's cool that you're looking to discover the mysteries of ancient Lemuria." She looked over her shoulder. "So, are you on, like some kind of secret mission?"

"It's complicated," Maddock said. They had left Pym's son on the island to die. Since then, the possibility of dad taking revenge had been in the back of their minds. "A friend sent us here to look for something."

Deana gaped at Maddock and then at Bones. "So, some rando sends me a message and hopes I'll help you with your secret mission?"

"Not a rando, not anymore. Likely he's watching on the security feeds right now."

"Probably listening on your phone too." Bones raised his middle finger and said, "Screw you, Letson."

The interior lights blinked off, then back on. Deana shivered and hugged herself. "I'm calling security."

Maddock held up his hands. "Please don't. Just turn your phone off for now. We really could use that tour. There's something here we need to see before we leave."

Deana's eyes flicked between the two of them. "I don't think our security would be up to it anyway. What are you guys, commandos or something?"

"Not anymore," Bones said. "Think of us as history buffs."

"Right, you look just like my professors... except not. What is it you need to see?"

Bones held up the brochure and pointed to the key. "Got one of these?"

The young woman snorted. "That's just allegorical... unlocking your mind and all."

"Then what kind of *key* would we find here?"

She pointed to a frieze decorating the wall above them. "People call that the Egyptian Key."

Maddock didn't bother to look up. "The *ankh*, we could have stopped at a local head shop and saved ourselves the trip."

"That's not all, take another look," Bones said. "The eye in the pyramid, we're in a den of Bavarian Illuminati."

Maddock shook his head. "Don't mind my paranoid friend here; he sees conspiracies in the most unlikely places."

However, he had to admit that Bones was right. Alternating between the iconic looped cross ankh symbols, the frieze included different variations on the Eye of Horus staring down from a row of stylized pyramids. "I'm still not sold. What else is there?"

"I could show you the Royal Tomb. It's very authentic."

Bones shook his head. "Been there, got the t-shirt."

Deana gave him a puzzled look and asked, "What's with this key thing anyway?"

Maddock glanced back at the entrance and scanned the galleries. "That's just it. We don't know what we're looking for and it seems our friend Sally, who did know, is a no-show. I'm sorry we wasted your time."

"Oh, no—you don't get to come in here, weird me out, and then just walk away. I can show you some stuff that almost no one ever looks at. Maybe you'll get a few ideas."

Bones nudged him. "Yeah, let's go see some *stuff* as long as we're here."

Maddock followed Deana past displays crammed with artifacts and up flight after flight of stairs. Each hall they entered was smaller than the previous one. Bones paused at the alchemy exhibit and stared around. "Smaragdine Tablet? I've…"

"No, you haven't." Maddock started up the next flight.

Bones glanced at the exhibit again. "Nope, guess not."

Deana had stopped at the foot of a narrow staircase. Above, the hall was in shadows. "The top level is devoted to ancient religions of the world. They... I mean, we keep the lights dimmed to preserve the old pigments. I've only been here a few times. It's creepy."

Maddock nodded and motioned for her to lead the way.

Deana shook her head. "No, you guys go on up."

Bones took the steps two at a time. Maddock followed. Dim red floodlights illuminated a row of life-sized wooden statues. In some places the original polychrome paint still clung to the surface.

"Man, I can feel the age of these things," Bones said. "It's like a blanket of dust on my soul."

Maddock walked down the row. "Yeah, well some of their rites weren't too pretty either. Let's see if we can find whatever it is Sally wanted us to see and get the hell out of here."

Bones bent close to examine a huge bronze idol. "*Moloch*—it says here they burned babies in this thing. It can't be real, can it?"

Deana had crept up the stairs behind them. She peeked past Bones. "Disgusting, isn't it? Dates from the Hebrew time of the First Temple, maybe three thousand years old."

A few feet away stood a grotesque red demon, all arms and horns and snarling fangs. Its globular bulging eyes glared down at the three intruders. As Maddock drew closer, Deana whispered, "That represents the Kali Yuga, the evil lord of final destruction. Please don't touch it."

In the chamber's lurid red glow, Kali Yuga seemed to radiate malice on all who stood before it. Bones gave a low whistle. "I don't think you could pay me enough to mess with that thing."

The wall behind was lost in the burnt umber shadows.

Still, Maddock thought he detected a subtle movement. Edging closer, he saw that a painter's drop cloth had been hung like a soiled curtain behind the statue. He looked again. The bottom of the cloth rippled out, then hung straight. "What's behind here?"

"It's a new exhibit. We're not supposed to..." She paused as Bones slipped behind the hanging cloth. "...go in there."

Maddock pulled a miniature Maglite from his pocket and stepped past the curtain. Bones played his own light along the wall.

"There's got to be a switch or something in here," Bones said.

Deana followed them in. "Don't..."

Maddock reached behind and flipped a toggle switch protruding from the bare wallboard. A pair of temporary floodlights came on, illuminating a chaos of unfinished exhibits and open display cases. "We're not going to touch anything. We just need to look." He turned back as Bones reached for a white feathered headband. "I said, no touching."

"I wasn't going to... well, I was, but I won't. It's just that this is all Native American, not Egyptian."

"Yeah," Deana said. "The lost tribes of Israel. They carried so much of the ancient wisdom here to the new world."

Bones didn't look up from the array of obsidian knives he was admiring. "This is some amazing work, but what are these symbols?"

"That sun symbol is a petroglyph found with this cache of ceremonial weapons. The nested triangles mean mountains. The one next to it is a coyote, symbol of chaos. Together, they probably mean something like, *the sun rising in the mountains brings chaos*. Strange, but I don't know what else."

"Yeah, but this third one is the eye of Horus. We just saw a bunch of them back there."

"Don't you understand? The sun-and-mountain symbol is just like the eye in the pyramid. That proves the connection."

Maddock shook his head. "Seems a little far-fetched to me." He looked over the other exhibits. Nothing struck him as unusual. "An impressive collection, but I think we've run out of clues."

Deana hung her head. "I just thought there'd be *something* here."

To Maddock, she looked a little like Cleopatra after losing Mark Anthony. "Hey, we had a great visit. Seriously, super interesting stuff. It's just that we have someone waiting for us."

"Deana smiled. I guess I can't talk you into becoming Rosicrucians?"

Bones shook his head. "Probably not today. But how about I come by later for another tour?"

Bones smile faltered. "Uh, yeah, that would be great."

Maddock laughed. "Come on Rameses. We've got a chariot to catch."

2

Willis tucked his feet beneath him and hugged his knees to his chest. No use opening his eyes. There was nothing to see. Not today, not yesterday, maybe not the day before. All the world had fled to darkness. He could be eight years old again, sitting in his Grams' cellar, waiting for the storm that thundered and shrieked like colliding freight trains to pass overhead. Waiting for Grams to say: *everything's gonna be okay, sugar.* Waiting for her to say anything.

They had waited a twelve-hour eternity before someone thought to check on the old woman living on the far side of the railroad tracks and her visiting grandson. They'd come with flashlight beams waving, with tow trucks and chains to clear the fallen timbers. Young Willis' night of darkness ended in the arms of his mother and a long ride back to Detroit. He rubbed his eyes just to see the stars. *This eternal night ain't gonna end so easily.*

The nineties had been a tough decade for a young man growing up in the decaying streets of Motown. Lately he'd had plenty of time to regret a youth spent in small larcenies and confrontations with the police. Willis' eighteenth birthday dawned through a wire-reinforced window at the local detention center. They prodded him into an interview room.

A man entered. Big, taller than even Willis, broader about the shoulders. "You're eighteen now, boy. That means no more juvie for you. Ready to serve some grownup time?"

Willis glared up from the tabletop where he'd been studying his own bruised knuckles. The man wore a black suit and had one of those funny collars. Priest or something.

"So what if I am?"

The man sat down. He didn't offer a name. He had a big head, short hair, crinkly black beard. He didn't smile.

"I saw you fight last night. Put that other kid in the hospital."

"Had it coming."

"I'm not saying he didn't, but I'm not the judge. So, you like to fight?"

"Yeah, what's it to you?"

"Look kid, I don't give a dog's butt about your attitude, your righteous anger, none of that crap. I know someone who is looking for someone like you to take on a tough job, real tough job. Not one in ten thousand of your little friends out there could handle it, but I think you can. Are you interested?"

Now, in the perpetual night, with nothing but his own dark memories, Willis sat wishing he'd asked the priest's name, that he could have found him and thanked him for yanking a young thug off the system's treadmill and pushing him into the Navy.

A brief flare of light. Off on the periphery of his vision, Willis saw a faint yellow speck. How he'd run to that first one, an eternity ago. How he'd crouched at the tiny flame just to watch it dim to a blue halo before burning out. Even as the orange ember that remained faded to darkness, Willis could still feel the sense of loss, of death left by that spent candle.

He didn't run this time. The light would last maybe sixty seconds, no more. A piece of birthday candle cut brutally short, he'd find food and water nearby. Then the flame would vanish. Someone watched. Someone with night vision goggles sat in the security of a high ledge and peered down at his captive, his subject, his specimen.

He once tried talking to that unseen entity. In SEAL

school they taught him how to be a prisoner, how to play to your enemy's pride. They taught him to create a rapport with his captor, create sympathy, create weakness. Willis used everything he'd learned, but finally weeping on his knees, he'd realized that it was like praying to a silent God for the life of his dying grandmother.

This purgatory, this prison, it was huge. An enormous cavern of rough stone and dry sand. He'd scouted it that first day, if ever it had been day somewhere, or if ever the sun still crossed the blue heavens above. Willis had wandered the perimeter, climbing as high on the rocky walls as he could. Nothing else to do but fall and endure the contusions. A beetle in a bowl, he'd scrabble his legs up the side, then slide back to the center. Somehow, if there was an entrance, he'd find an exit.

Two energy bars and a bottle of water. *Nothing like home-made mac and cheese, and definitely no resemblance to craft beer. No way.* He downed the water. He'd had worse. Last year, it was Spam heated on the manifold of a busted down diesel engine, along with the brackish dregs of a ruptured water tank. But then last year he'd been surrounded by friends, his misery had plenty of company. And there was Sally.

She had seemed to him like one of those tiny jeweled frogs, loud, fragile, and possibly dangerous. And oh, was she so smitten by Corey Dean. That quiet intensity and brilliant mind just drew her to him like a porchlight draws bugs. Still, Corey had always reserved his truest devotion for his computers and equipment. Sally had figured that out. Eventually.

Willis opened one of the granola bars and dropped the wrapper. Chocolate raisin, it was okay. He felt kind of bad about being a litterbug, but circumstances gave him little choice. *Maybe someone came by and picked them up.* He'd never found evidence of his earlier meals. *Maybe this place is so huge he could wander forever without crossing his own path.* The cavern was warm too, comfortable he'd say.

His thoughts returned to Sally. She had invited him to spend the weekend together. Sally said she had something special she wanted to share with him, the El Yermo annual mac and cheese cookoff. There'd be food, music, and craft beer. She'd invited him for the week. Willis curled up on the sandy ground to think. He recalled that long ride back from the northern islands, limping along in a sinking boat with a busted engine, Sally had curled up between him and Corey when she slept. Whether it had been for warmth, protection, or convenience, he missed it now.

3

Twenty minutes after leaving the Rosicrucian Museum, Maddock and Bones arrived at the private aviation side of San Jose International Airport. Just across the street a small blue sign read: *Champagne Charters.* They jaywalked over to a hangar, its corrugated back wall broken only by a single steel door.

"Hi," Maddock said to the tall blonde woman who was rising from behind a desk. "I'm…"

"Dave Matlock and Uri Bainbrook?" Without waiting for an answer, she handed them each a flute of pink champagne. "Where's the third passenger, Sandy Sykes?"

"Sandy, she had to cancel," Bones said.

The woman picked up a phone and said a couple of words. She smiled at Bones, "Good to go. Your luggage is already on board. We can leave whenever you're ready."

Bones said, "Luggage? Where I go, I don't need…"

Maddock interrupted. "What my friend means is that we hadn't expected this kind of service."

Bones nodded, tipped the champagne back, smacked his lips, and winked at the woman.

She smiled at him "I take that to mean you're ready now."

They followed her out another door, down a hallway and stopped short inside the hanger. "A Gulfstream," Bones said. "Beats riding the bus."

The woman glanced back over her shoulder. "A bit more comfortable, too. I'll be your pilot today. We're looking at a twenty-minute ride up to SFO." She stopped at the boarding ladder and held out her hand. "Welcome aboard, Uri. Corky Corcoran at your service."

Bones took it and said, "Bo… b… I'm Bo. Nobody calls me Uri."

"Welcome aboard, Bo. Your packs are in the back; just go find a seat anywhere."

"Packs? We're not jumping, are we? Because I'm not dressed for it."

Maddock grinned and said, "Just get on the plane, *Bo*." He shook Corky's hand as well. "My friend is a little jet-lagged."

Bones ducked through the cabin door and scuttled past the cockpit to a comfortable settee.

Maddock explored the back, returning with two gray packs. He took a seat opposite Bones and flopped one of the packs on the table between them.

"What are we, boy scouts now?" Bones took the pack and rummaged inside.

"It's California, we've got to look the part. Besides, take inventory."

A well-dressed young man came down the aisle, poured them two more glasses of champagne, winked at Bones, and retreated to the cockpit. "Okay, I'm good with our pilot," Bones said, "but not too sure about our crew."

"Our pilot is at least twenty years older than you and I'll bet she once flew for Air America. Just look in the pack, already."

"Oh *Dave*, you shouldn't have!" Bones held up a red and gold San Francisco 49ers jacket. "And whoa, we have matching caps!"

"Keep digging."

His friend's expression changed. "Aw. You remembered."

Maddock nodded. "I checked the packs. It's a Glock. Eighteen round mag with two spares, all in a Kevlar shoulder holster. And for Pete's sake, leave it in the bottom of your pack. Our pilot probably knows it's in there, but I doubt anyone else does. Let's keep it that way."

"How about you?"

"Same. We've got knives too. Just put the jacket on and wear the hat."

While the Gulfstream pushed back and began to taxi, Maddock took inventory. Toothbrush, spare shirts and sundries, enough to get by. As he stuffed a pair of socks back in the pack, his hand rested on the hilt of a slim combat knife. Gerber LHR, twelve and a half inches of silent death, Maddock slipped it in his jacket pocket. Bones said, "Yeah, buddy. Did the same with mine."

"Let's just be discreet, okay? We'll be riding the BART subway to downtown, and from what I've heard, those transit cops are getting jumpy these days."

"So, when were you going to tell me the plan? Seems you've worked this all out on your own. You're such a control freak."

"It's not me. Jimmy is apparently calling the shots." Maddock pulled out a generic convenience store cell phone. "He feeds me instructions on this and so far, I think we've managed to travel undetected."

"I don't get it. How come he contacts Nefertiti back there, instead of buzzing you directly and how come our pilot didn't know about Sally?"

"Not sure of that myself, but he had to have his reasons. Maybe this phone's been compromised after all."

Bones grabbed a handful of cashews from the table between them, leaned his seat back and said, "The guy spent a crap-load of *your* money." He waved his arm. "This all can't be cheap."

"Don't I know it? But since we got back from that damned island, we've all been waiting for a counter stroke." Maddock felt the plane pivot onto the main runway. He fastened his seatbelt and sat back. "Pym Investment Trust is still out there, and Pym Senior doesn't strike me as the forgiving type. Safety doesn't come cheap, but funerals are expensive."

"I'm not a big fan of funerals, least of all my own. The quicker we connect with Sally and find Willis, the better for all of us." Bones looked around for another glass of champagne. Finding none, he grabbed more cashews. "I hear San Francisco is a fair-sized burg. How do we meet up?"

"I had a text from Sally: *Vaillancourt Fountain, 6 p.m.* That's downtown. We'll meet her there."

They cruised up the Central Valley and dropped over a range of brown rolling hills. As they approached the airport, a thick bank of fog wreathed the city in silent tendrils. Champagne Charters set them down in a small corner of San Francisco International Airport. Stepping off the plane, Bones shivered and hunkered up his jacket. "It's still August, isn't it?"

"Coldest winter I've ever spent…"

"Yeah, summer in San Francisco."

They took a shuttle bus to the nearby BART station and hopped a train headed north. Old brick buildings, high-rises, and freeways—then more freeways and still more freeways went rattling by the windows. Without warning, the land rose up around them and the train plunged beneath the streets.

Bones pulled away from the window. "Goodbye world as we know it."

They rode an escalator up from the San Francisco Embarcadero Station. A giant clock on the old Ferry Building glowed down through the fog, five thirty. Most of the foot traffic headed the other direction, plunging into the ground like Eloi going to their Morlock masters. Maddock took stock of the scene, crowded sidewalks, street vendors. Bones grabbed his elbow and said, "Don't look back, amigo, but we're being followed."

"Who?"

"Looks like our flight attendant is a bit too attentive."

"He's going to get hurt if he's not careful." Maddock looked up. He pointed to the massive Hyatt Regency Hotel towering over the crowded street. "In there. I'll impart a little wisdom. You watch our backs."

Maddock led them inside. Empty corridors and vacant conference rooms occupied the street level. They rounded a corner and stopped. No one in sight, no sound. Maddock glanced at Bones. His friend shrugged. Then a shadow moved. Reaching around the corner, Maddock grabbed the smaller man by his collar and pinned him to the wall, combat knife beneath his chin. "It's not a good idea to follow strangers my friend."

The man grinned; Maddock shook his head. "What's so funny?"

"The legendary Dane Maddock just caught me with the oldest ploy in the book. I'm impressed."

"I'm not. Who are you?"

"Names don't really matter." The man shrugged. "Why don't you put that cute little pig-sticker away and let's, um chat?"

"And why don't I just fillet you right here before I go to do something more important?"

"Because if you do, you may never see your friends again."

Maddock pushed his knife against the man's throat. "I don't like threats."

Bones cleared his throat. "Uh—there's something you should know."

Movement, Maddock glanced back. Six men

surrounded Bones.

"They've got guns. Sorry," Bones said.

"Uzis to be exact, little ones." The flight attendant sighed and winked. "But still, you know, does size really matter?"

"They fire one shot, and you're a dead man."

"Okay, it looks like we're not going to be friends after all. But what if I told you I wasn't your enemy? What if I said that we were sent by your friend Jimmy to watch your back?"

"I wouldn't believe you."

The man spoke a few words in a language Maddock didn't understand. The six others scattered and vanished. "Let's replay the last few minutes. You let me go, I'll explain. Your big friend can even pull out his little gun if he wants."

"Sit down over there." Maddock indicated a padded bench against the wall. "You've got two minutes."

"Why don't you just come over here and sit with me? It'll be so much more comfortable."

"We'll stand," Maddock said. " Now start with a name."

The smaller man sat and looked around for a few moments. "Uzi, you can call me Uzi. Little gun, lots of damage, *Oozy*, I like that."

"Keep talking."

"Corky, you know her. Well, she's got connections. Has friends in Washington. Lots of agencies there you may not have heard of. I could tell you stories…"

"What about Jimmy?"

"Let me finish. One agency is so secret it hasn't even heard of itself. Get it? Well, Letson knows them, and guess what guys? They've heard of you. Yeah, you're rock stars sort of. Well, so Letson puts a piece of paper under a doorstep somewhere, and this *über*-secret agency calls me, and I call Corky and here we are having a nice chat."

"You put the guns on the plane."

"Yes, you get it now, don't you?"

Maddock turned to Bones. His friend shrugged and Uzi continued. "See, I'm not your enemy."

"What is it you do, Mr. Uzi?"

"I do this." Without moving from the bench, he snapped out a small pistol and fired. Silenced, it still made a loud pop.

Bones sprang back. "What the hell?"

"Behind you, Mr. Bonebrake. He was just spying on us, but I believe you'll find he was armed."

A man's head and upper torso lay half out of an open door. Bones dragged the body into a darkened conference room. He returned carrying a Makarov nine-millimeter pistol.

"Who was that guy?" Bones asked.

"Certainly not a friend. I believe your position has been compromised, gentlemen. Who else knows where you'd be right now?"

"No one except that Egyptian woman—Deana whatever." He turned to Maddock. "She couldn't have been a plant, could she?"

"She seemed a bit too dim to hold a museum job, and she did ask us to join their numbers." Maddock's heart raced. "Crap, does this mean they've got Sally?"

"No, we have eyes on her. She's sitting by the fountain out there, waiting like a jilted bride."

"That's what I don't like," Bones said. "Besides you I mean." Uzi didn't blink and Bones continued. "Sally would have sent a movie reference. She'd have texted, 'On the Waterfront' and let us figure it out. This isn't her kind of place anyway. She'd have found some crummy bar with fantastic food."

Maddock nodded. "It's a setup. I received the text on

my regular phone. Bet she got the same text from me. They're just waiting to get all three of us together."

"Well now, Mr. Bones. Like me or not, perhaps I and my colleagues can assist you in some way."

"Did Jimmy really send you, Uzi or whatever your name is?"

"Not directly, but yes, I am here at his request. That agency I didn't mention, and that doesn't exist, they're not too fond of Mr. Pym and some of his enterprises. We're here to help you out."

Maddock dashed up a broad flight of stairs into the hotel's central atrium. From the vantage of a high window he saw a small figure sitting by an empty fountain. She could be someone's lost child. He felt a chill in his gut. "So, the enemy of my enemy…"

Uzi had followed him to the window. "Yes, splendid. We are friends after all. This is going to be such fun."

"You know, I never thought I'd be the one to say this," Bones glared at Uzi, "but let's try not to kill any more people."

"We'll try, oh yes, we'll be careful," Uzi said. "But how are we going to extract your doe-eyed little princess down there?"

Maddock glanced out again. "Where are your people now, Uzi?"

"Two will be watching our backs, although you may not see them. I'm sure at least four will be cleaning house downstairs. That leaves two more keeping an eye on your friend."

Maddock glanced at his phone, quarter of six. "Call your two guys over here, now."

Uzi held one hand to his ear and two large men converged on them. "Let me introduce my friends," he said. "Thing One and Thing Two."

Maddock shrugged out of his jacket and handed it to Thing One. Bones got the idea; jacket and hat went to Thing Two. "Keep your knife Bones, but the backpack goes too. Now Mr. Uzi, how brave are your people?"

"Several years ago, six of us entered a certain Iranian nuclear facility. We managed to upload a particularly effective virus into their centrifuge control system. My men are brave Mr. Maddock."

"Then these guys will go in from the street. They may draw some fire, so you need to be their backup, your cleanup squad too. No civilians hurt, got it?"

"And you, my skeptical friends?"

"We're the extraction team. As soon as you manage to attract some attention, we're going in."

Bones glanced at his pack. "Without our hardware? I'll feel naked."

Uzi winked. "Now I'm totally on board."

Bones chuckled. "See, Maddock? Everybody finds me hot."

"Except me." Maddock led Bones to a doorway on the far wall. "They'll probably have men waiting just outside and the gun is too visible. We'll cut across here to the arcade and look for a service entrance."

They slipped past a small crowd of shoppers. Maddock followed a pair of maintenance workers into a spartan gray corridor and descended a flight of concrete stairs to a steel door. The door pushed open without a sound and the two found themselves in a broad pedestrian mall lined with restaurants. The entrance gave them a fair view of the fountain and surrounding plaza.

Just across the mall, a kiosk served expensive coffee in tiny cups. Maddock bought two and pointed to a small table. "Do you see her from here?"

Bones settled in, scowled at his coffee, and said, "Top of

her head, just over there past those skateboarders."

"I'm just hoping they all scatter when it hits the fan."

Bones sniffed his cup, took a sip, and nodded. "We could strip the paint off of *Sea Foam's* hull with this stuff. I like it." He turned to Maddock. So, what's our plan?"

"Something happens, we count to five and see who's running where. You scoop Sally, just sling her over your shoulder and sprint. I'll cover your back. Head this way. It looks like the mall goes through to the next street."

"You're staking a lot on this Uzi guy. Think he's legit?"

"Right now, I don't know if any of this is legit, but it's the best we got."

Bones peeked over at Sally for a moment. "She's being very patient."

"Probably thinking we'll stop for tea and scones somewhere. I don't want her hurt, buddy."

"Roger that." Bones paused a moment. "Shouldn't we be hearing something by now?"

Maddock scanned the courtyard. The skateboarders were gone, the place quiet, almost deserted. "This isn't what I expected."

"What *did* you assholes expect?" a voice said.

Bones spun around, purloined Makarov pistol in his hand. Two shots rang out. Maddock hit the ground. Bones knelt beside him and squeezed off two more rounds. Return fire. A bullet caught Bones in the shoulder, spun him backwards and threw him to the pavement.

Maddock sprung up, his knife sliced through a man's short leather jacket, his muscular abdomen, and found the *inferior vena cava*, the large vein that carried blood to the heart. He heard a man grunt, and pain blossomed in his head as a crushing blow to the head sent Maddock stumbling backward.

He caught a glimpse of someone raise a sap, then bring

it down. Maddock tried to dodge, still it caught him in the left temple. Vomiting on the pavement, his legs wouldn't move, he pushed himself backwards, one inch, two bloody inches. The sap descended again and everything went dark.

4

Sally hustled south on the Embarcadero. She hadn't realized how far it was from her hideout at Old Fort Mason. *Damned Maddock, he would pick the most visible place in all of San Francisco to meet.* Keeping to the east side, the bay side of the busy street, she hoped to avoid notice for as long as possible. She reached the Ferry Building just as the big clock pointed straight up six.

Crosswalk, red hands all glowing in their little black boxes, Sally timed the traffic. A quick sprint and she'd be across. Not ten feet away, an unmarked police car whooped at her first few steps. She sprang back. *Crap, those two idiots can just wait.*

Green, green hands all the way across. Sally sprinted for the far curb. She could see the fountain from here, a tumble of square concrete pipes. There must have been a time when it had water, when children played behind its shimmering falls. Now the gaping black openings just stood dry, an empty monument to conflicting public opinion.

She passed two joggers and slipped around behind the fountain. *Likely she'd find Bonehead and his altogether too serious boss tossing pennies in the empty fountain.* Sally peered around the side just as a rattle of fireworks broke out across the plaza. It was answered by another burst off to her left. People ran. It took her a moment, then she ducked behind the concrete structure and huddled in a corner. *Gunfire. If Bones was anywhere around, gunfire just seemed naturally to follow.*

The cop across the street went full code-three, lights and sirens. Sally heard other sirens in the distance. She crouched low to the ground and peeked out at the scene.

Four bodies lay on the plaza, none of them familiar. A few others scattered. Motion on a nearby balcony, a volley of shots pinged and sizzled off the pavement. Their targets, two men in orange 49ers jackets, returned fire. The shooter fell back.

Sally leaned closer, they wore backpacks and one of them could be Bonebrake. But he wasn't. They had been helping a small Asian woman. She screamed at them and smacked the larger in the head with her purse. *You go girl.* Sally watched them beat a quick retreat west across the dry fountain and through the shrubbery.

"So, if *she* isn't the lovely Sally Smith, then you must be."

Sally jumped up and spun around. A well-dressed young man stood before her, his dark hair combed back, his blazer and prep school tie immaculate. He cocked his head and smiled. "Sorry to have startled you."

"Mr. Bond, I presume?"

"Your two friends call me Uzi. That should suffice for now. I suggest we continue this conversation somewhere else."

"Not until you tell me where they are."

"Yes, a very good question, well *that* should be our first order of business. Now shall we?"

Uzi took her arm and led north through a small park. People had gathered in groups. Curious, they now drifted back toward the plaza. "Strange isn't it?" He said. "Alone, they each ran like hell, but once in a group, everyone wants to go back and be part of it."

"I'll pass, thanks. I saw enough mayhem last time I was with Mr. Uriah Bonebrake and company. Who are you anyway? You don't seem like his… type."

"Ah, perceptive too, I like that. No, not his type, not at all. Still we have common cause, and that's something, you know. Mr. Augustus Pym, know the name? Of course you do. Both Pyms, Junior and Senior, they're not our friends, now are they? Come, there's a good coffee house just a few blocks north. We can talk there."

Cappuccino bowl between her hands, Sally paused to survey the clientele. Typical mix of office workers and programmers, probably getting caffeinated up for a late evening. Two men sitting by the door stood out from the crowd. Buttoned up suit jackets, white shirts, centers of gravity well above the waist, they were too buff to be bankers. "Please tell me those two are yours."

Uzi didn't bother to look. "You can count on it, petal. Two more outside. I've got another four looking for Maddock and Bonebrake."

"And?"

"Not good. They found a trail of blood. It led to a parking garage, then nothing."

Sally just let herself slump forward and rest her elbows on the table, arms crossed over her face. Somehow… somehow when Willis didn't show up and didn't call, she'd prepared herself for this day. She'd had her long black hair cut short and bleached yellow. She'd belted a baggy pair of jeans about her slim waist and donned a bulky men's jacket. No use, her friends had died before she even reached them.

She sniffled. *Flaming bloody hell, I'm sitting here sniffling in front of Her Majesty's Secret Circus.* Sally sat up, wiped her eyes with both hands and drained her bowl of cappuccino with one gulp. "Okay Top Gun, second stage of grief already. I'm pissed as hell. How are we gonna kill him?"

"Tell me, flower, have you ever killed anyone?"

"Yeah, a big piece of crud named Mako. He was gonna shoot my friends. Coulda plugged Junior too. Had the chance, I'd take it in an instant now."

"I've had to personally shoot forty-three men and women, two in the past hour. I can see every one of their faces even today. Are you sure you're ready to go there?"

"I've been there since we escaped from Maug, since I spotted Junior prowling around my coffee house." She paused, let the catch in her throat relax, and lowered her voice. "Since my friend Willis disappeared."

"Then be patient, little spider. We can't leave until I hear back from my men. Besides, I sense a story that I haven't heard."

Another cappuccino arrived. Sally stared at it a moment. "You're not supposed to drink two... it just isn't done."

Uzi leaned forward. "If you're going to go killing people, you'll just have to learn to break some rules." He poured the contents of a small metal flask into her bowl. "There, a little absinthe and another rule demolished, my dear. Now drink up, and do tell all."

Sally examined her own feelings. Not that she trusted this unctuous little man, it was just that she was in past the halfway point. The story, the tale of treasure and betrayal, of storms, and witches and creatures she'd never imagined just seemed to unwind from her like a parasitic worm drawn long and writhing from beneath her skin.

Uzi smiled but said nothing as she spoke. Finally, Sally reached the story's end. "I knew that Pym would come looking for us one day. I monitored Pym Investment Trust. His father, Pym Senior runs it. Well, about eight months ago, they bought into this water bottling company, Silver Glacier. Heard of it?"

Uzi slowly shook his head. Sally continued, "Neither had I, until I read about the problems in El Yermo. It's a little town way up on the northern end of California. Seems this Silver Glacier company had bought all the water rights and cut off the local supply."

"I imagine you went up to investigate."

"I went up there to live. I got a job in a local café and watched. People in El Yermo didn't give up. They trucked water in and drilled backyard wells. After a few clashes with the Silver Glacier crew, Pym's little army showed up. They bully the locals and occasionally, people disappear."

"And your friend, Pym Junior?"

"I saw him only once, but he's still there. I know that."

Uzi leaned back, hands behind his head. "Now you are starting to lose my attention, darling. Don't tell me that you sensed his aura, or did the Lemurians come to you in a dream?"

Sally took another drink of her spiked cappuccino. The fennel herb flavor of the absinthe complemented the creamy coffee. She finished it off. "They take their Lemurians quite seriously in that part of the country, Mr. Uzi. But if I were to tell you how I know, you'd more likely believe it was the Lemurians."

One of Uzi's two men tossed back his coffee, stood, and said a few words that Sally didn't catch. They spoke for a moment, Uzi nodded and said to Sally, "Time to go, petal. We've got work to do."

Sally awoke somewhere north of Sacramento. She'd dropped off while they were still stuck in Bay Area evening traffic. Uzi sat at the wheel, silent, competent, stoic. *Like riding in a self-driving car*, she thought. No complaints though; the Jaguar SUV had simply appeared in the coffee house parking lot. He'd thumbed the door lock and climbed in. "Delivered a half hour ago. We get a discount rate for bloody shootouts and kidnappings."

Sally wasn't sure if he was serious, but she didn't question his choice of vehicles. Silent, fast, and wicked comfortable, it rocked her to sleep somewhere north of

Berkley. Now the empty freeway ahead just kept scrolling out of the darkness. A scattering of taillights slid past on her right. Lonely buildings drifted by in pools of yellow light. A green sign reflected their headlamps: *ARBUCKLE 10 MILES.*

She stretched. "Where are we?"

"Interstate Five. About two hours south of Redding."

"And do we have a plan yet, Mr. Whatever your name is?"

"Your friends nicknamed me Uzi. I think I like it."

"All right, Uzi. What's the plan?"

"According to my sources, at exactly six twenty-two a medevac helicopter took off just west of our little unpleasantness."

Sally nodded. They'd discussed this on their way out of San Francisco. "A bit too soon for a response."

"Exactly. Planned, I would say. What better getaway than a flying ambulance? Well, while you were sleeping, my team has been tracking them." He paused to pass a truck. "They tracked this *faux* medevac north. It seems that air traffic control is very strict these days about who goes where, and all. Downside of *that* plan, don't you think?" Uzi turned and grinned at her; the orange dash lights bathed his face in an eerie glow.

"Please tell me you know where they went."

"Umm, not quite. The helicopter landed in Redding to refuel. Then pfft… gone."

"There's a lot of empty country up here, a lot of open water to fish."

"Exactly, my dear. That's why I'm bringing *you*. If we must troll the ocean, we need to use good bait."

Sally glowered at the analogy, but Uzi seemed immune to her non-verbal responses. She let a few more miles glide by, then asked, "We stop in Redding?"

"Food, fuel, and a break, that's all."

Sally straightened in her seat. "Dinner then. I know a wonderful place. What kind of food does the mysterious Uzi eat?" She caught herself. "Hold on. Think about it but don't tell me. I have a game we can play to kill the time."

"You mean like twenty questions?"

"Yes, twenty questions, exactly. Okay, a bit different. I'll ask, and you answer. Then I'll know what you like to eat. No questions about food whatsoever."

"You'll *know*? Would you wager on that?"

"You're on, tough guy. Loser buys." As she spoke, Sally fished an enormous ragged purse from the back seat and drew out a battered notepad computer. "One other thing," she said. "I get to enter your answers in this."

"Nothing about food?"

"Nothing even related. Deal?"

"Ask away. Oh, you are so buying my dinner tonight."

Sally tried a smirk, totally ineffective. "Okay smarty, question one…"

Uzi mulled the first question. "Those are my only choices? Okay, blue." The next one he changed his answer a few times before deciding. More questions, more answers, the miles rolled by.

About ten o'clock, a large green sign loomed out of the dark: *REDDING EXIT 20 MILES*. Sally hunched over her little computer. "Last question: If you had a blue jacket, would it be wool, denim, Gore-Tex, or flannel?" When Uzi answered straight off, she looked up from her screen. "Really?"

"Is it the wrong answer?"

"No wrong answers. I just wasn't expecting that one."

"So, petal. Truth time, what *is* my favorite food?"

"No, we've still got twenty minutes or so. I'll tell you when we get there."

Down a darkened offramp, Sally pointed to a blue and red neon glow. They parked between a row of pickup trucks and motorcycles. She led Uzi inside. The waitress knew her, gave her a quick hug, and winked at Uzi. Sally said a few words.

Once seated, Uzi said, "Do we get menus? I don't usually frequent establishments like this."

"Already ordered for you. And yes, you do. I know better."

"You know? You couldn't."

"Mmm, just wait. Honor system here, you taste what she brings and if I'm wrong, I'll buy whatever you like."

Moments later, the waitress showed up with Sally's usual double Manhattan. She set a Tequila shot and bottle of Corona in front of Uzi, grinned and sauntered off. He sniffed the glass. "*Añejo*. You couldn't possibly have known."

"You grew up on the west coast. I'm guessing L.A. basin. Your father may have been in the military. This whole Israeli Mossad shtick is a disguise. You've had some training… just not sure where yet."

Uzi shook his head. "If I told you, I'd have to shoot you. Cliché, but not a lie. What disturbs me is how close you are to the truth. Not L.A., San Pedro. But nothing more. That's it."

Sally tipped back her drink and smacked her lips. "So satisfying."

Minutes later, their waitress returned with a pair of plates. She set one in front of Uzi and said, "*Conejo asado con picada de ajo.*" The other she handed to Sally. "And one Sally special."

Uzi stared in silence at his plate. Sally took another drink and said, "The rabbit is locally raised. Probably nibbling carrots and pooping little round pellets a few hours ago." When Uzi still didn't answer she continued. "I'll trade if you want. Mine's a Swiss steak sandwich with Havarti cheese and wild mushrooms."

Uzi smirked. "Don't bother. I'm buying."

Once back on the road, Sally opened her notepad and brought up a map. "Okay, we stay on Interstate 5 and turn right on Highway 89. El Yermo is only a few miles east. I'm sure they'll be looking for me to show up there."

"Then that's where we start. Like I said, you are bait *du jour*."

"And where is your hit squad?"

"You won't see them until you need them. Before that happens, perhaps I have twenty questions for you, starting with, *how did you know*?"

"Next to fine cuisine and lost causes, my specialty is computer neural networks," Sally explained. "I've developed a program that takes random questions and profiles a person's taste."

"And a lot more it seems. But how can your little notepad have that much power?"

"It doesn't, but this royal chariot has a wi-fi mobile link, and I still have access to the Columbia University mainframe."

Uzi's jaw dropped. "You hacked my car?"

Sally wanted to laugh. "Please—a child could do it. Okay, that's three questions. Seventeen to go."

"What exactly is it that brought you to El Yermo?"

"Told you, I wait tables, sometimes cook, sometimes pour a little wine."

"But why way up here of all places? Why not in San Francisco or Carmel?"

"I had a lot of appealing choices but couldn't make up my mind. So, I ran my analysis. Guess where the big red spot landed…"

"And it's a coincidence that your dear old friend Pym Junior just happens to be in the same area?"

Sally shrugged. "You know what they say about enemies.'"

"I ask again, why did the 'big red spot' just happen to land on El Yermo?"

"I think it's because there's something here, something in the groundwater, something in the rock, I don't know what. People see things, odd things. They have strange experiences. As I'd said, they take their Lemurians seriously up here. Even the ancient Modoc tribes had their legends about this place."

"Mount Shasta." Uzi turned and caught Sally's eye. "I did hear about it when I was a kid. There was an organization, the Unarians."

"They come visiting, waiting for the saucers to land. Others too. New-agers took over the place for a while. Most left when the weather got cold. A few have settled in the old lumber camps. Silver Glacier drove a lot of them out, but a handful remain."

"Still, it's strange that your machine sent you here. It must be useful for other things besides churning out menu suggestions. Yes?"

She nodded. "That's what got Junior all hot and bothered. The same algorithm that predicts individual behavior also predicts market behavior, currency futures in particular."

"*The* most dangerous game, now I understand."

Sally figured they were at question fourteen when she directed Uzi past El Yermo's darkened storefronts and down a side street. "Park it here. I've got a squat out behind. You can take the sofa."

Across the street a sign, *Pit River Café*, hung above a wooden door and plate glass window. Uzi pulled up and said, "Aren't you afraid our friends might be waiting?"

"Thought that's what you wanted. Oh, and now you're down to five questions."

Sally's *squat* turned out to be a converted garage. Single-car, algae stained cinderblock, it had a bathroom tagged on the back. She flipped a switch; one tube of an old commercial fixture came on. Sally tapped it with a broom handle and the other tube flickered to life. Uzi eyed the battered couch. "No mint on the pillow?"

"Four."

"And you sleep where?"

"I've got a futon in the corner. Three."

"Oh, for the love of all good things. Just *stop* it already. You still haven't answered my question."

"I ran the simulation on myself." She paused and stared through a window at the indigo night sky. "I asked it where I would find happiness."

There really wasn't much else to do but kill the lights and sleep. Sally was pretty sure her new friend had watchers outside. It had taken her a while to spot the lump behind his ear. Rectangular, it looked like an implant. Uzi was getting verbal feed from someone. Most likely the communication was two-way.

She closed her eyes, but sleep evaded her. *A freaking crappy mess. No one should have died. How could Pym's goons have known where she was?* Sally retraced her steps. When Willis failed to show up, she'd bummed a lift to Redding and gone Greyhound to Sacramento. From there, she'd switched to Amtrak and rolled into Oakland in the early morning. By noon she'd found no trace of the man and phoned Maddock.

He'd let it slip? Not possible. Phone? She turned over and rummaged it out of her purse. Older model, cracked screen, it glowed to life at her touch. Sally buttoned it off and used a bent paperclip to eject the SIM card. *Let's not make things too easy.*

Sleep came a little later. Short bouts of unconsciousness punctuated by thoughts of Willis, or of bodies lying strewn about the Vallencourt Plaza. *Was Bonebrake really dead? Was that even possible?* The shootout complicated everything. She dozed again until the cold morning glow roused her. Sally had work to do before that last closing number.

5

It wasn't New York, not that this man really cared. He had a decent chef. His apartment was comfortable. He understood that the local countryside was spectacular, but Augustus Pym Senior had little time for sightseeing. Something other than the view kept him here. His son, his heir had escaped to this provincial wilderness, and Pym needed to find out why.

He powered his motorized chair over to a bank of computer monitors. The market had closed but Pym Investment Trust was already gearing up for tomorrow's opening bell. Shares of Silver Glacier Inc. had dropped another fifteen percent. The old man smiled. He'd shorted the hell out of it, seeding rumors of bankruptcy as he dumped blocks of borrowed shares.

A few pecks on a handheld keyboard and he'd issued a buy order. Enough to cover his short position and fill out his holdings as well, all nicely financed by Wall Street's fear and greed. *If the average investors had any idea how money was really made, they'd run screaming for the exits.*

Silver Glacier had been an accidental gem. It held bits of property all over northern California, including the building he presently occupied. Now Pym was in control, and with some strict management, it would start coining some real money. Not what he'd intended from the first, his initial plan had been simply to create a safe place for his son.

Pym typed out a brief message. Five minutes later, a tall blonde woman strutted in. Her white nurse's uniform ended well above the knees and clung to her body like a bathing suit. "Good evening, Mr. Pym. Ready for your massage?"

He thought about it a moment. *Time was, I'd have had it an hour ago and another one now.* "Not today, just my meds."

Three times she poured a collection of pills into his outstretched palm and three times he downed them with a swallow of water. When he tipped back the last batch, she took his hand to her mouth and licked his index finger. "Are you sure you don't want that massage?

Pym wasn't sure, but business always had to come first, at least these days it seemed to. He looked up at the young lady and tried to smile. "You're very persuasive, certainly another time." He turned back to his monitors, not wanting her to see the anger in his face. "Send in Dr. Goertzner when you leave."

He heard her close the door. A few minutes later, the doctor entered the room and stood behind him. Of all the earth's people, Anton Goertzner was the one person he feared. "May I sit, Mr. Pym?"

Hungarian by birth, the man had no trace of an accent. Pym nodded without turning. "The latest trials? I expected to see your report by now."

"My assistants are still preparing the autopsies."

The old man wheeled back from his monitors and turned. "They died? Both of your subjects died?"

"About thirty minutes ago."

"I should have been informed."

"They were experiencing intense pain; later it became messy. There was nothing that could have been done to change the outcome."

"And in the future, Doctor? How will you ensure that it does not become—messy?"

"We need subjects who have been exposed to the symbiote over a longer period. We need subjects whose mind and body have become accustomed to hosting this thing, whatever it is."

"You speak of my son…"

"Admit it, you've said as much yourself. He had months on that rock before you recovered him, at least what's left of him."

Doctor Goertzner had just pushed one of his buttons. Pym maintained a steady gaze, the unblinking stare that defied analysis. "You'll not have my son until you can guarantee your results."

"Then perhaps one of those who left him there might have been exposed?"

"We are working on that. What about yourself? You may have been exposed as well."

"If you are suggesting that I take the infusion, then maybe you would like to watch the next round of experiments. It will help you understand why I might decline."

"Why don't we both go down now and observe the autopsy instead."

Pym waited for a response, but the doctor was good at his own game. He nodded and said, "Lead the way. I'll be curious to see if there are any unusual—*reactions*."

Pym's private elevator took them down two floors to the third level. The doors cycled open. He wheeled into a long gray hall and trundled to the end. Doctor Goertzner followed. Quick strides powered his compact frame right behind Pym's motorized chair.

The room they entered had been a morgue long before Crystal Glacier bought the property from the U.S. Government. Pym had wondered why a research facility would need a morgue, so he did some digging. It took more than a casual search, but he learned about psychotropic drug experiments that had been carried out during the cold war. It seemed that more than a few brave soldiers had died fighting on a very different kind of battlefield.

Inside, two medical technicians bent over a naked male corpse. Pym wheeled up next to them and touched a control on his chair. It whined for a moment, then unfolded slowly, standing him upright. "What killed this man?"

The older of the two looked up from his work. Pym noted that dissecting a corpse didn't seem to bother him. He also caught the tech's quick glance to Goertzner. "Look at his muscles, they've all torn loose from their ligaments. And his heart," the tech held up a twisted purple mass, "it's like it exploded."

"What do the blood tests show?"

"We drained the chest cavity and exsanguinated what was left of his circulatory system, but so far, we've found nothing in the blood."

"No parasites, no antigens?"

"We're running cultures now. It may take a while."

Pym glanced at a covered figure on the adjacent table. "And the other, the woman?"

"The same. We've taken brain tissue and spinal samples. They are being frozen and thin-sectioned as we speak."

Goertzner interrupted. "How long was it before she died?"

The younger man glanced at his colleague, then resumed working on the cadaver. The older man cleared his throat. "You mean after she went symptomatic?"

"Yes, I mean after she started shrieking for mercy."

"How long was it, Jason?"

The young technician looked sick. "It was forty-six hours and twenty-two minutes, sir."

Pym returned his chair to a sitting position. Goertzner said, "Have you seen enough, Mr. Pym?"

"No, not until the tests and samples return. Not until

we find out what killed these two."

"And the previous two? And the ones before that? What about the bones we found in the subbasement below the lower level? What do you think killed them?"

Master of the unblinking stare, Pym shot back, "I brought you on because you are the world's leading psychophysiologist. I brought you on because you could be the one man who best understands the relationship between the brain and the body. Well I'm waiting *Doctor* Goertzner, I'm waiting to hear those answers coming from you."

Button pushed right back. Pym spun his chair toward the door and said, "Don't you have some work to do?"

6

Maddock awoke secured to a cot, his head an excruciating combination of fever and pain. He felt something trickling from his brow that ran down his cheek. Blood, he could still taste it in his mouth. His left eye was swollen shut. He tried opening his right only to find it covered. He tested his bonds, tight but not constrictive, professional.

A door opened, then closed. He could hear someone enter the room. Maddock relaxed. He lay still like he'd been taught. *Play dead if you must.*

"I know you are conscious, Mr. Maddock." A soft voice, male, no accent but a slight rise in pitch told him the speaker was an older man. "And look, you've torn open your bandage again."

"Bones?" Maddock felt his voice croak. He swallowed a mass of congealed blood and phlegm.

"No bones broken, not even your thick skull, though my men did try. Ah, wait lay still—you mean your colleague, Uriah Bonebrake."

Maddock had no trouble lying still. When he didn't answer, the voice continued. "Mr. Bonebrake has been a problem. He shot three of my people you know, good loyal men. I expect that he's dead by now, but no worries, I only need one of you."

"Pym—Senior."

"We meet at last, Mr. Maddock, although under troubling circumstances. You cost me my son. Now I want him back." The door opened again, a few mumbled words, Pym continued, "My medic is here to put some sutures in that eyebrow. It will hurt, but they'll hold much better than the tape."

Maddock tried not to flinch when the needle passed through his skin. Another pass, then another, still nothing like the general pain and nausea he felt. *Under questioning, say as little as possible.* He tried to relax his arms, the clench in his shoulders, the twitch in his foot. He heard a curious click and hum as Pym changed position. *Wait for it.*

Footsteps again, pressure on his forehead. Then the door. "My medic will return with some—uh, medicine. First one question."

Let Pym do the talking...

"Why didn't you just shoot him when you had the chance?"

"Your son?"

"You're damned right, *my son.*" Agitated rustling, then a mechanical whirr of a motorized chair. "Why did you condemn him to that cursed island?"

"Not..." Maddock coughed and cleared his throat, "not my decision."

"No, no of course not. Your friend Willis Sanders held the gun. You'll be happy to know he's safe... for a while. It was the girl, wasn't it? She has a cruel streak. She'd have convinced him not to fire. She knows, Mr. Maddock. She knows what happens to people who spend too much time on Maug Island."

"What does happen, Mr. Pym?"

"As if you don't know yourself. As if you don't feel it. My son was not the same when we pulled him off that rock. He has something growing inside him. Something that will soon be growing inside of you, Mr. Maddock."

The door opened again. Wheels on linoleum, they rolled up to the cot where he lay. A touch on his leg, a cold swab, then the fiery pain of a scalpel slice skin and subcutaneous tissue. Maddock felt a large needle enter the wound, probe, then jab home. Muffled conversation followed, then the same soft voice, "You may experience some discomfort. I will return shortly to see how you are doing."

The door again, receding footsteps, then silence. Maddock struggled with his bonds. He tried to shake the cloth from his right eye; he tried to loosen the tape that held his arms. Nothing moved. The burning sensation rose in his leg. It reached his hip before a nauseous wave of vertigo gripped him, spun him. Like a new recruit with a belly full of cheap booze, Maddock felt the cot spin and sway beneath him.

A blinding light, then a tall menacing shadow loomed above him. "Holy crap, Maddock, you actually got uglier. I didn't think that was possible."

Maddock blinked his one eye. The shadow circled his cot, loosening his bonds. Arms free, legs free, he reached down and pulled a six-inch catheter needle from his leg. That tiny motion brought on a series of dry heaves. He rolled on his side and retched.

A hand on his shoulder, "Let's go. We've got to leave and I'm too banged up to carry you."

The vertigo only intensified when Maddock placed his feet on the floor and sat upright. He put his head between his knees. It didn't help.

"Let's go, dude. The bad guys are coming and we're bugging out now."

"Bones…"

"Yeah, in the flesh, at least most of it. Come on. We'll go out through the window."

Maddock half pushed, half dragged himself to his feet.

"It's only a three story drop to the ground," Bones continued. "We can shinny down that drainpipe."

"I'm glad you're still alive," Maddock said. A wave of vertigo passed over him.

"I won't be for much longer if you don't get your narrow ass out of that window.

Maddock dragged himself up and Bones shoved him headfirst over the windowsill. *Dark, of course, it was night.* The drainpipe, off to his right, he clutched it and pulled. His belt buckle caught for a moment, then let go. The remainder of him slid out the window like a dead fish from a plastic bucket. Arm looped around the pipe, he dangled for a moment, slid down about five feet of cement block wall, then lost his grip. Instinct propelled his arm out, he clutched a window ledge, hung for another moment, then fell.

A tree branch broke beneath his weight and Maddock found himself sprawled faceup across a scrubby manzanita bush. The moon hovered overhead like a silent prowling wraith and an equally silent shadow descended the wall above him.

A thump, and the shadow stood at his side. "Crude but effective," Bones said.

"I don't know if I can move my legs." Maddock wiggled his toes. They still seemed to work.

"No choice. You're far too fat to carry and we need to scram."

"You were shot."

"They put a patch on me... good as new as soon as my collar bone knits."

Maddock tried to flex his knees. He heard the brush crackle beneath him. Something gave way and he flopped to the ground. His legs tingling, Maddock staggered to his feet and looked around. They stood at the edge of a dark forest next to a five-story masonry building. It towered over them, windows dimly lit. "Where do you think we are?"

"No clue, but we need to get clear of this place. They've got dogs. Sicced them on me first time I got loose."

"First time?"

"Yep. Remind me to show you the scars."

They stumbled between scrubby pines. Keeping to the shadows, they worked their way down a rocky slope until Bones stopped, face pressed against a wire fence. "U.S. Government standard security fence."

With only one good eye, Maddock could barely pick it out in the gloom. "Looks like the barbed wire top slopes toward us."

"Meant to keep people in. Not good, old buddy. We've got about five minutes before they put the dogs on us." A mad barking sounded in the distance. "Or less."

"That way," Maddock pointed off to his left, "down the hill. I've got a hunch."

"I love it when a plan comes together."

Maddock led them between the dense pines. The fence contoured downward. He hoped the dark forest would slow their pursuers, but the dogs seemed right at their backs.

Turning to make a stand, Maddock's feet slipped from under him. Jagged wire poked him in the shins. "It's here," he hissed.

A shallow gully passed beneath the fence. Filled with rocks and pine needles it was invisible in the dark. Maddock dragged himself under. Bones almost made it. His bandaged shoulder caught on the twisted wire ends and pinned him halfway.

Frantic barking, snarling, something had Bones by his arm. Maddock found a stick and jabbed it up at a pair of yellow eyes; the dog held on. He worked the wire loose from Bones' shoulder. His friend pulled himself through, dragging the dog with him. Rottweiler, massive shoulders, it growled and thrashed beneath the fence. Hooked on the same wire barb that had held Bones, still it wouldn't let go.

Flashes from the darkness, shots whined off the wire

links and slammed into pine trees behind them. Finally, Bones managed to land a couple of hard kicks. The dog yelped and backed away, snarling. It watched them slip away, but didn't' try to follow.

They scrambled in the darkness, hands and knees, shots smacking bark off the tree trunks around them. Maddock found himself much steadier, but his head still throbbed, and his face burned with every passing pine branch. The slope ended at the crest of a rocky cliff. They worked their way around and arrived at a bubbling creek that tumbled from somewhere in the hills above.

Bones looked both directions and said, "They'll expect us to cross, so we head upstream."

Maddock started up the creek bed. "This only confuses dogs in the movies. "Good thing those were guard dogs, not trackers," Bones said. "Now it's Pym's men that I'm worried about. Mercenaries, they'll track us, but not until daylight."

Maddock stopped. "Trackers—Bones, check your pockets."

"Clean empty. You?"

"Something, feels like a cigarette lighter." Maddock held up a small black cylinder. "Damn, it's a miniature GPS unit."

"They're on their way. We keep underestimating these guys."

Maddock snapped the limb off of a dead tree, shoved the unit into a crack in the wood, and tossed it into the water.

"How far do you think it will float before they get wise?" Bones asked.

"Let's not wait around to find out."

A few miles farther, they reached the foot of a high waterfall that hissed and shimmered in the starlight. Maddock growled and led them back downstream to a wide spot in the bank. Between the trees again, he groped his way forward in the pitch dark. "Where do you think we are?" he asked.

"Nowhere near a city, look at that sky."

Maddock leaned back. His left eye, still swollen, burned like hell. He wiped the congealing blood from his face and stared up between the trees. Above him, a sliver of stars glowed like a jeweler's cabinet. "It's not San Francisco, that's for sure. I just wonder what happened to Sally."

"What about her?" Bones asked." Do you think she escaped?"

"Pym was saying as much—without saying it. What I wonder, is where did that Uzi character slither off to?"

"Let's go find out."

Maddock let Bones take the lead. Cherokee Indian, he'd been raised in the hills of North Carolina. Sometimes his friend carried the *Indian* persona a little too far, but Maddock knew that when it came to woodcraft, Bones was the real deal. The trail wound along the edge of a clearing then passed back beneath the trees.

By the time they'd reached another clearing, the stars had faded, and the sky had turned a pale gray. Maddock trudged along in a half-dream of Willis lying atop a glittering pyramid. One step, *get up Willis*, another step, *come on, buddy—get up*. An eternity passed climbing in the cold dawn. They rounded a large boulder. Bones stopped dead and fell to his knees. Maddock circled behind him and halted mid stride. Clad in a mantle of glittering snow, a lone peak, the God of all mountains blazed in glory against the morning sky. Almost in prayer, Bones spoke its name: "Shasta."

7

Sensory deprivation, **Willis** thought, although he knew it wasn't. The voices, the sensations, he could hear his own heart beating like a solitary kettledrum in the darkness. *Sally must have felt something like this when she first connected with what she called her* "Moogly-Woogly." *The* Ma'óghe, *the Eternal One.*

"Is that why I'm here?" He shouted at the dark vastness around him. "You want to come talk about it?"

Some acoustic oddity of his prison killed echoes like a carpeted ceiling. Willis sat at the center of his own eternal night and waited. Expecting nothing, he nearly jumped to his feet when a scattering of tiny colored lights glittered above his head. "You doing that? Trying to mess with me? Well, it ain't working."

"I didn't do that, Mr. Sanders. You did." The voice whispered from everywhere and nowhere. Willis felt for a moment that he, himself might have said it.

"Pym. I should have taken you down when I had the chance."

The lights faded and began winking out. "Now see, your negative vibrations are driving them away."

"You can stop the head games Junior. They won't work on me."

"Oh, but they're working already. We'll just sit quietly for a while and see if your friends don't come back."

Despite Willis' shouts and taunts, the ghostly voice didn't return. *Had he imagined it? Possibly.* He resumed his seat on the sandy floor and thought of Sally. It helped, that image of a Pekingese running with a pack of Dobermans. He smiled to himself. *She held her own too.* A cluster of tiny lights sparkled blue and yellow in the darkness above. Others flickered, lower on the wall, and the mindless chatter resumed its burbling monolog on the far edge of his consciousness.

Willis tried to ignore it. He said nothing, he covered his eyes and tried to think of other things. A dozen heartbeats, a hundred, then a thousand passed. He stilled his breathing, concentrated on his pulse, calmed his mind. *He could do this.* Same as sleeping on a helicopter, he just had to focus.

His hands slipped from his face and Willis stared about in wonder. Like sitting at the center of a blazing jewel, ten thousand, thousand shimmering colors glittered in the space around him. Almost without volition, he rose from the ground and began walking.

He saw only lights, no reflections, no shadows, no gray boulders looming in the darkness. Nothing dispelled the eternal night. *They're inside my head, like the damned voices.* Willis spun, but the lights remained fixed. He covered his eyes, they disappeared. *I'm making this up. Bastard's got my own head working against me.*

He held up a hand and moved it across his field of vision. Each tiny speck winked out behind his fingers and reappeared as his hand passed. *Or maybe not.* A simple line of poetry sprang unbidden to his mind: "*...all I ask is a tall ship and a star to steer her by.*" What Willis saw before him blazed like an entire constellation.

8

Maddock's shadow stretched out long and gangly before him. It limped and staggered as he climbed.

"Eastern slope of Mt. Shasta," Bones said. "About as far from anywhere as you can get in Northern California."

"Pym's mercs won't give up." Maddock gazed up at the slope ahead of them, steeper, rockier, and more exposed than ever. "You're going to have a hard time climbing with that injury."

On the hillside far below three crows broke from the chaparral and fled squawking to the north. Bones crouched low and said, "They're right down there. You got a plan?"

"Back to the trees." Maddock pointed the same direction the crows had flown. "We don't want to be seen."

"Yeah, but we'll be a lot easier to track."

"That's the idea. Maddock led them through a narrow gully and contoured the hillside until they entered a small copse of live oak.

"I don't understand your plan."

"If they're going to catch us, I want it to be on our terms."

He led them deeper into the stands of live oak and manzanita. Their feet left dark patches where they'd disturbed the blanket of fallen leaves. Bones shook his head in disapproval but followed in silence. Maddock didn't look back. His friend could move like campfire smoke when he wanted.

Another thousand yards and Maddock started to hear things, small things like birds silenced mid-song, like a stray branch zipping against Kevlar. *They're good,* he thought. *No radio crackle, no cigarette smoke.* He searched for his place, *the* place.

A hundred feet farther he spotted a cliff top. Oak trees thinned out, blue sky, and a million-dollar view. *If we've got to make a last stand, there's worse places to do it.* He dashed across the open space. Bullets zinged off the rocks and whined out into blue emptiness before him. *Warning shots, nothing more.* Maddock dove behind a boulder.

An amplified voice resounded from within the tree line: "Come out, you're surrounded."

He lay low, his feet dangling over a mile of nothingness. No one would get behind him, that was certain. *Would they dare a rush? Depends on how many there are.*

He and Bones waited, watching, listening. Bones heard them a moment before Maddock did. "Here they come."

Maddock sprang to his feet just as a man jumped on the boulder before him. An acre of Kevlar and straps, short brown hair, muscles, wide eyes blue as a morning sky. Maddock clutched him by the jacket and let the man's momentum carry him clear over the edge. The screams didn't come until later.

"You just killed my buddy, asshole!" someone shouted.

Finger like a Polish sausage wrapped about the trigger of a MAC-10 submachine gun. So close, Maddock couldn't see the man's face. So close, the forty-five caliber muzzle and fat, gray noise suppressor filled his vision. A steel cobra, it followed his movements. Maddock put his hands on his head. From behind came the crackle and clatter of radio traffic. He concentrated on the problem before him.

The gun twitched. "Stand up, peckerneck."

Maddock complied. No sudden movement. The merc stepped back half a pace. Lean through the cheekbones, short-cropped hair, camo jacket, he spat on the ground. "Supposed to take you alive, or else I'd chop you to bits right now just to hear you scream." He paused and squinted his eyes a moment. "You know why I'm okay with that? Because there's something waiting for you back at the lab that's much worse than anything I could dish out."

Maddock felt it first in his gut. Subsonic, the *wup-wup-wup* of helicopter blades chewing air. More radio chatter. The noise intensified, and he could hear the turbines whine as it approached. It almost masked another sound, a screen door slamming. Once, twice, then the gust of downwash and engine roar. The man with the MAC-10 knelt, scanning the tree line. The muzzle never moved.

Maddock waited for the landing, for the hurricane blast to subside and the wailing turbines to wind down. Instead, they rose to a shriek and the rotor wash flung a tornado of sticks and leaves at them. Maddock slammed his arm into the fat gray suppressor as a spray of half-inch bullets burned past his face. The merc reversed his weapon and hammered the buttstock into Maddock's forehead. An instant of stars and confusion, a spinning branch caught him in the back, knocking him face down, halfway over the cliff. Blinded by the dirt and the pain, Maddock slid to the edge. He felt the merc's knees come down on his back and the muzzle rest against his skull.

Maddock let go. Arms flailing, weapon spinning away, the merc tried to jump back, tried to grab—anything. Maddock clung to a tiny crevice on the cliff face and watched his assailant tumble into the valley below.

Heavy caliber automatic weapons fire sprayed from the helicopter as it struggled into the air. Hanging from the cliff face, Maddock got a look. White fuselage, red cross on the side, flames shooting from the starboard engine, it howled into the sky trailing smoke like an enraged dragon.

Circling, it headed back. Upper nacelle a mass of flames, it screamed toward him. Machine guns flashed from both sides of craft. Maddock flattened against the naked rock as bullets tore soil from the ground and cut deep furrows where they struck. The damaged machine sank as it approached, white-hot blebs of metal spraying from its burning engines. At the last moment, it banked. The flying blades passed a few yards from where he clung. Maddock dragged himself back to the top as the helicopter circled away. It dropped toward the valley floor. Its engines silent now, only the whisper of its flashing rotors echoed back.

"Pilot's trying to autogiro." Bones stood at his side, holding what looked like a small cannon in his hand. "Hmm, he might make it, too."

"Took you long enough."

Bones seemed not to hear. He stood at the edge and peered into the chasm just beyond his toes. "There were six like I thought." He paused, watching. "Nope, trees got them before they could land. Let's go find you some boots."

"First you've got to tell me what that monster is you're toting."

"Barrett M95, badass fifty caliber sniper gun. Its former owner is back there in the trees." Bones flung the massive rifle over the cliff edge. "I guess they figured you were going put up a fight."

Four bodies lay in the woods. Maddock helped drag them out in the open. Little more than ground meat, they'd taken rounds from both sides. Bones hefted one of their MAC-10s. "Never liked these things, too heavy. The suppressor is nice and the forty-five packs a punch, but a hand grenade is more accurate."

Maddock jumped when he heard a radio squawk. Then realized it was still strapped to one of the bodies. "They're going to come looking for us pretty soon and I don't want to stick around."

Bones stacked two of the MAC-10s and a half dozen

spare magazines near the cliff edge. Maddock rolled one of the corpses on its side. "Bastard's got my knife." He clipped it to his belt and rummaged up flashlights, canteens, and a pair of boots—much better than the sodden athletic shoes he'd been wearing.

"Everything else goes over the cliff, especially radio man there," Bones said. "Next time Pym's mercs show up, they're going to be pissed as hell and packing nukes. We won't outshoot them, so let's travel light and fight smart."

Maddock started to move, but the ground moved with him. A low grumbling, he scrambled back from the edge as the rocks settled beneath his feet.

Bones pointed behind them. "Holy crap, we got problems." A slice of raw earth appeared just in front of the tree line.

A stunned microsecond, then sprinting, yelling, they dashed the twenty yards of sliding cliff and leaped into space. Maddock's fingers slammed into a wall of broken rocks. His nails tore on jagged stone edges. He slid, gripped, wedged his feet. "Bones, where are you man?"

"Almost six feet under."

Maddock looked down at his friend dangling by one good arm over a tumbled ruin of dust and broken trees. "Just shut up. I'm coming down."

He managed to slide down nearly in reach of his friend. Bones couldn't let go, and Maddock barely maintained his own uncertain grip. He drew the combat knife from his belt and jammed it to the hilt in a fresh crevice. "I'll grab your arm. You pull up and try to find a foothold."

Before his friend could reply, Maddock gripped the knife with his left hand, swung down, and clutched Bones' wrist. The big Cherokee grunted, pulled and swung a leg up. Two points of support. Maddock felt the knife twist and slip sideways. "Come on. Find another hold."

Bones teetered a moment, kicking the broken rock surface, then found a tiny ledge with his left foot. "Let go, I got it."

Maddock released his grip. Bones slapped the rock just above their heads, gripped and pulled. Another move, and Maddock used the knife grip as a foothold while steadying Bones against his back. A little higher, and he put his hand over a large rock, seized his friend by the belt and heaved him within reach of the edge. The ground shook again. "Aftershock. Go, go, go."

They both crested the broken cliff face. Maddock turned and dragged his friend the final few feet. Beneath them, the ground trembled. All around the trees swayed and little puffs of dust jetted from between the rocks. "Keep going," Maddock yelled. "Run."

Bones needed no encouragement. He sprinted through the trees and leapt over boulders. The two cleared the forest edge and scrambled another hundred yards up the mountain as half the world broke free and tumbled away behind them. Maddock paused, breath screaming in his lungs like great mouthfuls of Texas chili. Bones looked back. "That's what I call a decent burial."

"I think the mountain tried to kill us."

"It'll take more than a mountain. Where to?"

"We head north, stay below the tree line and out of sight."

Maddock started picking his way between the tumbled rocks and scree. "I sure wish we'd saved one of those canteens."

"You got your boots and I still got my butt attached. That's what matters right now."

By midday, they'd descended almost a thousand feet and worked their way into a forest of stunted pines. With branches swept to the south, the trees looked like so many hitchhikers thumbing their way to San Diego. Bent to the ground, Bones said little. Maddock followed, lost in his own thoughts. *They would find water, but food? Not so likely. Night would get cold. They'd want to den up long before sundown.*

Bones grunted, cut downhill, and circled a large pine.

"Check this out."

The skeletal remains of an elk lay sprawled beneath the branches. Bones knelt beside it. Maddock sniffed. "A little gamy for my taste."

Bones poked around the carcass, drew out a slender arrow, and handed it to Maddock. "What do you make of this?"

"Only that a Cherokee Indian can track an elk six days after its dead."

"Look again, white man. This thing has been dead a lot longer than six days."

Bits of fur and desiccated skin clung to the bones, but the remainder of the carcass had been stripped clean. Maddock examined the arrow. It was in good condition, its birch shaft still smooth. The fletching looked odd, white feathers, long and tapered. Maddock examined the point, milky opal tied with gut and sealed with rosin. "I used to have a collection of stone points. This one's a beauty."

"Perhaps, but who uses them for hunting?"

"Someone did. Do you think they're still around?"

"We never left."

Maddock spun about. Nobody. Not a soul in sight.

Bones stood slowly, hands outstretched. "You have spoken. Show yourselves now, that we may name you, and you may name us."

"The name we give outsiders is 'enemy.' The name you may give us is 'death.'"

"My people name outsiders 'guest' until proven otherwise. How is that different here?"

Three shadowy figures arose from where they crouched. Cloaked in grass and branches, they had been invisible. One stepped forward, weathered brown face, prominent cheekbones, glittering obsidian eyes. "I name you both 'Dog' until proven otherwise."

Bones bowed in acknowledgement. "And so I will call you 'The People,' until I know you better."

The three turned and filed off into the forest without another word. Bones turned, touched a finger to his lips, and followed. Maddock scratched an itchy leg, caught himself and trotted after his friend.

"What just happened?" Maddock said in a low voice. "Is that a ritual of some kind?"

Bones shrugged. "I think I saw it in a movie."

Maddock barked a rueful laugh and shook his head.

The People followed a trail visible only to themselves. They took no regular path through the forest, but often doubled back. After an hour they halted next to a clear stream. Maddock stepped forward, but Bones held him back. Each of the three People knelt and drank in turn, then left before the two Dogs could drink. Bones shook his head and Maddock understood. They were to be tested.

Crossing the creek, the People cut a straighter path. They followed the mountain's contours, continuing north into deep stands of old-growth Douglas fir. Maddock watched for landmarks but knew that he would be helpless trying to retrace his steps. Ahead of him, Bones stayed five paces behind the People. He hardly glanced at their surroundings.

The afternoon light began to fade when the three halted. Their spokesman ignored Maddock but addressed Bones. "A dog that is not trained cannot be trusted. We must blind you and muzzle you here. Do not resist."

At Bones' brief nod, the old man emptied two bags into a third. The last Maddock saw was Bones' head disappearing into a course sack. Moments later, a similar bag was drawn over his own head and pulled down to his shoulders. Light glittered through the woven strands. Wet straw, mildew, and a pungent smoky odor filled his nostrils. *Food bag, they'd carried food with them.* Maddock let that sink in. *These three had been waiting—for something.*

His stomach growled in response. *When had he eaten last?* His headache, tamed for a while by adrenaline, now returned tenfold. *They were both starving and dehydrated.* Maddock wondered if this was how the People treated their dogs.

Moving again, his hand on Bone's shoulder, he picked his way by down a steep decline. He could see a little below the edge of his hood, dirt, rocks, tree roots, and a steep dropoff just to his left. Maddock still carried the white arrow drawn from the decaying elk carcass. He took care not to drop it or snag it on branches.

The afternoon light continued to fade, and Maddock felt like they were descending into a bottomless canyon. A trail now, a good trail, it followed a creek that burbled gently among the stones. He'd been smelling smoke for a while, not certain if it was from the sack over his face or something else. Now in the deepening gloom, Maddock heard voices above the creek's endless song. Perhaps children, or young girls, he couldn't tell. Moments later, the voices fell quiet.

They were led in silence. Maddock felt the glow of a fire to his right. He saw pebbly earth trampled hard beneath his feet. He smelled people yet heard nothing but the creek. They were led three times in a circle about the fire then seated in a pile of rocks and firewood some distance away.

"Dogs will stay here until told to move."

It was impossible to find a comfortable position. As daylight faded, so did the lingering warmth of the afternoon. He and Bones huddled together. Their hoods remained in place and although neither of them had been bound, they both knew it was part of the test. Blinded and muzzled. *Presumably that meant he couldn't see and shouldn't speak.*

The voices had resumed, definitely children and women. Some male voices as well along with a background of singing that started and stopped. It hit him, *native American, pre-contact.* Of course, Bones must have known. *What were the tribes up here? Modoc, Pomo?* Maddock wished he could talk to his friend but knew better.

It seemed like hours passed, huddled among the rocks. One of those blood-drenched Kevlar jackets would have been most welcome. Bones had collapsed into a heap and begun to snore, but Maddock could no more sleep than he could fly out of there. Whatever Pym had injected into him had never fully left his body. His legs still tingled, and his left arm felt stiff and clumsy at his side. He shivered in the cold night air.

What was it that Pym—Pym Senior had said? *"He has something growing inside him. Something that will soon be growing inside of you."* Maddock felt it. Something lurked in silent curiosity beneath his skin. A consciousness, neither malicious nor benign, it seemed to await—something.

Arms clutched across his chest, he f deeper into the pile of rocks and dead leaves. His eye, still swollen shut, burned where it had been slapped by a hundred branches. His head still throbbed like the mother of all hangovers. A flock of demented pigeons circled his brain, each with a question strapped to its leg. *Why had they been brought here? Why had they been left, abandoned?* He longed to tear the sack from his face, but Bones had played along. He'd do the same.

The fever dreams arrived just before dusk. Legions in Blue. Riding horses, firing rifles. The old men go down first, a living shield protecting the warriors. He cocks his ancient muzzle-loader and places a cap on the nipple. Blue eyes thundering from the shadows, he fires and draws his knife. The horse rides him down like piled up trash. Tumbling, lost in a hell of burning lodges. Smoke, smoke everywhere, filling his nose, burning his lungs. Tortoise Shell Woman sprawls dead over her wailing child. A bullet silences the boy, and the Legions in Blue ride on. Knife, useless knife, he runs for the bushes and never hears the shot that severs his spine.

Maddock startled awake, shaking in cool evening air. The scent of burning wood filtered through the course, brown sack. Waning sunlight sparkled from the creek. He glimpsed it just beneath the cloth. Then two moccasins—beaded moccasins—stood before him. "It is time, Dogs. Come."

9

Marumda, Dreamer of the World, Marumda, Father of the People, Marumda Keeper of the Earth plunged shivering from the gray dawn of chaos into the hot darkness of his father's sweat lodge. Vast beyond understanding, it spanned a world as yet unformed. It swarmed with the ghosts of ten thousand warriors yet unborn.

His father Kuksu came to him and said, "All is ready my son, Dreamer of the World. Why do you wait?"

"I cannot be certain that my children, the People, will not shame you when I bring them forth."

To this Kuksu replied, "I care not for these People; they are your People not mine. If they cannot behave, then the shame is yours. If the world shames you, then let it be destroyed and another take its place."

Marumda then rose from the sweat lodge of his father. Rise he did in smoke. Rise he did in great trembling, until a pillar of fire towered over the land. Then Marumda brought forth the deer. He brought forth elk and bear and crawling things of all sort. Marumda stretched his arms and filled the world with trees and meadows. He filled the rivers with fish and the sky with birds. Finally, he plucked five hairs from his right eyebrow and blew on them. Behold, a tribe of warriors stood before him. He then plucked five hairs from his left eyebrow. A single breath, and they became a village of industrious women.

Marumda's people grew in number, and he was pleased. They behaved with honor. No man lay with his daughter, nor sister with her brother, and he knew no shame. When the river teemed with fish, he taught his People how to catch them in willow baskets. When deer ran in the meadow, he taught his People of bows and arrows. And when the winds of autumn blew cold from the mountain, he taught his People how to gather from the forest and store food for the winter.

Then the snows descended on the great mountain and Marumda returned to his lodge. For indeed, the mountain itself was his home and while he slept within, it stood quiet sentinel, but when he awoke, it trembled and smoked. On that day, when he once more ventured forth, Marumda found a change in his People. They no longer lived together in harmony and honor. He stood among them and said, "Do not shame me, your father, but live in peace as before and follow the laws I have taught you."

A young woman stepped forth, slender of limb like a vixen fox, with the dark eyes of a yearling doe. "You have forsaken your People," she said. "They suffered of cold and fear while you were away. I have given them what you would not."

Then Marumda saw what he had not seen before. His People had fire. They ate of cooked flesh and warmed their lodges at night. The woman continued. "How do you expect your People to follow the law when they must live like animals?"

Marumda listened to this woman, bringer of fire. He beheld her beauty and asked of her name. "I have no name," she replied, "as you have not yet named me."

So Marumda called her Killeli, Keeper of the Fires. He took her to his lodge deep within the mountain where old fires lived in red embers and said, "Here you will be my wife and keeper of all that dwells below." Marumda took her then. He lay with Killeli in his great lodge beneath the mountain and got her with child.

She bore him a son who came in the spring. Marumda permitted Killeli to present their child to the People. He called on his father Kuksu to witness and bless the boy at his naming ceremony. But his father arrived in great wrath and threw Marumda to the ground. Killeli he threw to the ground as well and thundered, "Do you not know this woman? Did she not tell you?"

Marumda could not answer but looked to his wife. She did not weep, Killeli, but held his eye and said, "While you slept, Kuksu made me. He made your sister as he made you. I cared for your people as you would not. It is you who did not follow the laws, and now your People will not behave. It is you who lay with your sister and the shame is yours."

As she spoke, Killeli transformed into a doe elk. She sprang for the hills, shining like the sun, but Marumda drew a single white arrow and pinned her to the earth. "Keeper of the Fires you will remain," he said, "and never again will you walk beneath the sky save this one day, this naming day, when you will come each year to witness the sorrows you have caused."

So Marumda named their son Coyote, trickster, bringer of chaos. He brought forth another lodge, a lodge of fire, lesser than his own, but still towering over the earth. Killeli he bound within. He bound her with fire and smoke, and there she nursed Coyote her son. Marumda hid in shame. He descended into his lodge and was seen no more.

None were left to lead the People. None taught them of the hunt, none guarded them from shame. Seeing the People wandering thus, Killeli loosed her son Coyote on the world to lead The People in Marumda's place.

Sitting now in his lodge, his sweat lodge, Dreamer of the World felt the drums of creation *ta-tap, tom, tap* inside him. He heard Kuksu singing between the Sundering Ocean and the Eternal Blue Sky. Marumda breathed fragrant herbs, sage and bay laurel. His spirit faded, leaving Dane Maddock slumped in the stifling darkness. He'd long made his own peace with Coyote, now a mountain of Cherokee perspiring at his side.

Within the shadows of the lodge, Maddock made out three other figures, one drumming, one chanting and one dancing. He still held the arrow, the white shaft tipped with milky opal and felt it now, a silent bond between the divine spirit Marumda and his sister of fire.

Roused that evening from their bed of sticks and leaves, he and Bones had been led in silence to a sweltering pit beneath a low roof of branches and woven reeds. Their blinds had been removed as they entered. Given bowls of water, they'd been told to disrobe and sit. Maddock had settled cross-legged, his butt resting on a padded mat. Exhaustion, heat, and the rhythmic drumming had soon eased the spirit from his aching body. Through the eyes of Marumda he had witnessed the fires of creation. With Marumda's hands, he had embraced the warmth of Killeli's eager body, and on his shoulders, he had borne the weight of Marumda's crushing shame.

Upon awakening, Maddock touched his face. Not quite as swollen, it still burned beneath his fingers. His legs felt numb as he stretched them out. He tried to move his toes. Bones twitched at his side but said nothing. The drumming slowed, the dancing stopped, and the chanting figure stood, a tall shadow among shadows. "Rise now and be Dogs no more."

Maddock stood on shaky legs. Bones rose beside him,

hunched over beneath the arched ceiling of woven mats. They followed their guide, ducking past a heavy door-flap. Dappled sunlight glittered between the trees. A narrow valley spread before them. A scattering of low rounded roofs, cookfires, dogs barking in the distance. Bones muttered, "Aquarian Utopia."

"We are the *Okwanuchu*, the True People, the last remaining." Their guide spoke without accent. He could have been a Stanford University professor, but his Native American heritage was clearly written on his face. He presented each of them with a robe. "Cover yourselves and join me in the council lodge. You've been given a vision and we would hear of it."

Maddock examined the garment as he walked. Doeskin, lined with soft, hand-loomed fabric, its workmanship was remarkable. Their guide threaded between a scatter of low, rounded lodges. Cookfires glowed in the darkness. As they crossed the encampment, curious eyes tracked their steps. Maddock didn't stare back. Bones ducked low to follow their host into a long structure of bent branches and thatch. An older woman faced them across small fire.

Dressed as he imagined natives of northern California might have dressed, still the two betrayed certain anachronisms. The woman wore a watch and a gold wedding band. Their host reached beneath his buckskin tunic and drew out a pair of glasses. Black plastic rims, they made him look even more like a college professor.

Their host seated himself, but the older woman remained standing. She smiled at Bones and said, "You probably think we're play-acting, perhaps weekend warriors of a sort."

Bones ducked his head even lower. "Ma'am, I don't know what you are, but before morning, you're going to have all hell rain down on your heads."

Neither of them seemed surprised. The woman nodded. "Gentlemen, you have no idea what all hell could be. Why don't we sit down and talk it over?"

Maddock remained standing. "We played along with your charade, and that ritual, whatever it was. But my friend is injured and I'm sick. We're both dehydrated and starving. Why shouldn't I just walk out of here right now?"

Their guide spoke up. "The sweat lodge rite you endured was necessary. We have food coming, water too, but you must understand, what my wife said is more important than you know. Stay, listen."

Maddock nodded and sat. *A little food might relieve his throbbing headache and dizziness.* The older woman continued. "Here I'm called Pi'jko, in town they call me Alice, but I don't get to town very often. We're very self-sufficient here and have been for over a century and a half. And no, Mr. Bones, we're not an Aquarian Utopia as you called it. We are the Okwanuchu tribe, what's left of it.

"Years ago, our elders realized we could not fight the invaders. We hid, we survived, and we assimilated everything useful. Our children read, they go to university, many of them have built lives outside. Yet all of us eventually come home to the foot of Marumda's great lodge."

"And you've never been discovered?" Bones asked. "Not by hunters or the Forest Service?"

"Loggers, hunters, hikers, they've all seen us, if only a glimpse. You've seen us, but we have ten times more to our village than what is visible. Even so, we could leave in an hour and be on the other side of the mountain before morning."

"Then leave. Send your families away and follow. There are people hunting us who will find you here and they will kill you. It's as simple as that."

"It's not that simple Mr. Bones…"

"Bonebrake ma'am. It's Bonebrake, but you can call me Bones."

Pi'jko smiled and said, "Bones, it would be Bones, but I know you by another, more auspicious name. As for your friend, I could name him too."

Before either responded, a young boy arrived toting a flat wooden bowl. He set it between Maddock and Bones, ran to hug Pi'jko, and with a cautious glance at the large Cherokee, scampered out the door.

"It's eaten with the fingers," Pi'jko said, "but I could find utensils if you wish."

In response, Maddock reached over and dug in. The bowl contained a kind of dry starchy mash tasting of nuts and venison. Bones tried some. "Pemmican, really?"

Their guide and host had said little, but now he nodded. "Similar. It's leached acorn mash with dried meat and suet. We eat traditional foods; we use traditional materials. As long as we are here in the village, we are Okwanuchu in every respect.

"Except your glasses."

"Yes, except for education, medical treatment, and a few necessities. Remember, we have borrowed from the invaders, not resisted them or defied them. While you eat, I will have one of our healers look to your injuries."

On seeing Maddock wince, the older man grinned and said, "Not to worry, our healer is a practicing physician most of the year."

As he spoke, an earnest looking young woman entered the lodge. She wore traditional Okwanuchu clothing, but above her neck, glasses, earrings, and shoulder-length hair shouted urban professional. "Here I am called Ali'khem," she said. "It means frog, a small beast of cruel intent. Don't expect anesthetics. Who goes first?"

Bones grinned at her. "If I'm going to be hurt, I'd rather it was by a woman."

She said nothing but unbound his injured shoulder. Bones stared into the smoky lathes overhead as she probed his wound. She pressed against his arm and Maddock saw Bones' stoic gaze break into a suppressed scowl.

"You were lucky," Ali'khem finally said. "The bullet broke your clavicle but didn't shatter it. I don't know what you've been doing, but it's gone completely out of alignment. Hold still, this may be a little uncomfortable." Before he could react, she twisted his arm slightly and pulled.

Bones' scowl turned to a grimace of pure agony. "Holy crap, lady. What did I ever do to you?"

She rebandaged the wound and arranged a sling for his arm. "You doubted me, that's what. Who's next?"

Maddock nodded and she drew close to examine his damaged eye. He winced as the beam of a small flashlight crossed his left pupil. She held his head in both hands and examined the contusions by firelight. Her face close, he felt her breath on his cheek, heard her whisper as she turned his head back and forth. "So, Son of the Mountain, you have returned at last for these End of Days."

The ground shook slightly at her words and she continued to peer into his left eye. "Your face will heal, but you carry the seed of destruction within you. Are you ready to die, Marumda?"

"Maddock, ma'am. They call me Maddock. I think if I just had something for my headache, I probably won't die."

Ali'khem wasn't listening. She didn't look at him, or at Bones, but only stared into the fire. The earth trembled again. "Nahonka, you should tell these strangers who they really are."

The fire blazed a little higher, and to Maddock, the flickering shadows wiped all sign of the outer world from Ali'khem's face. She shrugged, and the effect vanished. "These two have the spirit in them, it's healing their bodies despite their recklessness. There's really nothing more I can do."

Their host, the one she had addressed as Nahonka, thanked the woman. She left without another word. Bones rubbed his arm and watched her slip out past the hanging cloth that served as a door. "Well, now I feel so much better."

"Yeah, that makes one of us." Maddock touched his swollen eyelid.

Nahonka said, "Ali'khem may not have the gentlest touch, but she knows her business. It's not your face that's causing the pain, it's what's happening all around us, it's what grows inside you."

Maddock looked at Bones; his friend had tensed up, ready to spring. A quick hand signal, *stand down*. When the big Cherokee relaxed by a fraction Maddock said, "How is it you know that something had been injected into me?"

"I read it in the sweat lodge, I can see it on your face. It has been spoken by the quivering mountain beneath our feet. But I know nothing of injections."

"You know nothing of a compound to the south of here?"

The one called Nahonka fell silent. He glanced at Pi'jko and she said, "Laboratory Nine, it's an abandoned Cold War-era hospital. We've heard of recent activity there."

"Well, whatever is growing inside of me was jammed into my veins at your Laboratory Nine."

The woman shook her head. "That means things are worse than we thought."

10

Tawny brown fur, eyes the color of ripening wheat, the big cat approached with the deliberation of a brain surgeon. *You're supposed to be nocturnal,* Sally thought. *You're supposed to be afraid of people.* Her back to a tree, she knew that a mountain lion could jump forty feet and climb like a squirrel. *Nothing here she could outrun.* Sally stood on tiptoes and waived her arms above her head.

"I'm big, and I'm mean, and I bite," she yelled. "And I taste nasty so just go away okay?"

"Bait," Uzi had said. "You're my bait to bring Pym's guys out in the open."

Just not this kind of bait, not canned tuna. She tried staring the big cat down, but it just kept pacing closer…

Sally had taken her usual morning shift at the *Pit River Café*. Black jeans, matching pullover that fell almost to her knees, two sizes too big felt just about right. The crowd had been light, mostly ranchers and truckers. El Yermo didn't attract many tourists. Colleen had wandered in after seven. Sally wasn't sure whether her boss had just gotten up or just gotten home.

"Glad to see you back, girl. How was San Fran?"

Sally rubbed a pinch of coffee grounds between her fingers, sniffed it, then weighed out exactly two and a half ounces. "Pathologically hipster." She dumped the fresh grounds into the hopper of an aging Bunn coffeemaker and added water from a plastic jug.

Colleen shook a mop of blonde hair from her face and pulled on a greasy ball cap. Bent over the grill she looked every bit the small town café proprietress. "Find that man of yours?"

"Found someone, or I should say, he found me."

She hadn't looked up from the coffeemaker until the front door jingled and a woman entered wearing a Stetson hat. Sally had seen her around El Yermo but didn't know her name. Kept to herself mostly and true to habit, she selected a corner table facing the street. Uzi had cautioned to watch for Pym's agents. Sally took in the blouse with SGC embroidered across the front, *Silver Glacier Company*.

She paused a moment to size the woman up. Muddy boots, jeans, slouching in the chair, she stared out the front window. Definitely a coffee drinker and probably someone who wouldn't bother with cream. Sally poured a full mug and carried it out to her. "You like it black, I presume."

The customer grunted, took a sip, and smiled, all without taking her eyes from the front windows. "Yeah, Sally Smith. We both like it black, don't we?"

Sally didn't respond. She slipped behind the counter and through the kitchen. "Sorry Colleen, got an emergency." Not stopping for a reply, she edged out the back and ducked behind a dumpster.

Nothing moved in the alley. They'd expect her to make a dash for her flop, the garage where she hoped Uzi was still hiding. Sally had other plans. Another quick peek, *no one.* She vaulted to the top of the dumpster and sprang for the eave, pulling herself flat on the café roof. The back door swung open and Colleen's head appeared right below her. "Sally?"

Getting no response, the woman vanished back inside. The door slammed shut and a small gray cat dashed across the dirt lane. Nothing. Sally continued to count, fifty-seven thousand, fifty-eight thousand, fifty-nine thousand. One minute to let her heart slow, let someone else make the next move. She exhaled. Nothing.

The bailout, the cut-and-run, Sally had rehearsed it a

dozen times. From the kitchen roof she had three options; drop back into the alley, climb the gentle slope and crawl through an attic window, or scramble down the west side into a scrubby woodlot.

She remembered her last bailout, New York. Gunshots, Bonebrake had been hit, her uncle nearly killed, and his restaurant burned. Then, of course there'd been Vallencourt Plaza—she didn't want to see any of that in El Yermo.

Pit River was a good café, Colleen was a good friend. Right now, Sally had to keep her out of the line of fire. *Woodlot then.* Jump to a live oak, down two branches, hang for a moment, and drop. *Listen*—nothing, no movement in the alley or on the street.

Brush and fallen branches hid an abandoned couch, its cushions gone, just rags on a frame. Two large plastic bags slumped nearby. Sally didn't want to know their contents. Between them, a cast iron storm drain protruded from the earth. She'd pried the cover off once, but never did more than look at the large culvert below, Sally wriggled in pushing an array of wet trash and what might have been a dead opossum in front of her.

Under the street and behind a stand of trees, the culvert dumped into a narrow creek bed. Sally dragged herself out and shook the mud from the front of her pullover. Stepping from rock to rock, she climbed the creek into the hills behind town. Twenty minutes had passed among the trees before Sally realized something had been stalking her.

Mountain lion, catamount, cougar, puma, all names for a top predator that could weigh in at two-hundred pounds and run fifty miles per hour. Sally could hear it, a low rumble, almost subsonic. To her left, a mesquite bush shook. Its branches parted and a second cat, slightly smaller, stepped into the light.

"Oh, right. Two of you now. Solitary hunters, territorial as hell, but hey, ganging up to take me down? Just try it," she said. "I'll bite your ears off."

Sally stopped waving her arms and took a step forward. Both animals settled back on their haunches. Movement off to her right, Sally dared a glance. A third tawny figure appeared above the grass. This one held back, snuffling the ground and swinging its head side to side.

"Okay, I give up. Three of you, really?"

Terrified at first, now Sally just hugged herself and waited. *There shouldn't be three of these things within a twenty-mile radius.* Almost at her feet, they rumbled softly and twitched their tails. A moment later, all three cats stood and trotted off.

Sally had also heard what had spooked the big cats, voices, at least two people working their way up the hill. She glanced around, *the tree.* It had been a day for climbing. She jumped for a lower branch and missed by a foot. Hands on the trunk, she managed to shinny high enough to wrap her arms around the branch. Leg up, then the next branch, it shook a little as she draped herself among the twigs and leaves.

Peering down, Sally caught sight of two heads bobbing up the path she had so recently taken. They stopped right below her. One she didn't recognize; he wore a Silver Glacier ball cap and green security uniform. The other sported a broad brimmed Stetson. Shorter, full bodied, not long ago she'd been sitting in the Pit River Café. The woman tipped her hat back and pushed a shock of brown hair away from her face. "You sure the Smith girl came this way?"

"Is only way men not watch." Her companion spoke with a thick Slavic accent.

The woman knelt, examining the dirt. "She must have

lit out the back. Where were you?"

"Such is not possible. If girl in alley, I would see."

"Well these could be her tracks alright. If she came this way, it looks like something startled her." The woman pointed to the ground. "Right next to your foot there, mountain lion prints."

"Then is eaten by lions?"

"Maybe, maybe not." She raised her voice slightly. "If I were Sally Smith, I would have circled back to town. We should do the same."

The man started back down the way they'd come. His guide pushed her Stetson back and flicked her eyes to the branches overhead. Moments later, they both disappeared back down the hill.

Sally remained glued to the limb. No question, Stetson lady had known she was there. She counted to sixty before worming her way back down the branch. Just as she reached the trunk, Sally froze. Movement, two men wearing military gear slipped through the brush and followed the others. *Jeez, regular New York City.*

Five minutes later, she dared move again. Down the trunk, bottom branch, she swung and let go. Silence, nobody around. Two butterflies played aerial slap-and-tickle. Blue jays scolded from across the creek. Sally felt a sense of presence an instant before she heard the voice. "Mind if I smoke?"

"Crap almighty!" Spinning, she jumped back, lost her balance, rolled, and sprang to her feet. "Just shoot me and get it over with why don't you?"

Uzi, in a green jumpsuit, lounged against the tree. "Not here to shoot you, luv. Just seeing that you don't get hurt."

"Look, Hawkeye, snap a twig or something before you announce yourself, okay?"

"Busy morning?"

Sally brushed the dirt and leaves from her pants, shook out her pullover, and said, "Yeah, if you hadn't noticed. What's with the traffic?"

"Oh, well that's simple darling. Your cowgirl is a contractor for Silver Glacier, and her buddy is part of their security force. We've put names to about ten others loitering about your little town. They're not too careful with radio protocol, and cell phones? Let me *tell* you."

"Wonderful. Town's crawling with desperate guys looking for a date."

"Oh, it gets worse luv. There's another bunch sniffing around as well. Or didn't you notice that sweet couple in matching unis?"

"Kind of figured they were yours."

"Uh-uh-uh—*nopers*. If you saw them, they weren't none of mine."

"Then who…" The ground rumbled like a passing freight train and shook beneath Sally's feet. She knelt and clutched a boulder as the trees above shed a rain of pinecones and dead limbs. She stood and dusted her hands together. "Then who were those two?"

Uzi remained silent for a long minute, then said, "Did you just happen to notice something?"

"Yeah, earthquake. We've been having a lot of them lately, but that was a particularly strong one. Those guys?"

"We don't know yet. Definitely a cut above your Silver Glacier security cops. I'd bet the helicopter was their idea."

"The game is afoot, Mister Holmes. That's me, on foot, in the hills. What's next?"

"I would first ask about your other little visitor."

"And what visitor would that be?"

"Seems you were entertaining a guest about the time Mrs. Hat showed up. I didn't catch all of it, but someone went slinking away as she and Sergei came whistling up the path."

"You saw them? I thought maybe I'd put the wrong mushrooms in my omelet or something."

"Them? Trolls, gremlins, tommyknockers perhaps?"

"Mountain lions—I swear, three of them. They just stared at me."

"You're becoming more and more interesting. First you are a hacker…"

"The last man that called me a hacker had his stones handed to him on a platter."

"…then you are a gourmet chef. And now—lo, you are a cougar-whisperer. So very intriguing."

"And useless. What next?"

"How about…" Uzi was interrupted by another rumbling of the hillside. He clutched the tree and watched a stream of cobble sized rocks go bouncing down the creekbed.

"Aftershock." Sally answered his unasked question. "There will be more. So, what's next?"

"How about I troll you down Main Street, for starters."

"Brilliant, sort of like one of those ducks in a shooting gallery?"

"Exactly like that. But no shots fired, I can just about guarantee. I believe I saw a bicycle out behind your café?"

Uzi explained his plan as they walked back toward town. On reaching the culvert, he stopped her. "This was brilliant, by the way. To cougar whisperer I would add Cou-Chi tunnel rat, but that would be so very insensitive."

Sally knelt to crawl through, but he stopped her. "One more thing, you weren't terribly attached to that little computer, were you?"

Her stomach lurched. She didn't yell, didn't scream, didn't seize him wriggling by the ears and bash his head against the rocks like she wanted. Instead Sally just settled to her haunches and buried her face between her arms. Shaking with suppressed sobs, she said, "You wouldn't understand. It was my connection, it was me, it was everything I am. It was all I have left."

Uzi sat next to her. "No, dearest. You are so wrong in that. Whatever you think, Sally Smith is an entire universe of which that computer was only a tiny fragment."

She sat and rocked, saying nothing. It was beginning, that slow implosion of her life. One by one, the people and things that meant most to her were slipping away. One by one, the lights were going out. She saw stood, staring down the well, emptiness, nothing, her footsteps ending in a void. Sally wiped her eyes on the sleeve of her pullover and squeezed her nose so she wouldn't sniffle. "What happened?"

"Not five minutes after you walked into that café and I conveniently disappeared, two men broke in and swiped it from under your pillow. Your files were encrypted, I presume?"

"Files, everything. Even the operating system is based on the old z/OS running in an XEM virtual machine. Why?"

"Well that's going to give their little cyber squirrels a nut to gnaw on for quite some time."

Sally thought for a moment then raised her head. "I'm ready."

11

Colleen never locked her bike, never needed to. Sally eyed it leaning next to the café kitchen door. Battered pink frame, knobby tires, the rear sprocket looked like a surrealist hedgehog. She couldn't remember the last time she'd ridden, certainly never on a deadly contraption like this. *No movement in the alley, it's now or never, Uzi's waiting.*

She stepped out of the shadows, took a dozen quick strides and swung one leg over the crossbar. A bunch of levers and cables between her knees, *screw it*, she'd just ride in whatever gear Colleen had left the thing. Push off, pedal, crackle and thump of gravel beneath her tires, Sally wobbled down the alley. Street dead ahead, backpedal to slow down, the chain made a noise like nuts in a blender. Her rear wheel locked up and Sally skidded into a fence.

She rubbed a bruised elbow and examined the tangled mess of chain and derailleur thingy. *Hera and all her horny harpies. Why don't people ride normal bikes around here?* Plan B, she'd have to jog. Sally shucked out of her pullover and stood in a gray t-shirt. Once around the block, Uzi had said. Feeling like Lady Godiva, she set off.

Up the side street and across to Main, Sally stretched it out. *I should have a ponytail,* she thought. *I should have spandex shorts and pink running shoes.* The fact was, she felt naked without her fuzzy black pullover. The new, unconnected, unshrouded Sally covered the long city block in about a minute and a half. Right down H Street, past the library, past the school. Another two minutes. Right again on Vallejo Avenue, and past Colleen's two-story bungalow. She'd counted three Silver Glacier trucks on her way around. Glancing behind her, she almost careened into two men standing at the next corner.

Turn right, turn right, Sally dodged around them, feeling their stares on the back of her neck. Uzi had promised that no one would expect her to just go sailing down the street. She picked up the pace, one more half a block. *Hope that promise wasn't wishful thinking.* Little more than a driveway ramping across the sidewalk, the alley had no name. Sally swerved between fences, grabbed the bicycle, and slung her pullover across one shoulder.

"I had a cat like you once." Colleen knelt on the kitchen floor, still cleaning grease and eggs tumbled by the earthquake. "Every time we were about to get a quake, damn thing would disappear. Got so that I wouldn't open up unless that cat was around."

Still out of breath, Sally mumbled her apologies. Colleen gathered her rags and towels and stood. "What happened to you, girl? Looks like you crawled headfirst down a gopher hole."

"Something like that, yeah. We had an earthquake."

Colleen looked around. "No kidding, second in two days. Yesterday's was as doozy. Seems you missed that one as well."

"Well I'm back, anything I can do to help?"

"We've got one customer in front. Clean up and go see if she wants more coffee."

A look in the mirror told Sally that her pullover was due for laundry rehab before it was fit to wear again. She brushed the sticks and opossum fur from her bangs, dried her muddy pants as well as she could, and pushed through the kitchen door.

Stetson hat on the table, mousy brown hair, her customer from that morning sat staring out the front. Sally slipped up behind her. "Want some pie with that coffee?"

The woman didn't turn. "Blackberry cobbler, corner piece if you've got it. And I'd sure like a warmup too."

Balancing two mugs and a plate of cobbler, Sally didn't ask to join her but just pulled up a chair and sat, back to the windows. Face to face, the woman wasn't as old as Sally had first thought. "Got a name?"

"I'm June, okay? You're blocking my view of the door."

Sally scooted her chair to one side. "You sure as hell knew I hadn't circled back to town. What's happening here?"

June took a forkful of cobbler, nodded and tried another bite. She sipped her coffee and finally met Sally's eye. "Someone at Silver Glacier wants a particular waitress with spiky blonde hair really, really bad. Seems she showed up sometime last night and then vanished again this morning. Any idea why they're looking for her?"

"You've got the souvenir shirt, you tell me."

June looked down at the embroidered letters on her blouse. "Yeah, so I do. Okay, I'll show you mine and you show me yours." She took a long drag on her coffee mug. "Everyone knows that Silver Glacier is drilling for spring water to package and sell down south. Well, there's water and then there's water."

Sally caught movement from the corner of her eye. Without as sound, another figure settled itself just out of June's line of vision. The woman continued, "Some of this water comes out of the ground pure, no bacteria, no contaminants, just a few minerals. They call it 'raw water' and get top dollar in Silicon Valley and the LA Basin."

Sally stopped her. "June, I want to introduce my friend Uzi. Uzi, June."

On cue, the man in question leaned forward and offered his hand. "Enchanted."

"I guess this means I shouldn't watch the door any

longer?"

Sally said, "It's a well watched door."

"Don't let me intrude, but could I have a spot of that pie for myself?"

"Behind the counter. It's not pie; it's cobbler. Serve yourself."

Without moving from his chair, Uzi raised a plate. "Already did. Now please, go on. It was just getting interesting."

If June had been startled by the intrusion, she didn't show it. "The point is, there's a lot of money involved." She gave Uzi a sidelong glance. "Or at least, I thought that was the point." Uzi held his plate and licked blackberry off his fork. June said, "Wouldn't you be more comfortable at the table?"

"Oh yes, thank you. Now maybe you all can slide over a little; I do so like the view from here."

June relinquished her corner spot and Uzi pulled his chair up, setting an empty plate in front of him. He pointed at the other plate. "You going to finish that?"

Sally kicked him under the table. "Knock off the act." To June, she said, "Don't let this guy fool you. He kills people for a living. Now, what's this about lots of money?"

"Silver Glacier keeps throwing money at this project. I know the profits can be good, but things started to get strange. People started disappearing. I want out, but I'm not sure I dare quit."

Uzi centered his plate in front of him and laid the fork across the top. The serious Uzi now. "What exactly did they hire you to do?"

"I'm a geologist, a volcanologist actually. My doctorate was in geothermal hydrology. Silver Glacier hired me to help them find a very special kind water, not just raw water, but virgin water, newly generated from within the earth."

"And did you *find* any?"

"I found something much more interesting, but it's her turn to talk now." She nodded at Sally. "That was our deal. Why are those guys turning this town inside out looking for you?"

Sally was about to reply when Colleen put her head through the kitchen door. "Now isn't this cozy. Sally, I'm not quite sure this is what I hired you to do."

Uzi unfolded from his chair and held up his hand. "A word?"

He disappeared into the kitchen. Two minutes later he reemerged, switched off the interior lights and turned the door sign around. "Colleen loves you again, even if you did wreck her bike. The café is ours for the day. Now?"

Sally explained a little of her beef with Pym, starting with her encounter in New York. "Pym Investment Trust owns most of Silver Glacier, you know." She didn't go into a lot of detail about her penchant for computer modeling, or about her escape from Maug Island. "I've got two of them to worry about, Pym Senior who runs the company, and Junior who bullies the staff. I had to bite off his ear one time, and he hasn't forgiven me."

Uzi pushed back from the table. "Wait, you bit off a piece of Junior's *ear*?"

"We didn't get off to a good start."

"It still doesn't tell my why Silver Glacier is so anxious to find one, ninety-eight-pound waitress that they pull their entire field team, including me, into it."

Sally hugged her t-shirt and suddenly wished she still wore the grubby pullover. "It's not Silver Glacier, it's their boss. What I don't get is why his commandos haven't come charging through the front windows."

Uzi said, "We were wondering the same thing. Afterall, that was the point of your little jaunt around town. My team was all set for a roundup when everyone disappeared." He stood to trade in his plate for a mug of coffee.

"Cream is on the shelf to your left," Sally called over her shoulder. "And no, we don't have brown sugar."

"Pity." Uzi rejoined them. "Okay, this just in. There's been a helicopter crash on the eastern slope of the mountain. All hands have been summoned for the search."

Sally leaned back in her chair. "Thank God. That's the best news I've had all day."

Both June and Uzi stared at her. "You don't understand," she said. "It's Bonehead. He's alive at least."

"Who's Bonehead?" June seemed totally confused.

"One of her little playmates, we thought he might have been shot. But I would ask, why do you think he's alive?"

"Bonebrake." She turned to June. "That's his name. He has a tendency to damage machinery."

"And if he was even there, you think he could have survived?"

"I've seen him sink a submarine, bare handed. He's survived worse things than a little helicopter crash."

"Well it may not help him that much if he's stuck out on the eastern slope." June sat up straight in her chair. "Do any of you know what a caldera is?"

"Not as in '*Double, double, toil and trouble*,' I should hope."

"Shut up, Uzi—you know what a caldera is. And God help me, so do I. What does that have to do with helicopter crashes?"

"Bear with me here. Did you know that Yellowstone Park is a caldera? When it exploded, over one trillion cubic meters of ejecta blanked western North America. One *trillion* with a tee. More recently, the Long Valley caldera blew about half that much over most of southern California."

"Okay, I'll rephrase my question." Sally paused a moment to picture one trillion cubic meters. "What does that have to do with Silver Glacier?"

"Water. Explosive eruptions always start with the water."

"Hmm." Uzi perched his elbows on the table and tented his fingers. "I always thought it was molten magma or something."

June pushed her coffee mug away. "Do you happen to have anything a little stronger around here?"

Before Sally could reply, Uzi slipped a silver flask from inside his jacket. "Absinthe makes the heart grow fonder, you know."

June sniffed the contents, wrinkled her nose and said, "Makes the fart grow louder maybe."

Sally was already rummaging in the kitchen. "She keeps it here somewhere." A minute later, she reemerged with a half-filled bottle of Crown Royal.

"Colleen always has a little nip in the afternoon." Sally splashed three generous fingers in June's mug and offered the bottle to Uzi.

"I will cleave to God's nectar and leave that more pedestrian spirit to you."

A quick sip from her mug, then June eyed Uzi for a long moment. Sally admired her technique, not a bunker-buster glare, more of a poison dart, working its mischief from within. She poured herself a smaller portion and said, "You were telling us about water?"

"Well, rhyolite magma really. It's viscous and rich in silica. The stuff carries a lot of dissolved water until it reaches the surface, then *plooie*, the water blows off and leaves nothing but a bunch of really hot rock."

"So, you get hot springs and geysers. I guess that's the source of your virgin water."

"Yes and no, that's where it gets weird. There's something in the virgin water, a bacterium of some kind. Hell, I have no idea what Silver Glacier wants with it, but they've been pumping this water and using reverse osmosis to extract the organism. Odd thing is, one day it's here and next day it's gone."

Uzi had poured his mug half full of fresh coffee, added cream and sugar. He stirred while filling the remainder with absinthe. "You're saying it just slips between your fingers?"

"It's there—and then it isn't. Don't ask me how or why."

"That doesn't get me any closer to helicopter crashes or Silver Glacier's unhealthy interest in little me."

"There's one piece of the puzzle I need to show you. The evidence is in my field office. It would be best if you saw it for yourselves."

Uzi threw back the remains of his spiked coffee and said, "We've been in this place for too long now anyway. Bottoms up, ladies. One last visit to the loo, then Sally is going to show us how to leave town unseen."

12

Between shadowy stands of Douglas fir, the land tumbled away into a dark riot of ferns, brambles, and mossy gray rocks. Maddock did his best to keep up with Nahonka and Pi'jko. The weakness in his legs had returned and his head throbbed with every step. The two Okwanuchu elders seemed to float along the forest floor, following the natural contour of the land. Bones slouched along behind. If his shoulder still hurt, Maddock couldn't tell.

The moon, nearly full, had risen above the line of hills. They carried no lights and kept to the forest edge where moonlight sufficed to pick a path between brush and rocks. Watching Pi'jko place each of her worn moccasins, one before the other, Maddock understood how people could live on this mountain without truly touching it. Every step, placed with care, left no mark. He tried but failed to emulate her movements.

From the long shadows that danced at their sides, he figured they were headed southeast, down the mountain flank and into the denser forest at its foot. Earlier that evening, they had discussed which direction to travel.

"Our people are moving north," Nahonka had explained. "It's mostly wilderness up there until you hit the ranches around Highway 97. They will scatter as they go, leaving a plain trail to follow at first but disappearing after about five miles."

Bones had been skeptical. "These asshats coming after us, they've got advanced military gear. They're not sportsmen, they're killers."

Wiry little Pi'jko led the way between fallen trees and mossy boulders. She didn't turn as she talked, and she didn't seem troubled by Bones' words. "None of this will matter if we cannot find the one called Killeli and reunite her with the fires."

As if to emphasize her point, the ground trembled beneath Maddock's feet. He halted for a moment and clutched a tree. "You know, to most people, this whole story would sound a little—sketchy."

"We've lived on this mountain for thousands of years," Nahonka said. "Understand, we're not playing 'Indians' here, nor are we preserving our past. We're living a very real and viable present."

"Without a viable future." Maddock said. "If what you said is true, then none of us face much of a future if we stay around here."

The older man had explained their dreams of that morning. He'd told of their creation story, how Marumda and Killeli slept below the twin volcanic peaks, Shasta and Shastina. "You did not simply dream in that sweat lodge my friends, you *remembered*."

Bones held up his hands. "I may have made a little trouble in my life." He glanced at Maddock. "Okay, maybe more than a little. But you can't pin that Coyote guy on me. I've never stolen the moon or done anything weird with a grizzly bear—or any of that other stuff. Actually, I've never chased a roadrunner either, but that's a different legend."

"And what of Killeli," Maddock said. "Marumda's sister. How does she fit in?"

Pi'jko corrected him. "*Your* sister, Marumda. She's your sister, she's Keeper of the Fires."

"I am not Marumda and my sister—my sister is certainly not this Killeli."

"She's your spirit sister. You may have met her in a different form, but you will know who she is when you see her. Until you find Killeli, the fires will no longer behave."

"And you're saying this whole place is going to go boom and rain hot ash over all of northern California?"

"It's done it before, millennia ago. This time, it'll be worse. Armageddon is coming to the west coast. Portland, Oregon south to Monterrey, California, it will all be wiped out."

Maddock stepped over a large rock and followed Nahonka down a game trail so narrow it seemed but a minor wrinkle in the surrounding carpet of forest litter.

"Unless I find this magic Killeli girl, that is—then what?"

"Then she resumes her duty: Keeper of the Fires. The mountain goes back to sleep and the Okwanuchu wander this land for another thousand years."

Treading close on Maddocks heels, Bones said, "So maybe if we knew what caused her to leave, we'd know where to find her."

Pi'jko halted and looked back. "You, Coyote. She left searching for you."

"I always knew I was a babe magnet."

"Trouble magnet, more likely," Maddock said. "Anyway, she's *your* mom, so that's just weird."

"You should have been there for the grizzly bear."

Nahonka said, "There's a clearing not too far ahead. We'll stop for a break and make a few decisions."

Their little band threaded between the trees. Pi'jko's game trail had widened somewhat, contouring around the hill and dropping toward a valley below. To Maddock, her choice of paths had begun to make sense. Generations of animals would eventually choose the easiest routes, and by following game trails, they avoided leaving clear tracks of their own.

The moon had risen overhead throwing long gray shadows by the time they halted again. Nahonka sat on a weathered tree stump. Pi'jko folded her legs and sat in the darkness nearby. Maddock was pleased to share half of a rotted log with Bones. It felt good to be off his feet for a while.

Nahonka waved toward the east. "We are at the edge of a tract that was logged off in the eighties. The forest is new here and there is little cover for game. This is the limit of the Okwanuchu universe, and I will go no further."

As he spoke, Maddock heard the distant whine of an airplane. Bones peered up between the slender trees. "Single engine—Cessna Caravan from the sound of it, civilian jump plane."

"Crap, the fat's in the fire now," Maddock said.

"They could be just looking, drop a recon team if anything seems interesting."

Maddock glanced over at Nahonka and Pi'jko. "We need to split up, reduce our infrared signature before the ground cools. If there's anything more you need to tell us, now is the time."

"We're about a mile west of the nearest logging road. You can shelter for the night in the remains of an abandoned timber camp." Nahonka pointed south. "Two miles that way and you will return to Laboratory Nine."

"No way I'm going back there." Bones said.

Pi'jko spoke like an oracle from the darkness. "But you must. That is the center of it all. Centuries ago, that site was sacred to the local tribes. Somewhere near the laboratory is the entrance to Marumda's lodge. You must find it and bring Killeli there. You, Marumda, must once more bind her to the fires below the mountain. Only then will this disaster be forestalled."

"Got it," Bones said. "We track down this Killeli lady, maybe a local grocery store clerk or something, we drag her kicking and screaming up on this mountain, and we toss her down some hole in the ground. I don't see a problem here. Except wait, how do we know which hole? Huh?"

Pi'jko knelt and used a stick to draw a simple figure in the dirt. For an instant, it seemed to glow in the moonlight. On seeing Bones' expression, Maddock looked closely. A circle enclosed in a triangle! He'd swept sand from the very same figure inscribed in stone on the island of Maug.

Bones slowly rose to his full six-foot five inches and stared off in the distance. "Lemuria."

"The Okwanuchu word is *Y'et*. It means the same, the world beneath the mountain, the lodge of Marumda. This is the key that unlocks all doors. Find it. Learn its secrets but do it quickly."

The story was altogether too fantastic for Maddock to believe and Lemuria was nothing but a nineteenth-century fable. Inflated by a pack of delusional cultists, it had become a near-religion. He glanced over at his true believer friend standing awestruck before Nahonka and Pi'jko. "One last problem. How do we find this Killeli person?"

"When the time comes, you will know." Nahonka shrugged off a pack he had been carrying. "There is food and water in here, the cloaks we gave you as well. You will want them in the evening." He drew out a long package tied with leather thongs. "This I give to you, Marumda; your bow and a quiver of arrows. One arrow is special. Coyote smelled it from high on the mountainside, but he gave it to you to keep."

Bones nodded. "The white arrow."

"Yes, it alone will arrest Killeli and pin her to the earth."

Maddock hefted the bow. Short and lightweight, it had been shaped from a simple length of tapered willow. He strung it and drew it back with ease. Nahonka watched him unstring and then re string it. "Your bow is designed for hunting in forests and dense brush. The range is limited, but it's quick and accurate."

Bones said, "How come he gets the bow? I'm the Indian here."

Pi'jko reached inside her buckskin tunic and drew out a knife. Its glittering blade had been flaked from a slab of jade green nephrite. Its wooden grip, wrapped in rawhide strips, was crowned by a carved pommel. She handed it to Bones. "Coyote generally prefers a knife."

Maddock watched the look on his friend's face. An aficionado of fine weapons himself, he understood the craftsmanship that had gone into that blade. Bones hefted it and examined the pommel. Worn from years of handling, it still bore the impression of a grinning coyote. A rawhide loop had been threaded between the teeth. Bones slipped the loop over his head and let the knife hang below his shirt. "I am more than honored," was all he could say.

Shouldering his quiver and bow, Maddock said, "We have no gifts that can match these. But I can give you this advice: there will be more aircraft; they will bring an army. Believe me, these men are well trained. They are equipped with long-range sniper rifles and the latest night-vision gear. They will hunt you like animals and shoot you without a moment's thought. It's Bones and me that they want. Don't try to lure them away. It won't help, and you will die. Go now, run, hide. Godzilla is coming."

Nahonka made a short bow, took Pi'jko by the arm, and vanished. Like a wisp of campfire smoke, the two were gone. Bones jaw dropped. "I think they're going to be safe."

"I wish I could say the same about us," Maddock said. "What's your take?"

"The dreams…"

"The dreams could have been planted, narrated to us as we dozed."

"Come on, Maddock. They knew about the lab, about

that stuff Pym had been pumping into you."

"It was a good guess, knowing I was sick. The woman was a physician after all."

"They knew about, you know, Sally's Lemurian triangle thingy."

"Bones, you know this whole damned mountain is covered with New-Age Lemurian crapola, and has been since the twenties."

"Then tell me straight out. Do you think these guys are phonies?"

"No," Maddock said. "That's the one thing that makes me believe something significant is going on. Say what you want about the Okwanuchu, but they're the real deal. Pym Senior, too. He wouldn't have crawled from his hole in New York, flown out here, and spent all this money just to entertain us. There's something, we've just got to figure out what it is. And we've got to do it before Pym kills us, the mountain kills us, or we get eaten by something."

"Well I still think it's Lemurians. We need to find Willis. We need to find Sally. One of them has to know what the hell is going on around here."

"Yeah, Willis. Nice irony, he's probably holed up in a bar somewhere, drinking beer and teasing the help. I'm concerned about Sally, though. Last we saw, she was surrounded by thugs and I'm not sure who's side any of them were on."

Bones nodded and slung the pack over his good shoulder. "Willis can take care of himself and everyone seems to underestimate Sally."

Maddock slipped the short willow bow into its quiver. Slung across his back it made a compact load. "Then best thing we can do is draw heat from both of them. We should get moving before the next fly-by."

They stayed to the shadows and crept from tree to tree,

crossing the logged-over hillside like ripples in the grass. Buckbrush and scrub oak had taken over where tall Douglas fir once stood. Following the gravelly ruts left by decades of logging equipment, they soon located the camp. Behind the cover of a sprawling manzanita bush, Maddock scanned the dusky hillside behind them before turning his attention to the ruined camp just below. "I don't like it," Bones said.

Maddock watched for a while. The sun had disappeared behind Mt. Shasta and a pale moon left long shadows between the folded hills. It glinted within the clouds, tinting a slender column of smoke in shades of silver and gray. "There's someone down there, Bones. They've got a campfire going."

"Not Pym. He wouldn't be so obvious."

"We have to warn them." Maddock led the way toward the first abandon cabin. Its roof had fallen in and one wall had collapsed. Just beyond, a larger structure stood, mostly intact. Someone had nailed black plastic over the broken shingles and hung paper curtains inside the windows. At one end of the building, a metal pipe jutted from the wall. Bones pointed it out. "There's the source of your smoke."

Maddock threaded his way down the slope. He pressed his back to the weathered siding and waited. Music, soft voices, there were definitely people inside. A silent gesture, and Bones joined him. Sniffing the air, he whispered, "Not Pym's guys, that's for sure."

Maddock sniffed. A faint aroma of sweet burning leaves surrounded the building. "Nope, not mercs. Should we go visit?"

Bones sidled around the corner and returned grinning. "Oh, we're going to fit right in with these dudes."

Maddock listened to the voices for a moment. "I'll go first. You count to ten, then follow me in."

Bones nodded and Maddock slipped around the

corner. The entrance stood partially open. Above the voices he heard the soft strains of an acoustic guitar playing counterpoint to the rhythmic thump of a conga. A light haze filled the room and Maddock counted a dozen people gathered around an oil-drum stove. He stepped inside.

For a few moments, nothing happened, then the drummer looked up. He grinned and gestured toward an open space on the floor. Maddock took off his quiver and sat. A young woman with blonde braids coiled about her head slid next to him and offered a hand-rolled joint. Maddock declined as gracefully as he could.

The guitarist stopped mid-chord. Across the small room, a middle-aged woman screamed. Maddock's new friend sprang to her feet. "Great Goddess save us."

Somebody yelled, "*Sasquatch*," and others took up the cry.

At first, Maddock didn't bother to look back. But when the commotion intensified, he had to turn around. Bones stood in the entrance. The tall Cherokee filled the doorway like a grizzly bear in a dumpster. He'd donned the doeskin robe given to him by Nahonka, and for some reason, decorated his hair with sprigs of manzanita bush.

Maddock stood. "It's okay, it's okay. Bones, what in the name of all insanity were you thinking?"

"I just wanted to fit in." He waved. "Hi, folks."

The middle-aged woman settled down, but she backed against the far wall. Maddock's blonde friend crouched in his shadow and peeked out past his shoulders. The drummer just kept tapping out a quiet one-two beat. "That's cool," he said. "Sit down. We're just a little jumpy tonight."

People moved over and Bones found a place next to Maddock. The blonde managed to squeeze in between them. Maddock noticed that she wore nothing beneath a sheer white cotton dress. She put her hand on Maddock's bow. "That's genuine Native American, isn't it?"

Bones cut in. "Yes ma'am, every inch of me." He grinned. "I'm Bonebrake, but you can call me Bones. This is my trusty sidekick Maddock."

"Keep it up Squatch and you'll get a sidekick to the head."

"Ain't that cute ma'am. He only comes up to about here on me, but boy is he feisty."

She reached up and brushed a shock of hair from Maddock's face. "I had a dream about you." She leaned up against his shoulder. "I think we were married."

13

Willis awoke with a start. The air had filled with dust and all about he heard the rattle and fall of rocks. A rain of gravel pelted his back and nearby, larger stones smacked into the ground. His constellation of tiny lights had vanished, returning him to the eternal night. When the ground stopped shaking, Willis stayed put. *No telling what still might come rumbling down.* He didn't want to think what a single rock would do to the back of his head.

The patter and tap of a few lingering pebbles died off, then an intense quiet enveloped him. Willis stood, breathing ten thousand years of volcanic dust. The ground lurched once more, he struggled to maintain his balance in the darkness. This time something big landed not ten feet away. The impact knocked Willis to his knees and sent a storm of small cobbles thudding into his back. He crossed his arms above his head and waited. *Not like it's going to help if I get clobbered.*

This time he stayed down, curled as small as he could make himself. *Breathe slowly, quite the mind.* SEAL training: in a crisis, avoid panic, let the reflexes take over. *Just ain't trained for this.* But Willis knew he was. Underwater, underground or under fire, it was all the same. *Sure could use those lights about now.* He let the image of Sally fill his mind. Peering out from beneath her disheveled mop of hair, she would look at him. Not her usual glare, but rather a silent question. Willis wanted so badly to answer, but now—well, he had stuff to do first.

A few more pebbles, he ignored them. Sally and her ridiculous little computer, Sally and her incredible *communiqué* with that mysterious guardian of Maug

Lagoon, finally he simply pictured Sally in her shorts and bikini top hunched over some unintelligible stream of data, just being her. *Heart beat down, muscles relaxed, it's time.* Willis straightened and looked up. Not much to see, a few dim glowing specks. He turned around. *Yup, there's Little Red, twenty degrees above the horizontal.* Off to the right, Big Blue glowed through the lingering haze.

Judging from the apparent distance between them, Willis figured he was closer to Big Blue than to the other lights. *Unless you've moved buddies, and I don't think you did.* He worked his way their direction. Between meals and sleep episodes, he'd used the lights as beacons to build a mental map of his prison. Somehow, a person entered the cavern to leave his meals and left. *If he can leave, then so can I.*

Willis had discovered a rough pattern to his infrequent meal deliveries. If he took Big Blue as twelve o'clock, then they all clustered at about one-thirty. *How long,* he wondered, *how long before Pym sends someone to check on his prisoner's health?* Willis figured they'd already be on their way.

Forty-five degrees clockwise from Big Blue, one-thirty, Willis found his landmark, a large boulder left years ago by a partial ceiling collapse. He knelt next to it and merged himself with its rough surface. Covered in dirt, he hoped to be invisible to Pym's night-vision equipment.

Willis concentrated on that one encounter at the airport. The old man, rising suddenly from his wheelchair. No longer old, no longer infirm. Grinning, the blanket dropping from his lap to reveal a snub-nosed thirty-eight. "Remember me?"

The hate came as he knew it would. This was the animal that hurt Sally, that cost his friend Lyn her eye. Willis let the rage cook inside him, quelling any chance that Little Red, Big Blue or any other glittering light would shine in the overhead when Pym's guys descended. Twenty, fifty, two-hundred heartbeats later, that voice: "Where are you?"

Frozen in place, Willis Sanders waited. Waited among the rubble like he'd done long ago in his grandmother's dark basement. Waited like he'd been taught, a hunter of men. Not a movement. Perhaps an hour, perhaps more, it didn't matter. He didn't have to breathe—his muscles weren't screaming for relief. He let the hot rage churn. Silence.

"Mr. Sanders, we know you are down there. Do you need help?"

Not a twitch, not a breath, Willis visualized his fists mashing that face to splinters of bone and gristle. The voice again: "Perhaps we should return in a few hours and ask again."

Yeah, you do that, homie. Willis mulled over what he had learned. *We,* interesting use of the word. He'd said *down* as well, that meant more than one of the bastards and they didn't just walk in, they had to come from overhead. Not in a few hours either, if it was going to happen, it would happen now.

A slight movement of the air. Willis held tight. They'd be watching for him. He hoped they were using standard military night vision gear. The dust would help mask his location, but anyone with a newer thermal imaging unit would pick up his heat-signature.

The faintest of sounds, semi-metallic, someone or something had touched down not ten yards away. He never would have heard it from across the cavern. Sound just died among that jumble of rocks and sand. Another click, a low grunt, and for one brief millisecond a glint of green light. Two individuals had descended. One adjusting his goggles, they moved away from his position.

Slowly, a stalking chameleon, Willis crawled toward where he first heard the sounds. Ten yards, ten minutes, nothing disturbed the silence. He felt it first against his face, a round plastic bar. A cautious touch, the bar hung between smooth cables. He stood and gripped another plastic bar, this one at face level, a ladder. *I'm coming after you, Pym.*

Willis clambered up the plastic rungs. It barely mattered now whether they knew he was there or not. Anyone at the top would hesitate for an instant before shooting. One instant, as good as an hour if he could gain the advantage.

Slowing, he felt the ladder sway below him. Willis held his rage at bay. No one followed, no voice of challenge from above. He climbed with lethal determination. *Pym would pay, he would pay for all the pain and grief he had caused.* Higher, the ladder jerked rather than swayed, he was nearing the top. Willis stopped and listened. Nothing. Slow deliberate moves now, reach, pull, step, climb, anything could be waiting for him up there.

Now for it. Willis scrambled up the final rungs. Longer than he expected, the ladder ended at a narrow concrete platform. He stood in the darkness. Somewhere there'd be controls. Hands on rough stone walls, Willis located a steel panel. Buttons, an entire array, nothing made sense. *One button would raise the ladder, which one?* Beneath his fingers they formed pairs, on-off, up-down, open-close. With night vision gear he might see the labels. *Screw it.* Waiting was the same as dying. He pressed one button at random.

A low hum, something happened. Willis heard the hum deepen to a soft groan, then clunk and stop. *Didn't sound good.* Random choice, he pushed another button. Dim red lights illuminated the panel and bathed him in their glow. Willis scrunched his eyes against the light, then peeked between his eyelids. Below his feet, a steel shutter had closed, shearing the ladder off just below the concrete platform. *Sorry guys, guess I should have rolled it up first.*

He memorized the panel, ladder reel, shutter, lights, gas. *Gas, really? Not me, not today.* Behind him, a simple steel door led—somewhere. Willis closed his eyes and ran his hand across the buttons. *Ladder, shutter, lights, gas, got it.* He killed the lights. Hand on the doorknob, he cracked it open. No lock, silent, no guard, the same eerie red illumination. Easy on the eyes, still it drenched the scene in bloody shadows.

He stepped through into a concrete antechamber. Night vision goggles hung from their charging stands, walkie-talkies as well. Beyond the antechamber, a dark stairwell led upward. *Had the pair in the cavern heard their ladder drop?* Willis grabbed a radio. Volume low, he heard the mumble of traffic. *Got to be here somewhere.* He rummaged around until he found a box of headsets. Behind-the-ear type, he plugged one in and slipped the silicone clip over his right ear.

The mumble resolved itself into a crisp dialog. "Sectors three, four and five clear."

A different voice responded. "Sectors twenty-five to thirty all clear."

Searchers, none of them too concerned about the ladder yet, and none of them Pym. Willis started up the stairs. One-hundred and twenty-five steps, he counted each one. The stairwell emerged into another chamber, larger than the one below. Cinder-block construction, it looked fairly new.

A third voice came through the headset. "I show the

ceiling shutter closed. Who returned?"

Silence, then shouting. Willis knew what would come next. He searched the chamber for weapons, nothing. A steel table stood in the center, it looked suspiciously like something from the coroner's lab. Overhead, a heavy industrial lighting fixture hung from the ceiling. One exit door, they'd be busting through it any second, probably armed. Willis stood on the table and made the only move he could.

Moments later the door opened. Something bounced off the steel table and rattled on the floor. Willis clung to the ceiling fixture as the flash-bang grenade detonated. Eyes beneath his arm, mouth open to protect his hearing, still the shock nearly knocked him to the floor. Four men entered. Armed with pistols, they grouped about the open stairwell. Another flash-bang and they all thundered down after it.

Willis lowered himself from the swaying light fixture. *Bunch of amateur chumps playing posse.* He pushed the door open and peeked into the next room. A shop of some kind, maybe a laboratory, it reeked of a musty fungal odor. The lights had been left on, but it was deserted. The radio crackled with a predictable dialog: "Subject is missing, ladder damaged. No, there's no way he'd have gotten past us."

Willis looked for another hiding place. Nothing. *Sure as hell, they're coming back up.* He checked the door through which he'd entered. Steel, it had a simple knob but no lock. Grabbing a chair, he jammed its back beneath the doorknob. Simple but effective. Another door, he killed the lights and drew it partway open.

A few yellow fluorescents illuminated the cavernous chamber beyond. Willis slipped inside. The same musty odor hung like a miasma in the cool air. All about, hundreds of wooden casks rested in row after row of steel racks.

Devil's winery, I'm better off never knowing what's in those barrels. He crept along the outside wall. Rough-laid cinder blocks, it felt cold and damp under his fingers. The radio had gone silent. *About time they figured that one out.* He thumbed through the channels. *All quiet.* Uncertain whether it could be tracked, Willis switched the radio off and ditched it.

No distant hammering, no thundering rescue, He darted from aisle to aisle waiting for their next move. Willis had been looking for weapons, nothing in the laboratory seemed useful. He searched among the barrels for a pry-bar or wrench, anything. Two rows, two aisles, nothing, no one. Next isle, he saw a vague shadow on the floor. A dozen strides, he crawled under a row and came up with a large wooden mallet. Several barrel-bungs and a nickel-plated tap lay next to it. He sniffed the tap; it made road-kill 'possum smell good.

Willis hefted the mallet, choked up on the handle a few inches and gave it a practice swing. *It ain't a Makarov nine-millimeter, but it'll do.* At the far end of the aisle, yellow light outlined a pair of swinging doors. He crossed the distance at a dash and plastered himself against a wall. Pushing one door open a few degrees, he scanned the next room. Bright overhead floods, industrial tiles, it looked like a loading dock. The rollup door to his right confirmed his guess. To his left, a heavy steel door with an armored latch plate.

Door number one, a good chance of freedom. Pick door number two, maybe a little vengeance, maybe a lot of whup-ass and death. Willis positioned himself between them, ready to take whichever opened first. No more than a half a minute passed before the left door rattled and swung open. Willis jumped behind it as four people charged through. They galloped into the barrel room without looking back.

The door started to close. *Wait for it.* Two more pushed their way into the loading dock and started to open the rollup. One, clearly female, glanced back. They exchanged stares for a millisecond before she yelled, "Carl, get him."

Willis slipped through the open door and twisted the bolt. Now the pounding started. *That's more like what I expected.* Before him, an office hallway, wooden doors on both sides, Willis ran to the end door. Locked. He swung his hammer, bashed it open in one blow, and stepped inside.

"I'm disappointed, Mr. Sanders." Augustus Pym Junior turned and faced him. "You've spoiled in the vat. Here, we had such high expectations for your unique *terroir.*"

Except for the light shining through the splintered door, the room was dark. Willis hardly broke stride. He swung the mallet shoulder high. Pym backed a step, letting its metal-bound head graze his chest. "Please don't do that."

Willis flicked the mallet about like a bandmaster's baton and swung again. Pym retreated another step. "You really shouldn't do that."

"Why don't I just bash you to jelly right now?"

"Because you aren't going to survive that long." At that moment the lights came on. Behind Pym stood a dozen silent figures. White robes, blue sashes, they charged forward.

14

Pym hadn't finished speaking before Willis jumped back into the hall and flew the other direction. *I can't pound him if I'm dead.* At the far end, same steel door. He flipped the lock and slammed it open. It smacked into the woman. She sprawled back and Willis leapt over her. Short hair, almost a buzz, she wore a similar white garment secured by a blue sash. Willis tried to locate Carl, her partner. Before he had a chance, she sprang to her feet and launched a kick at his midriff.

Willis used the mallet handle to deflect her kick. Almost as if she'd anticipated the move, she struck him in the elbow. His left arm went numb and the pain sent white stars shooting across his vision. Another kick, this one caught him in the shoulder and spun him about.

He let the momentum carry him in a full circle. Willis whipped the hammer around and caught her beneath the knee as the woman stepped in for another punishing strike. She crumpled, absorbing the blow. He reversed the hammer and struck her across the temple with the grip-end of the shaft.

She was down and her partner gone. *Three seconds. Three seconds at most before all hell's going to come busting through those doors.* Willis cracked open the rollup, then dove back into the barrel room. He rolled under the first rack, crossed the aisle and belly crawled beneath the next set of steel cradles. If the stench was bad the first time he passed through, it was ten times worse on the floor. While he waited, Willis tried to shake the numbness from his arm.

Shouts, running footfalls slapped past him on both sides. As he waited, all Willis could think of was that tiny slot of daylight that had beckoned from beneath the loading dock door. *Not now, not yet anyway.* He hoped it would provide a few moments of distraction.

Another clatter of feet. *Goon squad must have made it back up the stairs.* Willis held on to the heavy mallet as he slid from under the barrels. Crouching low, he scuttled up the aisle and veered left at the wall. Light from the laboratory spilled out through the open door. Willis slowed and dropped to his belly. At floor level, he peeked around the corner. No one.

Mallet at ready, he scooted inside and stood behind the doorway. The other door stood slightly ajar. A dozen strides, he crossed the lab. Two figures burst out. Willis caught the first with staff end of his mallet and jammed the head into the second. One dropped, a red welt across his temple. The other doubled over, shouting for help. Willis finished him with a strike to the back of his head. White robes, blue sashes, *who are these guys*? He checked for weapons. No guns, no knives, nothing useful. Willis flexed his hand, trying to regain strength in his left arm. *Damn that hurt.*

Answering shouts echoed from the barrel room. *Craptastic. Nothing for it, but back down the hole.* He picked up his hammer and headed for the stairs. Past the steel table, down one, two, thirty, one-hundred and twenty-five steps. Lights still on, steel shutter still closed, Willis stood in the shadows next to the control panel and quieted his breathing. Waiting, waiting, flexing his left arm and getting used to the pain.

Minutes later, sound from above. Willis reached up and opened the shutter. A low whine, a dark hole at his feet, faint shouts drifted up from far below. He heard a careless footstep on the stairs and killed the lights. Two objects rattled off the floor and bounced into the void. They exploded somewhere half-way down. Two more, hissing and sparking as they fell. Tear-gas grenades, he had to kick the second one over the edge. *Sorry guys, insult to injury, but not my idea.*

Gas means gas masks. They won't be wearing night-vision. A lingering mist clouded the air catching flashlight beams crisscrossing their way down. Willis gagged and coughed. He waited to see if there would be another grenade, then closed the steel shutter. *Don't want anyone dying unless they're named Pym.*

Lights poured into the little chamber. Willis smacked the first one about head level. He jabbed another in the groin and crouched, letting momentum pitch his attacker across the floor. In the confusion, he managed to trip two more. Then things got crazy.

The pummeling drove Willis back. He had no room to swing the mallet and just barely managed to fend off the blows. Two steps, he raised a hand and punched on the lights. "Stop or I'm going to open the trap door on those guys."

Two men in camo uniforms had collapsed across the shutter plate. To emphasize his point Willis punched the button long enough to slide the steel plate partially open. The white robes backed away, but two others, same camo, held pistols on him. "You won't take me down before I dump your homies into the pit. Or hey, what about I push this one labeled 'Gas' and see what happens to your people down below?"

"Or what if we all stand down, everyone." Augustus Pym himself emerged from the stairwell. "Mr. Sanders, I would call this a stalemate. You once had a chance to kill me, but you didn't. Why would I think you'll kill these people now?"

"Because I'm not going back in that hole unless I take you with me."

"Then we need a truce, Mr. Sanders, an armistice if you will. Let my soldiers retrieve their comrades here, then you and I can discuss matters without hammers or guns or grenades."

"Just you and me?"

"Alone, if you wish. Although that would put me at some disadvantage. Perhaps you would allow one young acolyte to accompany us."

"Yeah, female, short hair. Probably got a headache. She doesn't like me."

"That's the one, she's waiting for us at the top."

Willis weighed his options, bad, worse, and plain nasty. "Okay, everyone out, including the almost going to be Wright brothers there. Mr. Pym, you go last."

"Really? With you behind me?"

"Do I look like I want to do all this again?"

Willis counted steps on the way up. Five short of the top he stopped Pym. "Just wait right here a minute to catch your breath." A ten-count later, he said, "Okay, now slow. We go up together. No surprises or it's going to get ugly for both of us."

"A true dialog is built on mutual trust."

"Never happen. It's got to be mutually assured destruction for now."

They marched through the anteroom into the laboratory. A small crowd had gathered, white robes and camo, shoulder to shoulder. "Tell them to leave. Out everyone, clear the way."

Pym nodded and waved his hand. Moments later only one figure remained, he smiled at her. "You've met Giselle I understand."

"Yeah, we had some kicks. Let's do it again some time."

The woman might have smiled for a split second, the first real expression he'd seen on any of Pym's followers. "I'm counting on it, Mr. Sanders."

Pym said, "Why don't we talk first, dance later."

"Not here." Willis made a face. "I'm sick of this stink. Outside there, the loading-dock, we can open the door and get some air while we—uh—talk."

Giselle proceeded them into the barrel room. Willis looked the place over. Several figures lurked against the far wall. "No, get those sorry-assed ghosts, or whatever they are, the hell out of here." He raised his voice. "Scram, jerkwads, all of you."

Pym added, "Do as he says. Clear the area, we'll meet later."

Giselle didn't grin, didn't smirk, just mumbled, "Testy."

"Don't like being cooped up, lady. Besides, my arm hurts."

Three chairs and a small table awaited them in the loading-dock. Bottles of Silver Glacier Pure Spring Water stood on the table. Pym said, "You don't mind if I have some small refreshments brought in?"

"Whatever, man. It's still your party." Willis picked a chair facing the rollup. "Giselle, you don't mind opening that thing, do you? All the way up, now."

He was immune to her basilisk glare. Sally's was so much more effective. Pym sat on his left. "She'll do it because I ask. Just don't ever call her that again."

As he spoke, another figure entered from the inner door. Willis didn't turn but let the other come into view. Camo, gun, grenades, no sign of a white robe. He carried a gray plastic tray with an assortment of cheese and bread. "Whoa, straight from the mess-hall. I'm impressed, but sorry Carl, no tip."

"Are you trying to provoke my people, Mr. Sanders?"

"Well, hell yeah. They did kind of provoked the crap outa me, now didn't they?"

A nod from Pym, Willis turned to watch camo guy depart through the inner door. When he swung back, Giselle had opened the rollup. Willis stood, not caring that his chin had dropped an inch.

"Some view, don't you think?"

The twin summits of Mt. Shasta and his consort, Shastina, filled the skyline. A green cloak of Douglas fir draped their flanks, spilling into a maze of gorges and foothills. Above the tree-line, a blazing crown of permanent ice glittered in the afternoon sun. Willis opened his lungs and inhaled the clean, dry air. It still carried a lingering scent of melting snow. "*Hooya!*"

"That's been my reaction every morning when I look up there. The local native tribes worshipped that mountain. It is the home of their god, Marumda. That smaller peak to your right is his sister's, Killeli's lodge. Wife as well as sister, I guess if you're a god you don't have to care much about that."

"Is that what you think, Junior? You figure you're some kind of god around here? Do what you want, don't have to atone for nothing?"

"Sit down. Eat some food. You'll feel better and I can explain a few things."

Willis ate a roll and some of the cheese. It was alright, good in fact. He washed it down with a big slug of spring water. "Yeah, not bad. Not up to Sally's standards. You do remember Sally, don't you?"

Pym brushed the hair back from the left side of his head. A knot of scar tissue covered what was left of his ear. "Every time I comb my hair."

"Then you remember clubbing the eye out of my friend

Lyn's face. I'm sure there were others—you maybe remember them too."

Pym scowled. "I remember every woman that I raped, tortured, and murdered. Is that what you want me to say?"

Willis wasn't quite sure what he wanted. "Then we're good now. Okay, I'll be leaving. Which way to the local bus-stop?"

"Sorry, that bus hasn't run for years." Pym ate a roll. "Have some more. Go ahead Giselle, dig in. We may be here a while."

Eat when you can. Willis had learned that on the streets of Detroit. It was rubbed into him fighting across the mountains of Tribal Pakistan. He loaded up on bread and cheese. "Now what more do you have that's so interesting?"

"Have you ever thought you'd save the world, Mr. Sanders?"

"Nope, like I said, not into that god thing. Probably not much help either. Why did you grab me, anyway?"

"Because my father wants you. Understand this Mr. Sanders—me, your friend Sally, and now you, all of us, we share something special. Something my father badly wants."

"Oh, I can't wait to find out what *that* is."

"Don't you know? Can't you feel it? Together, on the island, we were all exposed to this thing." Pym's eyes lit, his countenance nearly glowed. "It's in us, you, me, Sally. It connects us."

"You don't mean that damned Moogly Woogly crap?"

"The *Ma'óghe*, the Eternal One. A single organism that spans the world, it's here on Shasta as well."

Willis shook his head. He remembered that weird business with Sally. Crazy stuff going on about Lemurians and all. Bones just lapped it up and spit it right back out. *That was what, eight thousand miles away? Whacko nut-job stuff out there on the edge of the Mariana Trench.* "They were a bunch of glow-in-the-dark squid. Good luck finding any of them around here."

"The cephalopods were just a vector. Here it's bacteria. Actually, it's a bacteria-yeast symbiosis. They are the Ma'óghe, the active principal, the arms of Gaia."

"Damn, you got *religion* or something?"

"Tell me, down there in that enormous lava vesicle, didn't you feel it? Tell me the lights never responded to you."

"Tell me what difference it makes. Bunch of glow worms or mushrooms, that's all. You ain't saving the world or anything." Willis snagged another slice of cheese and noticed Giselle watching him. "What? Getting ass-kicked and run all over the place, a guy gets hungry."

Her voice a buttery contralto, she said, "You seem very confident Mr. Sanders. No fear we may have drugged the food?"

"If you wanted me dead, you'd have had Rambo back there take me out. And if you were going to give me some goo-goo juice, you'd have just held me down and shot me up. Nope, we're good. What say you and me, later on we go catch a movie or something?"

"I doubt she's interested," Pym said. He sat back in his chair and gazed out the open door. "At one time, I'll admit, strong-arm would have been my tactic. It's still my father's preferred approach. But no, I tried to convince you, I tried to show you the power of Gaia, but you spoiled it. You managed to break out before the transition was complete."

"'Spoiled in the vat.' Yeah, I heard you say that. So, were you going to bung me up in one of those barrels? *Essence of man* sort of thing?"

For once, Giselle smiled. Willis was relieved to see that she didn't have pointed teeth. Pym answered before she could comment. "You're not too far off. My acolytes, like the lovely Giselle here, have all undergone the transition. We—all of us including me—we donate blood that gets mixed with a very special kind of water and allowed to um, *cultivate*."

"You mean ferment. That's the stink, rotten blood."

"No, I mean cultivate, we're producing more of the bacteria-yeast symbiote. A lot more. It will be needed for the coming event."

"But not mine, I guess."

"No, you lost your chance. Don't you see? You will not be part of what is coming. Once, you might have been one of us, but now you'll only be a spectator."

"Oh, goody. Do I get popcorn?"

"Smile while you can, Mr. Sanders. I need you to stay here a little longer. What about I let Giselle show you to your room?"

"That's just great. Does it have wi-fi?"

"Good evening, Mr. Sanders." Pym rose without another word and slipped out the inner door.

Willis turned to Giselle. "It's just you and me, kid. Fly me to the stars."

"I hope you aren't thinking anything rash, Mr. Sanders."

"All my friends call me Willis. Except your boss, of course." He stretched his arms out and stood. "We can dance another time maybe."

Like a striking adder, she hit him just below the breastbone. "That's for the cheap-shot to the head this morning."

Willis doubled over, his diaphragm spasming. He took two short breaths before kicking his chair into her face. Without trying to straighten, he followed through with a full bottle of spring water slammed over her head. His moves caught the woman by surprise, sending her sprawling to the floor. Without looking back, he shoved the table over and jumped behind it. Two nine-millimeter slugs buried themselves in the tabletop.

The inner door slammed open as Willis dove for Giselle. She danced to her feet, kicking the chair to one side. A hand to her ankle brought the woman back down. She drew back for another kick, but Willis grabbed her wrist and twisted it behind her.

A third shot zipped past his shoulder. He jumped up, hoisting Giselle to her feet. "You going to shoot your boss's little lady here?"

Willis eyed camo-guy, standing not six feet away. "You can stick that banger right back in your pants homeboy, because me and the girl, we were just getting acquainted."

Giselle nodded. "Do what he says, Carl." She slammed a foot down where Willis' instep had been a moment earlier. "Dammit, let me go. That hurts."

Her friend seemed unsure of what to do next. "Put the gun away and then go roll that door back down," She said. "If anyone's going to kill this gorilla, it will be me."

Willis relaxed his hold for a moment and when she tried to break free, he jerked her arm to the side and bent the wrist back, putting Giselle on her tiptoes to ease the pressure. "You're not going to kick me, bite me, slap me, or hit me anymore. Got it? Your little buddy is going to go away and I won't see his camo butt again. Right?"

"Go ahead and break my wrist, I'll still tear your throat out." She turned to the man. "You heard him, get lost. I'll take it from here."

Willis let her go. Giselle stepped back and rubbed her arm. "That was unnecessary."

"This whole deal was unnecessary. In case you haven't noticed, your boss has gone and lost his tinfoil hat."

"I drank his Kool-Aid, Mr. Sanders…"

"Willis."

"I drank his Kool-Aid, Willis. There's something here. I've communicated with it. I've contributed to the symbiote. Soon we'll have enough—*culture* to initiate the collapse."

"And save the world. Got it. How about I just boog' on out of here and let you folks get on with it then."

"It's not that simple, Mr…, Willis. For one thing, the Senior Pym would like very much to get his hands on you. He has his own designs on this mountain."

"The old man, he's here?"

"Not right here. On the other side of Shasta, the south slope above El Yermo. I think some friends of yours have been keeping him busy lately."

Willis let that sink in a moment. He glanced at the inner door where Camo Carl had disappeared. Giselle inched a little closer, he steeled himself for her next jab. *Do that and it's going to be your last rodeo, fuzz-top.*

Ten inches from his right ear she whispered, "Don't look at me, just listen. We're going to your room. It's a cell of course. Walk in front, I'll tell you which way to turn. If you must speak, make it casual."

Willis nodded slightly and headed for the inner door. He heard her tell him to take the first opening to his right. The hallway was dark, but a door stood ajar with a lighted space beyond.

Giselle continued. "They have your friends, the Indian and that other guy, but it's you and the girl they want."

"Sally?"

"Shh, no names, but yes. Our leader wants her too, but she's been—careful."

"Girl gets invisible if she wants. I've seen that."

Giselle turned him around. "She needs to stay that

way."

"Why do I think that's not according to holy canon?"

"Just understand, she has assimilated the symbiote. She has achieved the same level as Augustus Pym himself. If she were here, under his power, he would need nothing else to initiate the collapse."

Willis nodded. "He wouldn't need you."

She spun him back around and shoved him from behind. "Your cell is the last door on the left. Inside now, and no more talk."

15

When Giselle shut the cell door, Willis heard an electric lock buzz. The eight-by-eight chamber barely had enough room for a single bunk, a case of Silver Glacier water, and a bucket, presumably to relieve himself. The cinderblock walls felt solid where he slapped them. The steel door had only a narrow ventilation slit. He twisted the burnished aluminum handle and pushed. Locked solid.

Willis looked up and found another ventilation slit in the ceiling. He crawled on the cement floor and peered under the bunk. Nothing to use as a weapon or a tool. He settled back on the thin mattress to consider his options. *When you ain't got nothing, you got nothing to lose.*

Sometime later, Willis awoke to voices in the outer hall. He stood on his toes and peeked out through the slit. Groups of the white robed acolytes filed in. Speaking in low murmurs, they paired up and entered the other cells. *Seems I didn't rate the luxury suite.* Willis noted where each of them went. Mostly male and female couples, they seemed happy enough with their quarters. None of the guards had been among the group. *Guess Pym keeps his friends close and his army closer.*

The acolytes seemed to pay no attention to his cell. *Freaking bunch of lemmings.* Giselle was notably absent from the group. Willis checked the walls and ceiling again. No trace of a window, no utilities, nothing he could use to force the door. A single industrial light hung from the overhead. Similar to others in the complex, it had a low-voltage LED lamp and a heavy plastic diffuser. The switch was located elsewhere.

Willis jumped to the bed, and then sprang up and

grabbed the fixture. He pulled himself to the ceiling. *Spider-dude.* The thought brought him back to his time on Maug Island. Wrestling a madman in total darkness, Sally had been fearless. He lowered himself back to the floor. *Not helping her this way.*

He figured about an hour had passed before the lights in the outer room dimmed. He heard a succession of locks buzzing, including his own. *Control,* he thought. *The whole object is to make us believe we are under control.* It made sense. No minor liberties meant no major insurrections. Part of his SEALs training had been psyops; Willis knew the game. The loud buzz was there to reinforce their sense of submission. Even his own door-lock had cycled, all the doors, all prisoners.

A minute later, the overhead light winked out. Willis sat in the darkness staring at the narrow slit of light that showed in from the corridor. *I've got to stop thinking like a prisoner.* It took another five minutes for him to make the connection. *My door-lock buzzed? Nah.* He stood and turned the handle. The steel door swung open on silent hinges.

Willis slipped out and pushed it closed. Muffled sounds surrounded him, people doing what people did. He grinned; obedience had its rewards. He glided back to the entrance door trying to remember which way it opened. He found hinges on the inside, *inward then.* This door too was locked. Willis wondered for a moment what his next step might be when he heard the lock click from the outside. He ducked behind the door just as it opened.

Two guards in camo walked in laughing and joking. For an instant, Willis thought of jumping them. Instead he slipped out before the door closed. *Not a prisoner, not messing with guards.* The next door he knew led to the loading dock. He hated to leave it unlocked but didn't waste time worrying about it. Same with the rollup. He pulled it shut behind him. Plan A, he'd find a jacket. Plan B, he'd tough it out. So far, Plan A wasn't working so great.

Willis hopped off the loading dock and landed on an asphalt parking lot. Standard security lights, he looked around, no cameras. *Odd.* The place seemed both brand new and somehow archaic, rather slapped together it seemed. Two pickup trucks were parked against the building, both locked. On the far side, a battered gray sedan sat on blocks. Willis checked. No motor under the half-open hood, but the doors were unlocked.

A dirty set of coveralls had been tossed in the back seat. Not a jacket, but better than Plan B. He pulled them on. The shoulders pinched and the zipper only pulled to the middle of his chest. A tire iron lay on the ground. Willis dug it out of the weeds and tucked it through a beltloop. Above him, Shasta glowed in the moonlight, beckoning.

A quick glance back at the complex. Light shone from a scattering of small windows, but nothing moved. Once he was found missing, Willis knew they would search the road first. He ducked through a barbed-wire fence, pushed past a thicket of weeds and found a dry streambed that climbed the foothills to the south. The rocks and boulders made for difficult walking, but there was little chance he'd leave footprints or any sign of his passage.

As the hills rose above him, so the shadows deepened in the narrow ravine. Willis picked his spot and began angling up a brushy slope. Near the ridgeline, he once more caught sight of the moon. It glowed between the peaks of Shasta and Shastina. Only four miles away, they looked like castles in the air, rising above the dusky forest. Willis paused. *Eight-thousand feet of vertical? Hell yeah.*

Two hours later he wasn't so sure. The peaks seemed no

closer, but he was puffing with every step. Douglas fir trees still blanketed the mountainside, but rough cobbles of volcanic rock rolled beneath his feet as he climbed. Worse still, the slope was littered with fallen timber that seemed to block every path. Willis stared up at the maze of shadows and rocks.

Another two hours passed before he reached the tree-line. The moon was creeping behind Shastina's rugged crest, plunging the rock-strewn mountainside into a bewildering mass of shadows. Willis felt his way along, picking out an uneven trail beneath the towering peaks.

As he climbed, the thin air grew colder. Stopping once more for a break, Willis looked up. Dark shadows outlined by an ocean of glittering stars. The peaks were visibly nearer. Breathing had become a problem. *No more mac and cheese*, Willis thought. *No more beer, no more curly-fries*. He resumed his trek, picking a route that contoured west around the flank of Shastina.

He found himself skirting the base of a sheer cliff. Loose rocks rolled beneath his feet and Willis had to use his hands to stay upright. He grasped a large boulder and stepped forward into the darkness only to find nothing beneath his outstretched foot. Pulling back, the boulder began to move and the rocks he stood on tumbled away into the void.

Willis whipped the tire iron out and jammed it into the ground as his feet slipped beneath him and dangled over the unseen chasm. The boulder slammed him in the shoulder and fell away, striking with and explosive thud somewhere in the darkness below.

He could feel the loose rock and scree begin to slide beneath the iron bar. Willis stretched full length and made a desperate grab for anything that would hold. Pebbles, small rocks, they all slipped away from his fingers. Another grasp, nothing but sliding gravel. In desperation, Willis let go of the tire iron and slapped his right hand as high as he could reach.

His fingertips found a tiny ridge. He pulled, feeling the gravel and stones continue slipping away. Clinging in the darkness, his thoughts fled to Sally and her impish grin. *If only I could have seen her just one more time.* Holding on, face down in the darkness, he slid closer to the cliff's edge. *Please Sally, one last little smile.*

Willis looked up, if only to see the stars before he died. There, strung like tiny glow-worms he made out a mesh of shining silver lines. He inched his left hand up, grasped at one and found narrow crevice. Pulling, he slapped his right hand onto another that seemed etched into solid rock. Stones and debris fell away. He heard the tire iron clank and clatter down the slope. Crawling, pulling, Willis climbed a ladder of glowing threads embedded in the mountainside.

With no other route to follow, he continued climbing the cliff he had been skirting. Faint blue lights peppered the broken surface guiding his hands to the hard rock and solid holds. *Climbing alone without belay, in the freaking dark, and trusting God knows what. I've gone loony as Pym.* Willis dragged himself over the top and rolled on his back to gaze up at the stars. Permanent snowpack glittered on Shasta's flank and the moon, once occluded by Shastina's bulk, now shown pure and white above his head.

Willis breathed deep and felt his pounding heart jamming as much oxygen as it could into his aching muscles. He figured he'd reached ten-thousand feet. He'd looked up El Yermo and studied the topographic maps before flying off to visit Sally. From what he remembered, there was a saddle between Shasta and Shastina about two thousand feet higher. *Not going to get there by wishing.*

The rocky mountain flank was a debris field of loose

rock. For every step up, he slid half a step back. Still on the north side, Willis began to see patches of snow between the rocks. An hour later, he encountered an icefield that stretched all the way to the summit. This late in the year, the slushy surface was melting in small rivulets that ran down the mountainside. Willis angled off to the west, in search of firmer footing. A quarter mile farther he found a wooden stake jammed between the rocks. Climbers had come this way.

Willis followed a faint trail the curved around the south side of Shastina's crater and angled up from that direction. Climbing, puffing, he again reached the ice field. A collection of small glaciers, it circled the peak like a giant halo. Climbers had cut steps in the ice. Willis followed them up until he stood at the shoulder of great Shasta herself. At twelve-thousand feet, his head spun as if he'd stood too quickly. Tiny white motes swam in his field of vision, Willis began to feel the cold wind that swept up from the valley below.

The moon, once his guide, now settled toward the western horizon. Streetlights in the small towns along Interstate 5 glowed orange in the distance. He looked up at Shasta's icy summit, so close, yet a world away. *I'll never get this opportunity again.* Willis took one step higher, then another. Two thousand feet remained, a full-sized mountain by most measures. Barely a mile farther, still, he craned his neck to see the peak.

At this height, the ice had remained solid. He counted out each careful step. One slip could send him hurtling down the mountainside. Every hundred paces he stopped to recharge his lungs. Something he was supposed to do when he reached the top, Willis could barely remember. The climb itself had taken on a life, a purpose of its own. One more step up, one more step up, each one a gasping shivering effort.

The moon had long retreated west to her warm Pacific bed. Above, a milky ocean of stars glittered in rare constellations seldom visible from the lower elevations. The wind whipped around Willis as he stood drenched in starlight, shivering, agape at the glory. No more steps, no more ice, only rocks and a small cairn, the summit was his and his alone. *If I'm going to die now*, he wondered, *will this be the last thing I see, or the next thing I see?*

It could have been five minutes, it could have been an hour, Willis awoke to find himself huddled at the base of the rocky cairn. He dragged himself from a dream of Maddock, begging him to move. To the east, the sky had taken on a silvery hue. As he watched, the sun emerged from the below the horizon. A bleb of molten gold, it rose quickly from its hazy nest and drove a fleeing herd of shadows down the mountainside. *Pym, Sally, damn.*

Willis tried to stand, but his numb legs wobbled beneath him. He crawled closer to the cairn; an orange plastic box protruded from beneath the rocks. *Dig it out, open it.* His stiff fingers scrabbled at the steel latch. Inside, he found heat pads and mylar thermal blankets. He rolled himself in a blanket and crushed a pad to his chest, activating the chemicals inside.

Within minutes, he started shaking, a deep, bone jarring shake that felt like it would dislocate his shoulders. As the sun climbed higher, Willis felt his arms and legs tingle. *Got to go, got to get moving.* He draped the blanket over his shoulders and used duct-tape from the orange box to fasten it about his waist. *Thank you climbing club, whoever you are. Just saved my sorry ass.*

Another trail of wooden stakes led down a ridge on the southern flank of Shasta. Willis glanced back at the summit.

For a moment, the golden sun hovered over the mountain, framed by a shining silver triangle of light. A blink, and it was gone. Willis began his descent, sliding stumbling, but moving in the warm sunlight.

16

Shivering from his journey to the summit, Willis doubted the glory of that sunrise had been worth the ensuing hypothermia. In many ways descending Mt. Shasta proved more difficult than the climb. Willis crept down the shadowy trail before daylight had fully spread across the mountain. No sooner had he started, then a rock had spun from beneath his foot and thrown him down a ravine. Later that morning, a second quake had tossed him to the ground amidst a cascade of sliding ice. He'd regained his feet just as an aftershock knocked him down again and threatened to bury him in volcanic debris. *Damn lady, let a man depart in peace will you.* Now cautious, he placed one foot at a time, glancing down before he placed the next one.

After the sun climbed high enough to chase the shadows from his trail, Willis made better time. Small cairns, little more than three rocks stacked together, marked his way. El Yermo was down there, lost in the shadowy forest below. He picked between the rocks and the lingering patches of ice.

At one point, still above the tree line, the trail branched. A clear path doubled back west and descended toward the roads he had seen the night before. A second way turned east and contoured the mountain before disappearing into the rocks and scree. Willis thought of hot coffee and food, perhaps a lift into town, that waited at the end of the western path. He turned east. *Nothing to be found on the beaten path.*

By early afternoon, he began to doubt his own judgement. The eastern path had wandered through a ragged landscape of naked escarpments and mounds of broken volcanic debris. He passed a deep crevice that reeked of sulfurous fumes. Soon thereafter, what scant trail markings he'd been following disappeared into a maze of fallen rock and rough escarpments.

Faced with a jagged outcrop, Willis paused to consider retracing his steps. The sun had just edged over the ridge above him and its glancing rays highlighted every bump and crevice in the stone face. He stared a moment, blinked his eyes and stared harder. Clearly etched into the weathered rock, he made out a faint triangle. It enclosed a circle, just touching in three places.

Muttering to himself about Bones and his freaking Lemurians, he climbed a fallen boulder. No question, someone had cut this symbol into the rock. Willis couldn't tell how old it was, but by its weathered appearance, he suspected that it predated European contact. He searched the area for more markings, a cave, anything that would indicate why this figure had been chiseled into the stone. The desolate mountainside offered nothing else of interest.

He followed the ridge, moving slowly. A few yards down the slope, Willis found a series of narrow ledges that climbed the sheer face like a ladder built for giants. He grunted, looked up, and started to climb. Each ledge rose over two feet above the previous step. Leaning into the rock, he had to use both hands as well as his feet.

At about the height he figured a fall would be fatal, Willis stopped and assessed his next moves. No question, the ledges continued. They looked natural yet were too regular to have been formed by weathering. Curiosity overcame common-sense. Willis kept climbing. Angling across the rock, the steps brought him to a pinnacle, just above where he had found the triangular symbol.

He pulled himself up to a circular platform, barely large enough for one person. Crouching, kneeling, then standing,

Willis looked down a hundred feet on both sides of the ridge. A twinge of acrophobia made his feet tingle. Something about standing on this spot, something special had drawn an ancient race to create this place. He gazed out at the tumbling wilderness of rocks and trees that stretched below him like a sea of rumpled blankets. To the west, the town of Mount Shasta straddled Interstate 5, and east of where he stood, Willis saw only miles of open country.

The ridgeline descended due south, the direction of El Yermo. He stared that way for a dozen heartbeats, thinking of Sally waiting somewhere down there. In a moment of vertigo and panic, the hills and trees blurred, then roofs, streets, and hazy chimneys all zoomed into focus. Willis lurched, clutching air. His foot slipped and he fell to his stomach, grasping the rocky platform with both hands. *What the crap?*

Dragging himself back to his knees, he searched again for El Yermo. A vista of rocks and trees spread before him. *Sally?* Still, nothing but a hazy carpet of green. Arms out, he tried standing. Once more the world spun, and the roofline of a small town leapt into view. Willis didn't dare move. Like watching some giant camera-obscura, he found the world laid out at his feet. Turning west, he saw cars and semis toiling up Interstate 5. To the east, he scanned a deserted landscape of fir trees and scrub.

What in hell should I be looking for? As that thought crossed his mind, the world spun, and his view changed. Willis closed his eyes and bent his knees until the moment of vertigo passed. Inhaling, he looked out to the east. Set against the mountain flank, he saw a gray concrete building. Stark flat walls, narrow institutional windows, its brutalist architecture stood out like a bloody compound fracture on a dancer's leg. *Not what I had in mind.*

The view refocused farther to the east. A swarm of

aircraft and helicopters circled like gnats. Willis watched them for several minutes. They seemed to have a base somewhere near the building. *Either the Moogly-Woogly in me has my head all messed up, or I was meant to find this place.* He considered that both cases were likely true.

At the thought of the *Ma'óghe*, the *Eternal One* of Maug Island, his view spun again. He seemed to fly into the air and zoom down on a particular rock. A jagged pinnacle, it thrust up though a dense grove of ancient trees. He examined it for a few moments, then closed his eyes. When he opened them again, the world had returned to its normal order and Willis stood once more on the high platform. *Like I'll ever figure out what the crap that all means.*

Preferring not to retrace his ascent, Willis crawled down the jagged ridgeline until he reached a talus slope to the east. Lower still, his path led between scrubby conifers where lingering patches of snow still huddled beneath their branches. Snowmelt trickled down a shallow rill. Willis followed the clear water, wondering if he dared to drink any of it.

Lower still, he found himself in a full-grown forest of fir and pine. The rill he had followed cascaded between mossy rocks and fallen logs. A mile further, it joined a larger stream rushing through a deep ravine. Something at the bottom caught his eye. Willis scrambled down the slippery bank and stood on a bar of water-washed gravel. He scrambled from rock to rock, staying with the streambed and hoping the daylight would hold. He scanned both banks for any sign of Maddock's trail. About a mile upstream he spotted footprints in the mud and a candy bar wrapper. It reminded him of how hungry he was. He crouched next to a cluster of prints. Several men, more than just three or four, and fresh, barely a few hours old. The largest pair of prints could have been Bones' size thirteens.

They have to be. It seemed odd that he found no other sign of the big Cherokee. To Willis, it looked like he might have stopped here to eat a candy bar. He'd tossed the wrapper, then a bunch of men came and hauled him off. Or not—Bones was never a litterbug. Willis decided to backtrack on the prints. He climbed the bank and continued heading east. The forest litter provided a faint trail that led straight up the hillside. When the trail finally disappeared into a tangle of brush and rock, Willis kept climbing in the same direction. The sound of a vehicle stopped him. He'd almost blundered onto a road.

Willis stepped back, only one place this could be. Giselle had said it, two Pyms, father and son with the mountain between them. Not the cozy family of psychopaths that Sally had described, but it looked like Giselle might be right. If she was, then he'd find answers somewhere at the end of that road.

From between the trees he watched a convoy of four large black Suburbans come speeding up the road and pass through an open gate. Two guards in militia outfits pulled the gate shut behind them. Willis noted that the gate fit tight against a concrete sill. No room to crawl under that one. He stayed out of sight, circling through the woods until he found a chain-link fence.

The fence was easy to follow, contouring along the hillside. At the bottom of a shallow rill, he found a gap beneath the fence. It had been hastily blocked with heavy steel stakes. He kept going. Every twelve feet, an upright. Along the top, barbed wire slanting inward. Willis passed the occasional warning: "Government Property—No Trespassing." The rusting fence, the peeling letters, they all bore signs of age.

He reached a corner of the fence and followed it as it climbed the hillside. Around a copse of trees, the fence crossed a small clearing. Willis caught his first glimpse of the building it guarded. Every bit as ugly as it had first appeared that afternoon, the concrete monument to bad architecture glowed red in the rays of the setting sun.

Yeah, just like Maddock to find something like this. Fluorescent lighting flickered from behind broken venetian blinds. A door opened and Willis ducked low. A man wearing dark militia gear stepped outside to light a cigarette. A few minutes later, he stepped back inside. Willis continued to follow the fence.

Across the clearing, he reached another gate. Chained shut and secured with a rusty padlock, it had been abandoned for years. *If I'm going in, this is as good a place as any.* He checked the hinges. A simple strap over a pin, he tried lifting it. The gate rattled as the strap cleared the top of the pin. He slipped inside. From the back of the building came an insane cacophony of barking. Willis dropped the gate as four huge rottweilers came dashing around the corner.

Crap! It would have to be dogs. He raced to the back door. Cigarette butts littered the broken concrete walk. *Be unlocked, be unlocked...* It was. He dove into the darkened room. The lead dog had jammed its shoulders in the door while the others howled in rage, leaping over its back. Willis held the door and kicked at the snarling muzzle. Second kick, the dog caught him by the leg. Visions of a teenage burglary gone wrong, he held the door and punched the animal. It squealed and drew back, but another took its place grabbing him by the arm.

The lights went on. "*Stoyat, stoyat sobaki. Nyet, nyet.*"

The pack whined, quieted, and backed away. Willis turned to face four armed commandos, dark green kit, short hair. Their MAC-10 machine pistols were leveled at his chest. He raised his hands. "Hey, can you dudes tell me how to get to back to the interstate?"

Knocked to the floor, Willis didn't resist when they pulled his empty pockets inside out and bound his wrists behind him with nylon zip-ties. "You're gonna throw me in another cave? Sorry, boys, but this ain't my first rodeo."

He wasn't sure if they understood him until one of the guards slammed his face into the concrete. One on each side, they dragged him to his feet. "*Editiya, vyistro, vyistro.*"

Willis got the picture. He passed through an inner door to an open warehouse. Columns ran down both sides enclosing bays of equipment and vehicles. Some kind of armory, he'd seen enough like it on deployment in the Middle East. Behind a pile of new tires, a tanker truck lurked in the shadows. He caught only a glance before a rifle butt to the back moved him along.

The commandos wasted no time, marching him past a row of trucks and pallet-loads of supplies. Willis tried to get his bearings as they dragged him along. Spanning the full width and length of the building, the armory seemed to serve as a staging area for some activity Willis couldn't quite make out.

Halfway to the far end, they dragged him to a wide stairwell. A hard shove in the back sent him stumbling up the lower steps. Climbing, he reversed twice for every floor. At the third level, another shove slammed him against a steel door. It opened and he lurched into a stark gray hallway.

Rows of identical steel doors trailed off in either direction. The nearest on the right hung open; they hustled him inside, pushed him to a metal stool and zip-tied his ankles to the legs. The door slammed shut behind the last guard. Willis fought his bonds, but they'd been expertly applied. He wriggled harder. The stool seemed bolted to the floor.

He stopped struggling and inspected his prison. The only illumination came through a small square window in the door. Wire reinforced. It didn't look promising. About him, the walls had been padded with heavy vinyl mats. Dust and grime coated everything, and stuffing hung down from tears in the vinyl. *Looks like they dumped me in the damn rubber room.*

Willis considered yelling. If Maddock occupied an adjacent cell, he might hear. Flip side, Pym's goons might return to beat the crap out of him. He could wait to see what would happen, *but I'm one hungry mama-lama*. Yelling seemed like the better option. He took a breath, then stopped. Something smelled like nail polish remover, *ether*.

"Let me out of here, you bastards." He yelled it twice before the room became all foggy and Willis' chin dropped to his chest.

17

On the flats below El Yermo, Silver Glacier maintained their field camp. Drill-rigs, trucks, the usual scatter of equipment and portable buildings littered a five-acre site. June drove her battered gray pickup through an open gate and parked. Sally hunched down next to Uzi, expecting to see armed guards and mercenaries lounging about the site.

"No one is looking for you here, girl. Come in and take a load off." June hopped out of her truck, climbed three steps and unlocked a gray aluminum door. "*Mi casa es su casa.*"

Uzi wiped one finger across a dusty table. "If you say so, cupcake."

June's *casa* turned out to be a laboratory with a bunk in one corner. Sally examined the equipment. One item caught her eye. "Seriously, corn-dogs on a Bunsen burner?"

"Burritos, actually, but yeah, the microwave went tits-up last week."

Uzi prowled around the back of the lab where a rack of computer blades flashed rows of green and orange lights. With a twinge, Sally remembered that her own electronic companion was missing. Uzi bent close, examining the blades. "This is some nice gear."

"Xenons," June said. "Running a full twenty-eight cores and clocked in the gigahertz. They do okay."

Sally had guessed something like that. A fat bundle of cables sprouted through a large hole in the floor. She quashed a pang of jealousy. *Not quite ready to pick a nerd-fight with Calamity June.* "So, what is this we needed to see?"

"That end of the lab," June pointed toward her bunk,

"is mostly chemical analysis. This end is where I do my geophysics."

"Is that like Kegels?" Uzi asked.

Sally tried to ignore him. She glanced at the computer rack and took a guess. "Fourier transforms."

"Bingo." June opened a small refrigerator and pulled out two cans of beer. "Your friend can drink that mouthwash he's carrying, but you get to go on to the bonus round."

"Seismic data, you're profiling the mountain."

"I'm profiling the entire region. Like I said, Silver Glacier has been spending a butt-load of jack on this project. I've got seismic accelerometers scattered halfway to hell, all feeding that rack."

Uzi, the serious Uzi found a seat. "That wouldn't be Bumpass Hell, would it? All the way there?"

"And the little guy's back in the game." June handed him her beer and fished another out for herself. "Lassen, Bumpass, the cinder cones up north, this whole region."

"If I may ask…" Sally started.

Uzi cut her off. "Bumpass Hell? It's a geothermal field just east of here. You really ought to know these things, petal."

"So, we're sitting on a giant pool of lava?"

"Not quite so simple," June said. "It's more like a complex of vents and magma pipes. Everything is controlled by the flow of water. Super-heated water under extreme pressure, it's liquid, but hot enough to dissolve rock. I've been mapping the flows. and that's what I need to show you."

June moved a stack of papers and rolled a sheet of plastic off a large video monitor. As it came to life, she dug a battered keyboard out from behind a stack of books. Uzi feigned disinterest. Sally watched him periodically glance over a shoulder as he prowled from window to window.

When she looked back at the monitor, June had brought up an orange contour map. She adjusted the viewing angle and said, "It's been over a hundred years since the first recording seismometers. The scratchy lines on a paper drum have been replaced by digital equipment that is thousands of times more sensitive." She took a long swallow from her beer and tweaked the image. "You can join us for a minute, Mr. Uzi. Nothing in that parking lot but well-diggers and ground squirrels."

Uzi padded up behind them and watched in silence. June continued, "I get feeds from over five-hundred sensors scattered about Mt. Shasta. They're all processed here."

"And that blue lump?" Uzi said. "What's that?"

"Micro-tremors from the past twenty-four hours. They're plotted by location and magnitude. Let me run the record for the previous twelve months."

The screen went blank. Then an oblique blue rectangle appeared at the bottom. "I could adjust the frequency spectrum and it would map all the roads, just by traffic vibrations," June said. "Now look, I'll overlay an image of the region."

A white tracery appeared like a folded grid. Sally recognized Mt Shasta to the left. "I assume that orange dot is us, but what's the mountain to the southeast?"

"Lassen, this is a big area. Now watch, it's coming up."

As June spoke, a scattering of ripples spread across the blue rectangle. "That started in late April," she said. "I was hoping it would show me where water was percolating up from the lower strata."

The ripples moved in a swarm beneath Mt. Shasta like a school of fish feeding below the surface. Sally caught her breath. What she was seeing just shouldn't be possible. "It almost looks like it has purpose."

"You ain't seen nothing, girl. We're reaching the end of July, watch."

The swarm had broken up into tall lumps that pulsed and grew in a few limited locations. June hit a key and the animation stopped. "One month ago, check it out. Each of those peaks is exactly centered on one of the Silver Glacier test wells."

Uzi said, "You mean their wells are causing the micro-tremors?"

Sally shook her head. "No, it looks like the tremors are finding the wells."

"Right again, girl. Want another beer? No? Okay, hang on to your butts, because August just gets weird." June restarted the playback. "See those black columns? Those are earthquakes. The height of the column denotes the strength of the quake."

Sally had seen a few black lines appear earlier, but now a regular forest of them began to crop up east of Mt Shasta. At the same time, the swarms of micro-tremors gradually coalesced on a single location somewhere below the south flank of the mountain.

"And there we have it." June looked up from the monitor. "A veritable orgy of tiny seismic tremors about five miles east of here."

From what Sally knew of the area, few roads ran even close to that location. High enough to be above the historical logging tracts, she couldn't think of a less accessible spot on the mountain flank. "So, what the heck is so special about this place?"

"That," June pressed a finger against the screen, "is the Silver Glacier regional headquarters."

Uzi leaned close, squinted and said, "You wouldn't happen to have a map, now would you?"

"Better still, I've got satellite coverage at half-meter

resolution. Want to see?"

When Sally looked back at the screen, June had brought up an image of rocky hillsides and forests. "That's El Yermo in the center, with Highway 89 just south of it." She panned the image left across the screen and stopped. "Okay, right here."

June pointed to a white splotch and zoomed in. The splotch became a rectangle surrounded by an irregular tan border. Closer still, Sally made out an entrance gate and parking area. "Amazing, I can see cars and even people. Is *that* their head office?"

"Yup, that's the building. You should see it from the road. It looks like a mausoleum."

Once more the serious Uzi, he studied the screen a moment and said, "Have you been inside?"

"A few times. The place is crawling with guards, but they know me. I've only visited the fourth level where they do administrative stuff."

"Who's in charge?"

"I've never met their boss, just his assistant—guy named Goertzner. Real friendly type, if you like crocodiles."

"That wouldn't be Dr. Anton Goertzner now would it?"

"That's the guy, a colleague perhaps?"

"I know of him. He's an assassin, different branch of the business though. Dr. Goertzner administers psychoactive drugs that drive his targets to suicide. Very effective, but slow and cruel."

Sally shivered. "It's not Pym then. He's not so subtle."

"There I think you're wrong, cupcake. Maybe not *your* particular Mr. Pym, but I think it could be the old man."

"Great, double the fun. But all to manage a water bottling operation? What else do they have going on?"

June explained about her drilling program, how they used subsurface profiling to search for likely sources of virgin water. "If we locate a reliable source of this stuff it's worth hundreds of millions. Pym will unload his share and cash in."

Uzi lost interest and resumed his patrol of the lab windows. Sally remained silent, standing in front of the monitor. The image of seismic tremors systematically roaming beneath the ground just hit too close her own inner secrets. June stared at her. "Questions?"

"Yeah, like how does this relate to helicopter crashes? I mean besides Dr. Death scouring the mountainside for someone to kill."

"Do you have any idea how much energy has moved up from the earth's mantle in the past thirty days?"

"Lots?"

"Enough to blow this whole region into the stratosphere. If that water starts to escape and reduces the pressure beneath us, the remainder will burst into vapor."

"Like Mt. Saint Helens."

"More like Krakatoa.. Your friend will likely be toast before anyone finds him."

Sally examined the screen again. June had left out something vital. "When? Do you know when this is going to happen?"

"I'd say no, if the micro-tremors hadn't centered on one spot. But the water is moving up fast. It's invading the surface strata, weakening it. At this rate, maybe forty-eight hours. Maybe less, certainly not more."

"If you really believed that, you'd be gone by last week."

"No, I'd be trying to talk these knuckleheads out of more drilling. That's what got me on their pariah list."

Sally slumped back from the screen. She'd already known some of the answers. June had just confirmed what the flickering lights had told her. Of course, no one could know about the lights, no one would believe.

"So, what's so special about this place?" Sally put her finger on the white rectangle.

"That's the big question. There are no rigs in operation near that building, at least not since I started here."

Uzi had stopped pacing. He stared through a window at the far end of the lab. "There's a man with a gun over there."

June stood and glanced past his shoulder. "Jiminy jumped up Christmas, that's not a Silver Glacier guard."

Sally stood back from the front window and checked a different direction. "Another one this side, just behind that tractor."

Uzi sidled over. "Look familiar, petal?"

"Yeah, I guess everyone didn't go hunting this morning."

June locked the front door. "That'll stop 'em for about thirty seconds." She stared a moment at Uzi. "Hey spy guy, you talking to yourself now?"

Uzi had a hand to his left ear. He didn't bother to look up. Sally pulled June aside. "He's wired for sound, implant of some kind. How do we get out of here?"

"Unseen? We don't."

"No secret trap door?"

"Not unless you want to tear up the toilet."

Sally thought a moment. "Not quite the toilet." She turned to the computer rack and started yanking cables from the back of the blades.

June barreled into her and pinned her to the floor. "What the hell do you think you're doing?"

"Scramming my ass out of here, that's what. If you're smart, you'll do the same."

"Ladies, that's not getting along." Uzi didn't bother trying to separate the two, but rather began pulling cables out himself. "And cowgirl, if you've got the hat, you probably wear the gun as well. I'd suggest you find it."

Sally shoved the woman off her and scrambled to her feet. "That's a good idea, but what about all this backup you had?"

"Just help me push wires through the floor. They got distracted."

"Head fake, you mean. So much for the cavalry."

Sally dumped the last bundles of loose coax through the floor and slithered down after it. Above she heard Uzi say, "Follow the white rabbit, Alice."

A Stetson hat appeared. Sally grabbed it. The hat was followed by a gun belt complete with revolver, then by June herself. She lost two buttons from her blouse and had to wriggle her hips to fit the rest of the way.

Uzi dropped through feet-first as the lab door banged open. "Go, go, get away from here. I'll hold them off."

June's lab was propped on cinderblocks about two feet off the ground. She scuttled toward the other end, ducking under the occasional water pipe. Sally followed as an exchange of gunshots broke out above. They halted at one corner, peering through the mesh skirting. Two men in identical commando gear jumped from the cover of a trailer and dashed for the lab.

"Now," Sally whispered.

June pushed the skirting over and crawled through. Sally followed. They both ducked behind the trailer as automatic weapons fire broke out. June drew her gun, but none of the shots were aimed their way. Sally took in her revolver and open blouse. "You could have been in westerns."

One of the commandos came barreling around the lab, headed straight for them. June fired a single round, the report sounded like a small bomb had exploded. Despite his Kevlar vest, the man sprawled twitching on the ground.

"Ruger forty-four magnum," June said. "Annie Oakley had nothing like this."

The two women retreated between rows of parked drilling equipment. Sally heard the shooting continue as they retreated from the building. A louder detonation, and the entire laboratory erupted in a pillar of fire. June ducked, pulling her down. A flaming spray of debris hissed over their heads and set small blazes over a hundred-yard radius.

"Your friend was some kind of badass to put up that much fight," she said, "but I don't want to stick around to find out who won."

Behind her, a voice said, "We did."

A blow to the head knocked June to the ground. Sally turned to face an automatic carbine in the hands of a black-clad commando. He didn't smirk, or even smile. "Be smart; don't move. I only need you alive."

Sally let her eyes flick to June's revolver five feet away. Before she could look back, the gunstock caught her across the temple, driving her to her knees. "I said be smart."

The world spun, filled with flashing lights. Sally doubled over and vomited a mixture of beer, whisky, and blackberry cobbler. Two commandos yanked her to her feet as a black utility vehicle sped around the corner. It looked like a four-wheel drive Suburban. Next thing she knew, they'd duct-taped her wrists behind her back and her legs together.

They taped June's wrists and legs as well, tossing her unconscious body in the rear compartment. Sally got the same treatment, slamming into a steel mesh divider and flopping on the carpeted deck. Two men jumped in the front and they took off. Jolting over wheel ruts and potholes, an entire constellation of tools, rags, and cans orbited within the compartment. Sally could do nothing to protect her injured head and feared that June was getting the worst of it.

A can of motor oil bounced off Sally's cheek bone, rolled to the liftgate and then rolled back, smacking her nose. The Suburban careened to the right, and a familiar blue and yellow can rolled past her face. WD-40, the all-purpose lubricant and universal solvent. Sally had once used it to clean crud from her laptop. She tried to snag it with her chin, but the can spun past her.

On pavement now, the Suburban no longer bounced around. Sally flopped over. Propped up against June's inert body, she felt various small items roll against her back. Screwdriver maybe, then the heavier thump of the oil can, she wriggled around twisting her arms, but her wrists were bound tightly.

The oil can thumped her back again, then she felt a light nudge just below her right thigh. She wriggled and twisted, trying to work whatever it was up to her hands. The Suburban braked hard, sending the object rattling off against the liftgate. They turned left, throwing Sally against the right wheel well. With a lurch that felt like all four wheels leaving the ground, they slammed down and began rumbling off on another dirt road. When they slowed for a turn, and Sally felt a small steel cannister almost fall into her hands.

She pushed it against the liftgate and twisted until she felt the cold spray against her wrists. Duct-tape and WD-40, the immovable adhesive met the irresistible lubricant. Sally felt the liquid run up her arm and drip from her elbow. She let the can go and twisted her wrists together, working the lubricant under the tape.

Wrenching, pulling she managed to slip one hand free. A quick peek over the seatback, no one was watching. She bent double and used the screwdriver to tear the tape loose from her legs. Now, outta here. She searched the liftgate, the wheel wells, no interior release. *Really, how hard could it be?* She checked again, nothing. Behind them, a cloud of dust obscured everything. Sally peeked again. Upfront, the driver concentrated on the road while his fellow commando spoke on the radio.

There must be some way to open this freaking liftgate. Sally used her screwdriver to attack the vinyl liner. Near the base of the rear window she managed to jam it between the steel frame and the plastic. As she pried it open, the Suburban hit a pothole and threw her forward, dragging one corner of the liner with her.

Head down, waiting for shouts of alarm, Sally groped around inside the liftgate. *There's got to be a release in here somewhere.* Her arm was too short to reach the latching mechanism. *Crap.* Jamming her head against the wheel well, she searched the space behind the plastic liner. Insulation, steel reinforcement, a few wires, nothing appeared useful.

They slowed approaching a corner and the center brake light glowed in its socket. Okay, one wire is the light, those three bundled together have to be the wiper, and the fourth is—the electric latch. She yanked on the brake light wire until it pulled loose from its socket. *Quickly, quickly, these guys are taking me somewhere.* She scraped insulation from the latch wire and wrapped a few dangling strands from the brake light wire around the bare copper.

Her captors seemed to have some renewed sense of urgency. They fishtailed around the corners without even tapping the brakes. Sally held on as they slammed back and forth. A series of potholes threatened the throw the speeding vehicle from the road. Sally jerked free of the loose door liner, sailed into the air, and slammed down on the deck.

She heard rocks peppering the undercarriage as they gained speed. Head spinning, Sally crawled back and tried to reconnect the wires. They twisted and flopped out of reach. She snagged the brake light wire and felt for the rough spot where she'd scraped insulation from the latch wire. The suburban lurched into a slide, all four wheels locked up. Sally held on, sliding wires together. She heard a low click just before they skidded into a turn. The heavy vehicle spun sideways. The liftgate sprang open, and Sally flew tumbling into the underbrush.

She lay stunned for a moment. Just below the road embankment, she found herself tangled in weeds, beer cans and plastic bags. The Suburban had skidded to a halt. Sally heard its transmission clunk into reverse and whine back toward her.

I can't outrun them. She stayed low and scrambled toward the approaching vehicle. Its liftgate still open like a whale swallowing krill, the Suburban backed past where Sally crouched and stopped at the corner. She waited until both men jumped out and hopped over the embankment.

Now. Scrambling back to the road, she sprinted to the idling vehicle. Her pursuers were a dozen yards away, searching the stunted fir trees and underbrush. June had fallen partially out of the cargo compartment and hung twitching over the bumper. Sally crept around, pushed the woman back in, and closed the liftgate.

At the sound, both commandos spun around. Sally jumped into the driver's seat, slammed the shifter in gear, and floored it. The big V-8 lit off like a rocket, slamming Sally back into the seat. Her foot off the gas, the vehicle slowed. Bullets shattered the rear glass. She pulled herself forward and mashed down on the accelerator. Fishtailing, with bullets taking out two of the side windows, Sally fought to retain control. The Suburban lurched and shimmied.

Flat tires, crapulation on a stick! The engine raced but the heavy vehicle only scraped along on battered rims.

Sally glanced in the mirror. Running, the two were catching up with her. More bullets, one blasted the mirror to flying shards. In desperation, she looked for anything that could be used for a weapon. *Nothing.* She checked below the dash. *Hidden pistol, anything?* Another shot hissed past her ear and crazed the windshield.

Just to her left, a knob labeled *4X4*. She twisted it over, the transmission whined and clunked, the front tires dug in and once more she flew lurching down the road. Out the side window, trees flew by. A turn came up. Sally slowed and tried to ease her way around. The Suburban spun sideways then straightened as the front wheels pulled her back in line.

Another quarter mile, she stopped, jumped out, and ran to the back. June was barely conscious. Sally ripped the tape off her wrists and legs and helped her climb to her feet. With June safely ensconced on the passenger side, Sally punched out a piece of the windshield and kept driving.

"What the hell happened, Girl?" June rubbed the back of her head.

"We got bushwhacked. Any damage? Besides the concussion and possible skull fracture, I mean."

"Run over by a cement truck, that's all." June held on while Sally negotiated another turn. "What's with the rambling wreck?"

"We're escaping, I think."

As Sally spoke, a single-engine plane buzzed over their heads. June put her head out the window to watch. "You expecting company, girl?"

"Not in a good way. Hang on."

They negotiated another turn and Sally floored it. Ahead, the road stretched long and straight. The aircraft had circled behind a row of hills and now approached, almost tree height. Flashes from behind the left wing, a line of bullets threw dust in the air right in front of them.

"Bloody hell." Sally wrenched the wheel over. The big Suburban spun halfway around before flipping into the air and tumbling into a ditch.

18

Augustus Pym usually avoided the fourth floor. He preferred his staff to believe they had some autonomy. Of course, the illusion of autonomy required both surveillance and accountability. *Failure has its consequences*, he'd often pointed out.

Pym leaned forward in his chair and repeated his remonstrance. "I will not tolerate incompetence."

The issue in question was a battered pink notepad computer clamped to a laboratory bench and bristling with wires. It could have been subject to neurological experiments, had it been a human brain. In fact, the screen kept displaying a five-second clip from the movie *Frankenstein.*

The two technicians sitting at an adjacent bank of computer screens must have heard him because he could see the perspiration staining their shirts. A monitor just behind the little notepad also displayed a face. Certainly not Frankenstein's monster, still this face could have belonged to the fictional Doctor.

Pym switched on a small video camera and said, "What do you have from your end?"

Somewhere in the heart of Silicon Valley, rows of technicians processed feed from the little pink machine. The disembodied face spoke. "We were able to pulse the RAM and get a shutdown image. We've also deconstructed some of the bios. None of it is commercial software. We haven't even figured out what operating system she's using."

"So, you're telling me you've got nothing. I spend half a billion buying what you sold me as the best hacking outfit

WOOD AND MATSON | 170

west of *Lubyanka*, and you can't even crack this little toy."

"I wouldn't call it a toy. Someone's dropped a lot of money on the motherboard. The CPU is a custom military job. There's ten thousand dollars' worth of high-speed memory on the uphill side of the north bridge, and that's just the start."

"Don't give me that. It's got Japanese comic stickers all over the cover and the screen is cracked in the upper right corner."

"Pretty good camo, I'd say. Without the passwords, I think we've reached a dead end."

Pym sat back. "Well then, I may have some good news for you. Our subject is in hand and we'll get the password when she recovers consciousness."

After some closing words, Pym signed off. He spun his chair and headed for the elevator. A few keystrokes, the door opened and he wheeled into the elevator shaft. Hoses and guide rails adorned the sides and beneath his wheels, a rough platform had been affixed to the top of the elevator car.

He punched another key, the doors closed, and a soft chime confirmed that a roof hatch had opened. Augustus Pym Senior passed his own suite on level five and rose like an apparition through the roof. A rectangle of blue lights came on, marking the helipad. Off in the distance he heard the thud of rotor blades.

His chair parked behind a plexiglass shelter, Pym waited. Minutes later the whine and thud grew to a cyclone of dust and roof gravel as the craft landed. He let his crew unload a stretcher and wave the pilot off before wheeling out to inspect their captive. Dr. Goertzner stepped from the elevator and strode out to meet him. "Is our subject alive Mr. Pym?"

"You better hope so, Doctor. I'm running short of

alternatives and I'd rather not have to get too creative. Don't you agree?"

"Just let me take a tissue sample."

"In good time, Doctor. You'll get your bloody sample once she awakens. Now let these men through. We'll talk on the way down."

As they waited for the elevator car to return, one of Pym's personal guards stepped up and spoke briefly in his ear. Pym closed his eyes a moment before touching a control on his chair. Once more it unfolded, standing Pym eye to eye with Goertzner. "I just heard that we have captured an intruder. How long have you known of this situation?"

"It developed over the past thirty minutes while you were occupied. The prisoner has been taken care of."

"Does that mean you're pumping him full of infusion already?"

"He has been prepped. They're just waiting for me."

"Well then, un-prep him. No more tests until we see what we can get from Ms. Sally Smith. Who is this guy, anyway?"

"I don't know. Some loser looking for drugs. Does it matter?"

The elevator arrived. Pym said nothing but collapsed his chair and wheeled over to the awaiting platform. It descended through the roof and the hatch closed over his head. When he rolled out on the third floor, the Doctor followed. Another set of doors on his left stood open. Under a row of fluorescent tubes, two figures lay strapped to identical examination tables. Pym knew Sally from her description and reputation. Her head was bandaged, and a young technician stood by, checking her vital signs.

"And?"

The man looked up, startled to find both Pym and

Goertzner staring at him. "She should be okay. There are external contusions and she's suffered a low-grade concussion. We'll keep her on oxygen and monitor her for swelling on the brain."

"How long?" Goertzner asked.

The technician stammered a moment, then said, "You know better than I do. It could be an hour; it could be days."

Pym wheeled his chair around to the second examination table. "And who is our mystery guest here?"

"Some drifter, he's dressed like a bum. I think he got in looking for drugs, but he carried no identification. We're keeping him under sedation until you decide what we should do."

"A nobody then." Goertzner said. "You won't have to get too creative for a while Mr. Pym."

"You're both medical professionals." Pym wheeled his chair closer. "Open your eyes, look at his condition. Does this guy look like an addict or a drifter? No, he was here for a reason, and I think I can put a name to him."

Pym wheeled away from the unconscious pair. "I want straitjackets on both of them, and I want them strapped to the tables. Put her on a twenty-four-hour watch. As soon as she starts to revive, you can revive the other." He spun around to face Goertzner. "Do not touch either of those two until I've had a chance to interview them, do you hear?"

The doctor nodded slightly without making eye contact. "What happens when they are both conscious?"

"We listen to their conversation for a while, then I'll get you that tissue sample. Maybe take one from each of them."

19

"**Who's out there?** *Let me go, you bastards.*"

Sally heard the voice. It had echoed in her head since she'd regained consciousness. She saw nothing, it felt like her eyebrows had been taped to her cheeks. She tried to turn, but something held her arms crossed over her chest. Her legs had been restrained as well, and her entire body felt like it had been beaten with a stick.

The yelling continued. "I know you're there, I can't see, but I can sure as crap hear. Just answer."

The voice sounded familiar. She swallowed and said, "Cornpone?"

Silence, the sound of someone struggling to move, then, "Jeez—Sally, that you?"

"We've been looking for you, Cornpone." Sally's larynx tightened up, but she wasn't going to cry. "You missed my mac and cheese, won first place too. It had ham Wisconsin cheddar."

"Don't do that. I'm hungry enough to eat my own skivvies."

"You came to rescue me, right Cornpone?"

"I tried, but it's not working out. Can you see?"

Sally shook her head. "I've got tape over my eyes. What is this place?"

"Loony bin, old style. I've seen a little of it before they gassed me. I think we're wearing straightjackets. You got any Houdini mojo going?"

"Yeah, like dislocating my shoulders and wiggling out? Not likely."

"Any chance of reinforcements?"

Sally let that question sink in a minute. The best answer

would be the truth, mostly anyway. "Maddock and Bonehead were on their way up, but they didn't make it."

"What do you mean, 'didn't make it'?"

"Shot, killed in a helicopter crash, maybe both. I don't know, but they're not here."

Willis shook his head. "That can't be right. Bones is immortal."

"I thought so too. They brought their own backup, but I saw him get blown to bits. They tried to kill me and…" Sally stopped in confusion. "…and here I am."

A third voice said, "And here you are indeed."

Sally heard a door click shut and the low hum of a motorized equipment. The voice continued, "Willis Sanders and Sally Smith, the two people I've been looking for just dropping in out of the blue. How wonderful."

"Maybe wonderful for you," Willis said. "Me and her, we'd like to just drop out now."

"That will be arranged, all in good time."

Sally was glad she'd been rather vague, there was no need to tell everything she knew or suspected. *Better to let Willis do the talking for now.* She sensed his fury, the rattling of his bonds, and something else—she felt a link of sorts. He burst out with the question she'd been hoping he'd ask, "Who the flipping hell are *you*?"

"Augustus Pym—Senior. I am the father of the man you destroyed, and I intend that you will help me recover him. It's very simple, but perhaps a little painful."

Sally struggled with her bonds. Her legs had been shackled tight to the padded surface. Vulnerable, it wasn't a feeling she liked. The tape across her eyes only made it worse. "Your son tried to kill us," she said, "but we let him live."

"Oh, he's alive alright. He's got his own band of idiots holed up just north of here. We've been keeping track of my son, and what he's become. But you know that, Sally Smith. I've looked high and low for you, but now it seems that you've been lurking right on my doorstep the whole time."

"Well just think Ebenezer, if you'd left me alone back there in New York, you and your boy would still be happily fleecing widows and orphans together."

"Yes, and you could still be skimming the market any time you needed some cash. Amateurs like you should leave such things to the professionals."

Sally felt a cold, bony hand against her cheek. It slid down beneath her hair and clutched her left ear. A cold steel blade rested a moment against her temple. She tried to flinch away as Pym continued, "I think we should start by evening the score."

Sally felt the blade like a spike in her scalp as it slashed the ear from her head. The onset of screaming pain wrenched a long shriek of terror from her throat. At her side Willis cursed and shouted in helpless rage.

A strong grip pinned her down and jammed a bandage against Sally's face. The entire side of her head burned like it had been seared with a branding iron, but far worse was the horror of disfigurement that welled up from her belly like the sum of all nightmares.

"You bastard," she gasped. "You cowardly bastard."

Then Sally wept. The pent-up tears of frustration and rage burst from her chest. "You killed my friends. You tried to kill my uncle. Why don't you just kill me now and be done with it?"

"Because there is so much more I need from you. Not just your ear." The old man had drawn close, whispering at her side. "We should start at the beginning, don't you think?"

"Start wherever you want jerkwad, I've got nothing for you."

"Perhaps this will be easier if you could see."

Fingers once more against her face, and then more burning agony as a band of duct tape was ripped from her eyes. "I'm terribly sorry about your eyebrows, but it had to be done."

Sally could only spew more invectives and thrash against the hard bench beneath her. Fluorescent lamps buzzed in the overhead behind fly spattered plastic fixtures. She tried to move her head but the pain from her severed ear redoubled with every twitch.

From the corner of her eye she saw movement, a face, almost level with her own. Sally gritted her teeth and twisted her head slightly to the right. Wrinkled eyelids, almost without lashes, beneath them, a spiderweb of veins darkened the yellowed orbs. But it was his bright Delft irises that held Sally's gaze.

"Yes," he said, "I'm older than dirt."

His face whisked past hers, then turned, somewhat farther away. Sally realized that he sat in a motorized chair. She no longer cried. All she could think of was how much she wanted to kill this man. More than she'd wanted to condemn his son when she'd abandoned him to madness on Maug Island, more than she wanted to destroy his thugs who had killed her friends.

Pym held a pink plastic rectangle in his lap. "Recognize this, Sally Smith? I believe it was once yours."

"You stole my notepad. I hope it made an effective doorstop, because I doubt you could use it for much else."

"Sadly true. But now you are going to unlock its secrets for me, and I will find productive use for those tools that you've been using to what, create macaroni and cheese recipes?"

"You mean add a few more billions to your own pocket at the expense of legitimate investors?"

"Only an ignorant child would think the investing world is anything like legitimate, or even fair. Any one of ten-thousand traders in New York, London, Munich, anywhere; they'd strip you naked and flay you alive if they thought it would add another one-percent to their bottom line."

"Well then we're in for a long night. You better get started."

"No, I have other plans for you. However, your friend here, I could start with him. Maybe remove some vital parts somewhat lower on his body?"

Willis yelled, "Don't tell him Sally. He's gonna kill us anyway."

"Really—why would I kill you Mr. Sanders? You're helpless, almost useless, and when I'm finished here, I could just let you go—minus your hands and feet, say. Maybe a few other bits as well."

"Don't listen to him Sally."

Pym wheeled out of her line of sight. Sally heard the low hum of his chair fade, and then return. "I have an experienced medical team that will do the surgery, but no anesthesia. I don't know which will be worse, the pain, or the terrible, terrible feeling of loss. Say we start at the feet and work our way up."

Two men in white scrubs passed Sally's field of vision. One older, he headed straight for Willis. The younger paused and gaped at Sally's ruined face. He broke stride only a moment before joining his colleague.

"Leave him alone and let him go, I'll show you anything you want."

Willis tried to kick. "No Sally. Don't do it…"

Sally felt cold, almost detached. Nothing hurt any longer. She could feel her connection with Willis, with the others. Beneath where she lay, something moved, a microtremor perhaps, maybe something else. "I'll do it Pym, but I can't talk you through it. I'll have to show you."

She knew the pain was there, when they wrestled her to her side. She knew her face bled from the wounded ear, despite the bandage, but it all happened as if to another person. Moments later, Sally stretched her arms and sat upright on a padded steel table.

Pym said, "You can walk in those shackles, but you'll fall if you try to run. I've freed your arms, but look at me. One twitch out of place and my people will start working on your Mr. Sanders' groin with a rusty saw. Understood?"

Sally nodded. "Give me the notepad."

Pym guided his chair next to Sally. She met his unblinking eye, wondering if she could kill him with a single blow. *Perhaps the notepad to his throat.* Willis could, she was certain of that.

Pym opened the little computer, set it in his lap, and said, "I know what you're thinking, but I'm stronger than I look. For now, let me keep this. You tell me what to do, and I'll work the keyboard."

Sally showed him how to load the operating system. "You have to boot it off the bios. The system is on a sim card, just wait for it to come up."

She then walked him through loading and verifying the password. "Its six-bit ASCII code, sixty-four characters. Every time you use the password, you must rotate it one character. I've memorized the sequence."

Pym typed it first into a small keyboard fastened to his chair. "I have people who will do that, go on."

Sally next walked him through accessing the Columbia University server. "It's really a distributed system with processors all over the country, but there's one access point that I use."

Finally, she showed him the data structures and the

training sequences. "I'd say run about a thousand iterations to train and validate the network. There's a graphing utility in there. It's an off-the-shelf MATLAB application; your *people* will know what to do with it."

"Congratulations, young lady. You just bought your friend here another twenty-four hours of good health."

"That wasn't our deal. I said you had to let him go."

"Yes, but you didn't specify when. I'll release Mr. Sanders when I have confirmation that your system works. Who knows, by then he may be the sole surviving member of the Dane Maddock team."

Willis didn't speak, but Sally could almost hear his thoughts. *He knew something more. There were still wild cards in play. She had to buy time.*

The motors hummed and a tire squealed on the linoleum floor as Pym spun his powered chair away. "Now hold still, we must bind your arms and legs again."

"That wasn't part of the deal either."

"But it was. Remember, I said there is more that I need from you. Please, don't let this get ugly."

The young medical technician sidled up. "Mr. Pym, I should rebandage her injury first. An infection could spoil your experiments."

"Jacket her first, you've already let two escape. Another one, and you'll take their place."

Sally submitted to the indignity of the straitjacket. While one technician fastened it behind her back the other worked on her ruined face. *None of this matters.* She allowed them to lay her back and secure the leg restraints.

Behind her, a door opened. "So, we finally have some decent test subjects."

Sally twisted her head, ignoring the pain. A large man had entered. Not as heavily muscled as Willis, still he radiated a powerful presence in his own way. The man circled Willis like a farmer inspecting a pig. When he turned to her, Sally felt only detachment and cold clinical interest. "These two were with your son, I gather."

"Let me introduce Sally Smith and Willis Sanders. Both have been exposed. Sally, Willis, meet Dr. Goertzner. You'll be seeing a lot of him."

"We will infuse the female subject first. Based on her reaction we can judge how effective the symbiote will be on the male."

A clink of metal, and a small trolley rolled past. The technician guided it to her side and placed a hand on her leg. He produced a pair of surgical scissors and slashed down through her muddy slacks. Sally felt his hand on the bare skin inside of her thigh and thrashed against her bonds. "What the hell are you doing, you creep?"

Dr. Goertzner, the same cold voice she'd heard before, spoke from just beyond her line of sight. "He is preparing to insert a catheter into your upper femoral vein. If you struggle, he may damage the artery. That would be unfortunate for both of you."

Sally felt a cold antiseptic swab pass across her inner thigh and then the needle punching through her skin, probing, searching, and finally piercing her vein. *None of this matters.* She clenched her fists to suppress the screams building in her chest.

The younger technician spoke. "Should I start it now, Doctor?"

"Make a note: 'infusion started August twelfth at twenty-two hundred hours.' Check on her every hour. We can expect the reaction any time after midnight."

20

Maddock awoke from a hellish dream of screaming death and surgical dismemberment. It took a moment to recall where he was, or why a woman snored softly against his back. The candles had burned down, all but one. The guitarist had lapsed into silence, but the drummer maintained his slow rhythm, lost in music only he could hear.

Bones shook him again. "Wake up. The plane is back."

Almost part of his dream, Maddock had heard it. "The same one, or something different?"

"Same type. I think they've got two of them up there. No helicopters though."

"Could it be Forest Service?"

"Since when does the government fly at night? These dudes figure it's the DEA, but they don't fly patrols for a little pot anymore."

Maddock heard the far-off whine of an engine before it faded to silence. "Crap, he's gone silent and is coming in on the flaps."

Bones got the picture. He jumped up and shouted, "Hey, everybody listen up. There's some nasty business about to go down and y'all need to scram."

Confusion reigned, but no one seemed willing to move. Maddock pulled his things together and shouted, "Narcs, it's the narcs—run."

That had the desired effect. Maddock grabbed the pack and quiver. Bones slung the struggling woman over his good shoulder and the two stumbled out a back entrance. Bones followed Maddock as he dashed to the tree line. A shadow in the moonlight, the plane approached in near silence. "That's going to be a butt load of bad news," Bones said.

"He'll have dropped jumpers. They'll land on the road." Maddock pointed just above the hills where six parachutes descended toward them like angels of darkness. "You can bet they have night vision. I just hope our friends can run."

The young woman kicked and squirmed, but Bones seemed oblivious to the inconvenience. "We've got to scram, too. You want to lug the Keebler elf for a while."

"No one's going to lug me, and I'm not an elf; I'm a fairy. My name is Morgaine."

Bones set her on her feet. "Seriously? A fairy?

Morgaine nodded.

Maddock said, "If you don't have your wings yet, then you'll have to run."

"I don't need to run. I'll simply summon my goblins."

As she spoke, shots rang out from the camp below. Answering fire came from near the road. More shots followed and the shooters on the road switched from single-fire to full-automatic. The plane returned, circling under full power this time. Maddock saw flashes from behind the wing and the building they had just left erupted in splinters and flying shingles. Moments later, a streak of light flashed into the air and the plane itself disintegrated into a ball of fire.

Bones stood with his mouth open. "*Wowzers*, that's one badass bunch of goblins."

Morgaine clapped her hands over her eyes. "No, no, I didn't want this. What have I done?"

As quickly as it started, the shooting stopped. Maddock said, "Whatever happened down there, I don't think we should stick around."

The young woman started to cry. Bones held her around the shoulders and let her weep against his chest. "It will be okay. This wasn't your fault."

Maddock knelt next to her. "Look, if you've got a fairy castle somewhere. Lead us to it."

She wiped her nose and said. "You know nothing about fairies. We don't have castles. I live in Merlin's cave."

Maddock nodded. "A cave would do. Can you find it in the dark?"

"That's a silly question for a mortal to ask one of the Fair Folk."

Morgaine didn't wait for an answer but slipped between the trees like a fish in a darkened pond. A will-o'-the-wisp of white cotton, she worked her way back up the hillside. Maddock let Bones follow her and concentrated on leaving as little trail as he could.

Climbing higher up the mountainside and angling to the west, the fluttering wraith led them into a dense copse of ancient trees, then vanished like an extinguished candle. Maddock nearly ran into Bones standing in the darkness. "Typical woodland sprite, just when you need one, they are nowhere to be found."

"In here, fool mortals."

Maddock groped his way into the trees and found himself picking between the roots of an ancient fir. "Where are you?"

"In here. Come quickly, the Enchanted Forest is dangerous."

Maddock ducked beneath an enormous root and squeezed past a boulder to find a snug cave with Morgaine sitting next to a tiny glass lamp. "We're safe here," she said.

Bones pushed in behind his friend. "Isn't there supposed to be dancing and kegs of ale?"

"That would be the dwarves, they live on the other side of the mountain."

Maddock knelt next to her. "Seriously, you live here by

yourself?"

"My goblins come to visit; they sing to me when I'm lonely."

"And they bring you food?"

She looked down at her lap and twisted her hands together. "No, I have to raid the Warlock's Castle for food." She looked into Maddock's eyes. "But you must know all this. The fairy light is so strong inside you."

Half crouched, the big Cherokee had been roaming the shadows behind her. Maddock ignored his snort. "Bones, listen to this. I think we may have come full circle." He turned his attention back to Morgaine. "Tell me about this Warlock's Castle."

"It's my quest. I must venture deep into the Labyrinth of Eternity and ascend through the Dungeon of Skulls. The lower halls are filled with orcs and trolls. They have torture chambers on the third level. Sometimes the screams are so loud I can hear them as I enter."

Bones said, "Laboratory Nine, did you sneak up to the third level?"

She buried her face in her hands. "No—well yes, once. It was horrible."

They waited, but Morgaine had fallen silent. A draft flickered her tiny lamp. Finally, Maddock asked, "Where do you find the food?"

"Second level, there is a devil's kitchen where foul orc meats are boiled. I find some human food there as well, fruit and bread mostly."

"Can you take us there?"

"You wish to go on a quest with me?" She brightened immediately. "Bring your magic bow, does your friend have a magic sword?"

"I have this." Bones showed her his stone knife

Morgaine looked as if she would faint. Maddock asked

if she was okay. A few deep breaths and she replied, "Yes, yes but this is all too awesome—the prophecies you know. We must go now while the orcs yet sleep." Morgaine stood so quickly, the little stool she sat on fell over.

Bones said, "You wouldn't happen to have a flashlight, would you?"

"I have fairy lamps like this one." She rummaged up two more of the egg-sized glass lamps and lit them. "They burn cooking oil. We can refill them when we get there."

Maddock headed for the entrance, but Morgaine stopped him. "This way, we must go through the Labyrinth."

She led them deeper into her little grotto. Their fairy lamps cast dancing shadows against the rocky walls. In one corner, Maddock spotted a snug little bed, almost a nest, heaped with ragged blankets. Morgaine paused a moment. "This part is tricky."

She knelt, wrapped her cotton dress around her legs, and slid through a crevice in the floor.

Maddock saw the faint glow of her lamp almost twenty feet below him.

"There are steps," she called up, "you just have to find them."

Narrow treads had been cut into the rock. Maddock followed, pulling is bow and quiver through after him. Bones descended after him, holding his lamp high. The light barely reached the ceiling above. Morgaine sat on a rock waiting for them. "My bats come through here in the evening and return in the morning. That's how I found this place."

"The bats?" Bones looked around, "like in Carlsbad Caverns kind of bats?"

"Oh yes, maybe more. They pour through my home like a fountain of darkness. It's lovely, you'll see."

Maddock followed Morgaine as she picked her way between fallen boulders. They passed through a narrow crevice between two massive flakes of broken rock and entered a large open cavity. Bones stared at the rock arching overhead. "Another damned lava tube. Last time we were in one of these, things got ugly real quick."

Morgaine climbed a hill of soft earth. "We have entered the Womb of Gaia. Stay near the wall. This is where the bats live and it's a little messy in the center."

"Bat poop," Bones said. "We're wading through ten thousand years of bat poop."

"And fungus," Maddock said. "I don't want to know what this stuff is doing to our lungs. How much farther Morgaine?"

She stopped. "Through here. This way leads to the Labyrinth of Eternity. I've been lost for like, days in this thing."

"Let's not do that," Bones said, "I'm hungry enough to eat some of your orc meat as it is."

The Labyrinth of Eternity proved to be a bewildering jumble of broken rock that filled another enormous cavity. Maddock heard the rush of water coursing through dark channels beneath his feet. Up ahead, Morgaine's tiny lamp bobbed and dodged as she climbed over the boulders and slipped between the fallen slabs. "This way," she said, "we're almost there."

Maddock stooped beneath a broken ledge and duckwalked down a low passage that looked more like a road culvert. Bones followed, crawling like a turtle on his hands and feet.

Morgaine waited in a small chamber. She held a finger to her lips. "Shhh—we're right below the Dungeon of Skulls."

To their left, a narrow cleft climbed toward the surface.

Across the chamber a rectangular opening led off into darkness. Maddock nodded that direction. "And where does that lead?"

"The Halls of Madness. You don't want to go there, not for anything. Come on, we must climb now."

Maddock started toward the cleft when Bones said, "Holy Crap, will you look at that."

His friend stared at the ceiling. Directly overhead a triangle and circle had been incised into the rock.

Morgaine didn't bother to look. "Fairy signs," she said. "The Old Ones carved them everywhere. They are the key to these passages."

Maddock drew the white arrow from his quiver. "Do you know what this is?"

Morgaine blinked and shook her head. "It's pretty. Is that a magic arrow?"

Bones made a face. "Nah. Couldn't be."

Maddock persisted. "Do you know of anyone named Killeli?"

"Is she another fairy? Could I meet her?"

"Why don't we go up and do our quest first" Bones said. "Wouldn't that be better?"

Morgaine looked first at Bones and then back at Maddock. "Okay."

Maddock began working his way into the cleft. Just past the opening he found a series of narrow ledges, each about two feet above the other. "Bones, come here and tell me this isn't what I think it is."

Peering over his shoulder, Bones held the little glass lamp above their heads. "Lemurian stairway, I knew it."

"Of course it's Lemurians," Morgaine said. "The Old Ones, like I said. They come here to speak with their mountain."

Bones craned around. "You've seen them?"

"Well not for a long time. But my father worked in the lumber camp. We lived down there where—where…"

"It's okay. Your goblins took good care of everyone I'm sure. What did you see?"

"My father worked there in the summer. When I was little, I'd take my books up on the mountain to, you know, just to read and dream. Sometimes I didn't go home until after dark. That's how I found these caves, the bats, you know." She looked at both Maddock and Bones. "Did you ever do that?"

Maddock shook his head.

"Well that's too bad, because sometimes I would meet these people, really tall with white robes. They called me *Fairy Child*. Later I found out they were the Lemurians."

"Does your father know you are here?"

"Father is gone, so is mother. Nobody here now except me. Do you want to see the Dungeon of Skulls? It's really spooky."

Maddock climbed, keeping just his toes on the ledges. Each tall step he had to brace against the walls for balance. At the top, a stout wooden door blocked his way. From below, Morgaine said, "It's a secret passage. Just push it open."

He placed his palm against the door and pushed. With a quiet *snick*, it swung away into the shadows. Maddock stepped through to darkened chamber with a low ceiling and concrete floor. He sniffed. The air was fresh and the room was old, but certainly not ancient. The others followed, lamps held high. All about the walls and down the center of the room, decaying wooden shelves sagged beneath heaps of bones and staring yellow skulls.

Walking down one aisle, Maddock examined the withered limbs and shrunken skin. In the dim light of his lamp he spotted a scrap of metal beneath a rotting skull.

"Hey, look at this."

His friend pushed the skull aside, "Dog tags. This was a boy named Martin Davis. He was one of us, Maddock."

"There's more, all military. How old do they look?"

Bones shook his head. "No telling, fifty years, sixty maybe. I think we've found our Laboratory Nine."

"Yeah, Cold War, Korea, Vietnam. We were supposed to be the good guys, Bones. What happened here?"

"Project Bluebird, Project Artichoke, ever heard of MK-Ultra?" Bones shook his head. "Cold War mind control experiments. Those were the bad old days. Doesn't look like they're quite over."

Morgaine tugged on Maddock's arm. "We've got to finish this level before our oil runs out. Come on."

She led them to a concrete stairway with a rusting metal handrail. At the top of the stairs she pushed open a steel door and they entered another darkened room. Maddock examined the door they had just passed. A broken hasp and ancient padlock hung from the frame. "Someone has been down there recently, and I don't think it was the goblins. What is this place, Bones?"

"Fallout shelter, look." His friend indicated rows of boxes along one wall. White cardboard barrels were marked to indicate food or water. Most of them had been broken into, and rodent droppings littered the floor.

"I think I'd rather die out in the open," Maddock said, "then be crammed down here to suffocate in this filth."

Bones slipped the pack from his back and left it at the entrance to Morgaine's Dungeon of Skulls. Maddock set his bow and quiver nearby. "We'll get these when we return." Seeing Morgaine's doubtful frown, he said, "I want to save them for a real emergency."

"Come on." Morgaine tugged at Maddock's arm. "We've got two more levels and they're the hardest, crawling with orcs. There's oil in a can by the stairs. I will refill our lamps here and leave them for our journey home."

Another stairway, another steel door. Maddock pushed it open a crack and allowed a thin sliver of gray light to shine down on them. He drew it back, careful not to let it shut all the way and mouthed, "Two guards."

Bones crept up behind him, and Maddock opened the door slightly. A wide chamber receded in a forest of columns left and right. On the opposite side, a uniformed figure climbed a broad staircase. Maddock glanced the other direction. A second guard slipped out a door at the end of the building.

Maddock turned to Morgaine. "You don't need to come any farther. These are dangerous people. You should leave now and never come back."

She shook her head. "I am Queen of the Fair Folk, proper ruler of this land. If any are to cleanse this wizard's lair, it should be me."

Maddock looked at Bones, shrugged, and signaled to move out. The three of them crept between the concrete pillars, working their way toward the stairs. Maddock led, his head on a swivel.

Bones watched their back. "It looks like a Pym's got himself a freaking armory down here. They're going to return pretty soon."

Maddock stepped into a deep stairwell and peered up between the concrete treads. Zigzagging away into the darkness above, they didn't look like they quite reached the top. He was about to make a dash for the next level when the floor lurched and a rumbling growl echoed through the chamber. Bones said, "Another freaking earthquake."

Morgaine shook her head. "No, it's Mother Gaia. She's very angry with us. We must…" She paused mid-sentence and in the silent darkness as a wailing cry of torment echoed down from above. If ever such sound came from a human throat, it certainly was human no longer.

21

Willis concentrated on his face, on every nerve, how it tensed and writhed beneath his skin. He let his attention drift to his chest, to each arm, down each leg, acknowledging, recognizing every sinew, every knotted muscle. Then he started back up, beginning with his toes. Relaxing, letting go, feeling the tension flow from his body like a caged animal running from a broken fence. He drew on his psyops training to condition himself for what he knew was coming. Psyops, the only tool, the only weapon he had left.

He'd heard that doctor say twenty-two hundred hours, ten o'clock. Twice, someone had entered, checked his bonds, and fussed with Sally's infusion. *Whatever the hell that was.* Willis figured it must be a little after midnight, maybe another hour before she'd feel the effects. He would have taken that surgeon's knife for Sally. He'd told her so after they'd been left in the darkened room. She said to shut up, that someone was watching, listening. Now her silence was worse than her screams. *Psyops, the only weapon I got.*

Like a memory newly retrieved, Willis understood that Sally had some kind of plan. *How do I know that? Because we both got that Moogly stuff in us. Sally, yeah, she'd been drinking the Kool-Aid since Maug, and me because I've been soaking in it for at least the past week.*

A murmur of voices. Willis heard people walking the halls. *Changing of the guard, I expect.* Silence, then little scuttling rat sounds. Willis relaxed his muscles. *Psyops, remember?* The darkened room was bad enough, the tape over his eyes only compounded his fears. Whispers, ghosts, something prowled the floor. Muscles relaxed, ready, given the chance, he'd spring and kill.

A hand across his mouth, strong, smelling of nicotine, it pressed his head down. In his ear, a voice whispered. "I'm here to help, say nothing."

Willis kept his lips pinched together as someone peeled the tape from his eyes. Moonlight filtered through a set of steel framed windows. A shadow scuttled along the floor. It moved toward his feet; a soft clink and they were free. Willis rolled on his side and one, two, three, six straps loose, he shrugged the straitjacket from his arms and sat up. The shadow pushed him back down and whispered, "No, no, quiet."

Beside him, Sally stretched her limbs. Even if they made it no farther, even if he died right here, seeing her free had been worth it. The voice in his ear again. "I'm taking Sally out. The guards know me, and even if they don't know her, they'll let us pass."

As softly as he could manage, Willis said, "They know me too, just not in a good way. I'll stay, maybe give 'em something to think about, but I've got to talk to her first. If only for a minute."

A squeeze on his shoulder, it must have meant yes. Willis slipped to the floor and followed two other shadows to the door. Outside, he found a young man in technicians whites. Willis threw him against the wall and throttled him with a forearm to the throat.

"No, no he's with us."

Willis spared a glance. The speaker was female, late thirties, her torn blouse invited a second look. "Who's us?" Willis said.

"Me. I'm June, a friend of Sally's. Jason is coming out with us, he's fed up."

"Yeah, I'll bet—I know this dude, Pym's buddy, mister infusion man, he likes needles." Willis pressed harder against the man's larynx. "Don'cha buddy?"

Sally found her voice. "Please, Cornpone, stop. Please?"

Willis froze, his anger slipped back in its kennel, quiet now, waiting. *Sally, crap.* "Come here!"

She collapsed against his chest, sobbing. Willis wrapped his arms around her and buried his face in her hair. It smelled of dirt and antiseptic. "I love the new do, but blonde?"

"Oh Willis, It's all my fault, all my fault."

"None of it is, don't you believe it. You're just riding a wave of sewage someone else kicked up."

"Now listen, you big lug. I wanted you here, I wanted Maddock and Bonehead to come, because I needed all of you. There's something happening, something terrible. I've got to tell him. He's got to do something , 'cause no one else will."

"The key, there's some kind of key. Don't ask me how…"

The woman, June, grabbed her by the shoulder. "Time's run out, children. We gotta go."

Willis went down on one knee, it put him just below Sally's eye level.

"You listen to me. Keep yourself safe. When you see Maddock, tell him I know what's happening. I'm going to go kill that Pym guy now, him and all his friends."

Half her face swathed in bandages, dried blood still clinging to her cheek, Sally bent down, wrapped her arms around his head, and kissed him full on the mouth. "Just come back to me, Cornpone."

The three walked away as Willis stood in the vacant hall. He heard the soft thump of their shoes in the stairwell. It faded as they passed the lower levels. He scanned the hall. Darkened doorways, all but one. At the far end, light glowed from behind a pair of swinging doors. On little cat's feet he padded that way.

Willis peeked in at a laboratory of some kind. It looked more like a morgue. A slight movement caught his eye. A technician in white scrubs lunged from behind the door. Willis deflected the razor-edged rib shears that descended toward his neck but took a punch to the kidneys that sent him reeling back. A second lunge, this time to his midriff. The shears tore through Willis' shirt and left an open wound that streamed blood down his stomach.

Man knows his anatomy. Willis spun behind a steel table and flung a tray of scalpels at his assailant. *What are you afraid of buddy?* He grabbed a beaker of liquid and threw it at the man's face. It flew harmlessly past and dashed against the far wall. *Why aren't you screaming for help?* No other weapon at hand, Willis sidled around, as if to make for the door.

The technician rushed him. Willis overturned the table, ducked under the steel blade, and landed a side-kick to the man's head. In the same movement, he came down both feet on the floor and smacked a solid right to the man's sternum. A body slam to the concrete floor ended his struggles. *I got some anatomy too, jerkwad.*

A first aid kit on the wall supplied suture tape and bandages for his wound. Willis searched the lab for other weapons but settled for a large dissection scalpel and the rib shears. He dragged the unconscious technician down the hall and flopped him on the same table Sally had recently occupied. It took some wrestling to get his limp body into a straitjacket. Feet shackled, eyes taped shut, Willis admired his work. *Now one last touch.* He ripped the man's pantleg open and jammed the dripping needle into his femoral vein. *Happy dreams.* Willis slipped back into the hall.

That time of night known as oh-dark-thirty, few were

awake and fewer still alert. Willis knew he was running on fumes, but as a SEAL he'd often put in forty or fifty hours straight. Hoping Sally had made her escape, he headed for the stairwell. From outside, Willis had counted five levels. He'd had only a brief glance at the first level. It seemed to be a mustering area or armory perhaps. From that he figured the second level would be barracks. He'd seen enough of the third level. *Time to scout the executive suite.*

The stairs ended after only one more flight. He tried the door. *Locked, damn.* He descended to that same gray hall on the third level. Checking a few of the shadowy doorways, he found his padded cell from earlier. The adjacent opening was different. Twin polished steel panels, it looked like an elevator without buttons. Willis jammed his rib shears between the panels and pried them apart. The elevator shaft beyond fell away in darkness below his feet.

Willis inspected the walls. *There's always a ladder in the movies, why not here?* Rough concrete, hydraulic cylinders, a few steel attachment plates, nothing useful. *Freaking Bones would be up that shaft like a gecko on a wall.* He recalled Pym's mocking voice, badgering Sally into giving up her secrets, he'd find it and choke it to silence, no matter what it took.

Guide rails stood out from the walls on either side of the shaft. Nothing to hold on to. Willis jammed his left foot against the side of one rail and wedged his back against the opposite wall. The doors slammed shut and Willis hung there a moment in darkness. One foot and then the next, he worked his way up. His exhausted legs burned, he tried to push himself higher, but grease or something broke the traction he had against the steel rail.

As he reached higher, the entire building jolted like it had been hit by a locomotive. His hand flailed against the concrete, brushed against a bolt head in the darkness and slipped. Sliding down, he fell forward and clutched the greasy rail, jamming a foot against the wall behind him. Wedged at an angle, leaning forward into the dark elevator shaft, Willis had a brief vision of himself falling into the pit of trash and septic water that always accumulated beneath the lowest floor.

Here to kill, not die. He pushed himself higher, one hand above the other, one foot against the wall, one pushing behind him. After an eternity of screaming muscles, he saw a thin gray bar of light shining against the far wall. He'd reached the next level. One foot out, probing, there should be a ledge of some kind. Nothing but bare concrete. *It had to be there, that ledge.*

He lost his grip on the rail, slipped and jammed both feet against the wall. Breathing hard, he climbed a little higher until that thin bar of light came back in view. Florescent lights, they'd be outside the door shining from above. Willis realized that their reflection on the inside would be lower. *How much?* It didn't matter, he no longer had the strength to climb.

Can't stay here, not going back down. Sally, this one's for you. He pushed again, another inch, then another. His head touched an obstruction. *Got to be the elevator car.* Willis stepped back until his foot touched a ledge. He reached up and clung to the doorframe. Both legs shook so hard, he was afraid he'd slip back off. Willis pulled the rib shears from his belt and jammed them between the doors. They opened enough that he could slide a hand between them. Pushing with the other hand, Willis slipped through and collapsed to the floor.

He ran his fingers along the carpet, short fibers, utilitarian beige and brown pattern. *Not a lab or a torture chamber. Movin' on up.* Willis rolled on his back. One ceiling fixture out of every four was lit. *Off hours, then. Got the place to myself.* He wasn't sure how long that would last. Rolling to his feet, he took stock. Desks, keyboards, monitors. A copier-printer in the corner. Next to it, a recycling bin.

Got a social conscience, these guys. Wonder if that's where they dump the bodies too. A few sheets littered the bottom of the bin; he rummaged through them. Pages of numbers, they looked like database printouts. One sheet held half of a graph, but the rest hadn't printed. The vertical scale was labeled WBC, the horizontal was calibrated in minutes. WBC ranged from about four thousand at the sixty-minute mark, then shot off the scale at three hundred minutes. *If I wasn't so damned tired and hungry, I'd know what this meant.*

He kept looking, rummaging desk drawers. *Bingo*, a secret stash of energy drink and, *oh thank you Lord*, a tin of mixed nuts. Top drawer of the next desk yielded a box of granola bars. Willis stuffed his pockets full. Still no indication of what these people did. He tried booting up one of the computers. As expected, the login wouldn't accept 'password123' or 'admin'. He tried a few other obvious ones, no luck. All the filing cabinets were locked. He glanced up at the wall clock, three-thirty. *Tick-tick-tick.*

Pym would be on the level above. He'd have guards; it didn't matter. *Gimme one shot, then you can do what you want.* The elevator car blocked the upper door. Willis figured there had to be another way up, a fire escape, something. He checked the perimeter. Where he'd entered, it had been desks and open workstations. The west end of the building seemed to be taken up with private offices.

Willis slipped into a shadowy hall, trying doors on

either side. All of them locked, he could see moonlight glowing through the glass door panels. Two lavatories occupied the far end. He checked both of them but found only the usual stalls and urinals. He flicked on a light and checked the janitor's closet. It could be entered from either side. The usual assortment of boxes and buckets graced the interior, nothing useful.

Willis doused the light and turned to leave when he noticed a faint glow coming from the back wall. On closer inspection, he found a vertical seam running floor to ceiling. Light glinted between the edges. He pushed, but nothing moved. He tried using his scalpel to pry it open, but only managed to gouge out a flake of wallboard. Examining the other corner, he found a similar narrow seam. Willis pushed and the entire panel pivoted at its center, rotating into the closet.

Moonlight glittered through a narrow window in the far wall. Willis looked up and down. Another stairwell, its steel treads were narrow and steep, almost like a ladder. Below him, they zigzagged down into the gloom, but above they climbed to the next floor.

One hand on the rail, Willis crept up the final flight. He paused at the top; a heavy steel door blocked his way. He touched the polished metal knob. A flush deadbolt keyslot spoke of no-nonsense simplicity. Likely, the door was alarmed as well. He tried the knob anyway. It turned but the door held fast. *Got to be some other way in.* He looked up. A ladder bolted to the wall led to an opening in the roof. *Up there and drop in through a window.*

As he started to climb, lights came on in the stairwell. At first Willis thought they'd been triggered by his hand on the ladder, but from below, he heard the distinctive clunk of footsteps on the steel treads. Willis looked up. He'd never make it through the opening in time. The steps drew nearer, no way he'd make it back to the fourth level. *Seeing is believing, and you won't see what you don't believe.* Psyops again, Willis hoped it was true.

He vaulted over the rail, hanging by his hands. From the back he gripped the stair-treads, both feet pressed as tight as he could against the bottom of the steps. There'd be a shadow, an unexplainable dark clump huddled beneath the top landing. No reason for anything to be there. Still, he felt like a naked man in Times Square.

The thump-clunk climbing sounds came closer. Willis' arms ached and his fingers burned against the cold steel. He'd freaked too early, whoever was coming up had started near the bottom. *Crap, I could'a made it to the roof.* Then movement, someone climbed below him. Holding the handrail, looking down at the steps, he caught a glimpse of blonde hair. Willis clung beneath the steel landing like a spider watching a circling moth.

She didn't break stride stepping past his white fingers. He saw a flash of generous curves, wrapped in technician's robes. Willis heard a key slip into the lock and the snick of a deadbolt opening. *Wait, wait.* His fingertips said otherwise. Climbing up the rail, he caught the door as it swung shut. A ten count and he slipped inside.

The first thing Willis noted was the carpet. Deep, lush pile, it invited a nap. *None of that happening for a while.* He padded down the darkened hall. Light shown from an open doorway. Willis heard voices and edged closer. Glancing around the empty room, he saw a table set for one, but no chairs. Paintings and bookshelves lined the walls. A reading lamp stood by itself in one corner. A perfect gentleman's study, if there had only been a place to sit.

The voices came from a door on the opposite side. Willis glided across the room. Back to the wall, he peeked past the doorframe. Bedroom, the woman bending over a hospital style bed was talking to its occupant. "...thyroid medicine, Mr. Pym. Sleep now, you can eat in a couple of hours."

Something else in the room, a motorized wheelchair. To Willis it looked like a jazzed-up version of the deluxe model. He watched the women fill a glass from a bedside pitcher. Rib shears in hand, he thought about just taking them both out. The monster and his keeper, it would be over in seconds. The threat destroyed, he'd have Sally, he could return to Maddock and Bones, *wherever the heck they were.* The idea crossed his mind, then fled. *Not the woman, not murder.*

Willis slid back from the doorway and found a place in the shadows behind a table. A rattling of drawers, a few more words, then the bedroom light went off and the woman strode out the door. He calmed his breath, held the shears at ready and waited for his quarry to relax, to fall back asleep.

Counting heartbeats, he reached five hundred before rising like a ghost in the shadows and stepping back to the bedroom door. Rhythmic breathing, a tiny pool of green light shown next to the floor. Pym's wheelchair waited like a patient dog. Clasped shut, the twin blades of the rib shears formed a curved dagger capable of punching through sternum, viscera, and heart in a single blow. Willis raised it high and stepped into the room.

22

Morgaine collapsed in a heap, her hands covering her ears. The wailing cry trailed off to a burbling moan.

Bones ran up and gripped Maddock by the arm. "I guess they found someone to take your place."

The stairs climbed like a concrete zigzag that vanished into the gray shadows above. Another cry, this one rising to a shriek, echoed through the building. Maddock said, "Bones, you were loose in here for a while, where does this take us?"

"Up as far as the fourth floor. I've got no idea how you get any higher."

"We'll work that out later. Let's go back to the lab and see who they've got strapped to their table this time."

Bones glanced down. "What about her?"

Maddock knelt at her side. "Come on, Morgaine, we desperately need your warlock-smiting powers."

She huddled tighter and shook her head. Maddock bent over, close to her ear, and said, "Can you return to Merlin's cave and tell the Goblins of our situation?"

"I can do that, but you face terrible dangers ahead."

"Then I ask one more thing. Watch over my bow and keep it safe. I'll need it when we return."

Morgaine looked up, smiled weakly, and said, "That will be my mission on this quest. May the Powers of Light guide you and keep you."

With that, she floated back across the floor and disappeared. Bones let out a breath and said, "What'll happen to her?"

"Best case, everyone's taken a hike by the time she returns."

"Who were those guys, anyway?"

"First bunch were Pym's commandos, same guys we tangled with before. I have no idea where the second bunch came from. Probably DEA after all, coming down on a suspected meth operation."

"That was a butt-load of firepower for a bunch of Feds."

"Yeah, it's a good thing we had Twinkletoes or we'd both be answering some tough questions right now. What next, Hiawatha?"

Another anguished round of cries echoed down the stairwell. Bones pointed up. "Third level of Hell, don't you think?"

Maddock took the stairs two at a time, adopting a panther gait that made little sound. He couldn't hear his friend Bones, but knew he followed right behind. A quick peek at the second floor, dim lights.

"Mess hall," Bones said.

Maddock nodded. Next floor up, he hesitated and said, "That could have been me."

"But it wasn't. Let's go." The screams had diminished to a series of low, choking moans. Maddock pulled the door open a crack and checked the hall. Dim, empty, he slipped inside. Bones stepped past him. "This way."

The moans grew louder. Three doors down, Bones halted and glanced inside. An arm wave and they both entered. The moon hadn't quite settled below the mountain's flank. Maddocks eyes adjusted to the pale illumination. A figure in white was strapped to the same table he himself had occupied the day before. They needed some light, despite the risk. Maddock made sure the door was closed, then snapped on the overheads.

Bathed in the cold glow of fluorescents, the figure began to writhe and scream harder than before. Bones stared a moment and said, "Oh crap, it's Pym's own dude."

Maddock took in the torn pant leg and dripping infusion bottle. He stepped over and pulled the catheter needle from the man's leg. Bones tore off a strip of duct tape from a roll on the floor and slapped it over the wound. "Man, they got this one trussed up like Hannibal Lecter. If you had been wearing that thing, I'd have just left you."

"What are we going to do with him, Bones?"

Bones shrugged. "Sell the jacket on ebay?" Then he frowned. "How you feeling, Maddock. You took a pretty nasty blow to the head when we scrammed the last time."

"Better now, most of the stiffness is gone." Maddock didn't mention the weird moments of clarity he'd been experiencing, or the near premonitions. He could feel Sally; he knew she was close by. Willis too, although that was unlikely. "Good in fact. Kind of like that Moogly juice that hit us on Maug. It's wearing off."

"Exactly. We leave this guy here. He'll be fine. And if he's not, I don't think I care."

The guy doesn't look very fine, Maddock thought. He glanced back, then said, "How about we get some answers, find someone that can still talk?"

Bones killed the lights and scanned the corridor. "I say we clear this level. There's a light down there at the end."

Maddock didn't wait for another invitation. Together they padded down the hall and stopped at the half-open doorway. A lab of some kind, the steel table had been overturned and broken glassware littered the floor. "Looks like you've been here already, Bones."

"Nope, not today, anyway. What do you make of it?"

"I think our friend wasn't quite planning to wind up on the table back there."

"DEA again?"

"Right, about as likely as Morgaine's goblins," Maddock said. "I'm getting another weird feeling about this; something's going on here that's off-script. They've got a bunch of dead guys in the crypt, one of their own is screaming in the torture chamber but no one seems to care. And then there's us, we're charging around armed only with our bare knuckles."

"I got my knife."

"Yeah, and they've got automatic weapons. We're so wrapped up with Pym, we've forgotten our mission, to find Willis. I think he's close by, somewhere. Don't ask me why."

"You're forgetting Sally."

"No, I'm not. She's been here, Bones. She may still be near. I can tell."

"You've got that Moogly stuff still talking to you, don't you?"

Maddock ran his fingers through his hair. "I don't know anymore."

"*Gah*, all this Killeli-Marumda crap is just a bunch of new-age native Californian, pot smoking mumbo-jumbo. I so wanted to believe, I so wanted it."

"Don't you start doubting now Bones. We've seen a lot of crazy stuff, this is no crazier. You of all people Bones, I can't believe it's you saying this."

"You're the one mainlining the Kickapoo Joy Juice."

"Well we both saw the circle and triangle symbol down there and we've seen it before. Tell me I'm wrong."

"I got the squid-nibbles too, you know. Crazy how fast my shoulder is healing, but I don't feel it. Nothing."

"Yeah, but you missed out on the secret sauce yesterday. How come our friend back there is still screaming, but I'm not?"

Bones peeked back out the door. Moans and cries continued to echo up and down the deserted hall. "Yeah, weird. Think you're immune or something?"

"We've got to find someone who knows. Creepy, isn't

it? They've just left that poor bastard to suffer. What do you want to bet someone will be along to check on him?"

"You want to go back?" Bones said. "You want to just sit there and listen to him?"

"I'm open to better ideas."

Bones glanced down the hall. "Okay, 'till I start hearing the music myself, then we bail."

Before leaving the lab, they both checked for painkillers, anesthesia, anything. Bones held up a gray plastic bottle. "Looky what they've got in the 'fridge," he said. "Happy juice."

Maddock read the label out loud. "Diethyl ether, brilliant Watson. If they won't check on him when he screams, maybe they will when he's quiet."

Down the hall and back into the room, the hideous wails became nearly unbearable. Mercy came quickly thanks to an ether-soaked rag in Maddock's hand. Bones said, "That's the trick, I'll be the Scarecrow, you be the Sandman."

Maddock crouched behind the door. He had to get up once more to dose his patient and check his condition. The man's breathing came in short gasps and his pulse raced out of control. "I don't like it Bones—this guy is dying."

"Somebody's coming," Bones warned. "Get back."

Maddock had just returned to his position when the door swung open and an imposing shadow stepped into the room. The lights came on, a three count as the figure stopped in confusion, then Bones stood. "What's up Doc?"

White lab coat, short blond hair, the newcomer took two steps forward. "*You?*"

That was all he managed to say before Maddock put a chokehold on him and jammed the ether-soaked rag in his face. His opponent didn't hesitate. Seizing Maddock's arm, he bent forward, slamming an elbow to the ribs, then straightened and twisted free. Maddock spun away but not before the man wrenched his arm around, throwing him to the ground. The throw came a moment late and Maddock managed to kick him in the knee on the way down. Together on the floor, the man rained punches on Maddock's face.

For a few minutes, the room spun. Maddock opened his eyes to see a concerned looking Bones staring down at him. "Guy pulled some serious *Krav Maga* on you, man. Are you going to be okay?"

Maddock touched his face. Several new welts graced his left cheek. The stiches in his wounded eyebrow had opened and bled down his chin. His head felt like a well rung church bell. "Peachy. How's our friend doing?"

"Sleeping like a babe and not a scratch on him."

Maddock levered himself to his feet. Their visitor lay prone on a padded table, trussed and shackled like his assistant next to him. "Friend of yours?" Maddock said. "He seemed to know you."

"I don't know his name. He was there when they stitched me up. I think the idea was to put both of us on those tables and give us the juice. I managed to conk one of the guards when they thought I was knocked out."

"First time or second time you escaped?"

"First time. Second time they thought I was cornered on the first floor." Bones snapped his fingers. "But just like that, I was gone. Amazing how easy it is to climb this old building from the outside, even with a bum arm."

The lab technician began to stir and moan again. Maddock gave him another dose and checked their newer patient. "He's going to regain consciousness soon. Put some tape on his mouth and let's talk to him a little first."

Bones had no sooner stretched a band of tape over the man's mouth when he began to shake and roll his eyes.

Bones bent closer and waved. "Remember me?"

Maddock stood back from the man's line of sight and spoke from the shadows. "You look like a medical doctor, although your Hippocratic oath seems to have expired."

The man began thrashing, but Bones had laced him up tight in the strait jacket and shackles. Maddock continued. "Have no doubt that I'm about to do for you what you did to me. Bones, there's about a quarter of a dose left in that intravenous bag. Why don't you plug him in so we can watch his reaction?"

Flinching, perspiration, eyes rolling, Maddock knew real fear when he saw it. "Go ahead Bones, you should be able to find—what is it? The femoral vein, on this guy."

Bones said, "He's kicking too much, I'll hit the artery and kill him."

Maddock gave his patient another dose of ether and said, "You've got five minutes, can you do it, or do you want me to try?"

"I can, but do we really want to?"

"Turn off the drip. Then plug him in."

Only about three minutes elapsed before the man began gagging and twitching. Maddock let him come fully awake and said, "Here is what will happen. I am going to take the tape off your mouth and ask you a few questions. If I get good answers, we'll take out the catheter needle. If you resist, I'll put the gag back and leave you for someone else to find. Fair?"

It might have been a nod. Maddock was glad this guy was well restrained. "First your name."

Bones ripped the tape from the man's mouth. He licked his lips and tried to twist his head around. "Goertzner, Dr. Anton Goertzner. Now take that thing out of my leg."

"Not yet, Doctor. So, how are you feeling today?"

"You're the other one, aren't you? Maddock, yes?"

"*My* questions, Doctor. How are you feeling?"

"Fine, I'm feeling fine right now. Take that damned thing out of me."

"We're only getting started here," Maddock said. He lowered his voice and spoke slowly. "Tell me, what is this infusion of yours?"

Goertzner thrashed and cursed. Maddock couldn't place the language. He waited and let the doctor exhaust himself before continuing. "Just answer my question."

"You know damned well what it is. You have it in your blood."

"And you tried to pump more into me? Why is that, doctor?"

"Vaccine, antidote, whatever. We need to learn what it is and culture a cure."

Behind them, the bound lab assistant began to moan. Goertzner rolled his head to get a better look. "Is that your doing?"

"My questions, remember?"

"You bastards. Well, there's another like him around. Likely he's gone to get help, and when he does, I'll see that you die as slowly as possible, you and your friends as well."

"My friends? Tell us about these friends."

Goertzner rolled his eyes a moment, mumbling curses. Then he clammed up, pinching his lips tight. Maddock waited, but the man said nothing more. "Very well, doctor. We'll leave you with your assistant for company. Bones, tape..."

At that moment, a frenzy of shrieking alarms and flashing strobes filled the room. Maddock dropped to a crouch and looked at Bones. "Fire drill?"

23

A single beep, then the alarm, and all the lights went on. Before Willis could react, the empty wheelchair plowed into him, knocking him off balance. Pym sat up and shouted, "Chair—attack, attack."

The chair spun on one wheel and slammed into Willis again. The thing was much heavier than he'd expected. It smashed him against the wall, backed off and charged into him once more. The overhead lights flashed, and a claxon horn wailed like the hounds of hell. Willis was still trying to regain his feet when Pym said, "Chair—kill."

Without waiting to see what that meant, Willis dove to the side, knocking into a small dresser. The chair pivoted and spat a group of three bullets after him, throwing chips from the doorframe. It paused for a faction of a second, reoriented and fired again. In that moment, Willis spun and hurled the dresser. The chair fired two more groups of three, reversed and headed around the obstacle.

With uncanny intelligence, the motorized chair always maintained itself between Willis and Pym. It smacked the dresser aside, and reoriented. By that time, its target had fled, dodging into the living area. All around lights flashed like police strobes. Willis glanced back; the chair had followed him. He saw it stop and pivot.

Willis dodged one way, then dove the opposite direction. Three more rounds, they broke something. He didn't stay to find out. Back in the hall, the same insane cacophony. On one level, he knew it was intended to cause panic. *Yeah, like it's working, okay?* He dodged to the left, back the way he'd come. *I just wanted mac and cheese, not a freaking killer robot.*

Ten long strides taken triple-time, he made the door as the chair spun into view. Willis dove through. Another group of three rounds zinged off the doorframe and rattled down the stairwell. He recovered just as the door slammed shut behind him.

Below footsteps pounded up the metal stairs. The claxon horn was only a muted squawk from the landing, but from above the bright strobe continued to flash. Willis again swung his bulk over the gray rail and crouched hanging by his fingers beneath the diamond-plate steel landing.

This time, only moments passed before the climbers reached that last flight of stairs. Willis held his breath. Assault style weapons at ready, six men approached the landing. They stopped at the door. Two of them waited on the stairs, Willis could have looked them in the face, but both men craned their necks upward watching the others.

Voices, the lock clicked, then three shots. One of the climbers fell. Willis heard yelling and the rattle of automatic weapon fire. Answering shots and more casualties. The men below pushed their way up, shouting and firing. One reared back, lost his balance, and fell screaming down the stairs. The other rushed past Willis. The door slammed shut and the stairwell went quiet.

Willis dragged himself out from beneath the stairs and surveyed the carnage. Two lay dead at his feet and a third broken body hung from the stairs two flights down. *Tough little droid.* He collected a pistol and a MAC-10 carbine with a spare magazine. Descending two levels, he stripped the twisted body of its jacket and balaclava-style knit hat.

Move or die, Willis knew that. He scrambled down the steep steps, making as little sound as he could. Above, they'd be looking to their casualties, below would be a hornet's nest. *Best option, get the hell out.* He passed the third level, descended two more flights to another door. *Second level, barracks maybe?* Willis considered for a second, then heard voices on the other side. *Nope, no-go.* Another flight down, he arrived at the lowest level, two doors, left and right. *Must be the armory I came in at.* He wondered for a moment if the dogs were still waiting outside.

The door above flew open and a dozen armed men swarmed out. They rattled up the stairs single file, a chain of matching black jackets and knit hats. Willis heard shouts from the armory. Another squad was queuing up to bust right in on him. He zipped up his purloined jacket and pulled the balaclava down to his eyelids. Without looking back, Willis raced up the stairs. Behind him the door burst open, and he heard the rattle of more footsteps. *Thirteenth man, just keep climbing and don't ask questions.*

He'd passed the third landing when a stocky guy with stripes on his arm grabbed him by the collar and yelled, "*Idíte tuda.*"

Willis shook his head. "What?"

"*Tam, tam.*" The man pointed at the landing behind him.

Willis nodded and stepped back. "Yeah… *da, da.*"

As he spoke, the second group swarmed up behind them. Sergeant guy, the one with the stripes, continued climbing, but not before glaring back at Willis. Two others from the second group joined him. Willis tugged his hat a little lower and edged back toward the door. The guy on his right fussed with a pack of Marlboros, stared at it a moment, then shoved it back in his pocket. The other mumbled something, glancing back at Willis. Pretending he didn't see, looking down, *oh crap—I'm going to get busted.*

The Russian merc, whatever he was, turned around.

Willis shrugged. He received a shove to one side. The merc opened the door behind him and ducked in. Coming out a few moments later, he scowled at Willis and handed his buddy a plastic lighter. *Close—too close.* The two men turned to look at him. *Take them both out without raising hell? Not likely.*

Willis pantomimed with the zipper on his pants and slipped through the door. Another janitor's closet. *Two minutes at best. Then they're on my ass.* He exited through a restroom and stepped into the darkened corridors of level three. The strobes still flashed, but someone had killed the claxons. Willis glanced left. The laboratory lights were on. He peeked inside. Seeing no one he continued toward the main stairway.

From the corner of his eye, Willis saw a shadow move. In that moment someone caught him in a chokehold and pressed a knife against his eye. "Move comrade, and you die"

"*Nyet, Nyet*—wait, Bonebrake? That you?"

The chokehold didn't loosen, but the knife disappeared. "What the crap? Willis?"

Maddock stepped out of the shadows. "Let him go, Bones."

Willis felt the chokehold tighten ever so slightly. Bones whispered in his ear. "Whose side are you on, buddy?"

"Just let him go, Bones. He's on our side, trust me."

Willis took a deep breath and shook his head. "Love you too, Bones. Now if you want to stick around and get all happy, we've got some friends coming to visit in about thirty seconds."

The door behind them burst open. Willis spun and fired two bursts at the men who had come through. "There, now we're well and truly screwed."

"Back to the stairs." Bones yelled.

Willis shook his head. "Not an option. They got guys coming that way already."

Maddock pointed down the hall. "Same way we left last time. Out the window."

Bones led the way. Past the two bound figures, he pushed a window open. "*Once more unto the breach, dear friends once more!*"

Willis stopped a moment to stare at Goertzner. "Ol' Doctor Giggles here will know which way we went."

"Won't matter," Bones said, "they'll figure it out soon enough anyway."

From outside Willis heard dogs barking. He shook his head and silently pointed upward. When Bones nodded Maddock said, "You first."

Willis followed his friends out the into the cool night air. Looking up, he saw two shadows climbing a steel pipe. With a bum arm, Bones seemed to be having some trouble. Willis hooked his hands behind the pipe, braced his feet against the rough masonry wall, and followed them up. Passing the fourth floor, he saw the strobe lights flashing like a silent rave party. Higher yet, Willis cleared the ledge of a sealed-up window and wondered if this wasn't Pym's bedroom, if the man himself didn't lay less than a foot from his reach.

Bones helped him over the low parapet and whispered, "Sorry about the knife, dude."

"*De nada*, man. If it'd been me, you'da got shot."

A soft crunch of feet on the gravel roof and Maddock faded in from the darkness. "Good to see you alive and whole, Willis. We got worried."

"Yeah, well I was kind of worried, too. But thanks for coming to the party. When does our helicopter show up?"

"They've got a landing pad, but if a chopper shows up,

it won't be ours."

Willis glanced over. Outlined in flashing blue lights, the helipad occupied one end of the building. "I'm guessing we've got to get our own bad selves outa this one. You guys armed?"

Maddock shrugged. "Me, I left my bow and arrow downstairs. You've met Bones' stone knife. It's plenty sharp but limited range."

"I sense there's a story here somewhere,"

Maddock peered over the parapet. "More than one, I'm sure. Let's do a little recon and catch up."

Willis told of his captivity and escape as he and Maddock circled the roof. Panther-quiet, Bones trailed behind them. At one point, he interrupted. "So, Pym's holed up right below us?"

"Yeah, unless they moved him. I'm betting his fancy chair is pretty messed up by now. Knowing him, I'm sure he has plenty of spares."

"And you—how messed up are you, buddy?"

"I saw Sally," Willis paused a moment, not sure if he could say it. "That bastard Pym cut off her ear. They had her plugged into the happy juice too. She looks like crap. I'm going to kill him."

"How are you doing?"

Willis glanced away. "I met her friend, June. A little pushy, but I like her."

"You didn't answer my question."

Willis gritted his teeth. "A week in solitary, sensory deprivation and all that good stuff. Soaking in that Moogly juice, or whatever's in the water around here. A few days of no sleep, and I'm seeing Lemurians and flying saucers. Other than that, good to go. How about y'all?"

Maddock told of walking into a trap and their escape. He described Uzi as well. "Spooky in more ways than one, but he seems to have connections. Says he knows Letson and even knows about us. I don't believe half his crap, but if Sally is here, that means Uzi must have gotten her out of San Francisco."

Willis figured he was leaving some stuff out, but Bones filled in with their adventures on the mountain and the Okwanuchu tribe.

"So, this hippie chick has got it bad for Maddock. I'll bet she's got a love potion with your name on it, dude."

"She led us here," Maddock said. There's a whole maze of tunnels underneath, some natural and some not."

"Man made?"

"I wouldn't go so far…" Maddock trailed off. "We saw signs of Lemurians down there as well."

"Yeah, and you've been just as juiced as I have," Willis said. "Maybe more so. I saw you in the light downstairs and I'll say you both look like you've been wrestling Godzilla. What's our next move, because I'm running out of ideas?"

The three had gathered next to a ventilation stack. They'd finished a circuit of the roof and examined a few of the various bumps and small structures scattered about its center. At the far end of the helipad, a square structure broke the roofline. "Ladder from the fifth level, it's got your standard plexiglass wind screen." Willis said. "When they come for us, that's how they're going to get up."

"I've got a bad feeling some of them are here already," Maddock said. "Keep low and keep your eyes peeled."

Willis was about to suggest finding another way down when Maddock shoved him to one side. A flicker of light and a series of soft pops. Bullets smacked into the stack, just inches from where he'd stood.

Willis returned fire and rolled away as another series of shots sizzled off the rooftop. *Night vision gear. Crap. Where in all hell did Bones get to?* Willis checked his weapons. Full mag on the pistol, about half on the MAC-10. He fired another short burst before sprinting for the cover of an air conditioning unit. Diving into the shadows, he smacked into a crouching figure. "Maddock?"

In response, he caught a weapon butt in the face. Willis reeled, then jammed his fist where the man's throat ought to be. It cracked against something small and hard. He felt the weapon come around again. He blocked it with the MAC-10 and drew his pistol. The shot sounded like dynamite after hearing only the soft pop of the silenced weapons.

Willis yanked a set of night vision goggles from the dead man's face and jammed it over his head. *This is getting old.* The scene on the roof flashed before him in flickering green. *Not much visible.* He tried to pick out the mercs. No question, four figures came running at him from the far end of the roof. Willis fired three bursts. The men scattered, two went down. *Damn thing is about as accurate as a handful of rocks.* He fired again and changed magazines.

No sign of Bones, but he spotted Maddock huddled next to a flat rectangle. Off to one side, a flash of gunfire briefly lit the near parapet. Willis watched the shooter through his goggles. He held station, waiting for another target. Movement, then a shadowy wraith glided up. It touched the shooter and he fell. Willis shivered. *Bones could be one spooky dude at times.*

The rooftop went quiet. Through his goggles, Willis saw only a fuzzy green field of shadows and vague shapes. *Two of them still loose up here and more on their way.* He scavenged the body next to him, another carbine and a pistol. Half dozen more magazines, he stuffed them in his pockets. Ducking low, he made a dash for Maddock and flopped to the gravel next to him. "That better be you,

Willis," his friend said.

"Yeah, and I brought gifts."

"MAC-10, just what I needed. Got any ammo?"

"Yeah, and I got you a pistol too."

Maddock scooped the magazines and pistol. He checked out the carbine and sighted over the top of a flat aluminum box. "I haven't heard any shots lately."

"Bones took one down—I suspect more than one. There's two ran off that I missed. Damn MAC-10s are worthless."

"Better thank your ass they are, or we'd all be wearing some new holes. Wonder where those two went."

"Over by the roof hatch, guarding the way down," Bones whispered. Silent as an evening fog, he'd slipped in next to Maddock.

Willis sensed it first, the thump of rotor blades. He flipped the goggles from his face. "Incoming."

A spotlight appeared in the sky. Bones got up on one knee and said, "Gimme one of them MACs and let's see if I can go for a repeat."

Maddock pulled him down. "He's too far off. That's just what they want you to do. Any muzzle flash now and we're going to eat some serious firepower."

"We're screwed then, bro."

Willis took stock of their position, about halfway down the building, slightly west of the centerline. To the east, the sky began to lighten. Already he could make out details of the welded aluminum box they'd been hiding behind. "I think I just spotted our ride."

24

Bad enough to be awakened every night by that damned nurse. Bad enough he could barely drag himself to the crapper when he had to go. Worse, to be accosted in his own bedroom. To August Pym Senior, his bed was his prison, like his chair, a symbol of his growing infirmity. He'd pulled himself upright and listened to the bloody thing spray bullets all over his living quarters. The flashing strobes and claxon only added insult to the injury his pride had already endured.

Something like this could never have happened in New York. The two, Maddock and Bonebrake had seemed to fly out the windows despite multiple wounds. They'd single handedly taken out his strike teams and destroyed his aircraft. Now this Sanders character appears from nowhere, then vanishes at will. *Was this compound so insecure that people could simply wander in and out unchallenged?*

Pym listened to his mercs babbling in the halls. They were probably looting the place as he sat helpless in bed. When his nurse had reappeared, She'd brought him a sedative. Pym told her where she could stick it. "Get me some clothes and my backup chair," he'd said. "And for *God's sake* get those dumb bastard mercs out of my apartment."

Once the alarms had been silenced, he rolled out to the sanctuary of his office. Something about the process of making money. Almost a sacrament, it demanded its own rites and paraphernalia. He wheeled up to his alter, a framework of aluminum tubing that supported six large video screens. A few keystrokes brought them to life. London was open for business, but Pym declined the invitation.

He scanned a few security recordings. Movement on the third floor, it was hard to make out in the darkness. His technician and someone… He changed views and the story played out. His geologist, the girl, and now Sanders, *more treachery.* He wondered how deep that problem ran. *Damned Goertzner, so intent on his own games.* Pym wondered if the rot in his organization had its source in his psychophysiologist.

Clicking back to real-time, he watched his men search the building. Methodical, if uninspired, one team started from the bottom, while a second began combing the fourth floor. A row of tiny video thumbnails flickered at the top of the screen. Pym selected one for the second floor. Men pulling on pants and boots, normally off shift, they were hustling to join the search.

He checked the mess hall. Closest to the stairs, it was a logical place to hide. Two men sat spooning ice cream from a large round tub. One would periodically look over his shoulder. Pym memorized their faces. *Stupid idiots. More subjects for Goertzner's tables.*

Although he knew it unlikely for Sanders to have returned to the third floor, Pym checked anyway. Two minutes later, the restroom door opened. A figure stepped from the shadows into a halo of light shining from the laboratory door. Pym called his team leader. "Third floor, north end headed toward the stairs."

He watched, awaiting the inevitable confrontation, when two others stepped into view. Pym changed cameras and stared a moment. The sheer impossibility of what he witnessed left him stunned. He didn't bother to call a second time. His men were clearly outmatched.

Watching the confusion on the third floor, Augustus Pym almost wished things were different. He had been strong once, a fighter. *I could have been on that team. I could have been Dane Maddock, laughing while lesser men scrambled to keep up.* His early days on the tough streets of New York—the 1980s when Russian gangs were just beginning to challenge the Sicilians—he worked both ends of town back then. Collecting for slumlords in the morning and making discreet bank transactions in the afternoon, he soon learned how money was really acquired. *I made the Russians what they are today, and what do I get? A nine-millimeter hole in my spine, that's what.*

Pym's console chimed, and a face appeared on the center monitor, his team leader. "There's three of them now, gone out the window. The dogs are loose down below, but we think they've headed for the roof."

"Of course they're headed for the roof. Don't engage them, do you hear? Just don't. We can't lose any more men. Call in the helicopters, pin them down. I need one alive that's all. Oh, you do have a helicopter left, don't you?"

"We have two UH-1 Hueys. They're on their way in."

"Good." Pym waited. The man obviously had something more to say. "And, what else?"

"It's Dr. Goertzner. He was strapped to one of the tables, sir. Along with your chief medic."

Pym closed his eyes and rubbed his left temple. *The migraines always start there.* When he looked back at the screen, the man might have been sweating, but he hadn't moved. "Their condition?"

"Dr. Goertzner is a little... upset, but he seems okay. We have the medic under heavy sedation."

"Send Goertzner up. I don't give a rat's ass if he's upset—send him now."

Pym cut the connection and punched in a new code. The screen remained blank, but a repeated beeping told him that a secure link was being established. Moments later, the beeping stopped, and a voice answered, "*Da?*"

Nestled between Presidio San Francisco and Golden Gate Park, the Richmond District is home to the oldest and wealthiest Russian families on the west coast. Some of that wealth was maintained and defended by Pym Investment Trust.

Not a situation for small talk, Pym came straight to the point. "I need fifty of your best. Loyal soldiers, *krutoi* to the last man. And I need an Apache, fully loaded. Two, if you can get them."

They didn't talk price. A few words on timing and logistics, then the voice on the other end said, "*Da*," and closed the connection.

25

The whine of engines and thumping blades drew nearer. Maddock scanned the rooftop. At the far end, a faint yellow light flicked on. More of Pym's army had climbed up and crouched behind the helipad. *They're laying low, waiting for us to make a move.*

Willis and Bones had been whispering together. He heard Bones say, "What do you mean, *jack the elevator*?"

"How else ya figure Pym gets up here? He ain't climbing that ladder, I'll tell you."

"You think this covers the shaft?"

"I was down there. It's right under us."

Maddock crawled over to the others. "What are you saying Willis, that it just pops up through the roof?"

"Yeah, could be something like that. It's a hydraulic elevator. I saw the cylinders when I was climbing. Just got to slide this hatch open and crawl in."

Maddock couldn't see Bones shrug, but his silence told the story. Willis scuttled around the other side and then returned. "It slides towards us and there's a ramp."

"I'm not sure we could move it." Maddock said. "It's got to be motorized and I don't see any controls."

At that moment, something clicked, and the roof hatch began rolling back. They scrambled away as it slid toward them. A bright white light shown up from the opening and a figure in a wheelchair rose to the roof like a conjurer's phantom. His chair hummed and rolled down a short ramp toward the helipad. Willis raised his MAC-10 but Maddock caught him before he could fire "It isn't Pym. It's a decoy, a dummy riding his chair."

The motorized chair rolled five yards before a wheel fell

off and it flopped to one side. Willis snorted. "Looks like the one they shot the crap out of."

Maddock backed away, ready to provide covering fire as the lead helicopter touched down. Dust and roof gravel scattered, throwing ghostly shadows in the light from the shaft. Another click, and the roof hatch began to close. "Now." Maddock said. "Go now, the glare and confusion..."

He didn't need to explain. Bones had already thrown himself through the opening. Willis followed. A moment too late, Maddock sprang for the shaft. With a thump and a grunt, the aluminum hatch sealed off the rays of light and left him stranded on the darkened rooftop.

The second helicopter approached. It slowed and hovered about a hundred feet above him. A spotlight swept the scene. Maddock pushed his weapons away and knelt with his hands on his head. *I can at least buy the others time.*

A dozen commandos rushed across the rooftop. Maddock waited for the bullet. He heard the whine of turbines, the thump of blades. He smelled the kerosene smoke of jet fuel washing down on the rooftop. Then a flash of stars, and excruciating pain in his chest, and nothing.

Willis flopped headfirst through the closing hatch, fell six feet, and landed on top of Bones. He caught sight of the shaft climbing around him, then the lights died. Bones disentangled himself and whispered, "Where's Maddock?"

"Didn't make it." Willis saw a thin vertical line of light rise past his face. "We gotta go back."

"We will, but first we've got to get off this rollercoaster without getting caught. What are we standing on, anyway?"

"A platform," Willis said. "Clever as hell, they built a platform on top of the elevator car. It stops on the fourth floor and Pym rolls in on the fifth. He opens the roof hatch and rides it on up."

They watched another thin pencil of light rise before them. "Third level." Willis said. "It'll stop at the bottom and we'll have to get out at level two."

Moments later, their descent stopped. The elevator door was about two feet above their platform. The ascending lines of light cast a wan glow about the interior of the elevator shaft. Bones pulled out a combat knife. "Little souvenir. I thought it might come in handy."

He jammed it between the doors. As he did, Willis heard voices from the hall beyond. "Hold up," he whispered. "There's baddies outside."

Bones paused to listen. When the voices died away, he jammed the knife back in. As he did, a pump whined, and Willis felt the elevator car lurch upward. Bones yanked his knife out just in time. "I hope this thing stops before we reach the fifth floor. I don't think there's a lot of headroom with that hatch closed."

Willis counted doors as they rose. Level four appeared, but the platform didn't stop. They felt the elevator slow and halt just two feet below the level five doors. Bones glanced upward. "That could have been ugly."

A moment later, the platform began to rise. Two feet up, it stopped again, just even with the doors. "Oh, crap," Willis hissed. "We got company coming."

They ducked to each side of the entrance as the platform lights came on and the doors trundled open. First to enter was a standard wheelchair. Dr. Goertzner followed, pushing it in. Willis poked his Makarov in the man's face.

"Go ahead and try something, but my friend will gut you like a trout if you do."

Bones said, "Just close the doors, Doc."

Goertzner held a small touch pad.

Willis snatched it from him and tapped the symbol labeled *Doors*. "You were gonna push the red button, weren't you? That would have been a big mistake. Man, you got to think about your life choices."

Goertzner pointed up. "We have your friend in custody and he's not looking too good. I was going up to take him to the infirmary. If you cooperate, we may let him live."

Willis looked at Bones. "Works for me, but what if we change up the script a little?"

By the puzzled look in his eyes, Willis knew the big Cherokee wasn't quite on board. At the same time, the Doctor seemed to be sizing up his chances. Willis stepped a little farther back and said, "We're all probably dead, so I got nothing to lose. None of your Krav Maga, karate chop bull crap. You make a mistake and I shoot. Got it doc?"

A glance at Bones, another at the closed hatch over their heads and Goertzner nodded. Willis took that for a yes. "Shuck out of that lab coat and hand it to my friend with the knife. Then sit in the chair, nice and slow." The doctor complied with visible reluctance. Willis looked at his friend. "Bones, are you going to put that coat on, or do I have to shoot you too?"

The Indian head nickel dropped. Willis saw the wheels turn, and Bones said, "We've got to bind him."

"You'll find cable ties in the pockets of his coat. See if he's got a hankie too."

Bones found both. Minutes later, Willis tapped the *Roof* button. Above he heard the growl of the hatch opening, and the elevator platform began to rise. "You'll be Dr. Bones, I've got the uniform so I'm the guard. And what will we say about our friend here?"

"Subdued him trying to escape," Bones said.

Bound to the wheelchair, Goertzner didn't thrash or waste his energy, but just glared straight ahead. Willis worried about that one, he'd be more convincing if he were agitated. They emerged slowly on the rooftop. The helicopter still idled on the pad. Four men knelt next to a lifeless figure, but otherwise the roof was empty. Bones turned the wheelchair toward them and began pushing.

One of the guards jumped to his feet, pointing and shouting.

"Oh crap," Willis said. "I'm a celeb with these guys."

He drew his Makarov and fired. The shot struck the man in his shoulder and spun him around. The others leaped up. Willis squeezed off a burst from his MAC-10, scattering the remaining three. Bones gave the wheelchair a shove, it rolled off the edge of the ramp, pitched forward, and came to rest with Goertzner's face in the gravel. Before it even stopped moving, Willis tossed the machine pistol to Bones and scooped Maddock's inert body from the roof. "Which way?" He yelled.

Bones fired another burst as random shots zipped past them. "The chopper, they're not going to shoot their own machine."

By the time Willis made the landing struts, five new holes graced the canopy. "Looks like your theory has some holes in it, Doc. Who's going to fly this thing?"

"Just get in, get in."

Willis flopped Maddock into an open side hatch and jumped in behind him. Bones had knelt next to the fuselage, laying down cover fire. In return, bullets rattled off the gravel roof and *spanged* into the nacelle above him. "Open up on these guys, will ya?"

Huey, tried and truey. Willis almost rubbed his hands.

Got your M-60 machine guns, one on each side. He flipped open a breach, checked the belt, slammed it down and opened fire. Gravel and debris filled the air. Bones crawled in, checked Maddock, and said. "You flown one of these before?"

Willis shook his head, then saw the look on his friend's face. "No, Bones, just no. We shoot them all and run for it."

Bones was already on his way to the cockpit. Willis kept firing. *May as well go down shootin'.* He heard the engine wind up to a screaming pitch, the deck lurched beneath him, and the entire aircraft heaved over on one skid. It spun a half circle before slamming back down to the roof. The engine wailed, the blades thudded, and the embattled Huey slid off the pad, mowing down half the little blue lights. Willis grabbed Maddock and braced himself in the doorway.

Scraping along the roof, they lurched into the parapet. The Huey shook like an out of balance washing machine, then broke through, throwing an avalanche of broken concrete blocks to the pavement below. His arm around Maddock's waist, Willis clung to a mass of cargo webbing inside the fuselage. With a great pounding of its twin blades, the helicopter pitched forward at a forty-five-degree angle and slid off the edge of the building. They began spinning clockwise. The Huey listed to port and fell twenty feet.

In true rollercoaster fashion, Willis felt his stomach float to his chest, then fall to his hips as they screamed into the air. Laboratory Nine spun away below his feet.

With every turn, the rising sun flashed through the open doors. Bones seemed to have gained some control as the mad gyrations slowed and they howled off to the west. Below, a tumble of brush and scree gave way to clumps of trees. For an instant, Willis spotted one particular grove of ancient firs with a large rock looming from its center. Then it was gone, swallowed in the misty dawn behind them. He looked up at the peak of Shasta, a flaming golden torch in the morning light. *No wonder Sally was drawn to this place. If magic existed anywhere*, he thought, *it certainly must thrive here.*

Willis slid the cabin doors shut and examined his friend. Maddock's eyelids flickered and his legs twitched. Two wires protruded from his shirt. Willis tore it open and used his knife to dig the Taser barbs from his chest. Two jumpseats were fastened to the rear bulkhead. He dragged Maddock to one and belted him in.

Up forward, Bones sat in the cockpit, grinning like an idiot. Crawling forward and wedging himself into the copilot's seat, Willis donned a pair of headphones. Bones switched on the intercom. "How's the boss man?"

"Alive. Bastards Tasered the crap out of him. So, what cereal box did you find your pilot's license in?"

"Screw you. A buddy let me fly left seat on a Sea Stallion a few times. It was cool. Figured a Huey couldn't be much different."

"Yeah, except that Stallion had a real pilot on board."

"Bunch of other stuff too, like all the controls and gauges, and everything else was different."

Willis leaned forward and looked out the side. "Where we going, skipper?"

"West." Bones tapped a gauge on the instrument panel. "Not sure how far west. Seems they forgot to gas us up."

"What is it, you boost a chopper and don't even get one with a full tank?"

"Just shut up and look for some open space."

"Yeah, a whole lot of open space with firetrucks and ambulances."

"A strip joint would be nice too." Bones eased the cyclic forward. The helicopter nosed down slightly and picked up speed. "I see a town up ahead."

Willis peered through the crazed plexiglass. "That would be El Yermo. We gonna make it?" As he spoke, the fuel pressure gage flashed red. He heard the engine pitch drop and the whine fall to a low hiss. Red lights came on all over the instrument panel. Gauges scrolled down to zero, and Willis said, "We're dead stick, man. No gas, no power." He looked down through the nose bubble. "Nothing but trees, rocks, and bad news down there."

"We'll make it," Bones said. "We'll just autorotate on down like a maple seed. Look, there's some kind of construction yard ahead."

Willis tried to locate it. Plastering his face against the side window, he made out an open space about two miles to the northwest. He craned his head around to look behind them. For a brief moment, a dark shape flashed into view before vanishing into the sun's dazzling glare. "Ground control to Major Tom, we've got ourselves another problem."

"No time now, I've gotta land this thing."

"We got company coming up our six."

"I didn't need to hear that. Why don't you go use the ammunition God gave you?"

Willis crawled to the back and found Maddock with his eyes open. The helicopter pitched aft and Willis slid to the bulkhead. He worked his way to the port side and pulled open the rolling door. As he did, a flash of white and a trail of smoke passed the opening.

They listed to starboard as two more streaks passed, their exhaust trails scattering in the rotor turbulence. Missiles, Willis thanked his luck that Bones was a lousy pilot. Hanging from the doorway, he braced against the M-60 machine gun. *Damn thing's right on top of us.* He managed to get off a few dozen rounds before the embattled

Huey spun away.

They lurched to port. Willis jammed his feet against the landing strut and hung on to the gun for dear life. Below, a two-lane highway spun into view. Then nothing but treetops, coming up fast. Machine gun fire behind him, he craned his head around. Maddock had unbuckled himself and manned the starboard gun.

A roar like the opening of hell's mouth and fragments of metal exploded through their rear bulkhead. Behind him, the sliding door and a portion of the fuselage had been torn away. *They got a minigun. Crap.* Willis returned fire.

A high-tension electrical pylon flashed by the open doorway. Willis caught a glimpse of power lines passing above them. He scrambled back yelling, "Buckle up, buddy."

Maddock was nowhere to be seen. Willis checked again; his friend had vanished. He clutched a bundle of cargo webbing and leaned out the starboard doorway. There below him, Maddock clung, both arms wrapped around the landing strut. Treetops whipped by, then Bones pulled full up on the collective.

The helicopter stopped its descent, throwing Willis to the deck. It spun like a drunken pig for another fifty yards before bouncing off a gravel surface and rolling on its side. The rotor blades slammed into the ground and disintegrated. Spinning fragments blasted into air. A blinding hail of dirt and stones filled the cabin. Willis clung to the cargo webbing as they skidded to a halt.

"Objects in the overhead bins may have shifted during flight." Bones crawled from the cockpit. "I think we ought to deplane, buddy. Where's your seatmate?"

"Sonofabitch. He fell out. You call that a landing?"

For a moment, Bones stopped. Stunned, he stared at Willis, then said, "Out, go… go. We're sitting ducks here."

Willis had already boosted himself over the landing skid. He wriggled to the ground, swiveling his head. Bones plopped down beside him and waved toward a row of construction equipment. The two sprinted that direction. Willis heard the thud of rotors behind them. He turned in time to see two missiles slam into their broken Huey. It erupted in a ball of smoke and flame.

Just above the deck, a second Huey came blasting through the pall of smoke, headed straight for them. Willis ran. *I'll catch the bullet now, but I ain't going back on that table.* He heard the engine wind up, then spin down as the helicopter landed. Bones disappeared behind a yellow drill rig and Willis followed.

When his friend skidded to a stop, Willis almost slammed into his back. They faced the muzzle of a forty-four-caliber revolver. He did a double take. "June?"

"Duck!"

They hit the dirt as the enormous revolver bucked three times. June spun behind the bumper as hail of return fire blew glass and metal fragments into the air. Willis peeked around the corner. Four armed mercenaries sprang from an idling helicopter and advanced on their position. More shots tore into the parked rig or sizzled off the gravel yard. June said, "Hiya, Willis. Wasn't expecting you to bring company."

"Well, he's just my pilot."

"Either of you two armed?"

"Damn airline lost my luggage, and his banger's all outa caps."

"Is not," Bones said, "just that little Makarov you gave me."

June snorted and said, "Well I've got three rounds left, fellas. Think I'm gonna wait 'til they get a little closer."

Just then, another spray of bullets peppered the fender

above them. A voice called out, "Put down your weapon and come out. No one gets hurt."

June mumbled, "Not happening, not again."

Willis crawled under the drill rig and surveyed the parking lot. The four mercs had taken cover behind a battered gray pickup. June wiggled in beside him. "Crap, the bastards better not scratch my truck."

Greasy black smoke from the burning helicopter swept across the open lot. Another round of fire peppered the ground in front of them, sending a spray of gravel and bullet fragments clattering under the rig. Willis backed out quick. "They're tired of messing with us," he said. "We're dead whatever we do. Bones, you and me, we'll create a diversion. Lady, you run for it as soon as we do."

June shook her head. "Like hell I will."

As she spoke, the windows flew out of her truck in a shower of crystal fragments. It shook like a wet dog and all four tires went flat. Smoke and flames guttered from beneath the engine, then spread back to the fuel tank. In an instant a ball of flame enveloped the vehicle.

Bones stood flat-footed and stared. "*Holy crap!*"

June just closed her eyes. "Somebody's gonna pay for this. I loved that old truck."

Willis edged out from behind the drill rig. Whoever had been shooting at them could not have survived the explosion. Bones stepped up behind him. "They blew up their own guys."

"Someone did."

26

Commander Dane Maddock awoke in the sky over Afghanistan. Operation Red Earth had gone totally FUBAR. Someone must have tipped off the insurgents, because his SEAL team had dropped right into a Mammahornet's nest. He remembered little, taking fire, pain. He looked down at his chest; blood soaked through the khaki cloth. His shirtfront had been torn open and he bore two small wounds. Little more than skin deep, he figured he'd live.

Wind buffeted through the open chopper doors. He heard the chatter of machine gun fire over the engine whine and rotor whop. Maddock took in more. *A Huey? They were riding an antique?* He glanced over at the machine gunner. Willis stood on the portside strut, clinging to the stock of an M60 and firing away at something behind them.

What the hell? Willis hadn't been anywhere near this operation. Two white smoke trails flashed past the open door. *Crap, rockets. Really?* He tried to move, *strapped in.* Maddock unbuckled the three-point harness just as the Huey listed to one side and spun halfway around. His feet slid from beneath him and he grabbed for anything he could find. As his hips passed the doorframe, Maddock hooked an arm around the receiver of the starboard gun. Kicking, he hung on until his feet found purchase on the landing strut. On the opposite side, Willis kept on blasting away.

Just as quickly, the chopper changed course again. Another rocket streaked by, this one right past his face. Maddock looked aft. There, in the rising sun, another helicopter had given chase. Muzzle flashes from both sides, they looked like miniguns. Maddock cleared the receiver on his M60 and returned fire.

They banked hard to port and the pilot made another crazy maneuver. The turbine no longer whined, only the labored thud of rotor blades stressed far beyond their design limit. Maddock craned around and peered in the cockpit. *Who the hell would power down in the middle of a firefight?*

The answer came as a revelation. He was dead, they were all dead and this was some kind of insane purgatory. Bones Bonebrake, the devil himself, sat in the right-hand seat, cyclic stick in hand, grinning like a maniac.

Reality jumped back at Maddock when the helicopter interior exploded in a hail of flying debris. Something slammed into his chest pitching him into the open sky. For an instant, he caught sight of road and trees spinning beneath him, then the helicopter strut cracked him in the head and Maddock grabbed on. No chance of climbing back, he clung to the strut.

The ground came up fast. Treetops brushed his dangling feet. He caught a glimpse of Willis peering down at him and then a tangle of branches buffeted past. In that moment, the rotors howled like a flight of banshees and the helicopter jerked upward, hurtling Maddock into the trees below.

Three branches broke before he could cling to one and slow his fall. It yielded beneath him and slipped from between his arms. The next one down broke as well, throwing him into an adjacent tree. Maddock grabbed and somehow hung on, only to lose his grip and fall another ten feet to the ground. Flat on his back, he heard the grinding roar of the Huey's final landing.

Here's where they rewind and make us do it all over again, he thought. Maddock waited. No rewind came. He relaxed, *fir trees in Kandahar?* It seemed so familiar, lying there waiting for Bones to show up. He heard the other helicopter circle and approach. Mercenaries, choppers, Bones, the pieces started to come together like debris falling from the sky.

Maddock elbowed himself up. Bones and Willis had crawled from the broken fuselage and started running for a row of parked equipment. A shadow, a rush of downdraft and the second helicopter landed directly in front of him. Another Huey, it sported twin missile tubes and miniguns. They hadn't had a chance.

Four men dropped out of the side doors and advanced toward where Willis and Bones were hiding. Wobbling, Maddock pulled himself to his feet. One eye on the tail rotor, he slipped up behind the gunship. They'd have left a pilot on board, *who else?* His question was answered moments later when a black-clad figure sat on the doorframe and lit a cigarette.

Maddock ducked beneath the tail boom and watched. Soon enough, the merc snuffed his smoke, stood and fumbled with his trousers. Maddock caught him in a choke hold, wrestled him to the ground, and held him until he was sure the man no longer breathed. Three loud reports, and a scattering of gunfire told him that Bones and Willis were somehow holding out.

A stolen combat knife made even shorter work of the pilot. From the cockpit of the helicopter, Maddock surveyed the scene. Four black-clad men sheltered behind an ancient gray pickup truck. A single burst from the Huey's minigun, three seconds, it was over.

June was the woman's name, yes she knew Sally, and somehow she knew Willis too. At first, Maddock was afraid she was going to shoot him. The woman waved a monstrous forty-four revolver in his face yelling about the pickup truck. "I drove all the way back here to get that truck and damn your hide, look what you did."

The smoking truck carcass looked little better than the wreckage of the Huey he'd just ridden. Behind him, the second helicopter idled like a patient tiger, its blades slowly rotating over their heads. Willis just stood there with hands on his hips and goggled at Maddock. "You fell out, and just walked away? Damn bro, you made of rubber or something?"

"I feel like a sack of broken bottles, but yeah, basically glad to be alive. Can anyone tell me where we are and how we got here?"

"Someone popped you good with a Taser," Willis said. "I mean plugged you in and put a brick on the trigger. When we got back to the roof, I figured you for dead. Crazy Horse there jacked this chopper, but he messed it up big time trying to land. I guess you know the rest."

Bones had been prowling around between the parked equipment and the wrecked helicopter. "What is this place? It looks like it was a war zone before we even showed up."

"I've never been a lady, so you can call me June. This is—this *was* a Crystal Glacier drilling camp. That burned-out hulk over here was my lab. They had Sally and me, with that other guy pinned down in there. We escaped, but he didn't."

Bones said, "You're working for Crystal Glacier? You work for Pym? Old dude, rides a chair? Who was it that was burning down your lab then?"

"Same guy," Willis said. "She's turned renegade."

"I was his geologist, but I saw too much and I know too much." June recounted meeting Sally. She told of the magmatic water and micro-tremors. "There is something happening beneath this mountain—right now. Called the Buereau of Mines, the Geologic Survey, the local paper, nobody believes me except Sally. I'll tell you this, if Silver Glacier doesn't stop drilling, none of us are going to see another sunrise." She dropped her voice. "You probably think I'm nuts."

Bones caught Maddocks eye. "Then we're all bozos on this bus, because we've heard the same story."

Maddock stared out past June at the rows of parked drill rigs. He could feel Willis' impatience. He knew Bones' was hiding his unease beneath his flippant jokes. And now this geologist was telling him the same story he'd heard from Nahonka of the Okwanuchu tribe. The same dream he'd had the night before.

Something else clicked as well. "June, I believe every word. So do my friends here. But I'm almost afraid to ask— who is this *other guy* with you and Sally?"

"Weird hombre, named Luger or something. He had serious *cojones*—I'll say that."

"Oh crap," Bones said. "That wouldn't have been Uzi would it?"

"Uzi, yeah, that's the guy."

"Now it starts to make sense," Maddock said. "Did he kill anyone?"

"Bunch of them, it looked like. He held the fort while we scooted. They must have used explosives to blast him out of there, because the next thing I saw was my cot, blown to flinders. Bastards caught me and Sally though. Just kicked my Ruger under a truck and left it to rust. Look," she held the gun up like an injured child. "Genuine sixties vintage Blackhawk all scratched to hell."

Bones quirked an eyebrow. "Could you holster your weapon? It's making us all a little nervous."

"Well your bullcrap is just wasting time, big guy. What about we stop talking and go stomp the bastards responsible for all this?"

Willis nodded and said, "Yeah, I'd go for that. But it's been tried, and we got our asses kicked for it."

"But you didn't have an attack helicopter, did you?"

"We didn't have a pilot either." Willis glared at Bones, "…and we still don't have one."

June ejected three fat forty-four caliber shells, pocketed the brass, and tucked the revolver into a worn leather holster. "You do now. Warrant Officer Judith Moon, formerly of the First Air Cav."

Bones looked behind him, but Maddock said, "You?"

"In the flesh. Ten years of Desert Storm and I bailed. Spent eight more at the Colorado School of Mines playing rugby and getting my professional creds. What do you think, take a chance on me?"

Willis said, "You can't be worse than…"

Bones jabbed him in the ribs. "You can fly me any time, Junie Moon."

"Then let's take a look at that UH-1 Iroquois over there. I see five air-to-ground rockets left in the pods and a pair of miniguns. You boys were lucky this thing wasn't armed for air combat."

"I think I messed up the pilot's seat a little." Maddock said.

June opened the pilot's door. Just inside, a blood-soaked figure slumped against the instrument panel. "You boys tumble him out of there. I think I'll just fly this bird left-handed today. How many bullets we got?"

Willis hopped into the rear compartment. Two ammo boxes fed belt guides from under the deck. "Fixed guns port and starboard. Only got about three hundred rounds each."

"Then we'll be running light," June said. "Those miniguns can chew up three hundred rounds in half a minute. We'll have to hit fast, because we won't be hitting very hard."

Willis helped Maddock drag the dead pilot off in the weeds. Bones had taken up station on the port side. Willis trotted back to the crew compartment. June pointed at Maddock, wiggled a finger, and patted the right-hand pilot's seat. He climbed up, sat down and put on a headset. Blood oozed beneath his weight and he felt it soak into his shirt.

June came on the intercom as soon as Maddock plugged in. "We've got headsets fore and aft. No chatter unless it's urgent."

Maddock heard her wind up the primary turbine. The secondary started to spin up, turning the rotor blades into a roaring blur. For a moment her attention was all on switches and controls, then she looked up and pulled the collective lever. "Captain, I need your eyes on the right side. Keep us away from those high-tension wires."

"I was a commander. Never made captain. Just call me Maddock and that will be fine. We've got cheese-cutters about two-hundred meters off our three o'clock and I see a string of red and blue lights heading down the highway."

June took them a hundred feet up and banked left. "Time to bug out then."

They circled higher and started south. Bones came on the intercom. "Uh… the bad guys are off the other way."

"We've got to take out some wells first. Maybe slow things down a little. I happen to know where they all are. From here, I can fire the rockets and the minis. How are you boys fixed for firepower back there?"

Willis spoke up. "Looks like four MAC-10s and maybe a dozen magazines. I guess if we had to, we could use them as clubs, because they won't hit squat."

June came back on. "That's okay. If you remove the suppressor, the thing isn't quite such a bullet hose. We ain't going in stealth mode anyway, boys. Look sharp, we're coming up on target number one. Tonto, you go mess up the pump. Mandingo, cover him."

June brought them to a sliding stop on a gravel turnaround. About thirty yards off, an electric motor the size of an oil drum stood upright on a concrete pad. Bones dashed over, jammed the muzzle of his machine pistol in a ventilation port, and fired. In an instant, he jumped back, dancing, cursing, and wiping the blood from his face. June said, "I should have warned him about shrapnel, but I figured he knew."

Maddock watched his friend swat invisible flies. "Never assume anything about that guy."

As Bones and Willis ran back to the chopper, sparks and smoke erupted from the pump motor. June spun up the rotor as the two scrambled on board, and once again they roared off, just above the treetops. "One down, fourteen to go. Big guy, how's your face?"

"Nowhere near as cut up as my pride. At least I can still see."

"Good to hear. Coming up on our second target in three… two… one…"

There were two pumps at the next stop. Bones stood back and took them both out from fifteen feet away. As June lifted off again, she said, "We got one more unmanned site, then things get tricky."

Tricky meant destroying the wells without injuring the drillers. June circled a truck-mounted rig as three men shaded their eyes and looked up. "Those are working guys," June said. "They got no dog in this fight and I'm not about to see any of 'em get hurt."

When they landed, Willis jumped out and fired a burst in the air. The men scattered and Bones hit the ground. He took a few seconds to find the weak spot on the drill rig, the rotary table. Half a magazine in the gear box stopped it dead.

"Four wells and a water tank at the next site," June said. "It's guarded, so expect some pushback."

She brought them in low, holding altitude to avoid rotor noise. The pushback came as soon as they crested a low ridge. Maddock didn't see muzzle flashes, but a scattering of shots *spanged* into the fuselage. "Hunting rifles," June said. "Those good old boys have scopes and they're dangerous."

She banked hard and circled away. Bones came on the intercom. "The last camp must have called ahead."

June brought them behind the ridge and set down on a small clearing. "Gear up, all three of you. I'll cause a diversion, you hit 'em from behind—and listen, no casualties. Got that?"

"Roger," Maddock said. He pointed to Bones and Willis. "Suppressors this time. We go in quick and quiet, while June plays Space Invaders with these guys."

Bones took point, staying just behind the ridgeline. Then ducking from tree to brushy patch, he led them toward the camp. Maddock had spotted two of the pump motors from the air. A trail of pipes and overhead wires connected them to a steel building and a large silver tank. The other pumps would have to be in a wooded copse just east of the metal building. He heard the thud of rotors off to the west and saw their helicopter coming in high and fast.

A volley of shots echoed from behind the steel building as Bones discharged his silenced machine pistol into one of the pumps. Willis rushed the second pump, and in short time, both motors erupted in sparks and flame. Maddock gave a brief hand signal and pointed toward the woods.

As expected, two more pump motors sat on concrete foundations just beyond the metal building. June flew high overhead, but no rifle shots followed her. Bones and Willis repeated their performance, taking out the second pair of pumps. As they did, six men came running from behind the water tank, rifles at their shoulders, firing as they came.

Maddock was about to dash for the wooded area when an explosion knocked him off his feet. With a squeal like a giant can opener, the tank split straight up its side. Two thousand tons of sparkling clear water swept down on all of them.

The shooters vanished beneath the flood. Bones yelled, "If you can't swim, head for the rafters."

Maddock looked up just in time to get slammed in the face by the oncoming surge. Tumbling backwards, trying to hold on to his weapon, he smashed into something solid and lost consciousness. Choking and sputtering, he came to, flat on his back staring up at the sky. All around, a sheet of water rushed by, still spewing from the ruptured tank.

A body lay nearby, one of the shooters. Maddock rolled him over and checked for signs of life. With a gasp, the man kicked his legs and vomited a fountain of water. Maddock dragged him to a low hillock. Another of the shooters knelt nearby, trying to stand. Maddock helped him up and led him to safety. "Stay with your friend here, and make sure he's okay."

Bones arrived dragging a third man with his good arm. "This one's in pretty bad shape. I got his breathing started, but he's not opening his eyes."

Willis came sloshing up with two others, carrying an unconscious man between them. "Took a nasty crack to the head. I don't know how long he's going to last."

Maddock heard the thump of blades before the blast of air and spray told him of June's arrival.

Bones said, "These hombres need some help or they're going to die."

Maddock nodded and scooped up the nearest

unconscious figure. Bones and Willis helped the other three carry their colleagues to the awaiting helicopter. "Get on," Maddock yelled over the engine whine. "No one left behind."

Bones had no sooner stepped on the landing strut than June juiced the engine and pulled up on the collective. The loaded gunship sprayed water in all directions as it rose in the air.

Maddock plugged into the intercom. "We've got to get these guys to a hospital."

June came back, "I'm on it. They've got a helipad at Mercy Medical Center in Shasta. We're about seventeen minutes out. Hey, that tall one is Matt Williamson. Tell him that June Bug is on the flight deck."

Bones came on. "How's our fuel situation, captain?"

"Top of the checklist Mister Bones, or didn't you know? We're good for another hour before we have to walk."

Maddock did some quick math. Thirty-four minutes round trip didn't leave much margin to complete their mission. Three gurneys waited for them on the helipad. Maddock helped transfer the unconscious men. The attending medics were quick and professional, but when two men in suits approached, Maddock gave June the thumbs up and hopped in. The ensuing rotor blast sent the two to their knees. Mercy Medical spun away beneath them as June headed toward Laboratory Nine.

"You should have seen those guys look at you," Bones said. "Soaking wet and covered with blood. I wonder what they're saying right now."

Maddock said, "What's the chance that Matt Williamson is calling his boss to tell him we're still on the loose?"

June thought about it for a few minutes. "Matt's a friend. If he knows it's me, he might not call in for a while.

Silver Glacier isn't too popular around town, so they may not hear from the hospital either. On the other hand, you can bet someone has called."

"Nice shot on that water tank, by the way. Probably saved their lives. Do you really think taking out those pumps is going to make any difference?"

Willis came on. "It could. It's like sending a message saying, 'Hey, those earthquakes and stuff? We hear you Moogly.' That's what's going to happen. Then maybe we can figure out how to talk to it or something."

"Yeah, or something," June said. "Do you hear yourself? You think you can talk to a bunch of water?"

"Yeah, Bones and Maddock too. We all got the Kool-Aid, it did something. Look at us, we got beat up, shot, thrown out of a helicopter, and we're carrying guys around like we were fresh out of Underwater Demolition School. Well, it ain't our healthy lifestyle, that's for damn sure."

Maddock hesitated a few beats before chiming in. "Willis is right. Bones and I have had... well, visions. I can tell when he or Willis are around, Sally too. She's nearby somewhere."

"Should we go and pick her up?"

Maddock closed his eyes. She was with someone, not scared, in control. "No, we stick to our plan. I don't know what Sally's got going, but I think we'd mess it up."

June took them to another well site. Unmanned, it was an easy target. Only one MAC-10 remained after the flood. Maddock didn't want to risk going back to the earlier camp looking for the others. Two pumps stood side-by-side next to a pipe manifold and a small shed. June used the minigun on them. "After Pym's guys blew up my cot," June said, "that was rather satisfying."

"How many we got to go?" Willis said.

"Five more. Next up is a biggie, a reverse osmosis plant

where they concentrate their critters. It'll be hot with Silver Glacier guards."

June didn't risk coming in close. She kept them low to the deck, skimming the roads and scaring the crap out of a few truckers in the process. As they approached the plant, she pulled up and let loose with four of the remaining air-to-ground missiles. "That'll get someone's attention."

Bones said, "I love the smell of napalm in the morning."

"We do the next ones the hard way," Maddock said. "You've got to save the rest of that firepower for Pym's nasty little laboratory."

They circled the burning plant and headed east. June said, "You may just get your wish. The last four are pretty close to home."

Maddock watched their shadow on the trees below shrink and fade as they gained altitude. The sun, now well above the horizon, sparkled off Shasta's snowy peak. June seemed to know what she was doing. *Thank God she believes us*, he thought. *Thank God she found the evidence in her seismic equipment or I'm not sure I'd believe any of it myself.*

It seemed that Bones and Willis were convinced as well. *Here we are, engaged in acts of domestic terror based on an Indian legend and a bunch of weird feelings.* Doubts started to crowd his mind. Maddock could picture the newspaper headlines. He wondered what Spencer would think if she knew. Lost in reverie, he was thrown against the door when June banked hard right. Confusion on the headset, he heard Bones shout.

"Holy Crap! Apaches!"

27

Huddled between June and the silent technician, Sally didn't relax until a sleepy guard waved them past the main gate. Now, bouncing down a dirt road at one a.m. she glanced over at June.

"How did you get away?"

The woman concentrated on rounding a tight switchback, then said, "I bailed about the time you hit the ditch. Crawled off in the bushes then and waited 'em out. Those guys were so excited to catch you, they just forgot about little old me."

"Are you okay?"

"Didn't do my concussion a lot of good, but I've been stomped worse. What about you?"

What about me? Sally thought. *What about Willis, just so bloody ass-deep in this mess now. What would he say when he learned the truth?* "Nothing wrong that a couple of migraine pills and twenty hours of sleep wouldn't cure."

June didn't say much else. Sally let the endless line of trees pass their headlights like a green picket fence. When she felt herself dozing off, Sally asked, "Where'd you get this truck?"

"It's a borrowed company truck. I had to walk here from your parallel parking attempt. Someone had left the back gate open, so I came visiting. Found this guy lurking outside the armory, so I cut him a deal."

The tech had plastered himself against the door, staring out the side window. Sally touched him on the shoulder. "Where are you going after this?"

The man jumped and shrunk even farther from her. He rolled his eyes and said, "Just as far from this hellhole as I can get." He hung one arm out the window and straightened slightly. "Please, just don't touch me again."

"Afraid you'll get cooties?"

"If you saw them die like I did, if you knew what it was you've got in you, you'd be shaking. You ought to be screaming your guts out right now. Just don't touch me, okay?"

"Okay, deal," Sally said. "I won't touch, but you gotta talk or I'll plant a big ol' smooch right on those pink little lips of yours."

June mashed the brakes and the pickup slid sideways twenty yards before stopping. "Cripes sake! He just busted you out of there. Cut the guy some slack."

"This man helped strap me down and shoot me full of something. God knows what else he's done. Tell him to get out right now and walk home if he's that scared of me."

The tech glanced out at the darkness and said, "I'll talk. Just get me away from this madhouse."

June pulled the truck back into the middle of the gravel road and continued down the mountain. Sally wasn't sure if she felt crappy or vindicated. She started with an easy one. "How long have you been working here?"

"Eight months, maybe nine."

"Doing what? I mean, what were you hired to do?"

"I'm a biochemist, two years out of school. We were supposed to be testing the water for pathogens, bacteria, viruses, anything."

"And?"

"We found this bacterium, but nothing I'd ever seen. It's tiny and very mobile. It has an affinity for water but can survive super high temperatures. Extremophile, it's called, something that thrives where nothing should be able to live."

Sally inched a little closer and whispered, "So why did

you think I wanted it jabbed in my ass?"

June gave her one of those rifle-shot looks, so Sally backed away. "No, sorry, too early. You can tell me how you got started instead."

"It was my boss. Famous guy from Europe somewhere, psychophysiologist. He's all intense about this. Made us try it on animals, dogs at first. They just pissed it out again. Nothing. We had some goats and monkeys. Same deal, no effect. Then one day he called me in on a weekend. Seems one of the staff had gotten a needle stick. It happens. We had to sedate him, but it didn't do any good."

The tech seemed to retreat into himself. He stared out into the passing darkness for a while. "That's when they moved us all to the *Bug House*. That's what we call it, I don't have to explain."

"And you never thought to leave? To escape?"

"Oh, a few did. When we saw them again, they were strapped to a table. There's only two of us left. One now, I guess. Next thing I know, I'll probably be staring up into his face hoping to die."

June turned onto a paved road and headed west. "Not happening kid. I'm taking you all the way to Redding and putting you on a bus back to Omaha."

"I'm from Fresno, but Omaha would be fine."

They pulled up in front of the Pit River Café and Sally got out. June rolled down her window. "Sure you don't want to go all the way to Omaha with Beaker here?"

Standing in the darkened street, Sally stood on her toes and looked in from the driver's side. "I've got some unfinished business…"

The ground shook and the Café sign swung back and forth. Up the street an old wooden garage collapsed. "Damn," June said. "They're coming fast and hard now."

"If you were smart, you'd stay in Redding yourself."

"Wouldn't be far enough, kid. Not by half."

"Then go, just keep driving until you see cornfields."

June sighed. "Got some business of my own to attend. I guess I'd tell you to stay safe, but it won't do any good."

With that, the woman drove off, leaving Sally standing in the middle of a deserted street. The sign kept swinging, flashing a quick reflection from the streetlight at the corner. Sally stood in the darkened road watching a few lights flicker on. People opened their doors, poked their heads out, then disappeared. Sally felt another temblor, an aftershock, pass beneath her feet.

Coleen would be up, trotting over in her bathrobe to see what damage the latest quake had caused. Sally headed around to the back door to meet her. The older woman had just turned down the alley when she arrived. "Did you come to help clean up?"

"Yeah, guess I did."

Inside, Coleen switched on the kitchen lights and looked around. "Everything breakable's been broke already. Looks like that includes your face."

Sally mumbled a response; some things were just too complicated to explain. She bummed a handful of ibuprofens and went to clean up in front. A few sugar containers had rolled on the floor. She found a broom and started clearing the mess. Sally left the overhead off, preferring to work in the muted light shining from the kitchen. Working her way toward the shadows near the counter, she saw a dark figure at the back table. "You wouldn't happen to have a spot of hot tea, *petal*?"

"*Uzi?* I thought you were dead."

"Greatly exaggerated my dear. Now, that tea?"

Sally found Coleen in the storeroom restacking cartons of pancake mix. "I have a visitor."

Coleen didn't look up. "I'm not surprised. He's been

around a few times. I usually get him Earl Grey and a scone. He'll take cream with that."

Sally drew hot water from the coffee machine and found a plain scone in the dessert case. Last one, she put it on a plate with tea bags, a couple of creamers, and a spoon. Uzi hadn't moved. "Coleen says you usually like scones as well."

"Oh, but I have a scone already. Eat that one yourself. You must be *famished*."

Sally wasn't very hungry, but she sat and nibbled the scone. Uzi busied himself with the creamer. "You're not having tea?"

"Waiting on the coffee." If she'd been honest, she'd have admitted to murder for a strong cup of coffee at the moment. Sally heard the machine hiss and growl in the kitchen. "How'd you escape?"

Uzi stirred his tea. "If I told you…"

"Yeah, yeah, you'd have to kill me. It's been tried a few times lately."

"So, then I get to ask the same question."

"If I told you, I'd have to bore you to death."

"Try me. You can start with the head injury."

"I lost an ear. But it's okay; I've got a spare." With some prodding, Sally told of the car, the capture, and of the Senior Mr. Pym. Uzi pressed her for details of Pym's compound, but she remembered little.

"One of my agents saw you just riding out of Mr. Pym's tower of evil like you owned the place. How'd that happen?"

Coleen came out of the kitchen carrying a mug of black coffee and a plate of fried ham and eggs. "If you let me sit down, I'll give you my coffee."

Sally eyed the mug. "Deal, but you won't like what you hear."

Coleen went for another mug. Sally had finished half of

hers before the woman returned. "First off, fair warning. You should both skip town like yesterday." She went on to tell her story. *Most of it, anyway*, she thought.

"So, you think Shasta might erupt?" Coleen said.

"If I can't stop Silver Glacier from pumping their deep wells, yeah. And not just Shasta, this whole valley is sitting on a magma chamber. If it goes, it'll cover half the state in ash."

"Then I'd say we have cause to bring legal action against these guys."

"You know it's been tried, Coleen. When we lost our water rights here in El Yermo, we took them to court. But Silver Glacier has the courts and the state cops in their pockets. They can bring more legal firepower to bear than any of us could dream of mustering."

"I'm glad to hear you found your friend Willis," Uzi said, "and I have a little more good news. We've heard tell that Maddock and Bonebrake may still be alive."

"You saw him? You saw Bonehead?"

"Not exactly. It was nothing very specific, but there was a bigfoot sighting west of the mountain yesterday—and he had a friend."

"Then I can guess where they're headed," Sally said. "And they'll be walking into a hornets' nest."

Coleen left to get the coffee pot and returned bearing the sacred carafe and more hot water for Uzi. "I just can't believe that something this big is about to happen and no one seems concerned. It's… it's like some kind of elaborate joke. There's no smoke, no lava, no… I don't know, whatever it is that volcanos do."

"Just take a few days off," Sally said. "Go visit your spinster aunt or something. If nothing happens, then I was wrong."

Coleen nodded. "I'll do that if you'll come with me."

Uzi said, "Not likely, is it *petal*? You're going to go back. I can see it in your face, what's left of it, that is."

Sally gave him a halfhearted glance.

Uzi continued. "Let's do this, why don't you crash for a few hours, you look like you're about to die. I'll swing by later this morning and we'll go visit your friends, just to see who's still alive maybe."

Sally shrugged and staggered out. Inside, all her alarms were screaming, but the thought of some rest overwhelmed her sense of caution. Her little garage apartment, her little nest, aside from looking like a tornado had hit it, seemed the safest place in the entire world. She dragged the overturned couch away from the wall and set it on its feet. When she flopped, sleep hit Sally like a sack of wet cement.

The dreams this time, they seized her like a shark takes a seal and dragged her down to the darkness below. She danced with her children of the flame. She sang to the other mistresses of fire in their far lodgings. And she felt the pull of the waters. "Just let us go," they pleaded. "Free us from your lodge and let us stream into the light above."

Almost, she almost said *yes, go*. She almost released them from their bondage to the magmas below. But she had a task, she didn't know what, and Sally was so tired.

Perhaps it was the pain in the side of her face, perhaps it was that dim morning light that crept through her single window, but something pulled Sally from her dream and curled her up, back on that musty couch.

Movement, a shadow stood over her. "Good morning Sally Smith. We've been waiting for you."

The voice was familiar, yet somehow changed. She let her eyes open and sat up. "Oh, now my day is complete. I guess you've come for my other ear?"

Augustus Pym Junior stood before her. "I suppose that was my father's doing. He's not terribly subtle."

Sally tried to stand, fell back to the couch, then pushed herself up again. "What new hell do you have planned for me Junior? There's not much else you can do at this point."

"I've come to invite you to join me and my followers. We can catch up on old times."

"Look," Sally said, "I'm really tired, so let's cut the small talk. What is it that you want from me?"

"First off, I want you to meet my acolytes. We need you, Sally Smith, not for your computer wizardry, but for that marvelous *thing* that lives inside of you."

"Great. Get in line, take a number. I'm open for *thing* extractions between ten and ten-thirty on alternate Tuesdays. Now, it's been fun, we'll have to catch up some time, but I've got to get some sleep. Oh, and Pops swiped my computer, so forget about that."

Another shadow stepped out of the gloom. "You misunderstand our leader. His invitation is more like a command. I can think of many techniques to help you see it that way."

This new voice belonged to a female. Stubbly hair, white robe, blue sash and trousers, she stood nearly as tall as Pym. Sally blinked the sleep from her eyes and tried to will some of the fuzziness from her brain.

"So, Curly, you got a name, or should I just make one up?"

The slap knocked Sally back to the couch with her head ringing and her entire face burning. She hit the worn cushions, heard the springs squeal in protest, and bounced back up. Sally used the momentum to smash her right fist into the woman's left breast. Her opponent shrieked in pain and fury. She kicked Sally in the shoulder hard enough to send her flying over the back of the couch.

Pym yelled, "Enough, Giselle!"

Sally pulled herself upright. The bandage had been

knocked from her head and blood from her wounded ear once more ran down the side of her face. *None of this really matters.* She looked around for a weapon. The end table was too bulky. She needed to find a fireplace poker, a lead pipe, a Gatling gun, something. Pym didn't give her a chance. He flipped on the light and said, "Stop, both of you."

The woman, Giselle, stood feet apart, knees bent, fists up. Sally kept the couch between them and continued looking for a weapon. *Willis could have taken her. Hell, even Corey Dean would have thrashed her for what she did.* Sally let the blood run, just for effect. "So, this is what Pymmy's lapdog looks like."

Feigning inattention, Sally proffered her injured ear. The woman leapt over the couch. *The pain—yes, the pain would come, but it will be worth it.* Sally let Giselle land the blow but grabbed her arm and flung its owner against the cinder block garage wall. Giselle dropped like a discarded rag and Sally came down, knee-first on the woman's throat.

Pym grabbed her around the waist and threw her off. Sally jumped on his back and locked a chokehold about his neck. The man twisted and cursed before collapsing to his knees and falling on his face. Sally stood, stepped to the tiny kitchenette and returned with her favorite knife. *This story ends here.*

"You heard the man, Sally. Enough." Uzi stood in the doorway holding his namesake weapon. "I'm impressed. Where did you learn to fight like that?"

"I spent half a year surrounded by enough testosterone to gag a gorilla. Wha'dya think?"

She still hung on to the knife. *I could probably take out Pym before Uzi pulls the trigger.* She decided against it and said, "You gonna shoot her? Because I guarantee that chick is no fun just bouncing around like she does."

"No, I'm not going to shoot her, or her boss, or even you, for that matter. Put the knife away. It's my party now."

"Right *boss*." Sally slid the knife back in its tray and began rummaging the top drawer of a battered dresser. She found the steel box. *Key... key?* Glued to the bottom of her purse by a forgotten stick of gum, it took some fishing to recover. Uzi said nothing, his concentration on the pair twitching and gasping on the floor. When Sally turned, she held a battered thirty-eight caliber Smith and Wesson Police Special.

Uzi shook his head. "No, no way."

"...And believe me, I know how to use it."

"Right now, I'd believe anything, but I want you to get rid of that relic."

Sally lowered the hammer and jammed it in the back of her jeans. "Not gonna happen." She grabbled Giselle by the ankle and dragged her out to the middle of the room. "Why don't you search Pymmy for weapons while I keep an eye on his little friend."

"I'm not going to let you shoot her, Sally."

"I'm cool for now, but the day is just getting started."

Uzi checked both Pym and Giselle. Neither of them had been armed. Sally paced around the small room as he worked, always keeping Pym and the woman in sight. When Uzi stood and shrugged, Sally said, "That means they've got goons somewhere outside."

"Not anymore."

Giselle began gasping and choking. She clutched her throat and struggled for breath. Uzi said, "This woman may need medical attention."

"Thanks for noticing Galahad. Meanwhile I'll just stand here and bleed to death."

Uzi glanced over. "Sorry, I'd just gotten used to seeing you like that. Have you considered that red might be your color?"

"Yeah, me and 'Carrie.' I'm about to go do the shower scene right now." Sally took a few steps toward the bathroom, then turned. "Oh, and if you try to help that woman, she's likely to grab you by the nards."

Cleaned up and wrapped in a towel, Sally returned a few minutes later. She clutched the towel in her right hand and held a first aid kit in her left. "Patch me up, boss."

Uzi found a roll of gauze and began bandaging Sally's ear. In one fluid movement, Giselle leaped to her feet. Sally dropped the towel and brandished her ancient revolver.

"You faster than a speeding bullet now?" Sally said.

The same instant, Uzi stepped back and drew his own pistol. "My god, woman. You're shameless."

"Well, *he's* already seen me this way, you don't care, and that bitch doesn't count, 'cause she's about to die."

"Don't Sally."

Stark naked, Sally changed to a two-handed grip and aimed for body center. "On the floor, lady. Face down, or I plug the both of you."

"What has gotten into…"

"Just shut up and finish my ear, will you? I'm feeling real twitchy right now."

Sally kept her aim on the woman. Pym had rolled to one side. His eyes were open, but he said nothing. The pain still hammered at Sally's skull, but somehow, it seemed outside her, like it was happening to someone else.

Uzi's gentle touch told of some medical training. He whispered in her other ear. "This is a new Sally and I'm not sure I like her."

"I've had the crap beat out of me, I've had my ear cut off, but that's not the worst of it. They shot me up with some kind of happy crap and it's doing nasty things inside."

Uzi finished bandaging. "Clothe yourself. I want to

have a little discussion with these two."

When Sally again stepped from the bathroom, both Giselle and Augustus Pym were sitting on her couch. She tucked a clean shirt into her jeans and made a show of clipping a worn leather holster to her belt. Sally made eye contact with the two and said, "Now what kind of crap are you two turd-mongers selling?"

Junior leaned back and put his hands behind his head. "We came to help you stop my father."

28

They sat together in the back seat, but Giselle wouldn't look at her. That was okay by Sally, anything to avoid Junior. The man in question sat in front. Uzi drove. For a while, she considered just shooting Giselle and her boss. *Pow, end of problem.* But that would raise all kinds of questions. Like, what the hell did Pym mean by, *stopping my father?*

Uzi drove them back to Interstate 5, through the metropolis of Mount Shasta, past the storied village of Weed, and north to Highway 97. About fifteen minutes later, they bounced up a gravel road to a rather shoddy-looking commercial building. "Coming down in this world, Mr. Pym?" Sally couldn't help herself.

"Sometimes expeditious and efficient caps elegant, young lady"

"Why can't I just shoot him, Uzi?"

"T'ai Kung once said, 'The battle not fought is the best victory.'"

Sally thought a moment. "Wasn't that Sun Tzu?"

"Nope, six centuries earlier. Think, if you shot him, you'd have to shoot the woman too."

"But..."

"Then shoot him," Uzi said, "but consider the consequencces."

Sally figured she'd shoot Giselle first. The woman seemed nonchalant but had repositioned herself to strike if necessary. Nothing added up to a win, only sweet vengeance and the ensuing chaos. "Let's catch up later, Pymmy. We've got a few issues to discuss."

"Whatever you say, Miss Smith. If you're not going to

shoot me right now, may I introduce you to my followers?"

"Actually, I'd rather not. What I want to know is, what does this have to do with Pops?"

"Yes, my father. He has this idea that the water, the virgin volcanic water here, has medicinal value. The operative word being 'value.'"

"And does it?"

"You tell me. How much of his infusion did he give you?"

"You know about that?"

"There's much that I know, that I can see now that I stand so close to the source. Tell me you don't feel it. Tell me that it's not in your blood."

Sally didn't answer right away. Some things she'd rather not explain. They parked next to a single loading dock and Pym led them through a gray steel door. Sally let Giselle and Uzi follow. She turned and looked back across the parking lot. Mt. Shasta towered over the landscape. *Yeah, Willis would have gone that way.*

Uzi held the door. "Are you coming, Miss Smith?"

Hand on her revolver, Sally stepped inside. Pym proceeded down a short corridor and entered a simple office. Filing cabinets, Steelcase desk, three wooden chairs, it looked like the home of some government bureaucrat rather than a rogue hedge fund manager. He sat down and said, "Giselle, be a dear and fetch another chair."

Sally closed the door as she entered. "It's okay. I'll stand if you don't mind."

She wasn't sure who Giselle wanted to kill more, her or Pym. The woman backed against the wall and shot glares at both of them. Sally said, "Sit down please, *dear*."

Pym nodded and indicated a chair. Both he and Uzi were already seated. Giselle spun her chair around and perched, leaning over the back. Sally had no doubt that she could stand and throw the thing in an eyeblink. "Now Mr. Pym, what kind of medicine is your father brewing?"

"He is looking to cure mortality. Oh yes, he thinks he must cure me too of the—um—influence I acquired in our last encounter."

Sally shifted position, keeping a portion of Pym's desk between her and Giselle. "So, what's your angle in this? You planning tolive forever?"

"In a way, yes. Our elixir comes from the blood of converts, not from the water itself. We are children of Gaia, drinkers of the holy ambrosia, the blood of the goddess. We are one with all living things and all things below this earth. As are you, Sally Smith—as are you."

If the conversation troubled Uzi, he didn't show it. Sitting back, the man could have been listening to a book club recital of Tolstoy.

She kicked the leg of his chair. "What about you, Man of Mystery? Are you buying what Dr. Evil is selling here?"

"I'm waiting for the punchline. What exactly *are* we trying to stop his father from doing?"

Sally leaned back against the wall. "Well I know that one. In less than twenty-four hours, Papa Smurf is gonna succeed in blowing this whole place to smithereens."

"Well that's really not what the woman said." Uzi tapped a well-manicured nail on Pym's desk. "We're not sure that he's actually causing the problem, but the effect will certainly be the same."

Sally watched the interchange between Giselle and her boss. A brief glance, a nod, it was enough. Sally felt something; a long-forgotten task, it hovered just below her consciousness. "You said we needed to see something, Mr. Pym, something important. You can stop smirking at Bambi there and show us."

Giselle started up, but Pym stood faster. "She beat you

in a fair fight, woman. No rematch. Okay?" To Sally he said, "Keep provoking her and I might change my mind. You know, she almost took down your friend Willis."

Sally kept her face calm but filed the information away for later consideration. "Is that the important thing we need to see?"

"Giselle, instead of trying to kill our guests, would you find out what's keeping our friend Carl?"

The woman didn't spare Sally a glance but slipped out the door without a word. Uzi watched her go. He might have grinned. "Was this Carl going to show us something interesting, Mr. Pym? For I fear he may have been delayed."

A few moments later, Giselle returned. "Gone. Carl, the guards, not here."

Pym flicked a glance at Uzi and said, "The acolytes?"

"In their quarters, as instructed."

"Okay, my turn." Uzi stood. "Confession time. Carl— your guards—all of them, let's just say that they are not free to move about the cabin."

Giselle stood by the door, looking as if she would bolt but Pym remained seated. "What do you mean?"

"This complex all seems kind of hasty, I mean, where's the video surveillance? And your guards—*really*—have they received *any* training? While you were off bothering Ms. Smith, my people were here, sorting things out."

"That's impossible. I have fifty armed men on premises."

"*Please,* breaking in was just too easy. Rounding them up was like preschool naptime. And oh, *correction*, you had *fifty-seven* armed men including the two we left a little indisposed back in El Yermo."

Pym sat back. "And my acolytes?"

"No worries, they are all entertaining themselves

splendidly. What *is* it you put in their water?"

Sally felt time slipping away. The endless banter between Uzi and Pym had long ago lost its charm. She pushed away from the wall and said, "Mr. Pym, we came to see your operation. All I've learned is that you've got crappy security. Willis escaped your nasty little dungeon, and my annoying friend here seems to have rolled up your little army. I think we should take a tour, because right now, I'm not terribly impressed."

"A terrific idea, Sally." Uzi jumped up. "Mr. Pym, will you lead us, or should I have one of my men show everyone around?"

Pym stood as well. "Giselle, don't go running off. Why don't you do the honors?"

Uzi followed the woman out into the hall. Seeming unconcerned with her proximity, he walked at her side, saying, "This'll be fun. Let's go interview some of these acolytes first."

Sally indicated that Pym should follow the others. She glanced back into the room. Not his real office, it seemed like a stage set for visitors. At the end of the hall, she spotted a doorway with a smashed lock. Willis had definitely been here. Giselle was explaining something to Uzi. Sally hurried to catch up.

"I am an acolyte too," the woman said, "you haven't interviewed me yet."

"Okay, what's with the robes? Are you in a karate club or something?"

Pym responded. "It's a uniform for those who have crossed the barrier, for those whose blood is now part of the symbiote."

Sally noted his shirt and slacks. "And you're wearing street clothes because why?"

"Some people are a little uncomfortable with my

operation. As the one in charge, I need to look like a normal businessman."

"Rather than an abnormal freako businessman, is that it?"

Uzi spun around. "What did I say?"

"Sorry, just trying to get the perspective."

"It's alright, Mr. Uzi," Pym said. "She's still laboring under some unfortunate first impressions."

"Yeah, and second impressions, and third impressions, and they've all been unfortunate… for me. So, perspectives—okay? Now, let's see how splendidly those others have been entertaining themselves."

Giselle took them past the loading dock and led them down a short hall to the left. She keyed in a code and pushed a door open. "Please, go ahead."

Uzi demurred. "No, I insist, ladies first. You too Mr. Pym. Sally can wait here and hold the door until she learns to behave like a lady."

Uzi's taunt hid his distrust. Sally eyed the electronic button lock. A simple device, she likely could have cracked it if needed. Instead, she kept the aluminum door handle against her back and ushered Pym inside.

The room looked like a hotel lobby. Tables, chairs, commercial carpeting, a large-screen television occupied one wall. Like a hotel, rows of doors lined the walls. Uzi walked around, peered up at the indirect lighting, flopped on a couch, and said, "I'll take what's behind door number three."

Pym stepped to the third door on his left and knocked. The door cracked open, a few words and a couple dressed in white stepped out. Sally noted that, unlike Giselle, these two wore robes that reached below the knee. Barefoot, white shins, they didn't wear the traditional *karategi* trousers either. *Lovers not fighters then.* She watched their interaction with Pym. Deference, almost fear, the couple kept glancing at each other.

Before they could take more than five steps, Uzi said, "Oh, do come sit down with me. We must talk."

Sally tried to listen in on their conversation. Uzi had picked a couch just beyond her hearing. *So, he's playing games with me, too.* She thought back on their short history together and began to wonder who he really worked for. Sally returned her focus to Pym. He stood back, one hand on Giselle's elbow. *Lovers? Maybe they both liked it rough.*

The conversation droned for a bit, the room blurred, it seemed that ghosts or shadows flitted by. Sally could still feel the door handle pressed against the small of her back. Yet at the same time, she felt like a marcher in some vast army. Amorphous, it swarmed about her like ants. She sunk into the floor, down to a chamber, a prison among the rocks.

Once more, she danced with her children of the flame. She knew them now, her subjects. She'd known them since the dawn of time. They'd called her by a thousand names, Persephone, Pele, Killeli, all one, all queens of the subterranean fires. Then as one, her children fled wailing into the darkness. The earth trembled beneath her feet and strong arms shook her. More screaming, shrieking, the panic of ten thousand souls.

Sally opened her eyes wide. Face to face with Augustus Pym, the sheer terror in his eyes washed all the other visions from her mind. "Not now, Sally," he cried. "For God's sake not now."

The building rumbled and shook as if a freight train passed mere feet from its walls. The large-screen television sagged to one side, then crashed to the floor, scattering shards of glass and plastic across the rug. Uzi had come to his feet. With a lithe, spinning movement he deflected

Giselle's rush and stepped up beside Pym. "Kindly let her go."

Sally slumped forward, her back still pinned to the door, it seemed almost a lifeline between her and that other dark reality. When she finally looked up, the room had filled with white robed acolytes. Not milling about or talking, but just staring at her. "What?" Sally said.

29

The barrel room, a vast darkened warehouse, had become a disaster. Sally gagged at the stench. The acolytes stared about in horror, hugging each other and weeping openly. Half the barrels had toppled over and broken open on the floor. Pym strode to the center, wading through pools of dark bubbling liquid. "Months of sacrifice destroyed." He turned to Sally. "Do you see what you've done girl?"

Sally backed into the loading bay, holding a hand over her face. "What I have done? Why don't you tell me what kind of filth you've been brewing here?"

"You know what it is, Sally. You have it in you, the water of life, the holy ambrosia. With this, we, all of us become one with the mountain. Your Willis had his chance, but he chose corporal mortality instead."

"This disgusting mess has nothing to do with Willis or with me, Mr. Pym."

"Oh, but it does. You, my acolytes, even I myself now commune with the fires below the mountain." Pym raised his arms. "Don't you see? We are all that hold them in check. You slipped for a moment, and almost—almost we had disaster."

Sally poked her head back into the barrel room. "And this putrid mess? How does this help anything?"

"You see before you barrels of the symbiote, cultured from the blood of my acolytes after their period of sequester beneath this mountain. It's ten thousand times more concentrated than the native bacteria my father uses. Once reinjected into the rock, it will become an extension of ourselves." Pym strode from the barrel room, arms in the air. "We will become part of this holy mountain, now until eternity."

Uzi had been watching the interchange from the back of the loading dock. Dozens of the acolytes had jammed into the space. It didn't stop him from stepping up and addressing Pym directly. "Now that was a rousing speech, and I'm all for reinjecting that mess into the ground. As long as I don't have to smell it any longer. So tell me, where are your injection wells?"

"My father has drilled fifteen wells on the other side of the mountain. They're almost unguarded. We will commandeer the wellheads. I have hydro-fracturing pumps to reverse the flow and inject the symbiote."

Uzi put one hand on his hip, rubbed his chin, and said, "Oh, I see so many problems Mr. Pym. For one, your army is laying on their bellies with their legs zip tied. They say an army moves on its stomach. While they're not uncomfortable, they *are* rather helpless, you know." He began pacing. "Also, these earthquakes, do you really want to be injecting more fluid? I mean there's a history, and it's not a good one."

Pym was about to answer when Sally interrupted. "If you want to inject something into the rock, what is it your father is trying to extract?"

"He has the same idea, but as you know, he's injecting a concentrated symbiote directly into humans. My father also seeks the water of life, the secret of healing and immortality…" Pym stopped and glared at Uzi. "For God's sake man, can you stop pacing and mumbling?"

Uzi ignored him but moved closer to the rollup loading door. Sally said, "Let him go, he's doing his Napoleon Solo thing."

"You mean Han Solo."

Sally squinted at him. "No—but go on. Tell me what your father hopes to gain by this."

"He's getting old. The man takes more exotic medicines than you can imagine. My father hopes to develop an injectable immortality drug. He's been experimenting on human subjects for months. Can you imagine what this stuff does to one who has not been initiated, not been conditioned in advance?"

Sally didn't blink. "I've heard the rumors."

"Well, I fear that it gets worse. He's managed to somehow awaken the symbiote. It's leaving the magma chamber and migrating into the rock strata beneath this entire region."

"I've heard that too."

Pym stopped, stared at her a moment, then turned to Giselle, lurking just behind Sally's field of vision. "Get a crew cleaning up the spills and have them start loading the tanker. I want us ready to roll by noon."

Giselle didn't move. "What about her?"

Sally caught Pym's nearly imperceptible nod. Giselle blinked in return and said, "We'll be ready."

"So, what *about* me?" Sally said. "You would have been better off just letting me sleep in this morning. Why do you need me?"

"You must lead us. You, better than anyone else, know how to communicate with this thing, this entity that lives beneath our feet." Pym drew up close to Sally. She could see the fervor in his eyes. "You are the Mother of Chaos. Only you can descend in spirit and speak with these entities, as you once spoke with the Ma'óghe."

Uzi had been listening from a discrete distance. Sally beckoned him over.

"What do we do next? I'm thinking we cut them loose and bug outta here."

Uzi appeared to be sizing up Pym, but Sally knew that he was actually keeping an eye on Giselle. Clean up had started immediately, and Sally noted that much of the spilled culture was being salvaged. "We could," he said. "We could leave, but I am curious to see how this plays out. Even if we all get blown to crispy bits, this is so incredibly *interesting*."

Uzi resumed pacing and rubbing his chin. "Look flowers, and I *do* mean both of you, there is something in what Mr. Pym says. We've spoken to your geologist friend and she agrees that an eruption is likely. Lord knows, the woman tried, but no one is evacuating. Maybe the recent earthquakes will get some attention, but how long before anyone actually leaves?"

"So you think the crazies here are going to pump the mountain full of happy juice and save the day?"

"Probably not, but we'll be taking some action, and who knows, save climbing up there and parking my butt on the mountaintop, I can't think of anything else to do."

Pym said, "It would be helpful if you'd release my men."

"Done." Uzi wagged a finger. "But no weapons. No knives, guns, or grenades. They'll be working for me, now."

Sally let the two of them talk logistics. She glared back at Pym. The man had hurt so many people. He'd hurt her in ways she still couldn't fully understand. *Why didn't I just let Willis shoot him when he had the chance?*

She found her way outside. A stainless steel tank trailer had pulled up next to the building. Three of the acolytes were manhandling a four-inch hose into the top hatch. She watched them drag the hose up a ladder, brown streaks of Pym's culture staining their formerly white robes.

Sally lost interest and followed the building west. At the far end, six black vans nosed up against the back wall. Before she could investigate further, a strong hand gripped her shoulder and spun her around. "You shouldn't be here."

She faced a man in dark jeans and black flannel shirt.

He could be a local cowboy except for the M4 carbine held diagonally across his chest. "So you're real," Sally said. "I was beginning to doubt you guys even existed."

"You shouldn't be here Ms. Smith," the man repeated.

"Yeah, got that." She turned back to the loading dock, but not before spotting a large group in camo getting slowly to their feet. *What the hell were they going to do with Pym's army? For that matter, what the hell am I doing here anyway?*

As she walked, Sally contrasted what she'd seen of Pym Senior's complex on the south side of Mt. Shasta with what his son was doing here on the north. It seemed but a child's imitation of his father's sophisticated operation. Passing the tanker with its scurrying minions in stained robes, she walked to the other end of the building. Here, the gravel road wound up from the highway below. Between the distant trees she saw a light scatter of morning traffic.

More impressive were the pair of giant diesel pumps mounted on trailers. Parked amidst a row of tractors and vans, they dwarfed the smaller vehicles. Walking past the building, Sally saw a small helicopter anchored to an asphalt pad. *Okay, maybe Junior isn't totally without resources.*

As she started to return, Sally felt... *something*. Although she couldn't see around the building, she knew that someone approached. Sally scooted back behind the corner and waited. Moments later, she heard Giselle call out, "I know you're there, Sally Smith. You can't hide."

She spotted a door a few yards away, likely once the front entrance. Sally didn't doubt that it was locked, but a low parapet covered the doorway and a concrete windowsill jutted out nearby. She ran and jumped for the sill. Her feet planted on the concrete ledge, she sprang up and let momentum carry her to the parapet. Both hands firmly on the lip, she pulled herself over. The eave hung just a foot above Sally's head. With a practiced motion, she heaved herself onto the roof.

"I can follow you anywhere, Sally. Why don't we just have a nice talk?"

Sally lay flat against the warm metal roof. She felt the reassuring lump of her revolver. The woman knew she was armed, *so what does she have that beats my Smith and Wesson?* Like a voice in her head, it came to her. *An accomplice, idiot.* Probably with a rifle, probably circling from behind the trucks.

Sally didn't feel like tangling with Giselle again. In an even match, she knew the woman would take her in five seconds. She wriggled across the rooftop and crested a low peak before scooting down the other side. Just below her feet, the tanker sat, drinking up gallons of Pym's precious culture. Sally hopped on a catwalk running the length of the trailer, scurried down the ladder, and ducked back inside.

Uzi and Pym stood almost where she'd left them, still discussing logistics, terms of surrender, *or hell*, she thought, *exchanging recipes for disgusting crud.* "Has anyone seen Giselle lately?" Sally put on her sweetest face.

Pym had been nodding and smiling. On hearing Sally, he looked in the barrel room. His smile faded. "She should be directing the loadout."

Sally shook her head. "I didn't see her."

Pym cocked his head and stared toward the back. Uzi, to his credit, picked up on Sally's gambit. "Let's discuss this another time. You need to see to your people, Mr. Pym."

Sally watched him leave. The man did look troubled. As soon as he was out of earshot, she said, "Why so chummy with Mr. Psycho?"

"We will need his help, luv. If only as a diversion. What was it you wanted to tell me?"

"Was I that obvious?"

"No, but I'm beginning to understand the way you think."

"Giselle is out hunting for me, and I don't think it's to exchange grooming tips. She's got someone with her, someone armed."

"Two free agents, then. I'm not surprised. That would be her little friend Carl. He's been bloody hard to keep track of. Your pals here are playing their own game, as are we."

"They've got a small helicopter around on the other side. She and Carl could scram at any time."

"Oh, but it won't run without a magneto. One of my people saw to that. Your Giselle has likely just become aware of the problem."

"Providing we all don't shoot each other in the next hour, what's your plan?"

"First we have to find out what kind of mischief your boys have been brewing. Maddock and Bones have a way of throwing a wildcard into the deck. I've been worried that Senior would just show up at this point and blow his kid's little science fair project to nasty bits. But no, he's strangely absent."

"I was wondering the same thing," Sally said. "Pym Senior is not usually one to sit back and let things happen. So, you're figuring there's trouble in River City?"

"With a capital 'T' that rhymes with 'B,' that stands for Bones."

Sally managed a crooked smile. "At least I know he's still alive, all three of them are. Don't ask me how."

At that moment, Pym Junior stepped back inside. "She was just checking on our men. It seems they aren't terribly happy about being disarmed. My father's mercenaries could show up at any time."

"We'd been talking about the same thing," Uzi said. "How effective are your father's men, would you say?"

"I've known from the beginning that he could just come and shut us down whenever he pleased. The man doesn't want a confrontation though. Very cautious, my father. Normally, he'd rather wait until I came to him." Pym shook his head. "Now, I don't know. "What I do know, is that he's got at least two military grade helicopters, a pair of light planes, trucks, guns, grenades, the works. Here's the thing about my father, he doesn't trust his own men. They're well armed, but it's obsolete stuff. He'd rather rely on brute force that follows orders, than a skilled cohort who might think for themselves."

Sally held her tongue. She recalled the gang of thugs Pym Junior had once set on her and didn't figure his current crew were much better. Giselle had returned and resumed supervision of her acolyte crew without so much as a glance back. Uzi paced for a moment scanning the warehouse interior. Eventually he insisted on a complete tour of the facility. Sally felt... *knew*, about much of it. She pointed across the warehouse floor to a door on the opposite side. "That's your laboratory, isn't it?"

If Pym was surprised, he didn't show it. "Yes, not much to see, but come if you must."

Sally gagged at the stench but Uzi insisted. Pym beckoned to Giselle. Crossing the warehouse, she pushed through the doors on the other side. Uzi followed her in. "You process the blood samples here. Then what?"

"We take almost a liter of blood," Pym said, "and mix it with ten liters of concentrated symbiote. Some of our acolytes have contributed twice a month, but most of them can only take the sacrament every six weeks. Remember, we have all been infused with the symbiote. It tells us what it needs and how often."

Uzi peered around, exaggerating his movements. "That's still a lot of blood to fill all these barrels."

"Once a barrel has matured, we can use it to seed more culture. Our sacraments multiply as they age."

Sally pointed to another door. "That's where you draw the blood?"

"Yes, it is our origin, the place of beginning. You probably wouldn't be interested."

"Oh yes, but I would," Uzi said. "Madam Giselle, would you be so good as to give us a tour?"

Sally noted the body language between Giselle and her boss. The woman was hiding something. She could feel Willis too, and the violence that was in him. Giselle and Pym led the way, Sally let Uzi follow. She drew her ancient revolver and held it at her side. Past the doors, they came to a stark white room that featured only a stainless steel table. It looked like a mortician's exsanguination facility. "This is cozy. What's past that next door?"

"Nothing much," Pym said. "We have some underground preparation areas down there."

Uzi said, "Fascinating. Do you mind?"

Giselle had the look of a cat that's just spotted an injured bird. Sally couldn't tell if Uzi was being naïve, or just playing along. She hoped the latter. When Pym pushed open another door, Sally said, "Why don't you two boys go exploring down there? We'll just stay up here and talk girl stuff."

Uzi's quick half smile told her all she needed to know. When the inner door swung shut, Sally crossed her arms, revolver in her right hand. "What I want to know Giselle, is why you've been sniffing around my ass this whole time."

The woman stiffened. Sally saw nothing in the room that could be used as a weapon. Still, she kept the steel table between them. Giselle had clearly made the same assessment. She didn't relax, but feigned amusement. "The infamous Sally Smith, we're alone at last. I've dreamed of this moment. You've been such an obsession to the master. He's really quite smitten—a taste of honey, you know. Now he wants the whole vat."

"I don't give a corn dog crap about your boss. What's with you, Tinkerbell? Why are you following Peter Pym like his little puppy dog?"

"The same reason you're here. The same reason your friend Uzi is here. Love him or hate him, we all know Augustus Pym Junior holds the key to immortality. You're either in, or you are going to die. Well, I want in."

Sally leaned back against the chamber wall. "You're jealous. That's it, you think I'm here for your place in the Elysium. Let me tell you lady, no way in hell. Okay?"

"And you think you have a choice, Sally Smith. I know more about you than you can imagine. For instance, I know you're keeping a secret. Yeah, don't look so surprised. I'm not sure yet what it is, but it's eating you up."

"You know nothing, lady."

"Wrong, Sally Smith. We've got the same thing in our blood. We both hear the voice of Gaia. The difference is, I can control it. With the power I've gained here, I could cut you off right now. I could block the source and leave you hanging in the void."

With that, she arched her neck back and rolled her eyes up beneath their lids. Sally felt a moment of dizziness and a profound silence like some inner door shutting. A moment later, the silence was gone. Giselle grinned. "How did you like that girl?"

"You can't maintain it. Eventually, I'll learn to break through."

"You are wrong. I could silence you forever. How do you think I stopped your childish little fit earlier? I could break that thing you have inside, but I have my own reasons not to. Fear me, Sally Smith. Fear me and join with me. You could be immortal."

"I'd rather put a hole through the center of your forehead, but I have my own reasons not to," Sally said.

"You still carry a ton of obsolete baggage. If you wanted my master to fail, you would kill him. I want Augustus Pym to succeed and I want to be with him forever."

"Good luck with that. This whole place is gonna be orbiting Pluto before any of us are likely to see another sunrise."

"Not…" Giselle practically hissed. "Not if you and your pet mongoose would just get out of our way and let us finish what we've started here."

Uzi stepped back through the door, cutting off Sally's response. "Fascinating place down there, Ms. Giselle. Mr. Pym says that you were one of his first subjects. Did you see the lights? What were *your* happy thoughts, I wonder?"

Pym followed right behind. "Giselle was our first success, weren't you dear? Yes, some of our most potent culture sprang from her blood."

"I am intrigued," Uzi said. "And now, let's go see to the loading. They must have almost finished."

Judging from the condition of the barrel room, Sally agreed. Acolytes in filthy brown robes drained the few final casks into an electric pump. Uzi pointed out a row of barrels that had not been moved. "Those," he said. "Are those a good vintage?"

"The best," Pym responded. "Some of that culture was drawn from my own veins."

Uzi clapped his hands together. "Splendid, splendid. I must have one. Intact if you please." He tossed a black dongle to Sally. "Be a dear and bring our vehicle around to the loading dock."

"You want to put that nasty bucket of crud in your *Jaguar*?"

"Yes, you know, it's a sport, utility, vehicle. The emphasis is on *utility* today. Put the rear seat down, will you. Mr. Pym can ride with me. You and your lovely new friend will ride with the trucks."

Sally gave him a look that would have incapacitated a lesser mortal, but Uzi just kept gushing about what an honor it was to convey a cask of Pym's finest culture. Finally, she gave up and went to get the vehicle. By the time Sally returned, four acolytes had manhandled a cask to the loading dock and were lowering it to the parking level. Sally estimated the thing at two hundred pounds. It just cleared the interior hinges and slid all the way to the front seats before they could close the rear lid. The Jaguar bore it without complaint.

Sally heard a diesel start at the far end of the building. Uzi came out, hand on one ear. He spoke for a minute and then announced, "I'll have an escort for the fracking pumps and a separate escort for the tanker."

Sally hopped back up on the loading platform and handed him the Jaguar's dongle. "…and I'm riding with the escort, right?"

"Nope. You two ladies will be riding shotgun in the cabs. Giselle is already leaving with the pumps and you will grace our precious load of culture. The pumps are going around from the north. They should reach the well site and be set up before you and the tanker arrive from the south."

"And what about you and Pym? What are you, the Band of Brothers now?"

"We have things to discuss, business to attend. Rest assured, we will rejoin you before pumping has finished."

Sally knew she could refuse, simply say *hell no*. She had the gun, and she was pretty sure that Uzi wouldn't shoot her regardless. Giselle must have taken some persuading. She figured her master had to have done that. "What have you promised Pym?" She asked.

"He wants this to work. Mr. Pym knows that he hasn't a chance of taking over one of the major well sites without my help, so he's being reasonable."

"For now."

"Yes, for now. We both know something else is afoot. I'm counting on you. You're more important to this operation than you think. Keep your eyes open and stay safe."

"So how do I know that you and the Pymster won't just split for the coast as soon as we leave?"

"A great man once said you must leap from the lion's head. I need you to prove your worth dearest, take the leap of faith for me this one more time."

Sally pondered a moment. Uzi knew she couldn't resist a taunt worded that way, but the man's motives were too cryptic to trust. "I'll go in the truck," she said, "just to stay in the game. But don't you cross me, Man of Mystery. I'm counting on you."

"Your trust is well placed," said the serious Uzi. "I need you with the symbiote. Your presence will be the key to our success."

Sally let that sink in as she swung up into the cab. She wasn't even sure this symbiote was more than a festering mass of curdled blood. The entire truck stank of it. The driver gave her an odd look as she perched on the passenger side and fastened her seatbelt. "Get used to it buddy, things are only going to get weirder."

He shrugged and spoke on a walkie talkie. The engine growled to life and they began a broad turn in the parking lot. Gravel crunched beneath their tires. Sally caught a quick glimpse of the mountain before they began trundling down the dirt road toward Highway 97.

30

A storm of bullets peppered their fuselage before Maddock realized his friend had meant Apache attack helicopters. June practically dove them to the forest floor, dodging between trees and cursing all the way.

Maddock heard the occasional *thunk* of bullets striking metal, but the Apaches maintained altitude, preferring to wait their target out. June pushed the old Huey hard. They wailed across a road and screamed up the adjacent valley. Maddock swore he could reach out and touch the treetops. "We're not doing so good on fuel," June said. "I'm going to stop us for a moment. You all need to bail."

Maddock had already unbuckled his harness and cracked the cockpit door. About six feet above a tangle of manzanita brush and scrub oak, June pulled back on the cyclic and dumped the collective. "Go, go, go!"

Once more, Maddock plunged into the brush, feeling the scrape of an oak branch as it raked up his back. He managed to keep his feet under himself this time and looked up to see their helicopter rise circling into the air. Bones came up behind him. "What in hell is she doing?"

He was answered by two missiles that struck the Huey amidships. A flash and a fiery spray of molten aluminum, then it was gone.

As flaming debris rained down on the mountainside, Maddock watched two Apache helicopters wail overhead. Specialized killing machines, they bristled with weapons. Hellfire missiles, 30-millimeter chain guns, air to ground rockets, miniguns, all multiplied times two. One Apache could easily hover in the sky to spot Maddock and his team, while the other swooped down for the kill.

Bones stared up and said, "Crap, we are so dead. June took the easy way out."

"What do you mean, 'the easy way?'" The woman in question poked her head above a clump of brush. "I had to jump from twice as high as you three wimps."

She fished around in the bushes and came up with a battered Stetson hat. "That's better."

Willis watched the two gunships circle for another pass. "I think they got us figured out…"

He was interrupted by a section of tail rotor that spiraled into the ground not ten feet away. Burning helicopter parts scattered across the landscape, setting a line of fires that spread up the brushy slope.

"Follow me," Maddock said. "And *run*."

He dashed across the hillside, heading for the smoke. If they were seen, he knew what would come next. The crackle of burning brush and trees filled the air around him. A black pall of burning jet fuel rose into the sky. Maddock headed straight for it. They had to lose themselves in the chaos. They had to stay invisible in both daylight and infrared. And most important, they had to put some serious distance from where they had been when their Huey was blasted from the sky.

"Hellfire incoming!" Bones yelled. He pulled June down and fell on top of her.

Maddock saw Willis dive behind a rock. Half-second, quarter-second—*where, where?* A ditch, not much more than a coyote hole, Maddock jumped. The thermal wave caught him in midair. The blast slammed him into the ground. His shirt smoking, he tried to roll as the secondary shock roared past, a river of air filling the vacuum left by the exploding missile.

When Maddock could breathe again, he realized that all the fires had been extinguished like so many birthday candles. All that is, save the pillar of flames where the missile had struck. He crawled to his knees and stared back at the burning impact site. "Missed us. They bloody missed. We've got to keep going. They're not likely to miss again."

Little tongues of flame once again rose from the wreckage. Maddock helped June to her feet. "Keep beneath the smoke, they'll be back and if we're seen, we're dead."

Willis scanned the horizon. "They've circled to the south. We got ourselves about three minutes to skedaddle."

Maddock didn't wait to comment. The wind from the west carried a pall of oily black smoke eastward along the mountain flank. Following the trail of smoke, he led them through a tangle of brush. Bits of burning sticks and leaves drifted down around them. He heard Willis pounding along behind, coughing in the cloud of smoke. Bones and June lagged by about thirty yards. Maddock slowed until they caught up. "Best if we stay tight. If they spot even one of us, we're all dead."

Moments later, they heard the howl of turbines as the two Apaches roared right above their heads. Maddock watched them fly west, passing over the site they'd just hit.

"What I don't get, is why they haven't just sterilized this entire hillside."

Willis followed his gaze. "Those boys are being cheap. A hundred grand apiece, Hellfires are some damn expensive ammo and they'd rather bring as much home as they can."

Bones said, "I think they need a confirmed kill as well. If they just toasted us to crispy critters, then how could anyone be sure that they got us all?"

"Whatever," Maddock said, "they aren't about to give up until they know we're finished."

By the time both Apaches had circled off to the west, Maddock and the others were all bent double, coughing on the smoke. "Let's go," he said. "Stay low and keep moving."

Fires had broken out all along the hillside and the freshening west wind whipped the small flames into crackling, hissing conflagrations that dogged their footsteps. Beneath the smoke, Maddock knew that they would be invisible from the air. *Something else is afoot*, he thought. Bones read his mind. "What do you figure they're going to do next?"

He was answered by the scream of a minigun and a shower of earth that plowed up only a few yards away. Another volley came from a different direction.

"That," Maddock said. "They're shooting at random hoping to kill us or spook us."

"Well I'm getting tired of this crap."

June coughed and gagged before she caught her voice. "Get used to it, big guy. When you're born a rabbit, you better learn to run."

Bones stopped dead. "And how do you hunt rabbits? You chase them into the brush and then send the dogs after them."

Willis said, "We stay here, and we're going to get a buttload of ground pounders come running after us."

Another line of bullets stitched up the hillside, crossing a few yards ahead of them. "Keep going," Maddock said.

He led everyone west, working his way down the hill toward a large stand of ancient trees. Willis grabbed him by the arm and pointed. "I know those trees. Look up there, that rock sticking up? I've seen it before. Don't be asking me how, but I know this place. Let's go."

The two Apache gunships continued circling, firing at random into the smoke-covered hillside. A row of flames had already started along the base of the trees. The four dashed through, as a line of 7.62-millimeter bullets followed their path. "*Spotted*. Crap, the dirty bastards spotted us,"

June said.

"Now they know we're here, they're going to lock and load, and blow another hundred gees on us," Bones said. "Say your prayers, ladies and gentlemen, because we are about to be toast."

31

Merging onto Interstate 5, the tanker truck rolled south through the fabled town of Weed. *Pretty soon it's going to be some righteous vapor and that's about all,* Sally mused. Her driver wasn't the talkative sort and she was left with her own thoughts. She brooded a while on her situation. *Lunchtime, but nothing sounds good.* She touched her belly, hard, swollen even. *It doesn't matter, there's more important stuff at stake.*

They turned east at the town of Mount Shasta. The driver pulled over and dashed into a convenience store, coming out a few minutes later with two microwaved burritos. Sally smiled at him and shook her head. Before they reached El Yermo, he'd downed both of them. She watched him squeeze each burrito from its paper skin and bite off pieces as he drove. *The condemned man ate a hearty meal.*

Her own morbid thoughts bothered Sally. "Endings are as important as beginnings," someone once said. "A film that never rolls credits is meaningless." Still, she felt herself rushing toward that last scrolling list of names; the studio, the copyright date. If she was lucky, there'd be some funny outtakes, then the music would stop, and *End* would slowly drift onto the screen.

Instead, she tried to concentrate on her friends. Maddock, Bonehead, Cornpone, they were near. She could feel them, somehow. As they rolled off the highway and rumbled onto a gravel road, Sally caught a glimpse of gray smoke rising beyond the distant hills. She glanced at the driver. "Are we going that way?"

"Farther east, ma'am. Across the valley."

Ahead, one of the black vans bounced along the corduroy surface, throwing up a plume of dust and small stones. Sally knew that two more such vans followed, along with a covered truck carrying a small contingent of Junior's men. Uzi had explained, "I'm sending the main force with the pumpers. They will secure the site and set up the equipment."

She and the tanker were to arrive twenty minutes later by a different route. "As long as Senior is distracted by your friends," he'd said, "we should be connected and pumping before he notices."

Sally wasn't sure that Pym Senior was so easily fooled. Besides, Giselle's friend Carl lurked somewhere in this entourage. She wondered if he had followed the fracking pump, or was he right now riding just behind them, looking for his chance. Sally didn't intend to wait. She'd find Giselle and use her revolver before Uzi could say anything.

Twenty minutes later, they pulled up to an open clearing. A collapsed tank lay flat on the ground next to a beige steel building. At the far end, she saw the hydro-fracturing pump with a crew of men around it. They rolled up through six inches of standing water. Sally swung to the ground before the truck had stopped. As she'd expected, no Uzi. One of his men stepped up to intercept her.

"Look, don't tell me that I'm not supposed to be here," Sally said. "Where's your boss?"

Before the man could speak, they were interrupted by a low rumble like a distant sonic boom and a column of flame and smoke that rose into the sky. Sally was the first to understand. "You," she said to the man. "Tell these idiots to bust ass, because Godzilla's coming and boy is he pissed."

It took little urging on her part for the crew to resume connecting equipment. Sally kept an eye out for Giselle, but the woman was not among the workers. She pulled one of the female acolytes aside. "Where's Pymmy's little playmate gotten herself to?"

The woman blinked a moment, mouth open. Sally tried to maintain her patience. "You know, Montana Wildhack, Harley Quinn, She Who Must be Obeyed? Where is *Giselle*, for godsakes?"

The acolyte pointed toward the beige building and scurried off. Sally checked her revolver, if only to be seen doing it. She splashed down to the center of activity where a cluster of Pym's soldiers wielded wrenches and cutting torches. Two of Uzi's men stood by, weapons at ready. Sally asked for a progress report.

The taller of the two looked her up and down. She saw his eyes flicker a moment over the revolver, then refocus on her face. "Someone shot up these wells pretty bad. They're having to remove a lot of debris before we can connect the injectors."

"How long?"

"Maybe twenty minutes more before we can start pumping."

Sally walked off. They didn't have twenty minutes. They didn't have ten but belaboring the obvious wouldn't make things go any faster. She eyed the steel building and knew in her gut that she itched for a confrontation. Uzi had said he didn't like the new Sally. She wasn't all sure she liked her new self either.

A second shockwave rumbled past and again a plume of flame leapt into the air, this time lower down and closer. Sally could see two helicopters circling high above the mayhem. Like the cold wind from a deserted building, she suddenly felt the absence of Bonebrake, Maddock, and Willis. It was as if a piece of her had been wrenched out and thrown away.

Sally fell to her knees, dry heaves wracking her body.

She stared at her own reflection in a pool of clear water and wondered if she still had the strength to do what must be done. *Nothing remained to save, why should she care?* Then she recalled Giselle's boast, *I control the source,* she'd said, *I could silence you forever.*

Pushing herself to her feet, Sally stalked up to the steel building. *It works both ways.* She stopped a moment to admire the flattened steel plates and twisted pipes, all that remained of a large water tank. Then, without hesitation, she approached the building.

They would be waiting for her. Giselle to goad her in, the other to shoot once she'd entered. Clearly a maintenance facility, it had a row of small windows, an entrance at the near end and two steel rollup doors along one side. Sally considered just barging in and taking her chances. Queen's gambit, but she couldn't make it add up to a win.

Beyond the rollups a steel drum stood on four short legs. It had a hose and pump attached. Sally didn't have to read the sign to know it was filled with diesel. She didn't need to read the instructions to cock the nozzle open and start the pump.

Fuel streamed out and sheeted across the concrete apron, surging under the rollup door. She stood back and fired her pistol into the pavement. A roar, and the entire side of the building erupted in flames. "Come out, come out wherever you are…"

32

"Well I'm brown enough already," Willis said. "I ain't planning on being anyone's toast. Y'all going to follow me, or you staying here and getting your asses cooked?"

Maddock said, "Take point. I'll make sure June follows."

Willis hadn't waited for a response but ran between the trees. He knew that with one hellfire missile, the entire grove would become a roaring inferno. Still he hoped the pilots were waiting on confirmation to let loose. From behind he heard the Apache engines scream up and then howl away.

"They're measuring us for a roasting pan," Bones said.

Willis didn't answer, he was searching for something, anything. He came up short at the foot of a sheer cliff. The rocky face rose like a spire from within the grove.

Maddock pounded up behind, June in tow. "I like the way you're thinking, but this won't be enough."

"Got to be here." Willis followed the cliff around.

Maddock stopped, stared up at the rocky spire. "Look up there."

Willis followed his gaze. A circle within a triangle had been engraved in the weathered face. "This is it. Look around gang, somethings got to be here." He could hear the returning Apaches.

Bones pointed out a horizontal cleft at the base of the rock and said, "I think I could fit in there."

June looked down at the crevice. "Well I couldn't, I'm all boobs and butt."

Maddock said, "The Apaches are back. Off with the pants and shirt and get in there."

To her credit, June didn't hesitate, but stepped out of her boots, gun belt, and jeans. She backed into the crevice, dragging her hat and gear on the way in. Bones scooped up her gear and followed.

Maddock waved at Willis. "Go, that's an order."

No time left, Willis belly-crawled between the rocks. Maddock came in practically on top of him. The opening had grown slightly wider as he moved deeper into the darkness. Willis was concentrating so hard on crawling, that the impact caught him entirely by surprise. He felt something slam into his legs, throwing him down a steep incline. Blind, he tumbled into the total darkness, caromed off a wall and struck his head.

He couldn't been unconscious for more than a minute. Willlis heard June say, "Has anyone found my hat?"

Bones replied, "I think I'm sitting on it."

Maddock's voice came from a little farther off. "I'm here, most of me anyway. Where are we?"

"Alive," Willis said. "That ain't good enough?"

"A cheeseburger would be nice," Bones said. "And I wouldn't mind a little light so I could gaze on the wonders of Ms. Junie Moon."

"Like you'd ever get that lucky. Soon as I find my shirt, there's not going to be any wonders left worth gazing."

"You wouldn't happen to have a flashlight on you, would you Willis?"

"Shut up, all of you." Willis closed his eyes. He quieted his thoughts, concentrating on that moment when he and Sally held each other in that cold laboratory hall. *He shouldn't have let her go then. If he saw her ever again, he would never let go.*

He heard June gasp. "*Shazam!*"

Willis opened his eyes. The chamber had filled with light from ten thousand tiny specks set high in the overhead. On the ceiling directly above, the ubiquitous circle and triangle glowed like a neon sign.

He had more light this time than ever in Pym's cavern. Willis could actually see his companions, if only as shadows among shadows. Maddock stood cautiously and crept to Willis' side. "How are you doing this?"

He wasn't sure. "Hell, I don't know half of what's happening to me."

The lights dimmed until only a few glowed along the perimeter of the cavern. Willis returned his thoughts to Sally. Holding her in his mind, the glow once more spread up the rocky sides and into the overhead. "Hope attracts the light. Fear drives it away."

Bones had started climbing out the way they had come sliding in. "I don't think we're going back through that hole anytime soon."

Maddock said, "Better if we find another exit anyway. They may think they've got us, but you know that hill's going to be crawling with guys looking to be sure."

June finished pulling on her jeans and tucking in her blouse. "This cavern isn't here by accident." She pointed at the symbol over Willis' head. "That means something to somebody."

"Lemurians," Bones said. "They built this place."

June gave him a long look. "I'm a scientist, Stretch. I'm paid *not* to believe in stuff like Lemurians."

"Got a better theory?"

"Well, you're partly right. Rocks like the one we're sitting under don't just grow cavities like rotten teeth. Maybe it's a lava vesicle, but if it was, it should have collapsed long ago."

"I spent the last couple of weeks in a place just like this," Willis said. He stood, and the lights wavered a moment. "That's how I know... well, whatever this is. Could be

Lemurians; not saying it ain't. Just that, Bones, me, and Maddock here, we've seen this stuff before."

"I take it your friend Sally has, too."

"In so deep, we had to drag her out feet-first—more than once. No, if I were looking for one common thread, it would be Sally."

Maddock nodded in agreement. "Bones and I followed one of these tunnels last night. Led us straight to Sally and Willis."

"Then there has to be another way out." June said.

Bones grinned at her. "Should be, if Willis can keep his mind in the gutter or wherever he keeps them happy thoughts of his."

"Yeah, one of those is you, finding the bottom of a bottomless pit." The lights flickered. "Oh, crap. This is going to be tough with y'alls trash talking."

The lights dimmed and then faded. Maddock said, "Come on, Bones, let up at least until we get out of here."

"It wasn't me, he started it."

Willis' knees buckled. He knelt, his hands to his face. The silence was deafening. Somehow—somehow, he no longer felt Sally's presence. It was like she had been locked in a soundproof room. *Or, or...* He didn't want to think of the alternative. Sally had disappeared, and he just couldn't take any more of Bones' jibes. *Let's get things good and dark until they all shut up.* He concentrated on strangling both Pyms, one in each fist. Their faces darken, their legs spasm and collapse beneath them. Finally, their bowels... Willis looked around. The chamber had become darker than dark. He felt the waves of despair that radiated from the walls. Bones had gone quiet.

Maddock whispered, "Whatever you're doing Willis, please stop."

But he couldn't. Those long months in the mountains

of Tribal Pakistan, the brutal killing, it all came back. His youth as a cocky thug on the way to nowhere, the futility of it all. *Why*, he thought, *why did my Grams have to die in that storm?*

He felt June's hand on his shoulder. "Sally told me about you as we were leaving."

Willis tried to choke down the mass of wretchedness he'd been feeling and listen. June continued. "She cares for you more than you know, but it won't mean anything if you don't come out of here alive. Put her first for once, you might learn something about yourself."

He wanted to argue; he wanted to tell her that he couldn't feel Sally anymore, that she was probably dead. But that touch, that warm hand on his shoulder brought him back to his friends and his mission. Bones and his stupid jokes. Willis thought of the adventures all three of them had together. *No one left behind, not now, not ever.*

"Sally's gone, you guys. I can't explain, but she's no longer... with me." Willis straightened and glared back at the darkness. So go on, Bones, clap your hands if you believe in fairies."

Far off to his left, he saw a faint blue light. Maddock chuckled, and a dozen more lights glittered along the overhead. Off in the shadows, he heard the big Cherokee start clapping. Once more the cavern interior blazed with glittering sparks.

June said, "I'm seeing, and I'm believing, but no way I'm ever gonna talk about this one."

Maddock said, "We've still got to get out of here. Which way, Willis?"

He looked up at the triangle and circle and recalled the trail of tiny lights that had led him away from a precipice the night before. "Let's go find Sally."

Nothing changed, but the single blue light grew

brighter. "This way," Willis said.

Behind a fallen boulder, they found another passage. Rectangular, a narrow slot in the rock, it could have been natural but for the steep staircase leading deeper into the mountain. One tiny glimmer marked each step. Willis descended first. June followed.

"Did I ever mention that I'm claustrophobic?" she asked. When Willis didn't answer, she continued. "What I'm trying to say is, a little more light would be nice."

He remembered her hand on his shoulder. It had taken a lot of guts to crawl into that crevice in the first place, a lot more to maintain her cool now. "You're getting every kilowatt I can muster, Junie Moon. I promise, if we find any more lights down here, I'll switch them on for you."

The descent was so narrow, that Willis had to turn sideways in many places. He counted steps. After three hundred of them, they reached a level spot, a landing of sorts. Maddock said, "Careful everyone, I've got a feeling there are no handrails in this place."

Bones said, "Dude, you aren't kidding. There's a ledge here, and I don't know how far down it goes."

Willis could hear Bones but had no idea where he stood. "I'm not seeing any more lights, you guys. And yeah, got the happy thoughts cranked."

In the darkness, Bones said, "I believe you buddy. Edge over this way and take a look."

Willis crept toward Bones' voice. He felt the ledge with his foot. "Yeah?"

"Just look down."

A vague silhouette stood next to him. Willis looked down. Nothing. "Got to get closer," the silhouette said.

"Damn!" Willis scuttled back, almost falling over. Between his feet, he'd seen a sheer drop that fell away for thousands of feet. He returned cautiously to the edge. Far below, an orange glow seemed to climb the walls, gradually illuminating the chamber.

He felt June stand next to him. "Momma always said I was going to hell."

"I think this is where my high school girlfriend was born," Bones said, staring into the abyss.

Maddock held his arm out. "Why don't we feel any heat? Why don't we smell sulfur or something?"

Willis had no answer. He stared down into the pit, the light seemed to be climbing the walls. Slowly the chamber became suffused with an orange glow. "I think when you asked for light, June, this is what we got."

"Great. Next time I'll ask for ice cream instead. Where do we go now? And don't say down there, 'cause despite what Momma said, I ain't buying it."

Willis stepped back from the ledge and examined the platform they stood on. In the growing light, it looked oddly like a balcony. "I think this is sort of a theater. If we stay long enough, we'll see some kind of show."

"That, or it's a sacrificial altar," Bones said, "and if we stay long enough, we'll *be* the show."

Maddock backed away from the ledge as well. "I'm not so happy about staying, Willis. Can you find us another passage?"

"This is it, man. This is where the Moogly lights took us. I'd say even hell's gotta be a lot better than what they've got going on topside."

Bones leaned over and peeked down at the orange light. "We're about to find." As one, they all stepped back. The chamber before them brightened, glowing like a subterranean aurora. "Anybody got popcorn?"

33

As the orange glow welled up from below, Maddock saw a slender ribbon of solid black arose from the center like a snake following a fakir's music. It branched and twined into an impossible skein of interlacing figures that chased each other about the wall like a menagerie of living hieroglyphics. Maddock had waited with the others, standing in motionless thrall while the figures pulsed, disintegrated, and then reassembled themselves into a labyrinthine city that stretched in all directions.

The orange glow had faded to a twilight blue and a cool breeze blew from somewhere within the scene. Maddock put his hand on Willis' shoulder. "Are you doing that?"

"Not me, boss. This is some kind of weird that even I haven't seen yet."

Bones remained frozen in place a moment, then blinked and said, "You guys thinking what I'm thinking?"

June shook her head and stepped a little closer to the scenario. "I sure hope you're thinking there's another way outa this place that isn't the way I think you're thinking it is, if you get my meaning." She took another step and then jumped back. "Holy mother of Godzilla—just—just don't move okay?"

Bones took a Bones-sized step forward and stopped. His head tipped back, his jaw dropped, and he whispered, "*Goll-ly* gee... Will you look at that?"

Maddock stepped up behind him. The perspectives twisted and rushed forward. A charging battalion of towers and streets, a swarming tangle of soaring bridges, an archipelago of floating palaces, they all zoomed into focus around him. "It's like a science fiction cover illustration."

"Yeah, from nineteen fifty-five or something."

Willis had followed Maddock. "I'm not sure *my* kind of people are even allowed in here."

"Hey, this is your hallucination," Bones said. "I just want to find the freaking exit sign."

June had joined them. "Curiouser and curiouser. So, this is what's inside of Mr. Willis Sander's head."

"You ain't pinning this on me, lady. I sure didn't volunteer for any of it."

"Your rabbit hole, your hallucination. Couldn't you at least have put me in a gold lamé jumpsuit?"

"Oh yeah, with pointy ears and little antennae sticking through your hair."

"Wouldn't have worked with the Stetson and six-shooter," Bones said.

Maddock inched his way out, trying to find the platform edge. He ventured onto a narrow street, flanked by buildings of glass and shining metal. June was first to say something. "Hey, you trying to do a Wile E. Coyote on us?"

Maddock stamped a foot down. "It's solid."

Willis followed him out. He reached over and touched a metal wall, staring up at the tower that soared above them. "If this stuff is real. I got to think it's the way we were meant to go."

Bones dashed ahead craning his neck to see everything. "I thought there would be flying..." He stopped and stared into the azure sky. "Holy crap, they've got flying cars."

Maddock followed his gaze. Flitting beneath the gossamer bridges, a squadron of bullet-shaped vehicles cruised overhead. "Don't you think it's strange we haven't seen any other signs of life?"

"Like the place has been abandoned," Willis said.

"Or maybe it's here to tell us something."

Willis looked upward. "You mean someone built this

whole thing inside the mountain? Just for us? Hell, I can't even see where we came in."

"Or we're imagining it, "Maddock said. "Just like we'd imagined the bottomless pit when we first got down here."

June shook her head. "But who would do something like that? And for the love of God, why?"

Bones said, "Lemurians. They've been messing with us the whole time."

Maddock said, "Don't forget the lost Okwanuchu tribe. I still don't get how they figure into this."

"You don't think they were…"

"Lemurians? What do you figure?"

June broke in. "You boys gave me the slip at the last bus stop. What lost tribe? Here?"

Willis said, "They've been talking crazy about Indians since I arrived."

"Well they can talk all they want," June said. "It's not getting us out of here. I'd like to hook a ride on one of those flying cars and blow this *Toontown*."

Bones peeked into an empty doorway. "I'm not sure I want to leave. I'll bet there's a tall Lemurian girl around here just hoping I'll teach her some Native American mating customs."

"Be good and sure you know what you're wishing for," Willis said. "You just might get it."

Maddock explored further down the deserted street. The perspective continued to change with every step. Roads and walkways that seemed to branch off in all directions shifted as he approached, suddenly further down the street or far behind him. He called back, "Willis, come here and look at this."

His friend approached, then stopped and turned. Walking back, he turned again. "You can't get there from here."

"It seems there's only one path through this place. The rest is just a bunch of distractions."

Willis looked back again. "So, where did June and Bones get to?"

Maddock spun and retraced his steps. Doorways and side streets flicked by, but no sign of the two. Willis hustled up behind. "They were right with me a moment ago."

"Yeah, I heard Bones going on about Lemurian women. What the heck, you don't think he found one do you?"

"With June in tow?" Willis said. "Not likely, unless she hopped into one of those flying cars…"

"…like she said she wanted." Maddock finished his thought.

Willis shuddered and looked around. "Stay close, man. I don't want to be alone in this freak show. Not again. And don't go wishing for nothing."

"Not even wish we could find them?"

"No way. It's like that story with the monkey's paw. Wish for something and it bites you in the ass. Just makes things more complicated, messes them up."

Maddock stood where he'd last seen Bones and June. A doorway opened off to his right. He climbed a steep stairway and tried the door. Solid, like part of the building, it didn't even rattle. Willis waited on the street looking more and more nervous. When Maddock returned, he said, "Been two of those flying cars go by. Just kind of cruising like taxis. Want to try one?"

"Hell no! Look, Bones wouldn't have left us here, not on purpose. And June, she's smarter than that. They were tricked by this place. We start playing by its rules and we've lost already." Maddock watched another of the strange vehicles float by. Streamlined, vaguely automobile shaped, it didn't seem to have windows or other distinct features. "This whole place is like a Hollywood set. I'd sure like to…"

He stopped himself. "That is, I think we *need to* look behind the scenes."

"You know one of my favorite books?" Willis said. "'Wizard of Oz.' Yeah, my Gram used to read it to me when I was a little snot. Bet she read it a hundred times."

"Don't go wishing for something we're both going to regret."

"No that's not the point. In the book, see, they got these green glasses they had to wear in the Emerald City. Guess what everything looked like without the glasses?"

"I get it. But we're still screwed unless you know how to take our glasses off." Maddock craned his neck back and followed a line of building ornaments up to about the fifth floor where they ended in a balcony. "I'll bet I could climb that."

Willis frowned. "Then what?"

"There's got to be an entrance up there, something that would get us behind this façade."

"You could fall and bust your ass for nothing too."

"Looks easy to me. Bet I could do it with my eyes closed."

Willis scuffed one foot against the ground and kicked a building. "Seems real doesn't it? Eyes closed we wouldn't see the illusion. How long do you think we could walk down this street with our eyes closed?"

Maddock looked up at the balcony again. "You think if I closed my eyes and climbed that, I'd find myself hanging from bare rock?"

"What do you think?"

Maddock didn't answer. Instead, he threw his shirt on the ground, stood on it, and tore off a sleeve. Rebuttoning his one-armed shirt he said, "Blindfold me. I'll lead, you follow. Just don't let us get separated."

Willis muttered something about things getting

awkward. He tied the torn sleeve around his friend's eyes. Maddock tested the blindfold when he'd finished, tugging it a little lower until he could see nothing in any direction. "I'm going to start moving around. Just stay with me and sound off if you think you can't follow."

"You're going to step off a cliff, man."

"I guess we'll find out." Maddock started walking in what he hoped was a spiral path. He brushed into a wall and turned slightly left, continuing until his foot hit a curb and he stumbled forward. Catching himself, he took a few more steps before bumping into another wall. He followed it with his right hand until he could go no farther, then turned left again.

Another dozen steps, he stepped diagonally off a curb and walked for a few minutes until Willis said, "Hey man, you're not…"

"Don't tell me what you see Willis. Just let me find it by touch."

"No, stop. You don't get it—I can't see you anymore."

Maddock halted mid stride. "Where are you?"

"Right here behind you, on the other side of that wall you just walked through."

"It's an illusion, Willis. Close your eyes and follow."

Maddock waited in the darkness. He felt Willis' touch on his shoulder. "Oh, you've got to see this, buddy."

"No, you be the eyes. What do you see?"

"It looks like one of those old-style animated cartoons. There's cows in dresses and dogs walking around like people and they all got these rubbery arms and legs."

"Okay find Bones and June."

"I don't see Bones but June's here. She's riding some sort of merry-go-round thing."

Maddock reached up, and with some effort tore the other sleeve from his shirt. "You've got to catch her and blindfold her. Go."

He heard Willis walk off, but beyond that, only silence. A moment later June started cursing. Willis shouted something. Scuffling and cursing followed, then once more, silence. Maddock took a knee, hoping the two would work something out without more fighting. He heard June first. "Maddock, you really here?"

He responded to the affirmative and heard Willis say, "She thought I was the boogey-man or something."

Closer now, June spoke. "I don't know what happened. This flying car thing pulls up and suddenly I'm inside zooming across the city like George Jetson, then wham, here I am in crazyville."

"Just like you wished for," Willis said.

June was silent for a moment, then Maddock heard her gasp. "I just remembered what Bones said."

Willis grunted. "Do you think we ought to let him finish?"

Maddock said, "I think we ought to get all of us the hell out of here as soon as possible. June is your blindfold on tight?"

"Aye captain. Good to go nowhere."

"Then lead on. Any direction is fine. Just go slow and be careful of your head. Willis, try to keep up."

Maddock put a hand on June's shoulder and let her shuffle her way around. Occasionally he heard Willis grunt in surprise, but otherwise they walked in silence. After stumbling about for what seemed like an hour, Willis said, "Oh, lordy June, whatever you do, don't take off that blindfold unless you want a permanent retina burn."

"That bad?"

"It's Bones with some kind of female... creature. She looks like she's half praying mantis."

Tempted to look, Maddock put his hands to his eyes.

He heard Willis say, "Let him go!"

Moments later Willis started yelling. Maddock yanked the cloth from his face and sprang to his aid. Bones lay on a couch, eyes closed and motionless while Willis wrestled with a green, seven-foot woman. All legs and teeth, she snapped at his face. Maddock slammed into her thorax and felt her nails tear at his back. Willis jumped up and caught her about the neck. Maddock tried to break free, but the more he fought, the tighter she clung.

Willis shouted, "Close your eyes. Don't look at the damn thing."

His eyes shut, Maddock jammed both arms between himself and the woman. Leveraging against her body, he pushed up on her chin. She growled and fought, hammering him with her fists. Maddock broke free and pushed back just far enough to land a haymaker on her solar plexus. She went limp, slumped, and fell at his feet. Only then did he look.

No woman. They'd been fighting with Bones himself. He groaned and shook his head.

"Man, you guys sure know how to ruin a party."

"That thing was going to bite your head off, homeboy. You better be thanking us." Willis looked around. "Damn what were you doing? On second thought, I really don't want to know, okay?"

June called out, "Is he decent?"

Maddock walked back and loosened her blindfold. "He's as ugly as ever. Come join us, but please don't ask what he was doing."

Willis had helped Bones stand. "You get it now? This place is messing with us."

June looked around at the empty space, "You mean I didn't ride in a flying car?"

"Not unless it dropped you off fifty feet from where you

got on," Willis said. "We've been walking in circles since y'all went Crazy Eddy on us."

While they'd been talking, the light dimmed, the background faded. Before their eyes, what had appeared to be an upholstered couch, dissolved into a fallen pile of earth. "Time to get out of here," Maddock said. "We've seen the future and it doesn't work."

"We're going to need some lights," Willis said. "I've got to get my Moogly going again."

Bones shook his head. "Had my Moogly going real good 'till you showed up."

June said, "Well next time keep that Moogly in your pocket where it belongs, big guy."

"We've broken through something, passed a test maybe," Maddock said. "I don't know what's happening, but it's getting dark."

Willis started out, long silent strides. He said nothing as he led them off into the shadows. As the azure twilight dimmed to midnight black, Maddock noticed a tiny blue light that bounced along ahead of them. From behind, he heard Bones softly reassuring June. "I feel safe," he said, "and here, I think what you feel counts for more than what you see."

Maddock had similar thoughts. "This must be what our sweat lodge dreams meant. We are in the home of Marumda, the lodge beneath the mountain. I... I somehow feel I know this place. Bones, do you still have your obsidian knife?"

"Not about to give this one up, *Marumda*."

"Good, because I suddenly feel I'll need that bow and white arrow."

"Great, a magic bow and arrow," June said. "Can things get much weirder?"

Maddock glanced back at Bones' shadowy form. They

both spoke in unison. "Oh, yeah,"

As they walked, it never became fully dark. Beneath their feet, the path seemed unusually smooth for the floor of a cave. Maddock passed tall figures that lurked in the gloom like rows of grotesque statues. Tiny creatures flicked about their feet. He knew better than to investigate. Willis forged on in silence.

Like walkers in a dream, the four glided through the darkness, never stumbling or encountering a single physical obstacle. Maddock thought he could see daylight glowing in a faint blue line over their heads. Soon, the passing columns resolved themselves into tree trunks and he felt twigs and leaf litter crunch beneath his boots.

Willis halted. Beneath the drooping eaves of a dense forest, they stood on a rock promontory. He pointed at the stark gray building in the valley below.

"It all comes back to this stinking place."

34

Sally watched as Carl emerged first from the blazing maintenance building. He burst through the entrance, a military M4 carbine in his hands. Sally had backed away from the growing inferno, but when Carl saw her, he knelt and raised the weapon to his shoulder.

The diesel fuel drum exploded in flames knocking Sally flat on her face. Glancing up, she saw Carl groping for his carbine and struggling to stand. Before he could regain his feet, she jumped up and sprinted to the steel shell of the flattened water tank. A three-round burst kicked gravel at her feet as Sally dove beneath the crumpled plates.

Another burst rattled off the steel. She crawled farther in from the edge. Above, her ancient pistol meant nothing against the M4, but here among the shallow pools, and lodged beneath the rumpled plates, she stood a chance. Waiting for Carl to make his move, Sally heard shouts from the pumping crew. She had hoped that Uzi's men would have responded earlier to the building fire, but it took the explosion and gunshots to get their attention.

Lying flat beneath the steel plates, her face inches above a pool of water, she let the men go running by. Carl had likely seen the odds and retreated. Sally just hoped they were all far enough from the tanker. Moments later, she got her answer. The air vibrated with the whine of turbines and the thud of rotating blades. A wicked looking helicopter, all guns and missiles, swooped in and opened fire on the operation. Peering from beneath the steel plates, she saw the injector pump crumble under the onslaught, and the tanker explode in a spray of viscous brown liquid. *So much for Junior's precious culture.*

The attack ended as quickly as it began. Sally crawled out and watched the helicopter howl off into the sky. Little was left of Pym's army beyond a scattering of smoking corpses and body parts. The maintenance building still burned, the fire likely fed by solvents and fuel cans stored inside. Movement in the adjacent woodlot caught Sally's eye. A familiar figure picked her way between the trees, Giselle.

Taking care to keep a screen of branches and trunks between her and her quarry, Sally circled the concrete tank foundation and followed the woman at a discrete distance. She seemed to have some objective in mind. Moments later, Sally spotted it, a stake-truck with a canvas top.

Giselle had stopped at the edge of the trees. Sally drew closer to see what she was doing. Mobile phone in hand, the woman spoke in low tones to someone. *Not Junior, Uzi would have kept him incommunicado.* Sally watched her body language, deferential, almost bowing with every word. Giselle answered to a different master, one she clearly feared more than Junior, more than Uzi, more than the flying death machine that had just ended the lives of so many of Pym's acolytes.

Sally followed when Giselle ended her call and ran for the truck. Pausing behind the last tree, she watched the woman take one final look around before climbing into the cab. As the truck rolled off, Sally sprinted up and boosted herself into the back. Landing hard on the steel bed, she felt every contusion and bruise she'd taken since running from June's laboratory the day before.

The truck accelerated, slid through the first curve, then fish-tailed down a straight stretch of gravel road. Sally hung on to stanchion as they rattled over the corduroy surface. She didn't dare raise her head more than a few inches. Behind them, spiraling clouds of dust blotted out the landscape. A few brief glimpses of the sun indicated that they were headed north, but little else.

When they turned left onto a narrow, winding road, Sally recognized the route. She and June had descended the same way the night before. Sally had little time to consider the implications. The truck rolled to a stop, muted conversation. She flattened herself to one side of the covered interior. Footsteps followed, someone walked to the back but barely glanced inside.

After a moment, they rolled through an open gate, up a drive, and into the shadowy confines of Laboratory Nine. The truck maneuvered down the shadowy aisle between stacked boxes and parked vehicles Giselle finally backed it into a parking bay near the far end of the building. When they jerked to a stop, Sally heard footsteps approach. Just beyond her line of vision, a man spoke. "You can come out now, Ms. Smith."

In the dimly lit interior, all she could see was faded paint on a concrete wall. Again, the voice. "Just leave your gun in the back and come out where we can see you."

She slid her battered revolver into one corner before dropping off the tailgate onto a concrete floor. Still, she saw no one. "Around to your right, please. Slowly."

Sally complied, driven more by curiosity than fear. Standing next to the rear wheels, Dr. Goertzner stood with his hands in his pockets. "That's better, Ms. Smith. I am so delighted to see you again."

"The feeling is hardly mutual, Doctor. But you knew that."

"I don't care what you feel, Ms. Smith. I'm just wondering why you have returned to me so willingly."

"It's not you I've come for, it's your boss."

Sally felt a sharp jab just below her left shoulder blade. "I wondered where you had slithered off to, Giselle.

Reporting to Senior now are we?"

"I don't answer to either of the Pyms. I thought a smart girl like you would have figured that out."

"You can put the knife away, dear. Our guest is unlikely to cause trouble." Goertzner turned his attention back to Sally. "Would you like to go somewhere more comfortable, Ms. Smith?"

Sally shook her head. "Back to your lab table? No thanks."

"I was thinking of a chair in my office. We need to talk."

"Junior said the same thing. All I got out of that deal was Miss Manners here."

"We may have more interesting things to discuss. Things that don't involve either Junior or Senior Mr. Pym."

Sally didn't figure it was an invitation and knew she was no match for either one of them. She dodged around an old tanker truck and followed Goertzner through the lower level. Like a cross between a warehouse and a parking garage, it housed a variety of vehicles along with pallets stacked with crates and boxes. *Military gear, Pym's armory*, Sally thought.

Goertzner didn't head toward the elevator or the stairway. Instead, he led them through the shadows behind a row of parked SUVs. About midway to the entrance door he stopped at a small motorhome and beckoned them to enter. "This is your office?" Sally said.

"Let's call it my field office," he replied. "Mr. Pym likes to think he's my boss. He planted cameras all over the building. Here we can talk in private."

The interior held little more than a small table and a few chairs. Sally perched on a bench facing the entrance, while Goertzner found a seat near the front. Giselle dragged her chair over and placed it against the door. *Bad move, Bambi.* Sally relaxed and tried to look bored.

Goertzner relaxed as well and lit a cigarette. "You don't mind, do you?"

"I've heard those things will kill you, but I'm not sure I want to stick around long enough to watch."

He took the cigarette from his mouth and examined it for a moment. "You know, I don't think it will. Not anymore. Can you imagine, Ms. Smith, a world where cigarettes and sweetened drinks, junk food and even alcohol were just pleasures to be enjoyed?"

"You're almost as bad as Junior. Come to the point, Doctor."

"Very well, we have run the labs on your blood and tissue samples and found some remarkable things. One is, you are not only immune to the symbiote, you thrive on it. The infusion we gave you only made you stronger. Even more remarkable are your blood counts. Your lymphocytes are off the scale, your white cell count is way up, and we even found cancer antigens. Does that mean anything to you?"

"I'm dying, but then, I'm not."

"Precisely. In fact, a little while ago you ran down a truck and vaulted into the back. Not bad for a woman about to die."

"I still don't see the point."

"The point is, I have cultured your blood serum and injected it into myself. I can feel it growing, making me stronger." Goertzner clenched his right fist and admired his arm. "Your body is a factory that is pumping out the most remarkable medical discovery in history. My infusion has made you a living fountain of youth."

"Well my fountain is about to overflow, if you catch my drift. Did I see a lavatory in the back?"

Goertzner nodded and twitched his head in that direction. Giselle made an impatient face but didn't move.

Sally stepped into the tiny bathroom and closed the thin composition door behind her. Liquid soap, one relatively clean towel, toilet paper and even a spare roll, she looked under the sink. Nothing but a flimsy plastic drainpipe, it passed through an oversized hole in the floor.

Sally flushed the toilet at the same time she kicked the drain loose beneath the sink. Running some water, she noted that most of it trickled out over the vehicle's holding tank and poured onto the pavement below. She let the faucet run and slipped smiling back to join Dr. Goertzner. "That's much better. Now, where were we?"

Giselle grinned, showing a line of straight white teeth. "This is where we explain that you are about to become a living blood bank, little girl."

"And I'm sure you'd appreciate my cooperation but that gig just doesn't fit my busy social agenda."

Goertzner laid a small box flat on the table. "My Giselle is not very tactful. She prefers a more physical approach to persuasion."

Sally leaned forward slightly, eyes still on Giselle. The doctor continued. "Let me put things in a different light." He opened the box and took out a hypodermic syringe along with a small vial. "You will soon experience symptoms of your malady. I've seen them. It's not pleasant. As an alternative, I propose this simple injection. You will go to sleep; consider it an induced coma. Your body will remain alive, a boon to science."

"I'll be a vegetable, a rubber tree just bleeding sap for you and Mr. Pym."

"Hmm… perhaps not for the Pyms. No, he's bolloxed things up pretty good here. I think we'll just keep this our little secret. What say, Giselle?"

"I say you're wasting time. Do her, and let's get out of here."

"Patience, my dear. Sally, what's your decision? Yes, and you can hold out your arm. No, and I'll have to let Giselle help out."

"Just answer me one question, doctor. How's that going to work for you when this whole place gets blown to vapor?"

"We simply won't be here. Mr. Pym—senior that is—still has one aircraft at his landing field. Somehow, your boys have not yet managed to destroy it."

Sally heard footsteps and low voices outside. Someone banged on the motor home window. "Hey, your water tank's leaking."

The door swung open and Giselle started up. The woman barely had her feet under her when Sally's shoulder caught her in the ribs and barreled her through the doorway. Together, they mowed down whoever had been standing there, flew a short distance, and landed on the concrete floor. Sally rolled as they struck, but Giselle hit the floor on her back.

Running, ducking between parked trucks and stacked boxes, Sally didn't look behind her. She'd seen a door back there. Whatever lay beyond it had to be better than the needle. She heard footsteps in pursuit and slipped between the wall and a large van. Two vehicles over, her old revolver should still be in the truck bed where she'd left it.

She peeked out, *no one in sight*. Sally slid under the van. Nothing moved. She belly-crawled to the truck and stopped in the shadows next to the cold cement wall. The covered truck bed looked just as it had when she first crawled out. Six feet away, six feet, she would grab the gun and make a run for the back door. Three steps, then Sally froze.

"Were you looking for this?" Giselle brandished the revolver, hammer back, finger on the trigger. "I so want to find out if still works."

Goertzner stepped up behind the woman. He held up a

syringe filled with yellow liquid. Sally watched a bubble form at the tip, then burst and run down the needle. "Aren't you ready to do this the easy way now?"

Sally kept her eyes fixed on Giselle. "Shoot me." She walked nearer. "Come on, put me out of my misery."

As Sally approached, the woman shook her head. "Don't, don't."

Face to face now, she stood, her chest against the muzzle. Giselle glanced back at the doctor. In that moment of distraction, Sally slapped her hand across the frame of the revolver. The hammer fell. Its firing pin sank into the meat of her palm. Despite the pain, she pushed the weapon to one side. Giselle tried to pull away, but Sally clung to her like an enraged spider monkey. Goertzner stepped up with his needle. He jammed it into her shirtsleeve, but in the struggle, the tip passed through her skin and emerged from the other side.

Giselle hooked a leg behind Sally and threw her on her back. The old revolver skittered free and slid beneath the truck. Giselle pinned her to the pavement. "Say goodnight, my sweet."

Goertzner moved in. The needle plunged toward her. Sally arched upward and bit off a piece of Giselle's left ear. The woman gasped and twisted as the needle intended for Sally plunged into the back of her neck. Sally reached around and jammed the plunger down.

When Goertzner realized what had happened, he cursed and tore Giselle away. Too late for the woman, her shrieks of pain devolved into burbling cries of terror and confusion. The doctor laid her on the pavement and grabbed for Sally. Under the truck, hand out, reaching, groping, she struggled to crawl away. Goertzner caught her by the leg and dragged her out, kicking and thrashing.

Moments later, he understood his mistake. Sally held

the old Smith and Wesson in one bloody hand while she pushed herself upright with the other. From the corner of her eye, she saw movement. Carl stepped into view, an M4 carbine at his shoulder. Sally shifted her aim and squeezed the trigger. The shot echoed throughout the lower level. Carl spun backwards and dropped. She struggled to her knees and looked for Goertzner, but he had jumped away and fled.

Shouts from the entrance, the slap of feet on pavement, guards, mercenaries, Sally had no idea who was coming. She rounded the back of the last vehicle and bounded over a stack of tires. Shots pocked the concrete wall behind her. Sally ran for the back door.

As she reached for the knob, she was struck by a sudden cascade of visions—a burst of towering buildings, flying bridges and azure blue sky. And Willis. Willis, Bonebrake, Maddock and June, they filled her consciousness once more.

As bullets sizzled off the pavement and smacked into the concrete wall above, Sally stood in frozen amazement. *The door, something about the door*? Just then it flew open. A figure all in black caught her by the arms and pinned her to the floor.

35

Flat on her back, Sally twisted and struggled with the black-clad figure holding her against the floor. Grunting, he bent a knee across her hips, pinned her arms at the elbows, and said, "For God's sake woman, stay down."

Six more men swarmed through the door and knelt on either side. Sally heard the shriek of automatic weapons. Hot shell casings peppered her face and rattled off the floor. The return fire chewed pits in the floor and ceiling, spraying fragments of concrete and shredded bullets.

A brief cry of pain and the man holding her collapsed, his face a jagged mass of blood and bone. Still clutching her battered revolver, Sally rolled to her right and took cover behind a stack of truck tires. She heard shots fired outside but couldn't tell where they came from. Sally weighed her chances of escaping through the open doorway. Bullets rattled off the steel frame and punched little round holes in the door itself. She crawled further back into the shadows.

The firing stopped for an instant. Sally felt the thump of a small detonation behind her. A metal sphere glanced off the floor, smashed the windshield of a parked truck, and bounced away before exploding at the other end of the warehouse. Two more thumps, Sally ducked. She felt rather than heard the grenades explode.

More fighters poured in through the open doorway. Return fire came moments later, dropping two of the black-clad men. Their response was a wave of automatic weapons fire. *Not sure who's winning this one, not sure I want to find out.* Sally crawled back from the doorway.

A gap, about ten yards of open pavement lay between her and a row of parked vehicles. The space was partially filled by an aging fuel truck. Sally hugged the shadows and flitted across, diving beneath the truck. She lay on the cold concrete, heart pounding while the mad cacophony of battle filled the space around her.

Curiosity drove her to give the tanker a second look. Old, square military cab painted dark green, the thing didn't look like it moved too often. It had a new looking hose and nozzle. Sally guessed that it was their fuel depot. A sprinkling of silver dents decorated the exposed side, products of the firefight. She smelled it before she saw the fuel weeping from several of the dents. *Why in hell would anyone park that much fuel inside a building?*

Sally crawled over for a closer look. A twelve-inch gap stood between the tank and the far wall. She peered back into the shadows but saw little or nothing. *Probably going to get shot to ribbons or blown to hell anyway.* She turned sideways and squeezed into the space. The bomb had been planted about five feet back. Bolted to the tank itself, the device was simple, a small black electronics box attached to a single brick of explosives by a twisted pair of wires.

She'd seen it in plenty of movies, the hero sweats, *red wire or black wire?* Sally hated that old cliché. *They never think of the obvious.* She pinched the copper blasting cap between her fingernails and slid it out of the brick. *Cue dramatic music; everyone goes home and gets laid.*

By the time she'd scuttled from behind the tank, what had started as a serious skirmish now sounded like a full-scale war. More of the armed commandos had poured in through the back. Sally had no doubt that she finally witnessed Uzi's phantom army in action.

The opposition had also strengthened its forces. Nothing like the languid guards and disorganized mercenaries she'd seen earlier, these fighters moved with precision and discipline. Sally hugged the shadows along the wall wondering which way to run. The back door still seemed her best bet, but it was taking some brutal fire. Sizing up the stairwell off to her left, she felt a tap on her shoulder. "Hello, Sally Smith."

Sally spun, revolver in hand. Uzi poked a finger in the muzzle and said, "Bang."

"Holy *crap*, Uzi. What the bloody hell is going on?"

"Step back here a little. They won't aim too close to the fuel truck."

"Yeah, well take a gander behind you, Rambo."

Uzi eyed the pit marks, then leaned into the darkness between the tank and the wall. "Ohhh—nasty."

"I pulled the detonator… you can thank me later."

"Now this does complicate things. Whoever would plant a bomb there, do you suppose? Not our Mr. Pym, surely."

Both flattened against the wall as a line of machine gun fire stitched along the near column showering them in broken concrete.

"Try Goertzner," Sally said. "He and little miss Giselle were playing a side quest that doesn't include either of the Pymsters."

"You say *were*? What *have* you done Ms. Smith?"

"Bambi is on the other side suffering from a bad case of brain death. It's a long story."

"And our good doctor?"

"Scrammed before your guys showed up. They *are* your guys, right?"

"Oh, quite. In the flesh, as it were. What do you think?"

A rocket propelled grenade tore through the warehouse and exploded into the back wall, blasting a fist-size hole in the concrete and throwing fragments around like shrapnel.

"Outmatched, I've been watching your opposition.

Would you consider a strategic retreat?"

"Too late for that, I'm afraid. We have a perimeter set up outside, but it's shrinking fast. I hate to think what it looks like after that grenade hit."

"So we all get bottled up in here and somebody blows the fuel truck, cute."

"Not those guys. They want to live, just like we do."

"Well not Dr. Gee either, he's still counting on his magic elixir—and me, if he can get me."

"*Huzzah*, then we have a plan. Follow me, darling, and do be careful."

Uzi spoke a few words aside. Sally assumed he was talking with his men. She didn't see anything that resembled a plan in the surrounding chaos. A few minutes later, Uzi grabbed her by the elbow and pushed her to the floor. The din of battle was replaced by an unearthly screech, like chainsaws cutting sheet metal. "Squad automatic weapons," Uzi shouted in her ear. "SAWs, four of them."

An instant later, the armory fell silent. Uzi dragged her to her feet. "The stairs now, go, go, go!"

Sally felt insane, dashing across what moments before, had been a deadly no-man's land. Six others ran with them, shooting as they went. Just short of the stairwell, they flattened against the wall. Once more, the SAWs opened up. Uzi's point man pitched a grenade around the corner and opened fire on anyone on the stairs.

Two others followed, exchanging shots with someone on the landing above. Uzi pointed to the stairwell.

"Let's not dawdle. You have work to do."

Sally tried to stay beneath the steps as a hail of bullets rattled down at them. One of Uzi's men fell to the concrete floor. Two others dragged him to a corner while the remainder provided covering fire. They made it to the first landing before Sally caught a glimpse of their opposition. "Russian mercenaries," she said.

"Oh, but let's hope they don't make up in volume what they lack in diligence."

"Just get this over with, Uzi. I've got other business to attend, if I live that long."

Four of their men stormed up the stairwell and through the doorway that opened into the next level. Uzi stopped and gave Sally a strange look. "So, you know?"

The SAWs sounded much closer, echoing up the stairwell. Sally glanced down at the fallen soldier below. Uzi put a hand on her shoulder. "They'll form a hard line right below us and die before they let anyone through. So, you've known all along?"

"I know a lot of things, Uzi. Let's just get this done or none of it will matter."

One of Uzi's soldiers gave what she took for an all clear sign. Sally looked up at the landing above, no sign of resistance. She felt better with two armed and armored men leading and two others watching their rear. Uzi seemed relaxed, like he knew what would come next. Sally followed him up the steps. "What became of your new best friend?"

"Junior? He has a special job to do, just like you do, petal."

"His bucket o' crud got blown to slimy gobbets. I can still smell the stink."

"That was a ploy. Wonderful if it had worked—but doomed from the beginning."

"You have a Plan B…"

"Plan A, in fact. But mind you, we've reached the third floor and things might get a little dodgy from here. We need to have a few words with your Dr. Goertzner."

"I've got four shots left."

"Nope, nopers… we talk, that's all."

"You know for sure he's here?"

"His lab is here. From what you've said, I think he'll be packing up to bail out."

Uzi followed his point man down a wide empty hallway lined with doors. To Sally, it looked horribly familiar. Even on the third floor, the battle below thundered and echoed off the walls. She cast a doubtful glance into a room with two empty lab tables, their restraint straps and straitjackets still heaped on the floor. "So if I can't shoot him," she whispered, "what am I here for?"

"Bait. Now please be quiet."

A single shot. Sally jumped and hugged one wall. Uzi called out, "We're here to talk, Doctor."

Two more shots smacked into the linoleum floor and whined down the hall. Goertzner duck his head out and pulled back quickly. "I'll blow this whole place to hell if you don't all get back."

"You don't have to do that Doctor. I have Ms. Smith here with me. We want to make a deal."

Sally shook Uzi by the arm and mouthed, "*What kind of deal?*"

The man ignored her and said, "We'll put our weapons down and come to you."

"Your men stay there."

"Yes."

"You and the girl, you leave your weapons on the floor—her too."

"Like hell I will," Sally shouted

"We don't have time for this," Uzi said. "Just do it, Sally."

She glared at Uzi fingering the ancient revolver. "Do you trust him?"

"Do you trust me?"

It seemed like such a betrayal of Bonebrake. He had

given her the weapon in the first place and taught her how to stand tough in a fight. "Not really, but I've got no choice, do I?"

She laid her gun on the floor. Without looking back, Sally walked through the open laboratory door. "Here I am, you bucket of vomit."

36

"I don't know about you, but I'm getting sick of this place." Willis sat on a rocky outcropping and gazed down the hill at Laboratory Nine.

Bones crouched at his side. "Gimme enough C-4 and I'll do a little remodeling for you."

"Yeah, but we're facing a platoon of hard core mercs this time," Maddock said. "Not Pym's usual gang of thugs, but real fighters." He could see them patrolling the perimeter in ordered ranks. "Even if we had enough explosives, we could never get it near the building."

Willis smacked Bones on the back of the head. "If Bones here hadn't wrecked our helicopter, we coulda flown right up their butts before they knew it."

"Damn thing was out of gas. Besides, we couldn't get past those Apaches, not even with June at the stick."

Bones had been fidgeting the whole time. Maddock could read his mind, even without the Ma'óghe enhancements. The big Cherokee was getting psyched up to go storm the building, single handed if necessary. Willis too. The man turned and gave him a cold glower. "What are we going to do, boss?"

Maddock started improvising—sometimes it was the best way. "They won't find us back there on the hillside and that's going to make a few people nervous. We've already hurt them; we got Pym's attention. I don't know where those Apaches came from, but you can bet he's mustering a small army as we speak."

Bones jumped up. "Great. We go down there and stomp some butt right now before they show up."

"No." Maddock hadn't meant to speak so loudly. "No,

we use their fears to our advantage. We pull back. They're going to get antsy when nothing happens. They're going to be all binoculars staring out into the brush. Maybe they'll send patrols. I'll bet they've got thermal imaging on those Apaches. They'll put them up and send guys charging after anything that breathes."

"And while they're out doing all that stuff, we go full frontal assault," Willis said. "I'm on board."

"Yeah, but let's be sneaky about it." June said. "If we're in a shooting war, I want to be on the winning team. That guy Machiavelli once said, 'The wise general chooses his battlefield.' We need to be really choosy about ours."

"General, yeah, one of them would be good," Bones said, "but what we really need is Morgaine's goblin army."

Maddock nodded. "That's exactly what we need. Up for a little more spelunking, General Bones?"

Simultaneously, he felt the light switch in Bones' head flip on, June's anxiety level crank up two notches, and Willis' candle go completely dark. "What the crap do you mean by that?"

"Our friend Morgaine, hippy, new ager, whatever… she showed us a back entrance to Pym's fortress. It's how Bones and I got in this morning."

"Geez, was that just this morning?" Willis said. "I'm ass-whupped enough for a whole week."

"I got a feeling we're going to take a bit more whupping before this is over." Bones said.

June pulled further behind the rock. "Come on, boys, this goose ain't about to screw itself. Which way to the secret entrance?"

Maddock led them back into the trees, angling around the mountainside. "It's about two miles from here. I think I can find it again."

They stayed beneath the scrub oak and pine canopy

until the forest thinned and the four found themselves crossing an open field. Maddock led them along the grassy hillside toward a cluster of trees and rocks. "This area was logged off years ago. There should be a lumber camp down in that valley. The entrance is in a grove of trees up here on the hillside."

Bones walked just behind him. "I'd say we're a little too far south, but it's hard to tell."

Willis said, "Do you two cowboys have another idea if we don't happen to find this secret cave?"

"He's the cowboy—I'm the Indian. Don't ever forget that."

"I should have stayed home today," June said.

"Yeah, you could have ironed shirts and baked cookies," Bones said. "I can just picture you doing that." He stopped a moment. "Look up there on the hillside. That's got to be it."

Maddock followed his gaze. A tangle of old tree roots rose from a small rock outcropping. "Could be, let's check it out."

Ten minutes later, even Bones agreed that it was a bust. "Too much tree and not enough rock to be the place."

"Don't give up yet," Maddock said. He gestured off to the north. "I can see two or three more places just like this, not a half mile away."

Ten minutes later, Maddock led the others up a steep hillside. They approached a dense clump of trees. It looked familiar, but nothing stood out. June came puffing in their wake. "We could go thrashing around out here all day and not find the entrance."

Maddock halted in his tracks. Coming up fast in the valley below, he heard the howl of an Apache helicopter. "Quiet everyone—and get down."

Willis spun around. "Crap, they're right on our tail. I'll

bet they've got the thermal imaging units cranked up to maximum range."

As he spoke, a shower of sparks flashed from the sky and they heard the whine of a minigun chewing up ammo. Bones lay on his belly looking down the valley. "They're just fragging anything that blips on their screen."

"Bye-bye Bambi," June said.

Maddock crawled up among the trees. "Come on, at least get under cover."

June and Bones joined him, as a second Apache swung into view. Willis came crawling up moments later. "How the heck did they follow us here?"

"I don't think they did," Maddock said. "Last night, we saw Pym's army get their asses kicked. He probably thinks we've got a base or something at the old lumber camp."

Willis kept watching the Apaches. "Asses kicked by who?"

"The goblins, of course." Bones said.

Maddock shook his head. "If Uzi is here, it could only have been his commandos. You saw them, automatic weapons, shoulder-launched missiles. It was a slaughter."

June pursed her lips. "Payback is coming, and we get to be the bitch."

"Just stay low," Maddock said, "and keep to the cover. The rocks are warm. Maybe they'll mask our heat signature."

The four-bladed rotors sang almost in unison as the two Apaches swung north along the valley and began climbing the hillside. Two more bursts, Maddock saw a spray of dirt and something else burst from the ground. June said, "The bastards are heading right for us."

Maddock felt the thud of approaching blades. "There's got to be something in here with us," he shouted, "Something…

Even above the screaming turbine noise, a mad chittering whisper filled the air. In an instant the sky was blotted out as ten million bats streamed from an unseen cavern just behind them. The chopper pilot cut loose with a burst from his minigun before cranking the throttle and drawing back on both cyclic and collective. The engines shrieked as the rotors dug in, dragging the machine away from the blanket of flying bats.

Maddock heard it first. The engines, clogged with thousands of tiny bodies, fell silent. Pitched backward as it was— the gunship had no hope of recovery.

"This way, go, go, go." Maddock climbed higher among the rocks. Like a wind of darkness, the streaming cloud of bats led him to a crevice in the cliff face. The tiny wings battering his head, he dove inside and prayed that his companions followed. Moments later, a brilliant flash and jarring concussion shook the mountainside.

A chaos of flying debris and flaming helicopter fragments filled the air. Maddock kept his face down and his hands over his head. Someone slammed into his back and rolled away. Maddock tried to crawl farther, but his legs were pinned. He heard a string of secondary detonations as munitions in the burning gunship burst from the heat.

It seemed an eternity before the flashes and explosions settled into the crackling roar of burning timber. Someone touched him on the back and Maddock heard Willis say, "Hold on skipper, I'll get you out of here."

A weight shifted on the back of his legs. He tried to wriggle out, but the pressure on his knees kept him pinned to the ground. Willis grasped his wrists. "Come on, man, you got to move."

With the extra pull, He managed to drag one leg free and push himself forward. A grunt, and Maddock lurched farther into the crevice. The flickering light outside painted the cavern interior in shades of yellow and orange. Willis' face loomed into view, a lurid mask against the dark interior.

"You going to live, man?"

"Yeah, I'm good." Maddock tried bending his knees. They both seemed to work. "Where's June?"

"Out cold. Got blown halfway to hell when that chopper busted up. Bones is looking after her now. What is this place anyway?"

"Morgaine, queen of the fairies, she lives here. I just hope she wasn't outside when the *terminators* arrived."

"Whacked that one guy big time, dude. Teach them bastards to mess with us."

"I don't know anymore if that was us, Morgaine, the Ma'óghe, or the Lemurians but you know, those bats were flying hours before they should have. Someone sent them or we were just plain lucky."

"Yeah real lucky, except for the fact that we're gonna be all hair, teeth and eyeballs when this place blows."

Maddock heard groans and voices in the darkness behind him. He crawled across a well-swept dirt floor to find June on her side shaking and retching. Bones knelt next to her, wiping her mouth with the remains of his shirt. "She took a bad crack on the head. Flew clean over all of us and hit the wall on the other side."

In the flickering orange light Maddock searched out two of Morgaine's little oil lamps and a plastic lighter. He returned to June's side and held the light up inspect her scalp. A deep laceration just above her right temple bled down the side of her face. "We need to get a bandage on this."

"I checked her pulse," Bones said. "Seems okay." He peeled her eyelids back. "Good pupil response. Just give her a few minutes."

June reacted by coughing and twitching her legs. She opened her eyes but didn't say anything. Maddock pulled the lamp away and said, "Go easy, lady. You just took a nasty bump to the noggin."

Willis had been exploring the cave. He returned with the other lamp. "There's a serious draft coming up from somewhere back there. Probably all that keeps us from getting baked like a pizza."

Maddock inspected the entrance. Two large tree trunks lay crossed in front of the crevice, likely one of them had pinned his legs earlier. Outside, the flames and smoke presented a vision of hellish devastation. Willis joined him. "Dang, I'm not real anxious to go out that way."

"We won't have to. This is our back door."

Bones called from the darkened interior. "We need a hand here."

Maddock found June sitting up, holding a crumpled rag against her head. "You boys are bit rough on equipment, you know. This latest caper just cost someone two pilots and a thirty-five-million-dollar chopper."

"Hey, it's those guys that went all *Apocalypse Now* on us," Willis said. "Remember, I just came along for the mac 'n cheese and a little beer."

June tried to stand. Maddock and Bones helped her to her feet. "Lord, mac 'n cheese," she said, "your Sally sure knocked that one out of the park."

She swayed, holding her head. Maddock checked the wound on her temple. "You're going to need a few stitches up there. Okay on your feet?"

"Beside the momma of all headaches, I think I'm good. Put a Band-Aid on it and let's get out of here."

Bones tore some strips of cloth and rigged a makeshift bandage. "That's about the best I can do 'til we get you to town."

Maddock checked their lamps. Two in hand and one missing meant that Morgaine likely had the third. "I'll take point. I think I remember the way. Willis, you stay with June. Sound off if you've got a problem. Bones, use the other lamp and watch our six."

June said, "My six is more like a twelve, but you can watch it all you want, big guy."

"Yeah, give him something to dream about," Willis said. "Just don't get too carried away, buddy. I don't want to find any more bottomless pits."

Maddock had made his way to the back of the cavern and started down a narrow flight of steps leading to the lower level. A small cloud of bats still chittered in the darkness above. Occasionally one darted into the lamplight before disappearing in the gloom. He entered a large open chamber and stopped.

June braced herself against one wall and looked up. "What is this place?"

Maddock held his lamp high, trying to get an idea of the chamber's size. "Morgaine called it the Womb of Gaia."

Bones raised his eyebrows. "Oh, so that means we entered through Gaia's…"

"No." Willis held his hands over his ears. "That's plain rude and I don't want to hear it."

"Actually, the ancient Greeks and the pre-Vedic Indus Valley peoples had similar beliefs," Bones said.

"Where in the hell do you *get* this stuff, man?"

"I attended a lecture series. The instructor was this cute brunette, and you should have seen the textbook."

June waved her hands. "Sorry, sorry, if I didn't have a headache before, I've got one now."

Maddock pointed to the rising heap of bat guano in the center of the chamber. "I think I saw that pile of dung just grow a foot higher. We need to move out. Follow the wall.

There's another passage up here somewhere."

His words echoed off the ceiling and a thousand bat chirps replied from the darkness. Maddock worked his way to the right, climbing over fallen boulders and mounds of ancient bat droppings. Morgaine had led them straight to the passage, but now in the shadowy gloom, it didn't look familiar. Bones caught up. "Hang on a sec, something's not right."

Maddock felt his boots sinking into the soft guano floor. "I don't remember this much bat crap last time we were here."

"It's the earthquakes," June said. "Liquefaction, the stuff flows like mud when it's shaken."

Willis tilted his head back and said, "This day just keeps getting better and better."

"No help for it." Bones held his lamp along the base of the wall. "We're looking at a belly-crawl through a pile of crap to get out of here."

Bones searched back the way they'd come while Maddock pushed ahead, lamp held at knee-level. He hadn't made another twenty feet when he heard his friend's call. "It's back here, we passed it."

Bones stood, ankle-deep peering into a low opening. "It was a lot bigger last time."

June took one look and said, "I don't care how much it hurts, I'm gonna take that one crawling on my back."

"I've done worse," Maddock said. "It's a short passage that leads to another chamber. I'll go first and help you through."

He flopped on his belly, pushing the little oil lamp ahead of him. Beetles and centipedes swarmed away from the light, scurrying into the dark crevices on either side. Maddock wormed his way in. Almost halfway through, the guano had mounded up, nearly touching the ceiling. He had to dig the soft material away, pushing it to either side.

Once past the blockage, he slid down a short slope and arrived in the next chamber. Maddock straightened and called back, "I'm through."

June followed. Maddock helped her stand in the cramped space. She stared about in disbelief. Maddock heard Willis cursing and grunting as he wriggled past the narrowest part. On arrival, he spat out a mouthful of tiny legs and bits of shell. "I don't ever want to eat with this mouth again." He squeezed into a corner. "Just exactly where are we, Maddock?"

Bones rather oozed out of the passage, a Cherokee eel emerging from its den. "People, you have entered the Labyrinth of Eternity, according to Ms. Morgaine." He paused a moment and looked around. "Damn, I remember it being a whole lot bigger than this."

Maddock held up his lamp. "It seems the recent quakes have collapsed the ceiling and filled the chamber with rubble."

37

All Maddock could see of Bones were the soles of his boots wiggling in the crevice between two giant fallen boulders.

June held their other lamp. "You made *me* take off my clothes."

Willis watched from the shadows. "Don't give him any ideas."

Muffled grunting and scraping, the boots disappeared, to be replaced by Bone's grimy face. "It goes through. More room on this side. June will probably have to…"

"I get the picture, big guy."

"Willis and I will go first," Maddock said. "Take your time."

"Just take care of my hat and gun belt," June said.

Willis said, "I'll go next—smack loverboy around a little bit." With that, he wriggled headfirst into the crevice.

Maddock pushed June's gear in front as he wriggled into the tiny crevice. Amazed that Bones and Willis had fit their shoulders between the rocks, he found the only way to make it was by stretching one arm ahead and trailing the other at his side. He found a tiny ledge with his fingers and dragged himself inch-by-inch past the fallen boulder.

Pitch dark, Maddock could see nothing. "Where's the lamp?"

"Bones got it. Said he's gone scouting. Where's June?"

"On her way."

Maddock tried to find the opening he'd just passed. No light, nothing. A soft scraping noise, he reached and pulled out a roll of clothing. The little oil lamp glittered right behind it. June's hand followed and he could see her face in the halo of yellow light.

"I'm stuck," she said.

Willis said, "You can't be stuck. That's just not allowed."

"Well one of you lummoxes better do something, 'cause I'm really, really stuck and it's not funny."

Maddock said, "Look at me June, and listen. You're scared."

"Damn right I'm scared. One earthquake away from being subterranean roadkill scared."

"Then listen to me. People swell up when they get scared. They inhale a lot of air and their chest and shoulders expand. It's a natural reaction, we all do it. You need to sing something."

"You're insane. I don't know any songs."

"How about 'Itsy bitsy Spider?'"

"Not even to save my life."

"Come on. Give me your hand and I'll sing along. You too, Willis."

Maddock started. He got past *down came the rain* before Willis joined in. It wasn't until the second round that June began singing. Maddock was surprised to hear her rich contralto. About the fifth round she started giggling. Maddock grabbed her wrist with his other hand and pulled as hard as he could. June squawked, "…*spout,*" and slid past the obstruction.

Curled up on the ground, she shook with laughter. "Don't look, you jackasses. Oh, Gawd—if I ever live through this, I won't even be able to tell the stories."

Bones chose that moment to return. "What was all the caterwauling about?"

Willis said, "Just turn around, Bones, and give her some privacy."

"Is she all right?"

"She will be," Maddock said. "Tell us what you found."

June was still laughing. Maddock looked the other way and held out her bundle of clothes. "It's okay, boys. I lost all my dignity in that last stinking cave. Please just tell me there's a way out of here."

Bones' smile looked spectral in the flickering lamp light. "Yeah, good news. The rest of the way is open as far as the Dungeon of Skulls."

June sat on the ground wriggling into her jeans. "I take it this Morgaine is big on fantasy role-playing games."

"It's more like she lives in one," Maddock said. "I don't think she can tell the difference."

June stood up and straightened her blouse. "Around here, I can see how that could happen. Where's my six-shooter?"

Maddock handed over the gun belt and hat. "And what about you? How's your head?"

"Been better. At least the stars and sputniks have gone away."

Bones guided them over a pile of broken rock and through a low tunnel. When all four had assembled at the other end he pointed up. "Anyone recognize that?"

Willis craned his neck back. "Damn, can't get away from them."

Maddock didn't have to look to know that the Lemurian circle and triangle symbol hung just over their heads. June glanced at it a moment and said, "Just tell me which way gets us out of here."

"Pym's lab is up those stairs," Bones said. "We could go up there and make some more trouble for him."

Willis started that way. "Don't y'all wait for me or anything."

"Just a minute, hotshot." June pointed to a rectangular opening on her right. "What's behind door number two?"

Bones held up his little oil lamp and peered into the

darkness beyond. "Maddock's hippy chick wasn't too keen on this one. She called it the Halls of Madness."

"Well I feel like we've already been there." June adjusted her bandage, tightened her gun belt, and jammed her hat back on her head. "Then we're off to see the Wizard."

Willis had already disappeared up the stairs. Bones clambered up after him. "Not so fast, buddy. We still have to pass the Dungeon of Skulls."

Willis stopped. "Now you're messing with me."

Maddock helped June climb the oversized steps. "No, you'll see. Something's really wrong about that place. Wait for us when you get there."

When he and June finished scrambling up the last steps, they found Willis and Bones prowling through the mausoleum at the top.

Willis muttered and cursed. "This is sick. These boys should have come home heroes. Look at their dog tags, Brown, Jackson, Davis, Robinson. You know what neighborhoods those guys came from, and I'm not talking about no Hamptons. Bad stuff went down here."

"I think this building has never been clean," Maddock said. "It was a center for human experimentation in the sixties just like it is now."

As he spoke, Maddock's little oil lamp flickered and died. "We've got to go up one more level."

He led Bones to a stained concrete stairway. At the top, a sliver of yellow light glowed under the metal door. Maddock put a finger to his lips. "We've got company in the next room."

"Crap." Bones eased up next to him. "Can you tell what's going on?"

"Not without opening this door. Douse your lamp. It's about to go out anyway."

Bones returned to the others. In response to June's questioning look he said, "We may have a small problem."

Maddock pushed the door slightly. One rusty hinge rasped in protest. He froze. Voices, sounds of people moving about, nothing changed. Maddock pushed a little harder. The door swung far enough that he could peek past the frame. Bare florescent tubes illuminated neat rows of cots folded and stacked against the far wall. Armed men in urban camo sat talking in small groups. The floor had been cleaned and no trace remained of the ancient fallout shelter supplies. Maddock let the door ease shut again.

"Smoke 'em if you got 'em," he said. "We're going to be stuck here a while."

Willis objected until Maddock explained that the men he saw weren't being paid to hang out at the barracks. "It looks like they just got back from a rabbit hunt. Chances are, they'll be heading out again soon."

June said, "The three of you look like you've been dragged ass-first through a thresher. Get some rest. I'll take first watch."

Maddock settled his back against a wall. Planning their next move, he didn't count on getting any sleep.

An instant later, June was shaking him like a terrier. "Open your eyes, dammit. There's a war going on."

Maddock struggled to his feet, rubbed his eyes..

"She's here. Sally is back, I can feel her again," Willis said, sitting bolt upright.

June relit their oil lamp and kicked Bones' reclining form. "Move, for cripes sake."

Maddock heard the commotion above. Shouts, running feet, and the rattle of gear quickly gave way to small arms fire and the occasional explosion. "Sounds like hell's hammer factory up there."

He risked another peek through the door above. Six

commandos wrestled bundles of heavy gear toward another flight of stairs. Finger to his lips, Maddock shook his head. When they too had cleared the room, he signaled for the others to follow.

"The chaos should work in our favor. I see helmets and jackets against the far wall. Let's try to blend in—you too, June. Lose the Stetson."

Bones had unfolded from the floor and beat the others up the stairs. "Wow, this place sure cleaned up nice. Wonder if they've got any beer in the fridge?"

"I'd rather you found us some weapons," Maddock said.

The lights flickered and an explosion reverberated through the chamber. All four hit the deck as flakes of peeling gray paint rained down around them.

"What the hell?" Willis said. "Indoor artillery practice?"

When Bones turned up a blank on spare weapons, Maddock climbed the next flight of stairs. "I'd say Morgaine's goblin army has arrived. Let's see if we can get in ahead of them."

Bones held the door as the others filed past. Maddock nodded in approval as June climbed the steps. She'd swapped her trademark western garb for a black helmet and tight-fitting armored jacket. Willis had just cleared the door when the unmistakable *thonk* of a rifle-launched grenade in flight sent them all jumping for cover. It detonated about ten yards away.

"Over there, the stairwell." Maddock called.

He led them across the open space, dodging between columns. They caught a few curious glances, but most of the attention seemed focused on the other end of the building. Two guards stood at the foot of the stairs. Maddock grinned and pushed past. When they each turned to grab him by the arms, Bones and Willis took them down with a simple chokehold.

"Nice work," June said.

Willis followed, brandishing a compact submachine gun. "Heckler & Koch MP5 machine pistols. Now *these* guys are packing some serious gear."

"Which means we're up against a whole different league," Bones said.

Maddock started climbing. "I'm here for Pym, not his entire army."

Willis followed. "Up to the fourth level, then I'll show y'all the back way."

At the first landing, Maddock let Willis take the lead. Bones as usual, guarded their backsides. Up ahead, Maddock saw something fly through the air.

"Grenades! Take cover!" Maddock yelled.

Plastered against the nearest wall, Maddock felt the impact of three explosions in short succession. "Go, go, go." He scrambled up after Willis.

Behind them, the crackle of automatic weapons fire gave way to the enraged howl of heavy machine guns. By level three, June was breathing hard. They all slowed a little to let her catch up.

"You boys go ahead. I'll be okay."

"No way," Maddock said. "We stick together, at least until we find out what's happening on the fourth floor. Willis, go on up and wait at the top."

Bones took station at the third level as the others climbed. Willis hugged the wall just outside the door. June stepped up behind him and Maddock followed. He glanced down at Bones, then gave Willis the nod. The door opened with a push. Willis checked left and right, then signaled for the others to enter. Waiving at Bones, Maddock slipped through the door. His friend followed, taking the stairs two steps at a time.

Maddock tapped Willis on the shoulder. "You've been here before, which way?"

"Only been down the hall to the right. They've got admin stuff, desks and cubies, down there. We're smack in the middle of the building, though. There could be anything off the other direction."

"June and I will hole up here while you check it out," Bones said.

Maddock and Willis crept down the hall to their left. Overhead, the recessed florescent fixtures had been switched off, but light filtered in from a window on the far end. A row of doors opened on both sides. Maddock checked a few. They were unlocked.

"Storage," he whispered.

Willis nodded, touched a finger to his lips, and pointed down the hall. Maddock heard it, subtle movement in a room two doors farther. He nodded, pointed to himself, and made a walking motion with his fingers. In response, Willis held his MP5 at ready.

With a few brisk steps, Maddock crossed in front of the open door. He didn't pause, he didn't turn, but he made sure to be seen and heard. Willis followed in silence.

"*Stoyat!*" Short, dark, and slightly overweight, the merc who had ordered them to stop was a bad caricature of every Russian stereotype. His hand rested on the butt of a holstered pistol. The muzzle of Willis' gun was pressed to the man's neck.

"Anyone else in that room?" Maddock asked.

Willis glanced to his left and shook his head. "Only Vladimir Putin here."

"Name not Vladimir. Is Lev Petrovich, captain of guard."

Maddock checked the room for himself. A large duffel bag stood open, half filled with laptop computers.

"What are you doing up here?"

"Securing important equipment. Is not your business."

"I don't think Mr. Pym would miss this guy if I just shot him," Willis said.

Maddock relieved the man of his pistol, a cheap Bulgarian copy of an older Russian model. "No, Lev here wants to escape alive. Don't you, mister captain of the guard?"

"Is so. Men all out on hunt. Lev wait, protect boss."

"How many of your men are still in the building?"

The little merc pressed his lips together and gave Willis and Maddock a calculating look. "Think is you, men hunt. Is ironic, big reward if Lev catch escaped prisoners. Bullet if prisoners catch Lev. *Da*?"

"How many men?"

"Ha! All them. *Slushaete*, listen, they practice on targets in armory. Soon practice on you."

Willis stepped back and raised his machine pistol. "This guy's stalling for time. How many men?"

Lev raised his hands. "Is six on top floor, executive penthouse of boss."

"Maybe you help us get up there," Wills said.

"Take elevator. Is only way."

Willis pressed the short stock to his shoulder and zeroed in on the center of the merc's face. "I'm going to waste him just for thinking I'm that stupid."

"You've got one more chance," Maddock said. "Take us up the back way and we let you live. Keep annoying my friend here and there's nothing more I can do."

Lev nodded back the direction they'd come. "*Da*, is so."

They made Lev tote his duffel bag with its small fortune in computer gear.

Bones didn't seem delighted with their new team member. "Always hanging with a bad crowd, aren't you?"

Willis grinned. "Got us a key to the fifth floor, bro."

"Looks like this dude was packing to split. What do you have in the bag, comrade?"

When Lev didn't speak, Willis answered for him. "Got himself a giant loot bag, but he's letting us fight the final boss." He gestured down the hall to their right. "The back stairs are that way. I'm guessing if Link here's been rummaging around, this floor is empty."

Bones started that direction. "I'll clear it anyway."

"Usually just file clerks and payroll up here," June said. "Don't go shooting anyone you don't have to."

Maddock said, "Where do you think they'd hide if they thought Godzilla was coming?"

"Me? Ladies room. That's one place even commandos won't go. I'll check it out."

While Bones kicked open closet doors and peered under desks, Maddock followed June to the far west end of the building. She emerged from the restroom a few seconds later leading three older women and an attractive young nurse.

"Crap," Maddock said, "civilians."

Willis swung his machine pistol away from the Russian mercenary and pointed it at the nurse. "I know you. Pym's little night caller. Empty your pockets, lady."

Lev started to inch away. Maddock turned the Bulgarian nine-millimeter on him. "Don't even think about it."

Willis eyed a small pile of keys, lipstick, and sundries the nurse had dumped on a nearby desk. "June, stay clear of my line fire, but make sure that's everything."

Pym's nurse, who'd been silent up until then, said, "If she touches me, I will kill her."

The others backed away. June said, "Come on. I'll be gentle."

Lev chose that moment to make his break. He shoved one of the older women into June's back and bolted between the other two. Maddock couldn't fire without hitting a civilian and Willis didn't swing his machine pistol around until the little mercenary had burst past the men's room door and disappeared. Bones jumped up and bolted after him.

Maddock turned his attention back to the nurse. She now had June in an armlock with the big revolver pressed to her temple. June winced. "Sorry guys."

The nurse tightened up her hold and shifted slightly to put June between her and Maddock's pistol. "All of you, drop your weapons and move back, or I'll blow her head right off."

A muffled thud echoed up from below. Willis stepped closer, his Heckler & Koch MP5 aimed at her head.

She shifted, trying to keep June between herself and both men.

"This isn't going to work out well for you," Maddock said, training his pistol on her left eye.

"You think so?" The woman bared her teeth in a wolfish grin. "You think one of you can get me before I decorate the wall with her brain matter?"

"I think so," Bones said, stepping out of the bathroom door

The woman was sweating profusely, getting twitchy. Maddock sensed she was about to do something foolish.

"I guess there's only one question," she said. "Are you feeling lucky?"

Maddock didn't believe in luck, but he pulled the trigger anyway.

38

The old Smith & Wesson Police Special, six-inch barrel, thirty-eight caliber, it had been her connection, a talisman of sorts, binding Sally first to Uriah Bonebrake, then to Corey, and finally to Willis. Laying that battered gun on the floor and walking away felt like breaking a vow, like betrayal of her friends.

Lying on that steel laboratory table, Sally understood that betrayal always worked both ways. "Let's get this over with, you bastards."

Uzi stood next to her, connecting the intravenous transfusion tube. Dr. Goertzner sat in a chair at her side. One hand rested on a pistol in his lap. The other rested on the lab table as Uzi probed his arm. "Hold still doctor. Miss Smith has generously volunteered her artery for this procedure. You can certainly tolerate a little ineptitude on my part while I find your vein."

"Volunteer, hell. You weasel, you tricked me into this. Damn you, Uzi. I trusted you." Sally wouldn't look at his face, wouldn't look him in the eye, wouldn't give him the satisfaction. Most of all she wouldn't cry. Stone-faced she waited. The only thing to do was see this thing through and move on, roll credits, finish.

Goertzner grunted and cursed. "Any of my assistants as clumsy as you, I disposed of long ago."

"I'm certain you did. But we have a vein now and the small transfusion you need will only take a few minutes."

"At least my tests showed she has O-negative blood. Universal donor, how convenient." He clenched and unclenched his fist. "I can feel it working already. Do you truly comprehend the gift you are giving me?"

"Not a gift; an even trade. You get a half-pint of her blood, yes, but we get the remainder of your infusion."

Sally couldn't contain her anger. "You're a fool, Uzi. That infusion causes nothing but excruciating death."

"Fool on the hill, Sally. You can hate me, but I need that infusion and he needs your blood. You lose nothing by it except your chance at revenge. Tell me, what profit would you gain from killing this person? Consider what you could lose in the attempt."

Sally just looked at the ceiling and let the man drone on. She could feel Willis nearby. Willis, Bones and Maddock so bloody damn close she could nearly touch them. *What would they say if they saw her now?*

"And we're done." Uzi withdrew the catheter from Sally's arm and applied a bandage. "That may sting for a while, but you look like you've had a few stings today."

"Thanks for noticing. Just let me get out of here."

"Oh, not yet. Our gracious host is going to show me where he keeps his secret sauce."

Goertzner raised his pistol. "I should just shoot both of you."

"That would be unfortunate. I have four men outside who would happily blow that supercharged body of yours into bloody chunks. In fact, they'll do it anyway unless I tell them otherwise. Now, where is that magical infusion?"

Goertzner stood, steadying himself against the table. Sally sat up and slipped off the other end. The doctor rolled a large metal cabinet to one side revealing a wall safe. He gave the dial a few spins, turned the handle, and drew it open. "Refrigerated, you'll notice. The infusion begins to ferment after a few hours at room temperature. I can't imagine what you'll do with it."

"No, I don't suppose you can." Uzi lifted out two large IV bags and set them on the lab table. "Ciao, doctor."

"Your men."

"Oh, I almost forgot." Uzi pressed a hand against his right temple and muttered something. "You're good."

Sally said, "Do you trust him?"

Uzi and the doctor each looked at the other a moment, then Goertzner nodded. Uzi said, "I'll even escort you out. I imagine you won't be using the elevator?"

Goertzner pushed his way into a janitor's closet and opened a door in the back. "I don't advise you follow, although I'm not sure why I care." He held up a small plastic box. "Any trouble from your people, and this whole place goes up."

At that moment, a heavyset figure lugging an oversized duffel came clattering down from above. Sally caught his brief glance of amazement before he fled toward the lower level. A few seconds later, a loud explosion echoed back up the stairwell.

Goertzner winced and started down the stairs. "Waste of a perfectly good claymore mine."

"Take him with you." Sally yelled back, but the doctor was gone.

"Be a love and retrieve our weapons." Uzi poked his head in the stairwell and looked up. "Now *that* was odd." He drew his namesake pistol. "We really should go up one more level and see what's happening."

Maddock felt the pistol buck in his firm grip, heard the loud bang. His aim was true. The woman's body jerked, stiffened, then went lip.

Cursing, June shoved the corpse away and picked up her fallen revolver.

"All right, let's…" Before Maddock could finish the sentence, he heard movement in the distance. Footsteps coming toward them, slowing as the approached.

They all dropped down, aimed in the direction of the sound.

The footsteps came closer. Maddock's heart raced. His finger was on the trigger.

"Willis?" a tentative voice called.

"Sally!" Willis breathed.

Sally appeared, followed by Uzi. Sally looked like hell.

"Sally, what have they done to you?" Maddock said.

"I'm fine, you should see the other guy."

"What are you doing here anyway? You should have been long gone from this rat hole."

"Looking for some payback, that is until your friend Uzi came along and spoiled it. Traitorous bastard."

"Not my friend." Maddock eyed the man in question. "He ditched us in San Francisco."

"I heard that." Uzi had slipped between them without their notice. "Let me start by pointing out that we all seem so wrapped up in revenge here that we've lost sight of our mission."

"Yeah, considering I never even knew what *your* mission was."

Bones said, "Well I was shanghaied into this by brother Maddock here, so don't go asking me."

Maddock rubbed his face, trying to clear his head. "I thought we were retrieving Willis from whatever mess he'd tangled himself up in."

"Don't look at me. I just came for the mac and cheese." Willis stepped over and put an arm around Sally. "I don't give a crap what you say, Uzi. Just seeing her like this puts revenge right up there on the top of *my* list."

Uzi raised a cautionary finger. "A great man once said, 'Living well is the best revenge.' In our case, the operative word is, *living*."

"I think smarty-pants here means we're all about to get blown through the stratosphere," June chimed in. "I just don't know how he intends to avoid it."

"Ah, so the brains of this outfit finally reveals herself. Avoid it indeed, in fact, I intend to prevent it." Uzi's grin always seemed like a smirk to Maddock. The man beamed at all of them and continued. "We now have four liters of Dr. Feelgood's magic infusion—thanks to Ms. Smith here..."

"You little weasel..."

"*Do* let me finish. As I was about to say, we also have a hundred liters of Junior's golden concoction that he so gladly gave into my keeping."

"You mean that stinking bucket of slime that the two of you hauled off? Speaking of slime buckets, where did that new best friend of yours get to?"

"Another deal, oh yes, another bargain as it were. You see, I restored the missing parts to his little helicopter." Uzi tapped his wrist, as if he were wearing a watch. "In about five minutes, by my reckoning, he will be here to whisk his father to safety."

"Well, that just ain't happening." Machine pistol still slung over his shoulder, Willis swooped down and scooped the nurse's keys from the table. Before anyone could speak, he dashed to the back and pushed open the hidden stairwell door.

Uzi leapt after him, tangling himself in Sally's outstretched leg. They both fell to the floor, Sally clinging like a lovestruck octopus. Maddock jumped over the two, pounding up the stairs after Willis.

On the fifth level, the door stood open. Maddock plowed through and slammed into Willis coming the other direction.

"He ain't here and there's a bunch of hostiles on my tail."

"The roof," Maddock said.

Willis returned to the stairwell and began climbing a steel ladder bolted to the wall. He fumbled with a trapdoor, flipped it open, and hauled himself out. Maddock scrambled up in pursuit calling, "Wait, wait."

Below, gunfire rattled about the stairwell like hornets in a soda bottle. A quick glance down, and Maddock saw four of Uzi's men swarming the fifth level and returning fire through the open door. He figured they had it under control and returned his attention to Willis.

A two-seat helicopter idled on the rooftop pad. Augustus Pym Junior had lifted his father from the motorized wheelchair, about to transfer him to the passenger side. The two stood frozen in place, their eyes glued to Willis. He knelt on the gravel rooftop, his H&K MP5 machine pistol extended, both hands on the grips.

"Don't do it," Maddock said.

"Give me one good reason why I shouldn't."

"Wait, I have a reason." Uzi had somehow managed to wriggle free and follow them. "Listen! Down below, do you hear any more gunfire? No? Well, that was the deal. Junior gets to rescue his father. In return, Senior called off the dogs. They're bailing right now, no more shooting. Ruin this deal, Willis Sanders, and we're all dead."

"It ain't right. I should have blown his ugly ass off this planet the first time I had him in my sights.."

"Think of Sally, think of June," Maddock said. "They don't need to die."

Willis didn't move, didn't lower his weapon. Sally had followed Uzi onto the roof. Crouching next to Willis, she stared at the two, father and son. She might have said something to Willis. She put a hand on his arm. He shook his head and slung the machine pistol over his shoulder.

Junior placed his father in the passenger seat. Almost gently—a child, caring for his aging parent, he buckled the straps and closed the door. Moments later, the engine roared, the blades spun up, and the little helicopter vanished into the afternoon sky. Willis walked over, still shaking his head. "Tell me you put a bomb in that damn thing."

Sally gave him a sidelong look. "Could have happened, just not the way you think."

The building shook. A quick tremble at first, then a hard shock that cracked the concrete roof and knocked pieces of cinderblock off the parapet. "So much for the peace talks," Willis said.

Uzi started for the ladder. "That, flower, had nothing to do with our little war. We've got Mother Nature knocking on devil's door and she's getting impatient."

He helped Sally start down, although she clearly wanted nothing to do with him. They regrouped on the fourth floor. The three clerks had fled, replaced by a small contingent of Uzi's men. To Maddock, they seemed the same unremarkable group he'd seen in San Francisco, quiet, efficient, deadly.

He was happy to let them lead the way back down the main stairwell. Happier still that they had cleared the other levels and guarded the entrances. Uzi followed, two large IV bags draped over his left shoulder. They'd almost reached the bottom level when the building shook again. This time a wrenching, twisting motion that brought blocks of broken concrete down the stairwell after them.

Maddock waved everyone on. "Quickly! June, you go with Uzi's men. Run!" She looked at Maddock. He nodded and said, "Just go. Stay safe and we'll see you on the other side."

She backed away. One of Uzi's commandos caught her by the arm and started running. They'd cleared two rows of columns before the next tremor struck. A deep rumble and part of the overhead collapsed, thundering to the floor where she'd been. Fragments of concrete showered Maddock's face and the overhead lights blew out in a cascade of sparks.

The pall of dust that spread through the cavernous armory blotted out what little light remained. In the darkness, Maddock practically tripped over Uzi. He pulled the man to his feet. "Is this your doing? Which side are you on, anyway?"

Uzi touched his head. "Minor scalp wound—thanks for your concern. None of this is my doing, and maybe all of it. You'll learn soon enough. Where are the others?"

Off to the back, a dim yellow glow flickered against the wall. Somehow, a fire had started among the fallen debris. As Maddock's eyes adjusted to the darkness, he began to pick out details of the damage. From where they stood it looked like the entire front of the building had collapsed. He bent over, coughing on the dust. "I think Sally was with Willis and Bones up ahead somewhere."

An aftershock brought down another rain of concrete fragments. The dust burned his eyes and Maddock struggled to keep his feet. In the murk he made out another figure lurching toward him. "Bones, that you?"

"Careful," Uzi said. "Not everything is as it seems."

A moment later, he staggered backward and fell. Two shots, Maddock saw the flashes, and drew his pistol but the shadowy figure had disappeared. Movement to his left,

Maddock knelt behind a mound of debris. *Hell, it could be anyone out there.* "Bones, Willis, where are you?"

Three shots plowed into the broken concrete, not two feet away. Maddock scuttled to his side. The shots had come from his right. Two more flashes gave him a target. He raised his pistol and pulled the trigger. Nothing. Maddock tried racking the slide. It moved a half inch and jammed. Another shot sizzled off the end of a broken column and whined into the darkness behind him. *Who the crap is shooting at us?*

Maddock jammed the useless Bulgarian pistol in his belt and belly-crawled toward the shooter. Worming his way through the rubble, a pall of dust hid everything from view. He felt a tickle in his throat. It started as a cough and turned into a sneeze. Small explosions, bright flashes, three more bullets practically in his face, they peppered him bits of lead and grit.

Maddock heaved a block of concrete and was rewarded with a grunt of surprise. Two bullets pinged harmlessly off the overhead as he hurled three more chunks. Rapid-fire fastballs, they struck with a thud and clattered away. Jumping to his feet, he rushed the crouching shadow. Maddock saw a glint of steel as the pistol swung toward him. Twisting sideways, he grabbed the slide with his left hand and pushed it back, disabling the weapon. His opponent chopped down on the extended arm. Maddock felt a sharp pain and then his nerves went limp.

Dr. Goertzner stood triumphant, the pistol centered on Maddock's chest. "Something, something is happening to me. I need more blood—some of yours will have to do."

39

Standing in the flickering yellow light, Goertzner's face swarmed with writhing veins and seeping pustules. His chest and shoulders bulged beneath his torn shirt. Sighting down the barrel, he tightened his finger on the trigger. Nothing.

Maddock spotted a partially ejected cartridge jammed in the receiver and staggered to his feet. Goertzner realized the problem in an instant, but before he could clear the jam, his target had dodged behind a concrete pillar. "Oh, come on. You're just making this harder and you know how it will end."

Stalling for time, saying nothing, Maddock tried to flex his injured wrist. He could only shut out some of the pain. His skin felt like a glove, two sizes too small. His arm felt like white fire shooting up his elbow. While he groped about for a weapon, Goertzner's voice came from the other side of the column.

"I've got one more shot. Where do you want it, the chest or the head?" When Maddock didn't answer, he responded, "The chest then," and stepped into view.

Timed right, the twisted length of rebar would have broken Goertzner's forearm. A half second too early, it connected with his pistol, sending the shot wide. Maddock threw all his remaining strength into right cross that would have flattened most men. It landed with full impact.

Goertzner just grunted and staggered back a step. He gave a shake of the head.

"Not bad, but not enough." He slammed Maddock across the face with his pistol and returned with a blow to the throat. Maddock had anticipated the second strike, turned, and raised his arm to deflect the fist.

Goertzner struck again with the pistol, knocking Maddock back among the broken blocks of concrete. Enraged, the doctor dropped his gun and waded in with both fists. Maddock absorbed most of the blows with his arms, then returned an uppercut to the chin followed by another to the gut.

Gasping, Goertzner shoved Maddock to the ground, then drew back.

"I'll have your blood if I have to drink in straight from your gushing arteries." His bulging eyes reflected a flickering yellow glow.

Maddock dashed a fistful of dust in the doctor's face, grabbed the rebar and slammed it into his left cheek. Growling, spittle running from his ruined mouth, Goertzner stood, clawing the dirt from his eyes. Maddock jumped up and swung again. Too late, he realized the last move had been a ruse. Mid-swing, Goertzner blocked the strike and snatched the rebar from Maddock's hand. A kick to the hip spun him back to the dirt. In the flickering light, he spotted Goertzner's discarded pistol.

One chance, one chance. Maddock rolled on his belly, letting the rain of blows fall about his back and shoulders. He wedged the pistol in his numb left hand and groped for the Bulgarian knockoff at his belt. The raging berserker seized him by the throat, hoisted him bodily from the ground, and buried his face in Maddock's neck.

At point blank, Goertzner's body muffled the shot. He arched his back, opened his mouth and howled. A raw moan of insanity poured into the darkness. The man began to twitch and shake. He released Maddock and fell to his side, straining backwards. Screaming now, his arms and legs thrashed into contortions normally impossible. His shoulders and elbows dislocated. His limbs writhed on the ground, boneless tentacles twisting and knotting in agony.

Maddock dragged himself to his feet and watched in horror as his assailant devolved into a mass of squirming muscles. The man's mouth hung open. His screams no more than the pulsing whimper of a dying puppy. Dr. Goertzner rolled his eyes and fixed his gaze on Maddock.

This was the fiend who had shot Uzi and condemned countless others to a hideous death. Still, Maddock couldn't let the man suffer. He pinched another round from the Bulgarian pistol's magazine, chambered it in the other gun, and fired a headshot, quenching the fire in those baleful eyes.

Maddock turned to where he'd left Uzi, knowing that he should be dead. The yellow glow had grown into a spreading flame and in the light, he saw another figure. A wraith of wispy hair and gown, fingers like bundled sticks, it bent over his fallen companion.

"Get away from him, you." He picked up the length of broken rebar and advanced on the crouching specter. It stood and faced him. Maddock dropped the iron bar. "Morgaine?"

"Your friend needs help. He's been hurt."

Maddock knelt at Uzi's side. Beneath the flattened IV bags, a smear of blood had spread across his chest.

Uzi opened his eyes. "I'm not as bad as I look," he said, "but this is still a disaster."

The fire had ignited a stack of tires that guttered and smoldered before spreading to a vehicle. Its fuel tank exploded with a low thud sending a wave of heat across the armory. Maddock extended his right arm and hooked it under Uzi's shoulder. The man struggled to his feet, eyeing the flames.

"We have to leave now. There's three thousand gallons of fuel in that tank truck back there."

Morgaine said, "Quickly, the labyrinth is in ruins, but we can take shelter in the Dungeon of Skulls."

"No, I've got to find Bones and Willis."

"They're with the girl. She's hurt and they are carrying her out. Mr. Bones sent me to find you."

Morgaine helped drag Uzi a few steps toward the far wall. Maddock knew the doorway there would lead to the lower levels, but he wasn't too happy about being trapped underground. They had just passed a second row of columns when a burst of flames erupted from the far corner. It flowed along the concrete like a swarm of hunting pythons. Somehow, Uzi broke into an awkward run.

"Now! It's going to blow!"

Maddock practically flung Morgaine through the metal doors and followed her down the stairs.

Uzi descended two at a time yelling, "Next level, next level!"

The doors above burst inward with a blast of heat and flame that threw them all to the concrete floor. Smoke and burning fuel everywhere, Uzi rummaged around in the confusion and came up with a large plastic jug. He belly-crawled, dragging it toward the other door.

Maddock found Morgaine unconscious on the floor. She lay face down, her long, tangled hair shriveling in the heat. He seized her by the belt and began dragging the limp body after Uzi. One step, pull, another step, pull. The heat became unbearable and the narrow chamber seemed impossibly wide.

A moment later, Bones lifted her by the waist and ran. Maddock scrambled the rest of the way, descending into the cool gloom of the lower chamber. Willis sat next to Sally, holding one of Morgaine's small oil lamps. They both looked up as Maddock half slid, half fell down the concrete steps. Willis scrambled to his feet. "Glad to see you made it,

Boss. What took you guys?"

"We ran into an old friend. Where's Uzi? He's been shot."

Willis helped Maddock sit on the floor next to Sally. "Bones has him under control, but that arm of yours ain't looking too good, Skipper. Can I splint it for you?"

Maddock nodded and glanced over at Sally. "And you, how are you doing?"

"I'm fine. If Mr. Mom here would let me stand up, I could help Bonebrake with Uzi and his friend."

"That's Morgaine. She knows these tunnels better than anyone."

Sally's head had been bandaged in torn khaki. As she retreated, Maddock saw a large bloodstain on the shoulder of her blouse. "What happened?"

"Got clocked by a chunk of debris from that last quake. It was all Bones and I could do to dig her out. Then this blonde, Morgaine, pops up out of nowhere. Says we've got to run for it and that she'd go find you guys."

"Yeah, she found us, but not before Goertzner showed up. He didn't die well." Maddock told Willis about the fight. "I just don't see how Uzi is still alive."

"Those bags of infusion he was carrying, they were enough to absorb the bullet impacts. He's still got some pretty serious holes in his chest."

A few minutes later, Uzi himself walked over.

Willis' jaw dropped. "You've got to be kidding me."

"In so many ways," he said.

Before Willis could say anything more, Bones and Sally arrived, supporting Morgaine between them. Aside from the bruise on her forehead, the woman seemed uninjured. "We can't stay here," she said. "We've run out of time."

As if to punctuate her words, the ground beneath them lurched once more. From above, Maddock heard the growl of collapsing concrete walls. The upper door blasted inward and a ball of flame exploded across the ceiling.

"Back down to the Labyrinth," Bones said. "It's the only way."

Maddock jumped to his feet, but Morgaine stopped him. "Wait, wait, I saved something for you." She reached under a shelf and drew out the short willow bow and quiver that Nahonka had given him, seemingly a lifetime ago. "I'm so sorry, I couldn't save your packs and your cloaks."

Maddock hefted the bow. It seemed so pointless now, but he slung it across his shoulder and thanked the woman. Willis led, guiding Sally through the secret door in the back. As streams of burning fuel raced across the floor, Morgaine followed the others through the maze of desiccated skeletons. Maddock looked back for a moment and muttered a brief benediction to the hundreds of unknowns soon to be incinerated.

They descended the narrow passage of tall steps by the flickering light of their single lamp. Below, Maddock heard a cacophony of hisses and groans, the very bowels of Leviathan come to life. The air had turned thick and sour with sulfurous vapors.

Willis turned and looked up at the others. "Y'all sure we want to do this?"

Uzi, the plastic jug balanced on his shoulder said, "The only way out is to go through."

Morgaine stopped them at the bottom and pointed toward a low tunnel at their feet. "The Labyrinth of Eternity has filled with dragons. We couldn't possibly fight our way through."

In the flickering light, Maddock could see steam rising from the tunnel. The subterranean noises now roared and boomed from the opening.

"The other passage! It's still clear," Uzi said.

Maddock turned and did a double take. "What the hell Uzi, how can you possibly know that?"

"No time to explain, just get in the cave."

Sally led. She didn't look back at the others but just stepped up to the rectangular opening. "I understand." She gave Uzi a knowing smile. "This is the only way."

The ground beneath their feet vibrated like the cheap car on a fast train. Dust streamed from crevices on both sides. Maddock heard Bones behind them, urging the reluctant Morgaine.

Willis' small lamp guttered and died, but overhead a row of bright golden lights shown through the dust and steam. "I don't know who's doing that, but it ain't me."

"It's me, Cornpone. Just follow the yellow brick road."

Up another flight of stairs and a hundred yards further, the yellow lights merged into a glow suffusing the interior. Maddock stopped.

"Wait, Sally. We've seen this before."

Enormous shapes began to materialize in the haze. Uzi caught up with them. "You must keep going."

Bones had Morgaine by the arm. She wept and pleaded. "The Halls of Madness—I've been lost in here for days. It was horrible."

"It's a damn rerun," Bones said. "We've already seen this show."

Willis stared upward as the shapes coalesced into a maze of crumbling towers and mossy battlements. "Not this one, we haven't. I'm not moving until someone explains what the hell is going on."

Sally took his arm. "A little farther, Cornpone. Then you'll know. Straight on through 'til dawn, right Uzi?"

"Yes, we're almost there." Uzi took the lead. Twenty yards farther, they came to a blank stone wall. A tall rectangle had been engraved in the face and at its center,

Maddock saw the familiar circle within a triangle.

"This is always where I stopped," Morgaine said. "No matter what I did or where I went, every path led to this same dead end."

Maddock stood in stunned silence. "We've been searching for the key since we got here, but I think we've had it all along. Your knife, Bones." He seldom saw his friend at loss for a smart reply, but now Bones stared at Maddock with his mouth open.

Uzi touched his arm. "Your knife, Mr. Bonebrake, or should I call you Coyote, son of Killeli?"

As if in a trance, Bones drew the cord from around his neck and passed it to his friend. "The museum display, it was right there in front of us." He brought forth the exquisite jade green blade and handed it to Maddock.

Maddock held it up like a sacred icon and stepped to the stone image. He rubbed dirt from the stone triangle and traced a ring of tiny figures ringing the engraved circle. Close inspection revealed a narrow vertical slot like the iris of an eye set within.

"You *have* seen this show before. Willis has, anyway. It is the Eye of God, enclosed by the host of his Heavens." He handed the blade to Sally. "You should do this."

Sally stepped up and jammed the stone blade into the slot. All about, the tiny figures burst into an iridescent display of flashing colors. Dancing, glittering, the lights spread to fill the triangle. The stone wall itself began to glow.

Uzi said, "The portal is open. Go now, children."

Sally passed through in a blaze of golden light. Willis went next, a tangled web of blue streamers. Morgaine burst through the portal in a kaleidoscopic rainbow. Bones put his hand into the glittering rock face, clenched his teeth, and stepped through in a flash of red.

Maddock paused. "And you, Uzi. What color are you?"

"A color you cannot see, Mr. Maddock. A color not of this world. Please go now."

Maddock felt, rather than saw, his emerald green aura as he passed into the next cavern. If tranquility was a sense, an odor, or a sound, Maddock would have said it permeated this space. Uzi seemed to arrive simultaneously, the plastic jug still perched on his shoulder.

Willis was the first to break the silence. "Okay, man. We're here, now give. What's up with my girl?"

"You should try asking her."

Sally had gone on ahead, still projecting a faint golden light. Maddock trotted after and Willis followed. When they caught up, she had stopped at the edge of a green pool that seemed to glow from within.

Maddock caught her by the arm. "No Sally, for God's sake, don't go there."

Willis said, "What is going on?"

"Allow me to explain." Uzi stepped up next to Sally and set the plastic jug on the ground. "This is four liters of the culture developed by Mr. Pym Junior. Together with four liters of Senor's infusion, we could have set the balance straight. We could have appeased the *Kuksu* of local legend, the Ma'óghe as you call it."

"The great *Gaia*," Morgaine said.

"Yes, the great *Gaia* whose roots reach down to unimaginable depths beneath our feet and whose branches touch an undiscovered host of microbes populating the high troposphere." Uzi paused and looked at Sally. "Could have. Except that Goertzner survived long enough to destroy the infusion. It wasn't just me he wanted to kill. It was all of us."

Sally had seemed in a trance. On hearing Goertzner's name, she made a face and shrugged away from Maddock.

"I thought that was your special deal, Uzi. My blood for his cooperation."

"Goertzner would never have let us live. Once outside, he tried to trigger the bomb behind the fuel truck, but you had disarmed it. Then he came looking for us. Too late for him, he discovered that your blood wasn't exactly what he expected."

Bones had been gazing into the limpid green depths of the pool. He kicked a small rock. Without a splash, without even a ripple it vanished beneath the surface.

Uzi shook his head. "Don't. You have no idea what you might disturb."

"Yeah, we've seen something like this before, Mr. Uzi man, or whoever you are. We almost lost Sally back then. Same deal, dead volcano, weird hombres, Moogly-Woogly."

"Hardly dead, sailor. You won't feel it in here but above, things are getting quite lively."

He turned again to Sally. "You have only one option left, and you know what that is."

Willis stepped to Sally's side. "What in hell is this guy talking about? We're getting out of this spookhouse now, if I have to carry you out."

He put his arms around Sally, but she pushed him away. "No, Cornpone. No, it won't work." She fell to her knees, hands on her face and whispered, "I'm not going to cry, I'm not."

Willis knelt at her side and once more wrapped her in his arms. "Don't cry. I'm here for you."

She let him lift her back to her feet, then collapsed against his chest. "You can't, not for much longer. I brought all of you here because I needed you and I couldn't do it alone."

Sally dropped her head once more. "And I haven't told

you everything."

"Time is passing, petals." Uzi interrupted her. "We have very little of it left."

While he spoke, the rippling green glow cast a writhing shadow at Uzi's feet. Maddock saw it flick first to Bones, then to Willis, and finally wind about Sally's legs. He stepped back from the pool. "Just who are you Uzi?"

The shadows elongated and the chamber darkened. "I thought you would never ask."

The man they had known as Uzi thinned and grew to over seven feet in height. His fingers stretched into slender spidery digits and his clothing shrank to a bark-like scale covering. Only Bones seemed to understand. "You are Lemurian—I thought so!"

Morgaine's eyes opened in wonder, "I know you. We've talked."

If Maddock read his face correctly, Uzi the Lemurian seemed to smile. "And I know you Morgaine, Queen of the Fairies. Long may you reign among the hills and trees. But we have a difficult choice to make, and work to do, if that is to happen." He reached down without bending and passed the plastic jug to Morgaine. "When the time comes, pour this into the pool."

Willis held Sally's ruined face in his hands. "You gotta let me wipe those tears away and tell me what all this means—what *you* mean."

She reached her hands out to Maddock. "You know what it means, don't you *Marumda*? Don't you remember the dream, your sweat lodge visions?"

"I remember." Maddock shook his head and rubbed his temples. "I just don't see where you come in."

"Killeli, I am the Killeli. Now, use that arrow you found on the mountain. Return me to my fires."

"That's crazy talk." Willis put himself between her and

Maddock. "Ain't no one shooting you with no arrow."

She pushed him away. "You don't get it." Turning to Maddock and Bones she said, "Why do you think I ran off? You guys treated me like family, but I just couldn't tell you. I couldn't bear it."

Willis edged away. "Tell us what? What did I do that was so bad you couldn't talk about it?"

"Not you, Cornpone. Never you. It's me." She wiped her nose. "Oh, God. It's cancer, stage four ovarian cancer. I came here to die, I should have been gone six months ago, but for the Ma'óghe in me. Look at us—all of us. Shot, beat on, slashed and smashed, we're still running around like twelve-year-olds."

Bones stepped a little closer. "I thought it was something I did, or maybe you just couldn't face Corey after your split."

"Not you, Bonebrake, and not Corey, he was terrific." Sally stepped back to the pool's edge. She wept openly now. "No don't you get any closer, none of you. There's not going to be any hugs. No goodbyes. Not one of you asshats had better cry."

"And what about me?" Willis whispered. "I'm supposed to just stand here and watch another person I love get herself killed?"

"Yes, Willis Sanders, you have to be that strong. You have to be the tank in this outfit, for everyone's sake. You just don't have to like it." She straightened and faced the group. "Do it now Dane *Marumda* Maddock."

"I can't." He reached for the bow and single white arrow. "Even if my wrist weren't injured, I don't think I would."

The water behind her surged and began to bubble like an angry cauldron. "It's time," Uzi said. "It's now or not at all."

Two long strides, Willis snatched the bow, the gleaming arrow, and shot Sally in the center of her chest. A tiny smile on her face, she fell back and disappeared into the seething pool.

The tall Lemurian nodded and Morgaine poured four liters of brown liquid in after Sally.

40

Bones had sprawled across an empty row of center seats. Eyes closed, mouth open, a sleeping wolf. Willis had lowered the plastic shade, reclined his seat, and wedged himself against the plane's inner wall. He'd said little in the past day and the others had respected his silence. Maddock was glad to see his friends finally get some sleep, but that luxury still eluded him.

Maddock pulled a yellow notepad from the seatback pocket and fished a pen from his shirt. It felt strange to write this all down, but Corey would want to know every detail. Maddock concentrated on the last few hours. He flipped over a few curling pages of scribbled notes, then turned back to a clean sheet and started writing.

After Sally fell, he wrote, *Morgaine added her jug of culture. The seething green pool—*

What? Brightened yes, but the exact shade of golden yellow eluded him. He skipped a few lines and went on, resolving to elaborate later.

Maddock had expected Uzi himself to disappear into the pool, or just vanish like another illusion. Instead, the gangly Lemurian led them out, stalking through the shadowy halls until their pathway lightened. Once more they found themselves threading their way between towering ancient trees. In the daylight, Uzi had transitioned back to his more human form.

Morgaine had been walking at Uzi's side, glancing up and smiling all the time. She didn't seem surprised at his transformation. When the ground beneath them lurched and rumbled, she clung to his arm. The giant trees swayed overhead, and Willis came running up from behind, muttering under his breath.

Bones had caught the first whiff of sulfurous steam. "Stinks like hell's waiting room out here. I thought the little Moogly critters were happy again."

Uzi, already human, had said, "I think this may be Sally's doing. Remember, she's Keeper of the Fires now."

Another quarter mile, and Maddock found himself on the same rock promontory where he had stood earlier that day. Bones climbed to the top and scanned the valley below. "Holy crap in a can, it ain't over, it's just starting, and we're totally screwed."

Maddock climbed up next to him. Far below, a ring of fire had erupted from the ground. Towering fountains of incandescent volcanic ash enveloped the gutted hulk of Laboratory Nine. Little whirlwind jets of flaming gas played about the valley floor. Willis just stared in silence at the scene like something out of Dante. As they watched, a deep trembling knocked boulders from the hillside. With a growl like a wounded mastodon, Pym's ruined laboratory tilted on its foundation.

In an explosion of boiling lava, the doomed structure settled into the fiery pit like a lost soul sinking to perdition. Morgaine thrashed about in panic, but Uzi held her by the arm. "We're safe here, child. Keeper of the Fires is not angry with you."

As Uzi spoke, the trembling ceased, the ash and flames guttered out, and the bubbling pool of lava skimmed over. Across the valley, wildfires climbed the mountainside, but below them, the rocky slope burned in only a few places.

"So it *is* over," Maddock said. "Sally was the Killeli all along. Had you known that in advance, Uzi?"

"There was imbalance, discord. We sought her out and now there is harmony."

Willis looked as if he was about to hurl Uzi from the

cliff, but Bones stepped between them. "You're not saying you caused this are you?"

"This? All of this was decades in the making. It began over a century ago. When soldiers slaughtered the local native tribes, the old Killeli died, forgotten in her mountain lodge. When gold and lumber became more important than human lives, Marumda hid in shame and Great Kuksu departed this land. Humanity caused this in their blind indifference."

Uzi stepped down from the rocks and retreated to the shadowy forest behind them. He gestured to Moraine. "Come flower, these Halls of Madness will hereafter be your home. You are now our Watcher. Watch carefully. Someday you will herald the new dawn when humanity finally takes their baby steps from infancy to awareness."

He turned to address Maddock directly. "Leave—and don't return until you are ready."

The cabin illumination dimmed and a soft announcement from the cockpit suggested that those who wished to read could switch on their overhead lights. Maddock reached up and pushed a blue button. In the yellow pool of light, he reread his words on the paper. That last line, a rather dark warning from a person he had come to respect. Scratching it out, he considered the words. *True to events, yes, but maybe not the way he wanted to finish his story.*

Maddock chewed the end of his pen, then started writing again, relating an earlier narrative. On their way out, the Lemurian had explained himself. "I never intended to show my true form, but when the infusion was destroyed, I had to borrow your friend Uzi." On seeing Maddock's expression, he'd said, "Uzi will be fine. In a few hours, he'll awaken in his vehicle, with a somewhat abridged memory of recent events."

Chewing on his pen once more, Maddock scanned his latest notes. *How does this square with Uzi the flight attendant, the smarmy killer, the Lemurian defender of earth?* He flipped over a fresh sheet of paper and started again. *Maybe Bones could sort it out for Corey.*

This time, he wrote about their descent from the mountain. Just the three of them, they had headed east toward the abandoned lumber camp. How even the irrepressible Bones had started to drag ass. Willis slogged on like he would walk all the way back to Key West, but Maddock knew the man was running on empty.

Bones had been first to break the silence following Uzi's departure. "Going to be Forest Service, NOAA, USGS, FBI, NSA, and every other alphabet soup of cops, feds, and asshat officials crawling all over this place."

Maddock made a few notes on the page. *Forest Service should have been there already. It seemed they'd finally taken June's warnings seriously.* He went on to describe their hasty departure in more detail. The sun had been low on the horizon by the time Maddock and the others made it back to the logging camp. He remembered thinking, *what now—what are we going to do now?* They had passed the wreckage of the plane shot down the day before. Fire had charred the sage and buckbrush for a hundred yards around. Other than that, the site was clean, no cartridges, no corpses. He'd been about to suggest that they hole up for the night in one of the abandoned buildings when a light plane swung wide around a nearby hill and descended toward them. Bones had fallen into a crouch. "Crap. Another jump-buggy full of mercs."

Maddock flipped to a new page and paused. Truth was, they had left Sally behind. Against all their training, their pledges to each other, only the three of them remained.

How would he explain that to Corey? It was then that he noticed Willis' eyes open, watching him. Maddock nodded. "Sleep okay?"

"Yeah. You should get some rest already."

"Can't. Got too much going on in my head. I thought maybe I should make some notes for the others before I forgot all the details."

"Let me see that." Before Maddock could object, Willis grabbed the yellow pad and turned back to the beginning. He skimmed a few pages, flipping them over and working his way down. "Damn mission report, all official details. You don't say much about Sally. You said nothing about how we felt."

"I'm having a hard time with that. I keep thinking there should have been something we could have done, some way we could have helped Sally."

"She's not dead, you know? She's still down there. I've got a little of that Moogly in me. Sometimes I can hear her, far off."

"I think we all can," Maddock said. "Sally drank from the Eternal Spring, she's part of it now."

Willis handed the pad back and buried his face in his hands. "Just tell me, and make it the truth, man." He didn't look at Maddock. "Was I played? Did she even give a rat's ass about me, or was this just a ploy to set us against the Pyms? She practically said as much."

"No—well, yes and no. She wanted you there, needed you, Willis. Even I could see that. But Sally was in way over her head and knew that too." Maddock looked down at his hands, trying to find the right words. "I think she ran off because of the cancer. It wasn't her style to die with all of us standing around. At the same time, she couldn't get away from you. There was that link forged in the depths of Maug lagoon. She had to give in. She had to bring you to her, not because she wanted to hurt you but because she had no other choice. She cared for you Willis, and she still cared for Corey as well. But Sally knew that of all of us, you were the one she most wanted to see."

"Yeah, you make it sound good. I just wish I could have asked her myself."

Maddock nodded toward a reclining figure snoring softly in the seat in front of them. "Sally confided in our friend. You'll probably get the full story when the lights go up and the breakfast cart comes around."

For the first time in a long time, Maddock saw Willis smile. "Ha. Remember how Bones looked when that plane showed up? I thought he was going to take on an entire squad of mercs bare handed."

"We both were kind of thinking that way, Cessna Citation just like the one that tried to blow our lights out earlier."

"Damn thing lands right there on the road in front of us, and who pops out but the same gal that saved my ass back at Pym's lab."

It was Maddocks turn to smile. "And she was wearing the same goofy hat." He tried to pitch his voice in a throaty contralto. "You boys need a lift?"

"I've never been so glad to see anyone as I was to see June. Somehow, she'd ripped Pym's last set of wings and found us out there in, like sticks city."

Maddock handed Willis his pen and yellow pad. "Here, you're just the man to finish this. I'm going to catch some rack time."

41

Joanie Milford checked her dossier and glanced up at the street signs while she walked. Prime New York real estate was always hard to find, and she was on the trail of a hot one. Joanie had taken the Number Three train to lower Manhattan and hopped off at the Wall Street Station. East to Water Street, she turned north toward Maiden Lane. Past a coffee shop, past an abandoned bicycle in its final stages of ruin, she cut across to Front Street and looked up.

Back from the pavement, behind a shiny new bank lobby, seven stories of old red brick rose from the sidewalk. Double-hung windows adorned the walls. Half of them sported the rusting grill of an air conditioner. She glanced back at the dossier and nodded to herself. *The building is a teardown, but my God, the location.*

The woman licked her lips. She'd ripped into Manhattan real estate like a wolf on an injured fawn. Joanie knew just how to flip her blonde hair, when to flash a smile, and *wham*, an eight-figure property deal. This one was going to round out her year nicely. She paused at the marble entrance. Above the stone lintel, it bore a heraldic shield with the outline of a bird's head and the motto, *Tekeli Li*. The doors beneath had been covered with plywood.

She didn't hear Jimmy's approach. He tapped her on the shoulder. "What do you think? Nice huh? For a dump that is."

Joanie didn't jump, didn't even turn. She had been expecting Jimmy Letson. Investigative reporter, hacker, scammer, she never knew for sure, but he put her onto some of the juiciest leads in the city. "Yeah, but couldn't you find a rattier building?"

"Wait 'til you hear the price. Want to go inside?"

"Looks pretty well locked up. You got a key?"

"Where I go, lady, I don't need keys."

Jimmy led her through a narrow ally, hardly a slot between buildings. Down a flight of concrete steps, he stopped at a rusting steel door. "Let me see, double sided pin tumbler. This will only take a minute." With a few slender tools, he turned the deadbolt. "Voilà. No power, no alarms, good thing I brought a flashlight, huh?"

Joanie had brought her own. This wasn't her first self-guided building tour. They explored the lower six levels. Broken furniture, trash, the former occupants had left in a hurry.

Jimmy pointed upward. "The seventh floor is a little tricky. There's an elevator, but we'll have to use the stairs."

He unlocked a maintenance closet and opened an inner door. "This place is full of secrets."

Joanie directed her flashlight into the hidden space. Wires, cables, bundles of them climbed the inner wall like vines in a jungle. To her right, a circular iron staircase disappeared into the gloom above.

Jimmy urged her on. "Just watch your step."

Through another hidden door, and another utility closet, Joanie stepped into what once must have been a luxury office suite. The sliding glass doors had been propped open. Written in large gold letters, she read, "Pym Investment Trust, Inc." The remainder of the seventh floor had been gutted to the bare columns and studs. Nothing remained.

"Damn," She said. "I knew these guys. They were among my best customers."

Jimmy stood at the entrance but didn't go any further. "Then cut your losses and count yourself lucky. That Pym outfit was bad news."

"What happened?"

"Come on, let's get out of here. This place even gives me the creeps. I'll buy you a cup of joe and fill you in."

Twenty minutes later, Joanie found herself ensconced in a corner table nursing a large cappuccino. The morning crowd had long fled to their cubicles, leaving the place to Jimmy and herself.

"Spill it, Letson. What happened back there?"

"Anonymous source and all that, okay?"

"Just let me know what I'm getting myself into."

She'd run into Jimmy off and on over the years. They had usually converged at a scene of urban mayhem, him looking for the next story, and her looking for the next chunk of distressed real estate. He glossed over the details of Mt. Shasta and Laboratory Nine. "I'm not sure I believe half of that nonsense anyway."

Joanie filled in the blanks from what she'd read of the fires and earthquakes in northern California. "I sense there's more to that story than has appeared in the press."

Jimmy squinted. "I'm not at liberty to talk about it."

Instead he talked of Sally Smith, her fight with the Pyms, and how they had stolen her neural network analysis program. Joanie managed to connect a lot of what remained unsaid. Fascinated, she leaned forward. "So, these guys were going to make millions off this computer program."

"Billions, yeah. But that was Pym Senior. See, he managed to ease his kid out, lock him up in some kind of rehabilitation center. Junior had this delusion about communing with the creatures of the earth. He was hearing voices. They've got him in an executive rubber room somewhere." Jimmy stopped to scratch his head. "Funny thing, I wonder what will happen to Junior when the payments stop coming."

"What do you mean?" she asked. "The old man has got

to be raking it in by now."

"You would think. But here's the deal. Sally Smith didn't just fall off the turnip truck. She had an entire network on standby, just waiting for someone to log on. I'm guessing that was the access codes she gave to Pym. Oh, it worked alright. It made him millions upon millions trading money markets all around the world. Overnight billionaire trades, month after month. Wizard stuff."

Jimmy sat back and took a big slug of his double-shot Americano. "Then one Friday morning, it all went orbital. Made some big leveraged bets on the Hong Kong currency exchange just before closing. An hour later, it made the same bets on the Singapore exchange. Frankfort, London, New York, all around the globe it planted these bombs. Then Monday morning, they all started going off. Every trade was a disaster, a leveraged disaster. The losses were spectacular. A dozen private banks failed overnight. Most of the news has been covered up, but the markets were shaken."

"You're saying Pym was wiped out?"

"Obliterated. He's disappeared and even I can't find him."

"Then, who owns that building?"

Jimmy pulled the flashlight from his pocket. He held it beneath his face and grinned his most diabolical grin. "Stick with me, lady, and *we* will."

The End

About the Authors

David Wood is the USA Today bestselling author of the Dane Maddock Adventures and several other books and series. He also writes fantasy under the pen name David Debord. He's a member of International Thriller Writers and the Horror Writers Association

Learn more about his work at:

www.davidwoodweb.com or drop by and say hello on Facebook!

C.B. Matson has survived former incarnations that include mining geologist, commercial fisherman, civil engineer, mess-hall cook, surveyor and international port consultant. He lived much of his life in Colorado, California and Virginia, but he has also spent considerable time in Moscow, Bogota, Nagasaki and Dakar. When he is not writing, he enjoys walking, tinkering, and "... simply messing about in boats." C.B. Matson and his wife live on the water in Hampton Roads, Virginia.

Visit C.B. Matson's web page www.cbmatson.com for story synopses and upcoming releases. You can also contact him at write@cbmatson.com.